THE ACROS RAIDERS

DOWN
IN
FLAMES

SARA TUNDER

Crow's Nest Publishing House

The Acros Raiders: Down in Flames (2)

Copyright © 2025 by Sara Tunder

saratunderauthor.com

Book Cover Design by ebooklaunch.com

Map by Cartographybird Maps

ISBN: 979-8-9865415-5-6

Library of Congress Control Number: 2025902543

Dedicated to Max.
Thanks for supporting my dreams.

ALSO BY SARA TUNDER

The Acros Raiders Trilogy

From the Ashes (1)

Down in Flames (2)

CAST OF CHARACTERS

Scotty Sedgewig - Clansman woman. Short, brown hair, tan-grey skin, and grey eyes. Fallion trainer. Driven and protective.

Katze - Scotty's blue-grey fallion companion.

Reiner Samael - Average height snoskal with peach-fuzz hair. Passionate and aggressive.

Jean Kay - Leader of the Acros Raiders. Snoskal. Smooth black hair and piercing, icy-blue eyes. Serious and careful.

Aster Hawthorn - Deputy of the Acros Raiders. Mountainfolk. Short, brown hair, brown eyes, and tan-olive skin. Usually in his set of frosted steel armor, a poncho of worn metal. Holds loyalty in high regard.

Withorn Fae - Medic of the Acros Raiders. Mountainfolk and snoskal. Blond hair, tan skin, and captivating hazel eyes. Irritable and devoted.

Cosette Klein - Snoskal woman. Curly blonde hair, blue eyes. Weapons expert and quartermaster. Caring and determined.

Farsing Reddick - Dewick with shaved horns. Oldest member of the Acros Raiders. A loose cannon, literally, he's the explosives expert.

Jericho Martin - Young snoskal man. Curly blond hair, blue eyes, and pale face flecked with freckles. Prefers a crossbow in battle. Left leg is a prosthetic. Timid and intelligent.

Adelaide Merryweather - Tall mountainfolk woman with brown eyes and long, flowing black hair. Ambidextrous. Dual wields revolvers for range and cutlasses for melee. Charismatic and compulsive.

GODS OF SOHARISM

Yuna
Parenthood, Justice, Fertility

Forez
Life, Death, Funerals, Purgatory

Aurthuras
Healing, Love, Weddings

Gadias
War, Protection, Strength

Ludon
Beasts, Nature, Storms

Nikos
Plague

Cassius
Chaos and Lies

INGVAR

EDGEWOOD
PORT

FORT VAIL

HAYWARD CITY

OAK HILL
LAYTON

LESSER
ASPERETTI
MOUNTAINS

PALLO

RUSSET
PROVINCE

WEST
LORAIN

RIDGE

FLIGHT
STRONGHOLD

SALINA VILLAGE

PINEFALL
PROVINCE

FORT
BRINE

NETTLECREST

MAYHEW LAKE

FORT
LAKEBREEZE

LITTLE
BAY

WINGATE
PROVINCE

FORT WINGATE

VINCENT

TURLAN

VALENTINE ABBEY

OUELETTE

THE RUGGED PENINSULA OF

VALKO

AND

SURROUNDING LANDS

EVE
HALLOW

JAREATH

ASPEN

GREATER
ASPERETTI
MOUNTAINS

HIGHTOWER
HARBOR

TLE
KE

LITTLETON   CANNONSBURG

FORT
KIP   SNOWDEN

KIP LAKE   VALEN RUN

NORTH ASH

NEW NORTH ASH

GHENT   SIAMAK

SUNBELL CITY

NAHARAI

1
BACK IN ACTION

Alignment 26, Year 271.

The summer heat lingers in the air, but the clouds are a puffy grey with no promise of rain. Autumn is nearing already. Scotty frowns.

It's hard to stay calm as the seasons shift. Mike's execution at the start of spring is still fresh on her mind.

Five months since her fiancé passed and the fire in her heart has only worsened. She grows impatient. Hayward City needs to burn, along with Valko's High Priestess and her pawns.

She lets out a breath, the small filter in her mask letting out a slight hiss.

Little missions like these will get her closer to her goal.

The Raiders are tucked in the trees along a dusty road, the leaves rustling in the wind overhead. Katze is at Scotty's side, the fallion panting as she lays in the leaves. Jean and Jericho are on either side of the fallion and trainer. Jean's icy eyes watch the road, his gun clutched tightly as his trench coat brushes against the forest floor. Scotty looks to Jericho, her eyes trailing to the blond young man's prosthetic leg. This is the first mission Withorn has cleared him for. Scotty knows she should trust the medic's choice, but doubt lingers. The doubt is overwhelmed with shame.

She should trust Jericho.

Ren is on the other side of Scotty, the red-head throwing Jericho hesitant glances too. When Jericho thanked Scotty for saving his life in the raid on Salina Village, she was able to forgive herself for her teammate getting injured, but she knows Ren has some remaining guilt.

Scotty's hands tighten on her gun's grip, thinking about that day. That was when Hartwood's betrayal was revealed. On Commander Jean's orders, Scotty was tasked with weeding out the group's Valkoean spy. By a stroke of luck, not falling into Hartwood's traps, Scotty caught him in the act of setting bombs for the Raiders in Salina Village's guard house.

How Hartwood could betray years of friendship like that is beyond Scotty. Rage flutters in her chest as she thinks of the man's lack of loyalty. What could motivate someone to be so despicable?

Part of her doesn't want to believe Hartwood is the traitor. She's still haunted by dreams of her comrades turning on the team, the dreams so persistent that she expects it to come true any day.

Goosebumps crawl over Scotty's skin as she becomes all too aware of her comrades around her.

Are they secretly trying to sabotage this mission?

Scotty shakes her head, trying to bring her thoughts away from the doubts about her comrades. *They're good people. Besides, Hartwood was the traitor.* It was a shocking reveal to Scotty and the rest of the Raiders. No one else is capable of betraying them.

But why did Hartwood do it? It still doesn't make sense.

Hartwood was an apostle of Ludon, or it was a convincing lie that Scotty still believes. Why would someone so devout to a god of the Soharist Pantheon side with the Castist Regime? Maybe it was like Mike's family, Scotty's heart sinking at the thought of her late fiancé. The Brunswick family paid bribes to the Valkoeans so they could still practice Soharism. Did Hartwood strike up a similar deal?

Scotty's hand clenches around her ethner revolver's grip, anger swelling inside her as she thinks about Hartwood, the Brunswicks, everything about this gods forsaken war that led to Mike's execution.

She lets out a breath, trying to force the anger away. She needs to focus on the mission at hand: the caravan raid. Staying calm and getting this over with is how they get a step closer to taking out High Priestess Tapscott's Castist Regime.

On the other side of the road, Scotty tries to see the rest of her comrades through the cover of the trees. Aster's crew is hidden, she can't make out any of the deputy's team, which is perfect.

They've been out here for hours, waiting for a passing caravan. The team needs to intercept the carriages carrying ethner gear that will feed Valko's war machine. Farsing, the Raiders' explosives expert, stressed to them to not damage the gear. If one piece detonates, it will destroy the whole carriage, maybe even the whole caravan. The Raiders need to overpower the Valkoeans and bring the volatile gear to the rebel fort — Cannonsburg — a few miles east in the mountains.

It's just another run-of-the-mill raid. She's been on countless of these missions in the past season.

Scotty notices Ren yawn and Jean shuffles in place. She holds back her own yawn, the tiredness turning to frustration. These missions are an insult to their team! They're the Acros Raiders, an elite team from Ghent's Sunbell City Guild, not the rebellion's errand runners.

Scotty's eyes intermittently shoot back to her comrades, paranoia lingering in the back of her mind. She lets out a soft breath. Jean, Jericho and Ren can be trusted. All of her comrades are trustworthy. She spent too many of her early days with the Raiders skeptical of their trust, she doesn't need to be ever watchful around them still. They have been nothing but good to her, they're like the family she never had.

Katze's ears prick and she rustles at Scotty's side, the small party's attention piquing at her.

"They're coming," Ren whispers, brown eyes pointed at Katze.

3

Scotty's finger twitches near Tex's trigger, watching the road through her yellow steam-protectant goggles. First she sees the movement among the trees, then she hears the clacking from the hooves and the crackling from turning wheels. The winding woodland road reveals the guarded caravan.

Katze stands up and the rest of the Raiders ready themselves, Scotty checking Tex to assure the steam vents are properly aligned. Tex, a unique ethner revolver, was made by Scotty's late brother — It's more accurate and deadly than any gun ever made, or so her brother claimed. Tex is why she was such a successful hitman — and in turn, a Raider.

Scotty's grey eyes lock on her prey: three carriages, three coachmen, six valen, ten foot soldiers.

The soldiers are a mix of Mohkans and Valkoeans. The Mohkan dewicks, a bulky, hairy, and horned race, donned in typical garb — puffy brown pants and maroon long sleeve shirts. Their curved horns are painted in stripes of Mohkan's colors: brown, red, and yellow. Curved bayonets with bone handles are in their sheaths, Scotty having seen too many of the blades since Mohkan and Valko made their alliance.

The Valkoeans wear the blue, gold, and white colors of the country the rebels are struggling to liberate.

The valen trot along, the cervine creatures toting the carriages, unaware of the danger around. Their antlers bob atop their sleek heads as they walk. When they're parallel to the Raiders hidden among the trees, Jean points a sleeved arm towards the caravan.

Scotty aims at a Mohkan guard's thigh, careful to not hit the volatile ethner gear in tow.

Sss-sss-sss-hissss!

Gunpowder weapons boom around Scotty, the steam whelming around her from Tex. A veil of smoke and steam blotches the woods, obscuring Scotty's victim from sight.

Chaos ensues and the caravan foot soldiers respond with a volley of bullets.

Scotty snaps back behind a tree as hissing bullets splinter the wood, adrenaline rushing through her veins.

"To your left, Scotty," Jean says from the next tree down. "At the front. Two Mohkan soldiers. I got the left, you go right."

"On it." Scotty nods.

"Ren, cover fire!" Jean calls.

Ren gives Jean a grumpy nod and the three peek out.

Gunshots thump in Scotty's chest and she fires low at the rightmost silhouette flashing through the steam, the figure evading through the patchy visibility. She grits her teeth and snaps back behind the tree.

"The steam is covering the carriages!" Scotty calls to Jean. "It's not safe to shoot at them."

"We'll keep our distance as much as possible," Jean says.

"We need to move in," Ren argues.

"Keep firing," Jean says. "Focus the front carriage guards."

Scotty wants to argue, but she just nods and peeks out again, firing towards the silhouettes. The soldiers weave in and out of the carriages, returning fire. The valen snort and whistle, their antlers cutting through the steam as their heads move around, their handlers struggling to calm them.

"Go, go, go! Get the carriages out of here!" Scotty hears a Valkoean's voice call out over the steam and the carriages jolt as the valen break out into a run.

"Idiots!" Jean says. "The full carriages can't outrun us!"

"They can if the guards buy time," Ren says.

"Look out!" Jericho calls.

Battle cries call out as the soldiers burst through the steam, brandishing swords.

"Gah!" Scotty shouts as a curved Mohkan bayonet swishes by her face. She brings her gun up and fires.

Click click click.

Empty! Dammit!

She jumps to evade the Mohkan man's blade once more, her feet moving in a dangerous dance at each lash. She parries one blow with her gun's barrel, Katze latching her jaw in the man's calf. He yells as Katze yanks him back and Scotty jams Tex into its sheath, pulling her twin daggers from her belt.

The Mohkan man pierces his blade downwards, Katze yelping and releasing him when the sword slices her shoulder.

"Katze!" Scotty hollers.

Scotty lunges towards him with crossed daggers, the man thrusting his head down to meet her blades with his painted horns. Adrenaline surges through Scotty when she pulls back, her daggers not budging from the deep cut in the horns.

The man twists and yanks to the side, Scotty yelling as her daggers release. She tumbles, but regains her footing, scrambling to miss the man's curved blade swinging down at her, her heart racing. She spins and his blade is already swinging at her again. Gasping, she jumps back and the blade licks over her bicep, warm blood dripping down her arm.

"Dear Gadias!" she hisses

"Cry to your false gods!" the man says. "It falls of deaf ears!"

The man swings back around for another blow and Scotty brings her daggers up to parry, wincing. Rage flares in her chest. Castus is the only false god, and so many are dying because of him, because of a lie! *Mike* is dead because of a lie! A flash of grey catches Scotty's eye and Katze leaps up, locking her jaw on the dewick's sword-arm.

"Gah! Get off!" he grunts as he yanks his arm.

He turns and struggles to free himself, grabbing at her with a hairy hand. His back turned, Scotty yells and rushes forward, leaping and digging her daggers into his shoulders. He screams and falls with a thud, the noise cut short as he goes limp.

Scotty's heart races as she gets up, her heavy breathing slow.

Swords clash around her and she looks up at the battlefield. Jean dances around, his black trench coast swishing over the dusty road as he trades blows with a Valkoean. Ren is covered in blood, redder than his peach-fuzz hair, finishing off his opponent with a vicious snarl. She notices Aster's team on the road through the dissipating steam, Merryweather battling a Valkoean with her dual cutlasses. The tall, muscular woman lashes forward, overpowering the man with bladed fury. Her long black hair shimmers as she spins to meet another Valkoean in battle. Aster stomps forward in his Panzer Suit, a poncho of frosted steel armor. His helmet is emotionless as he slices his longsword over the shoulder of a Mohkan solder, another fleeing at the sight.

Scotty's heart lurches when she catches sight of Jericho. He's locked in battle with a young Valkoean soldier. Despite being weak on one leg, he's standing strong. Most of his motion is in his upper body, pivoting on his metal leg. Jericho has gained muscle since he joined the Raiders, but his build is still thin. He has adopted a fighting style that works for him, but limited mobility is still a massive disadvantage.

The young Valkoean sweeps low and sends his leg into Jericho's prosthetic, Jericho falling to the ground with a yowl.

"Jericho!" Scotty hollers.

Her feet scramble as she rushes towards the Valkoean, daggers clutched tightly in her gloved hands.

Her boots slide in the dust as she comes to a halt, Ren reaching the tussling pair first and sending his sword into the neck of the Valkoean. He gurgles and spits out blood, falling to the ground, limp.

Scotty rushes to Jericho's side, jolting him upright.

"Are you okay?" she presses, her heart thumping.

Jericho scowls at her and straightens his leg, pushing her aside.

"I'm fine!" he snaps. "I'm okay! I can handle myself!"

Scotty frowns under her gaiter. He's tried to be in high spirits since the amputation, but it's been a back and forth battle.

"You did good," she reassures him. "You held your own."

Jericho's gaze softens, but he doesn't apologize for his outburst. He extends his arm out and Scotty helps him stand up, averting his gaze.

"Don't lie to him," Ren says. "If not for me he'd be dead."

Rage whelms in Scotty's chest. She wants to bite at him and say that if not for Ren, Jericho wouldn't be like this. Jericho needs encouraged.

"After the carriages!" Jean shouts. "Don't let them get away!"

Scotty didn't notice the clashing of swords stopped around her.

"Stay here, Jericho," Ren demands. "You'll just hurt yourself if you follow."

Scotty races away, wanting to ring Ren's neck more from his remark. Arguing with him now wouldn't be good for the mission.

Her arm wound stings as she races after the carriages, Katze zipping at her side. Scotty catches Ren to her left out of the corner of her eye, Jean, Merryweather and Cosette to her right. Aster stomps far behind them in his armor along the rest of the Raiders, but the carriages quickly come back into view. Two guards are posted on the backs of the boxy carriages, each lifting ethner rifles up as the Raiders approach.

"Look out!" Scotty shouts out. "Guns!"

Hissing bullets stream towards the Raiders, everyone diving off the road to run through the woods. Plants slap against Scotty as she runs and bullets pierce into the trees around her.

Her heart thumps as she reloads Tex. Gritting her teeth, she lurches to the side and bursts out of the trees to race alongside the carriages.

Hissing sounds behind her and a bullet pierces wood, the rear-most carriage exploding into a cloud of steam.

"Gah!" Scotty yells as she stumbles and halts, wooden debris flinging around her. Acidic steam settles in her arm wound and she hisses in pain. The other Raiders shout out as the explosion stops them, the other two carriages racing ahead.

Scotty blinks, the steam swirling around as debris settles.

Was that an ethner bullet? Everyone else uses gunpowder. Did a Valkoean shoot the carriage so we don't get the supplies? Was it one of us?

"Careful!" Jean yells. "The drivers! Go for the coachmen!"

Scotty hardly has time to look at the steaming wreckage, the valen and soldiers a mangled mess. She buries her thoughts and races ahead.

The soldiers on the back of the second carriage leap off in terror, throwing their guns to the side and kneeling in fear as the Raiders run by.

Smart choice after seeing that.

Scotty and Ren are at the front, Katze tailing them. The second carriage lurches and jolts and Scotty's muscles tighten, anticipating another explosion.

She comes up alongside it and wide-eyed, the coachman yells out. She sends a bullet into his forehead and he thunks to the side on the coach box.

The valen slow and Jean runs up alongside the carriage, lugging himself onto the coach box. He grabs the reins and commands the antlered beasts to halt, the creatures snorting as their thin legs slow.

The carriage in the front also stops and the coachman and guards abandon it, running off into the woods, leaving their weapons behind.

"Smartest Valkoeans I've ever seen," Ren remarks.

The Raiders surround the two carriages, breathing heavily from the run. Aster, Jericho, and Withorn meet up with them last. Withorn tends to the wounded with gear from his large wooden medic's backpack. Thankfully, no one was seriously injured.

Aster takes his helmet off, the deputy's sweat-slicked maroon hair plastered against his tan face.

Farsing is already smoking a cigarette, the dewick with stubs rather than horns sharing his pack with Jericho after their wounds have been assessed.

"You two are addicted to those things," Cosette remarks.

"Really?" Farsing asks sarcastically, smoke spilling from his lips. "I hadn't realized!"

"It just helps us relax, Cosette," Jericho says, his blue eyes guilty as he looks at the blonde woman.

She purses her lip before sighing. "Sorry, the smell is just irritating after this raid."

"That was just terrible," Jean scolds. "We need to be more careful on missions like this. It should have been easy."

"This is volatile gear," Aster says, stepping up to his commander. "We should just be happy no one got hurt from the explosion."

"How'd that happen anyways?" Scotty speaks up. "An ethner bullet hit the carriage."

Aster blinks at her. "What?" he asks. "It was from the carriage jolting. You of all people should know how volatile this stuff is."

Scotty opens her mouth to argue, but a fearful voice speaks up.

"And we're expected to take these carriages all the way to Cannonsburg?" Jericho blurts out. Smoke snakes from his lips as he speaks, his blue eyes wide.

Scotty frowns as the conversation pulls away from her comment, the team falling into an argument.

Was it really from jolting? Did I actually hear a bullet? They're so quiet, it's hard to say. No one else seems to have heard.

Scotty frowns, certain it was a bullet. Did someone accidentally shoot the carriage while aiming for the guards?

Fear strikes her.

Was it a traitor trying to sabotage the mission?

Her eyes dart around to the arguing team, seeing menacing faces on her comrades.

No. Hartwood was the traitor. It was just an accident.

Her eyes fall on a flash of orange in the woods, seeing a sharfawks peering out at the arguing team. The little vulpine creature watches with amused brown eyes, its antlers looking like branches among the foliage. It turns to Scotty and its gaze peers into her soul.

It looks amused by the chaos of the team.

Scotty shivers despite the warm summer air.

"Quiet!" Jean shouts. "Let's stop bickering and get these back to Cannonsburg *safely*. So long as we take it slow, that won't happen again. These carriages need pulled into the fort by sunset, so we need to get moving now."

A scowl twists over Aster's face at the mention of Cannonsburg. "Can't the rebels there meet us halfway? Cannonsburg has been a tug of war, taking this gear there is useless. It will fall into Valkoean hands and back a dozen times by the end of the war."

"I know you have foul memories in Cannonsburg, but our orders are to take it there," Jean says. "It doesn't matter how trivial we think it is."

Aster's face stays twisted in a frown, but he nods at his commander and takes his place at the front of the second carriage.

Jean gets on the coach box on the front carriage and gestures the Raiders forward. "Let's get a move on," he says. "It's going to be a long evening."

2
CANNONSBURG

The Raiders ride through the rest of the evening, Scotty marching alongside Aster's carriage. Katze pads tiredly at her side, head hung low.

Scotty loses track of time as the sun crawls through the sky. Eating just trail rations and stream water along the way, Scotty longs for a hearty meal.

They meander eastward down Valko's woodland backroads, the terrain unforgiving as they near the Greater Asperetti Mountains.

They crest a wooded hill and the land slopes downward, the rocky Greater Asperettis peeking through the forest in all their grandeur. Through a pass in the mountains, the sun descends into Mayhew Lake, making long shadows over the land. Woven among the rocky foot of the mountains is a castle-like fort. Its walls are made of the same stones as the mountain, blending in seamlessly with its surroundings. If not for the unnatural shape of the fort, it would be invisible from here.

Aster huffs from the coach box, bags set under his eyes, his helmet resting beside him.

"What a sight," Scotty remarks.

"Ey, Aster that's where we first met ya at," Farsing points out. "Can't believe we're going back, and it's in rebel hands again!"

Aster hesitates. "That's just the nature of this place. I'm just amazed it's been built up again."

Scotty frowns as she looks at Aster, his brow furrowed as if lost in thought. She recalls Withorn mentioning that Aster came from a rebel fort around Littleton. Well before her days as a Raider, the team was supposed to help defend a rebel fort from an impending attack. They got there too late and Aster was what was left. Cannonsburg must be that place.

Aster told them there was a lot he regretted that day, but Scotty can't imagine the Raiders without him. He's more than made up for whatever mistakes he made. When Scotty first joined, Aster was adamant about her being perfect "Raider material" so the others wouldn't lose faith in Jean's decisions. Jean is lucky to have a deputy as loyal as Aster.

The Raiders' caravan descends the mountain, the trees hiding the fort from view, dousing the group in dappled shadows.

"So that fort sees a lot of change?" Scotty asks.

Aster glances down at her and nods.

"That's almost an understatement," he says. "The pass behind the fort used to be the main route everyone would take from the province of Wingate's eastern coast to anywhere in central or western Wingate. Because of this, it's a crucial spot for the rebellion and Valko alike. It's been destroyed and rebuilt countless times. I wasn't there for long, but I saw a lot of death there, rebels and Valkoeans alike." He scowls. "The best part? Because of how volatile the fort is, the pass isn't used much anymore. Everyone vies for the Little Lake pass up at the Pinefall-Wingate border or near Fort Kip down in the foothills. I hear the Valkoeans have started blasting a tunnel through the mountains with dynamis. Anything but Cannonsburg Pass."

"If the pass isn't used much, then why are we taking this gear there?" Scotty asks.

Aster huffs, grabbing the valen reins tightly in his hands. "That's what I'm saying!"

"We're taking the gear there because of the proximity to Hightower Harbor," Jean calls from the front carriage. The rest of the Raiders slump along next to the caravan, looking unamused by the loud conversation. "If the rebels weren't there, the Valkoeans would be. Regardless if the pass is used or not, it's an important foothold in the province of Wingate. If the Valkoeans get control of it for very long, it could quickly be the end of the rebellion. Stop your griping and just be thankful we get a warm meal tonight."

Aster snorts and frowns, not responding to the commander. His tired eyes stay trained on the carriage in front of him and Scotty falls back into the march.

The Raiders close the gap between them and Cannonsburg and the sentries open the thick wooden gates for the caravan. The newer gates are a stark contrast to the beaten, patchwork stone wall. Rebel flags flank the doors, the twisty grey symbol sitting between green and white fabric. The walls are about as thick as two houses. Countless cannons adorn the wall, Scotty seeing where the fort gets its name from.

A sentry leaves his post to lead the Raiders into the heart of the fort. Inside, there has been an effort to repair the place. Chunks of dirt have been upturned from where Scotty assumes pieces of the wall have landed. Attempts have been made to fill the holes, but others are dug deeper with dirt bags and barbed wire around the fronts and backs.

The fort walls sweep around the wide yard, meeting at an identical wooden gate on the far side. Entryways lead into the bulwark, rebels and Ghentian soldiers disappearing into the walls as the sun falls. Stables, makeshift carriage ports, and workshops are pressed up against the walls, the valen settling for the night. Beyond the gate, the looming mountains cast ever-darkening shadows.

A young rebel — in his early twenties like Scotty — notices the Raiders approaching, making his way across the yard to dismiss the sentry leading the team. A short clansman woman follows the young rebel closely, the woman much older than the man.

Bags line his eyes, and a receding hairline makes Scotty wonder about her judgment in his age. He has a young face but holds himself with a tired authority. Scotty notices Aster avert his gaze from the man, though he may just be admiring the mess of a fort.

"You sure made it in time," the rebel remarks, considering the setting sun.

"We made it by sundown," Jean points out, the caravan slowing to a halt.

The rebel sniffs in response, but Jean gives him no time to respond.

"You must be this fort's commander," Jean observes. "Melrose, correct?" His eyes point to the woman. "And Bramblewood, the second in command."

"Yes, refrain from calling me by my title," Melrose says. "I'm a citizen rebel, we don't care about titles like you militant Ghentians do, we just care about the end goal. I'm in charge of this place, that's what matters."

Scotty sees Jean's lip twitch in amusement. The Sunbell City Guild, the Ghentian criminal organization the Acros Raiders were hired from, doesn't care about military ranks either, nor do the Raiders. Despite Ghent's outright help to the rebellion, the Raiders still need to hide their origins lest it damages Lady Amala's reputation. If others knew the leader of Ghent hired criminals to try to get the upper hand in this war, it could damage Ghent's faith in her.

"I'm Commander Jean Kay," Jean greets. "Leader of the Acros Raiders. You probably assumed that, so skip the formalities I suppose. Where can we drop the gear off at? And where can my men find lodging?"

"Gear can go by the eastern gate," Melrose says, pointing to the one wall. "The bulwark has a fortified storehouse in it there. Beds are in the western wall."

Scotty glowers at the fort's leader. He can at least spare a curt "thanks" for the gear.

"Do mind the mess," Bramblewood adds. Scotty can't tell if the remark was supposed to be sarcastic, but she and Melrose step away soon enough, and the caravan continues on its way to the western wall.

Aster throws the fort's leaders a scowl before turning back, his hands grasping the reins tightly. She wonders if Aster knows Melrose from his days in the rebellion. Maybe there is a hint of jealously since the Raiders met Aster when he was stationed at this fort — and Melrose is clearly younger than the Raider's deputy.

Scotty shakes that idea away. Aster isn't spiteful like that, he is part of the Raiders' family. This fort just holds sour memories for him, like how Scotty feels about Hayward City, Valko's capital and her hometown. She spent her youth training to become a successful hitman for Hayward City Steel, owned by Mike's family, the Brunswicks. She would feel bitter if she were in the city and happened across one of their employees.

Her heart thumps hard at the thought.

Perhaps she would feel more than bitter.

The caravan halts by the storehouse entrance and they get busy unloading the supplies. They break off into small groups, Withorn and Cosette watching Jericho closely, much to his dismay, as they lug supplies out of the carriages. Farsing and Ren are heaving crates together and Jean and Merryweather have naturally paired with each other. Scotty sees Aster eyeing the commander with the taller woman, so she and Katze fall into place beside him.

They heave open the doors of the wooden carriage, crates of ethner guns, cartridges, and bullets in front of them. Scotty shivers at the sight of the volatile equipment, despite it being the gear she uses. Her ethner gun uses the same cartridges, mixing the water and ethner to make a highly pressurized steam to propel the minie balls.

Aster steps up into the one carriage and yanks a crate from the top, thrusting it down towards Scotty. She grits her teeth and recoils, but says nothing as she takes the crate into the storehouse.

The moons shine as the land darkens, already having taken their place in the middle of the sky. They pass crates around, Scotty growing frustrated with Aster's care of the fragile gear. Towards the end, Aster thrusts a crate of ethner cartridges into Scotty's arms. The metal vials clink as she stumbles backwards and the cap on one comes undone, the precious liquid spilling over the side of the wooden crate. Scotty lurches to the side, narrowly missing the toxic liquid. Katze jumps back at the sudden motion.

"Watch it, Aster!" Scotty hisses. "Be more careful, will ya? I've had my share of chemical burns and I don't want more."

Aster's gaze softens, and Scotty can tell he is studying the healed ethner scars on her face. He sighs. "I'm sorry. I don't want to be here."

"I can tell," Scotty remarks before taking the crate into the storehouse.

When she returns, Aster hands her the next crate more gently. She places it on the back of the carriage and lets out a sigh.

"So, what's wrong? I know you probably have bad memories here, but it's not worth blowing us up over."

"It's just... odd seeing this place alive again," Aster says. "That's all."

"Is the leader a rebel from when you were stationed here?" she asks. "Commander Melrose?" She knows she's prying and sees irritation flicker in Aster's brown gaze. She almost expects him to lash out at her like a threatened rattlesnake, but instead he shakes his head.

"The leader when I was here is dead. He died during the battle that I... survived in." His tone is dark, but any hint of annoyance has fled. "Melrose, he's just a kid. Truth is he doesn't take the title of commander because it's just another thing to put on his gravestone. He won't say it like that, though. Spirits are not high here at Cannonsburg." Aster's nose scrunches. "Some rebels take titles, usually the former military, but the default title for leaders in the rebellion is commander, usually reserved for uneducated divisions. The civilian divisions."

"You say that like it's a bad thing," Scotty says. "Jean's title is commander."

"Jean's a fine leader," Aster says confidently. "I'm not saying it like it's bad, it's Milos's title after all. He dropped his title of general after acting in defiance at Tapscott's new leadership. I'm not saying it's a bad title. It just makes the rebellion seem... messy."

Scotty frowns.

"You use the word civilians," she observes. "Were you in the military before joining the rebellion?"

"Yes, I was." Aster grabs a crate of his own and slides off the carriage. "I don't want to talk about it, Scotty. I just... want to get out of here. I just want to make it through the night and we'll be rid of this place in the morning. Can we leave it at that?"

Scotty nods. "Sure." Embarrassment flutters in her chest, maybe she pried too much. She picks up her own crate to finish unloading the carriage. When she turns around, she notices a flash of a lithe figure in the shadows. The poking antlers, the sleek vulpine face — another sharfawks.

It stares at her and Aster in the shadows, frozen mid-step. Scotty narrows her eyes at it. An odd place for a sharfawks to show face, but maybe the rebels feed it scraps.

As soon as it appeared, it slinks away into some rubble. Scotty shakes it off and helps Aster unload their carriage the rest of the way.

The Valkoean carriages are taken away by some rebels and loaded into the carriage ports, the valen calmed and sent into stables of their own.

The Raiders are sent to the barracks in the bulwark, heralded in by the night watch. Cots and bunkbeds line the walls of the dark, musty room. No free cots left, the Raiders are directed to hay piles dotted throughout the barracks. Scotty lays down on her pile, making space for Katze to curl up next to her. She looks up at the towering ceiling, thankful to at least have a roof over her head tonight.

It could be worse.

She lets out a breath and is lulled to sleep.

3
HIS CLAWS

The familiar corridors of Salina Village's guardhouse surround Scotty, the smoke of the dark halls invading her lungs and choking her. She staggers down the toxic halls, gasping and clawing forward against the cold walls.

Smoke spills down the hall into the entryway, leading Scotty along. Pictures of Castus sit on shrines, animated yet frozen in place. The false god's eyes follow Scotty as she stumbles towards the front door.

A piercing sensation overtakes Scotty's head, like the claws of Cassius, god of chaos and lies, are digging in her skull. Her heartbeat races, the smoke filling her lungs, her footsteps hastening.

The images of Castus contort and warp, Scotty's comrades, the Raiders' faces replacing them.

Fear strikes her looking at her friends.

Can she trust them?

But the traitor has been found.

Who shot the bullet that destroyed one of the carriages?

Was it just an accident? Was Aster right and there was no bullet?

Doubt and guilt overtake her.

She starts running.

She turns into a gaping doorway and a wall of flames swirl in front of her. Her boots skid on the dusty floor and she falls back, yelling in fear.

She averts her gaze from the bright light and stumbles to her feet, dashing back out into the main hall.

It warps around her, fading into a chamber, smoke brushing over the floor. Her feet trail over rebel gunpowder mines, explosions ringing out, her ears ringing, her head piercing in pain.

She staggers forward.

Hartwood looms in the center of the room, moonlight cutting through the windows, but the moons highlight another figure. Hartwood cowers and yowls out, a knife cutting into him.

Over and over.

Blood spurts, dousing his attacker.

Scotty freezes in fear, the blood-soaked figure turning its gaze to her.

Her heart thumps like its soon to burst out her chest.

She grabs for Tex, but it's not there.

Any icy gaze meets her own.

It's Jean.

An understanding is in his eyes, a kinship, but Scotty feels fear.

His lips move, but no words come out. Scotty's ears ring, a buzzing invading her mind, the piercing feeling pressuring her brain.

She shuts her eyes, she just wants it to end.

Her eyes snap open, staring up at the towering ceiling of the barracks in the bulwark.

Her heart thumps, but she's used to the nightmares.

She sits there, unmoving, praying that it's at least nearing dawn. A faint light spills into the halls, but she's uncertain if its from the shining moons or the rising sun.

That nightmares started once a week after Hartwood was outed as the traitor. Now, its nearly every other night. Some nights, she thinks she's used to it. Some days, she forgets about it entirely. Sometimes, it's all she can think about. The nightmares are usually different, but similar. They always include the team turning on her or Hartwood's betrayal.

She sits upright, a pounding sensation overtaking her head. She winces and hisses and Katze lifts her head. The fallion nuzzles her muzzle into Scotty, and she puts her arm around her.

"I'm okay, girl," she says. "Just a headache." Withorn should have something to make it better.

Reluctantly, she gets up and puts some fresh clothes on before finding the team's medic in the barracks. He's already up and dressed, crossed legged on some hay, his hazel eyes glued to the Good Book. His blond hair is messy, but it looks like he made somewhat of an effort to clean himself up this morning. His short cape is draped over his shoulders, held together just below his neck with the symbol of healers — a peony pin.

"You're up early," Withorn remarks, still engrossed in his book.

"I woke up with a headache," Scotty grumbles. "Do you have anything that'll help?"

Withorn looks up to her and shuts the book.

"If I break your arm, you'll forget about the pain in your head," he says with a chortle.

Scotty looks at him, deadpan, while he laughs.

"Eh, you're no fun," he says, turning to his medic cabinet. His hand fishes through the wooden backpack.

He produces a small vial and Scotty grabs for it, but Withorn quickly pulls it back.

"Is my pain just a game to you?" Scotty asks.

"Doctor's orders to also go take a walk in the fresh air," he says.

"I was going to do that with Katze anyway," Scotty says.

"Doctor-ordered walk *with* the doctor," he corrects.

Scotty leans down and snatches the vial away from him.

"Last I checked you're a *medic*," she teases. "I don't mind if the medic comes along, though."

Withorn's bulky nose scrunches, but he stands up, Scotty snickering along the way. She takes a small dose of the medicine, Withorn redoes her arm's bandages, and they head outside, Katze on their heels.

Cool morning air brushes over Scotty's face, a jacket barely enough to keep her warm in the mornings as fall nears. The rising sun douses the land in a faint yellow, the rubble-laden yard as busy as it was the night before.

Katze sniffs along the wall, halting to take in the smells at the stables. Scotty's nose twists at the valen dung odor, but whatever Withorn gave her is starting to make the pain in her head ebb.

"So, what's really wrong?" Withorn probes.

"What do you mean?" she asks, failing to hide a defensive edge to her tone.

He shrugs, stuffing his hands into his overalls pockets. "You've just seemed restless lately. Something seems different."

Scotty scoffs. "I don't recall ever being rest*ful*. Not since we've known each other."

Withorn raises his hands in defense. "Fine, I'm sorry, I'm just looking out for you."

She lets out a soft sigh. Withorn never knew about her mission to find the traitor, so she doesn't want to tell him about her distrust of the team. He wouldn't understand.

Withorn confided in her about the truth of his mother — he's the unwanted son of High Priestess Tapscott, the woman they're fighting so hard to take down. He ran away when he was young, so no one else on the team knows about Withorn's childhood. Scotty is thankful for the trust she shares with her friend, but something deep down makes her scared to talk fully about the dream. It's like if she says she fears there's still a traitor, it will come true.

"I've had a recurring dream," Scotty says carefully. "About Hartwood. Since he... turned on us." It's not a lie, but it's not the full truth.

Withorn raises a bushy brow at her, but says nothing.

"It's really like I'm reliving the Salina Village raid nearly every night," she tells him. "But it's okay, I'm used to it now."

"I'm just a medic," Withorn says. "I don't really know the inter-working of a mind, but it's been almost over a full season since then. I don't think getting use to it is normal."

"You're the one who asked what's wrong!" Scotty says in defense. "I'm just telling you what's wrong. I don't think it's normal."

"Don't get snappy with me," Withorn says. "I'm just concerned."

Scotty grits her teeth at the medic. She wants to tell him that there's more to it. She wants to tell him about how Jean picked her to hunt down the traitor in the group. She wants to tell him about the clawing paranoia that still lingers about her teammates. She wants to tell him everything, but a lump in her throat holds her back. The piercing sensation in her head comes back and she winces.

"Scotty?" Withorn says, extending an arm to her.

She forces herself upright, Katze turning from the smells at the stable to be at her distraught master's side.

"I'm okay," Scotty says through gritted teeth. "My headache is just acting up."

As quick as the sensation hits, her head clears, shouts and howls pounding on her ears. She looks to the ruckus at the western gate, Katze's ears pricking in the direction.

The sentries are shouting, rebels flooding to the gate.

Scotty's heart thumps hard.

Ambush?

Before she knows it, she and Withorn are joining the crowd, the two Raiders pushing through to the front, Cannonsburg's massive gates stretched wide.

Two sentries are leading a battered rebel man through the door, panting heavily as if he ran across the whole country to get to the fort.

"My team. They're all dead," he gasps. "All of them! The Valkoeans, they're pressing out from Kip Lake. Aurthuras save us all! It's only a matter of time..." Behind wide glasses, his eyes shut and he starts to go limp in the rebels' grasp.

"Do we have a medic nearby?" the one sentry shouts.

"Scotty," Withorn directs. "Get my cabinet from my bedroll."

Scotty nods and turns to push back through the crowd, Withorn rushing to the man's aid.

The blood pounds through Scotty's ears, the rebel's words heavy in her head.

Does this mean the Valkoeans will be attacking soon?

4
ON THE HORIZON

Ren fingers over his bronze locket, legs kicked up as he leans against the barrack's cool stone wall. The chain tugs at his neck as he digs a dirty fingernail between the two oval halves to pry it open.

A small smile creeps over his lips as he looks at the carefully painted portraits of his family.

On the left is Curlew, his wife, with beautiful curly brown hair, brown eyes, and the smallest smile — something she doesn't flash often. On the right is Rosie, their daughter, who has Ren's red hair and a stoic expression — something friends joke that she could have gotten from either parent.

His smile fades a bit. He hasn't seen them in two years. He wonders what his daughter looks like now. He missed her toddler years, he doubts she'd even recognize him.

His mind flickers to the neighbor — the next homestead a couple acres over — Treacher, Ren's friend and retiree from the Sunbell City Guild. Ren asked him to care for them, his daughter probably thinks of him more as a father than himself.

Maybe Curlew does too.

Ren's teeth grit as anger flares in his chest, and doubts swirl through his head.

He shuts the locket and tucks it back into his shirt.

Curlew would never be unfaithful.

He hasn't heard from his family since Amala took Cyrus, the team's messenger swift, from Jean. Since the Raiders get orders directly from Milos now, their new messenger swift is with Milos more often than Jean. Curlew wouldn't stop sending him letters. Lady Amala must have stopped sending the messages she receives to Commander Milos to pass along. The leader of Ghent just doesn't care, she has other things to worry about.

Ren's family means nothing to her. After all, the Raiders are just a tool to her to help get Ghent's land around Kip Lake back.

Sounds of shouts pound on his ears and he freezes for a moment to assess the noise.

No gunshots, no blades, only ruckus.

The rebels in the barracks stir, some rushing outside to see what's going on. Someone pushes through the doors, running inside — it's Scotty, with her mutt, Katze, on her heels.

Ren forces himself out of his restful position, getting up to follow after the rushing woman.

"Scotty, what's going on?" he demands, stepping behind her.

She's already by Withorn's sleeping spot, kneeling down to his cabinet.

"A rebel came in injured," she says, not looking at Ren. "We need Withorn's supplies."

"I can grab that," he tells her, the little woman struggling as she lugs the large cabinet onto her back. "Don't hurt yourself!"

Scotty grimaces as she stumbles backwards from the weight of the cabinet and Ren pushes himself in the way to make sure she doesn't fall.

"I got it!" she insists.

Ren snorts out a laugh, hands clasped on the wooden pack. "Clearly not!"

Scotty turns to shoot daggers at him, her scarred, greyish cheeks turning red in embarrassment. "Take it," she says, giving in as she slips out of the straps. The cabinet drops in Ren's arm and he hides a huff of shock as he's left supporting the weight. He slings it over his shoulders.

"Lead the way," he says.

He follows Scotty as she bursts out if the barracks and pushes into a crowd facing the western gate.

"Move, move!" Ren's booming voice cuts a path through the mob. They break into the front of the onlookers, Withorn kneeling next to an injured rebel, grabbing the cabinet from Ren.

The rebel has large, circular glasses widening his eyes — one brown, one green. His tan face is flecked with freckles, blood, and dirt, his short hair matted with sweat. A half-cape is draped over his shoulders, held together at his collarbone with a peony pin, much like Withorn's — this rebel is a medic.

Withorn goes to work getting him cleaned up, by now a massive group having congregated, including Jean, Aster, Melrose and Bramblewood.

"Connie!" Bramblewood exclaims.

Melrose steps forward. "What happened?"

"Commander Melrose, Bramblewood," Connie greets shakily. "They're all dead... Everyone is dead, even Preston."

Ren looks to Melrose and Bramblewood, the fort's commander and second-in-command unmoved by this revelation.

"Your scouting party was supposed to be set up far from Kip Lake's shore and far from Fort Kip," Melrose says. "Far from the railway, from the caravan roads. What happened? How did you engage them?"

Ren frowns at the fort's commander, but admires his brashness.

"Give him a break with the interrogation, will ya?" Withorn says.

Connie ignores Withorn's remark, and speaks up through gritted teeth as the Raider medic looks him over.

"The Black Glove Scouts," Connie says. "The airships saw us. They saw us and sent them... they sent the Scouts after us!"

"The Black Glove Scouts," Melrose echoes.

An uncontrollable shiver crawls down Ren's spine. The Black Glove Scouts, the team that the Raiders met their match with many times, the most devastating being at Fort Vail that took out thirteen of their members.

"That man in armor, he cut them down, he cut them down! The steam weapon... The screams! Oh, by Aurthuras, the screams!" Connie gasps, his eyes growing wider behind his glasses. "Preston's dead."

Ren recalls his first time meeting Commander Halcy, the man in frosted steel armor, much like Aster's. Impenetrable to bullets, the man is a force to be reckoned with. At Fort Vail, Halcy had almost overpowered Ren and if not for the Scouts taking prisoners rather than corpses, Ren would have never been able to make it out alive. If Halcy wanted him dead, it would be so.

It's a wonder this Connie is even alive if the Scouts got the jump on his team like they did.

Ren isn't sure what the steam weapon Connie mentioned is. The Scouts all have ethner guns. Is that what he means?

"Dammit," Melrose hisses. "We hardly have more men to throw at this right now. We *need* intel from Fort Kip!"

Ren scrunches his face at this remark. Even if true, why admit weakness in front of his men? No wonder this fort is doomed like Aster claims.

"We can investigate," Jean speaks up. "The Raiders are at your disposal. If the Black Glove Scouts are involved, that means Tapscott is taking the conflict seriously in Wingate and with precaution. We need to find out why."

Before Ren can throw out a harsh remark, a voice cuts him off.

"Jean," Aster asserts. "With all due respect, we need to get back to Hightower Harbor."

Ren hesitates. Is Aster scared too? He is the only one who stands a match for Halcy.

"Commander Milos said no such thing," Jean tells the deputy.

"This fort is hardly worth our time," Ren adds, stepping forward. For once he agrees with the deputy. Jean knows it's a waste of time.

"We are here to aid the rebellion," Jean says, his icy eyes shooting daggers at Ren. "Kip Lake and Cannonsburg are important landmarks. We have bested the Scouts before, if they're here again, we can do it. It wouldn't be right sending anyone else."

"You've never been one to give into hubris, Jean," Ren says, staring at the commander with cold eyes. "Surely you haven't forgotten about Fort Vail."

Jean glares back at him. "We've grown since then and the Scouts have shrunk. If anyone has a fighting chance, it's us. Besides, we are only going to investigate the troops, gather intel. We know how the Scouts work."

"You don't have stakes here, Ghentian, but we do," Melrose tells Ren. "It was a mistake bringing Ghent into the rebellion, there's no passion, only political gain."

Ren's hands ball into fists, he wishes he could strike this cocky kid down where he stands. No stakes! His hand is free of a tattoo — a symbol of marriage in Valkoean culture — he has no wife, probably no kids, but he might have a death wish.

Ren meets Aster's gaze, a surprising anger mirrored back.

Jean steps towards Melrose, his trench coat brushing over the dusty floor, slyly dividing the fort's commander from Ren and Aster.

"Do you want our help or not?" Jean asks, his tone clearly turned to anger by the rebel's remark. "We'll begin our trek back to Hightower soon if not."

"We'll accept your help," Melrose says with a nod. "Your team can—"

"Melrose, sir!" Connie asserts, his wounds treated. "I want to help them."

"Connie, you're not in any condition to go out again," Melrose says. "Especially if the Scouts show face again."

Connie stands up, hissing in pain.

"Hey, watch it!" Withorn says, standing up alongside him.

Withorn's hazel eyes point to Melrose. "His wounds aren't bad, but he sure is exhausted."

"I'm a medic too," Connie says, slightly leaning on Withorn. "I know to not overwork myself. I can lead them to where we engaged the Scouts at. I can... maybe put my team and my brother to rest too."

"I hate wasting time," Melrose says. "But rest up, Connie. You can lead the Acros Raiders to a good campsite tonight. Getting intel on Fort Kip is vital to Cannonsburg's survival."

"I'd be honored to, sir," Connie says with a nod.

Anger bubbles in Ren's chest. They don't need another impossible high-stakes mission like Fort Vail was! They should abandon these people. High Priestess Tapscott is in Hayward City, Valko's capital, at Valko's northern shore. Wasting time at the southern border is point-less. At least Fort Vail was near Hayward City. There's no point in risking another run-in with those damned Scouts!

The crowd parts and Withorn leads Connie back to the barracks for some rest. Scotty follow them close by, dwarfed by the two caped medics, her stupid mutt glued to her as usual.

The rebels disperse to their duties and Ren walks over to Jean and Aster.

"You really want to help them?" Ren asks when he's next to the Raider commander.

"Of course I do," Jean says. "Like I said, we are here to help."

"It went *so* well last time we were here," Ren remarks. "This fort is doomed *without* the Scouts' involvement. This is a recipe for disaster."

"Lay off him, Ren," Aster says. "The decision is made."

"Aster, you know better than that," Ren says.

"Enough, Ren," Jean says.

"He spoke out against your decision too," Ren says. "You don't want the input of your men, of your deputy?"

"He trusts the decision that I made," Jean says. "That's why he's my deputy. I considered it, but he's acting on emotion."

"What, so helping a place that's going to fall into Valkoean hands before we know it is acting on logic?" Ren asks.

Jean sighs. "I know you think you can lead the Raiders better than me, but I—"

"I never said that," Ren asserts. *But I probably could.* He bites the remark back.

"We will just help gather information, and be out of here after that," Jean says. "I have no intentions to stick around. They obviously need the help right now."

"That's a relief," Aster says.

Ren frowns, unsatisfied with the answer.

"And Ren," Jean adds darkly. "A good leader knows when to act on logic and when to act on emotion. It's not black and white like things are in your head."

Ren opens his mouth to argue, but Jean and Aster have already turned away, leaving him by himself. He contemplates giving chase and chewing Jean out, but he lets out a frustrated snort. It's not worth his time. Jean and Aster meet up with Merryweather, Jean smiling at his old friend. They laugh together, Merryweather's shrill voice piercing Ren's ears. Ren's hands ball into fists — they're too carefree, they aren't taking this seriously.

He turns to look at the forested mountains on the horizon beyond the gate, the sentries cranking the wooden doors shut. The trees are pinched from his view and he lets out a sigh.

The Black Glove Scouts.

The ones that killed Eliska, his friend and rival, the ones that killed most of his team.

The ones that almost killed him.

The image of Halcy flickers in Ren's mind, the armored menace having been the bane of his existence since late winter.

Ren shivers at the thought of engaging them again. He was hoping the fight at the railroad would have been their last. It ended in a victory for the Raiders, but how many times did they have to barely escape from them before that?

Hopefully Jean is right about this mission. They will gather intel, report back to the fort, and go back to Hightower Harbor to report to Milos.

Any mission the Raiders do will help keep his family safe, that's what matters. He'll follow the Raiders so long as his soul is on Harkive.

5
A BROTHER'S MISSION

The barracks are warm and dark, Scotty thankful to be in a dry place to repack her travel bag. Cannonsburg is depressing, she's actually looking forward to being on the road again with her team. She's grown comfortable with that setting over the past few months.

A few items are left scattered over the floor next to Katze, the fallion's flank rising and falling as she sleeps soundly. Her shoulder wound is healing fine, much like Scotty's arm.

Scotty shoves the rest of her fresh clothes into the middle of the bag, some jerky folded in parchment going in the top alongside some hardtack. She grabs at her remaining gear, her hands brushing over a cool chunk of metal, an etching prickling under her fingertips.

She picks the thing up and flips it over in her palm, frowning at the sight. It's Hartwood's lighter, the smoking gun that tipped him off as the traitor. A honeycomb symbol is etched into the simple piece of metal, the mark taunting her as much as it did the first day she laid eyes on it.

Scotty flips the cap open and gives it a couple clicks. After a few tries, a warm yellow flame flickers in the dark room.

The light is smothered with a click. Scotty found the lighter on the boat taking them back to Ghent when a lantern was lit to give away the vessel's location on a foggy night. In a hurry to get back to the Raiders' cabin, Hartwood dropped the lighter. It wasn't until Hartwood asked Scotty for a lighter for a ritual for Ludon just before the raid on Salina Village that Scotty even suspected the team's tracker as the traitor.

Her nose scrunches up.

He sure had her fooled.

Why such a devout follower of Ludon, god of beasts, would turn against the Soharist Pantheon is beyond her.

He was probably relaying information to the Black Glove Scouts, the team that had been tailing the Raiders since Scotty joined, and the team that they might soon have to engage again.

She places the lighter on the top of her supplies and finishes loading her bag up.

It's been nearly a whole season avoiding them, and she isn't looking forward to risking crossing paths with them on this mission.

Her brain buzzes as guilt overtakes her. Are the Scouts here because of the Raiders? She shakes that away. No, they can't be. Hartwood, the traitor, is gone. No one is relaying information to them.

This is a coincidence.

Scotty's arm stings and she figures she should go find Withorn to redo her bandages before the long walk. He should be watching over Connie now, waiting for the rebel medic to recover enough to lead the Raiders on their mission.

Scotty steps through the bulwark barracks, the odor of sweat and dirt heavy in the summer heat. Most of the rebels have disappeared around the fort for the day, but the night shift soldiers are settled into the beds, in a restless sleep in the heat.

She finds Withorn cross-legged on his bedroll, Connie passed out in a nearby cot. His wide glasses are neatly folded beside him, revealing dark bags under his shut eyes.

Jericho sits next to Withorn, the two playing a card game Scotty recognizes as matekart. Her brother, Grover, learned it from some friends when he went to the University of Eve Hallow and tried to teach Scotty when he got back. It involves a lot of math, something Scotty is not very good at. Jericho seems to be teaching Withorn the game, Withorn's bushy brows furrowed, his forehead wrinkled as he calculates how to win. Scotty smirks, it looks like he's having a hard time with it.

Jean and Aster are pressed up against the wall further back, murmuring among each other, paying no mind as Scotty and Katze approach.

Scotty's eyes point at Connie as she approaches Withorn and Jericho, careful to not wake the slumbering man.

"How's he doing?" Scotty whispers.

"He's really, really bad at this game," Jericho whispers back, not looking up from his cards.

"That's not what she meant!" Withorn hisses back.

Scotty laughs, trying to keep her voice low.

Withorn sighs and pulls his cards down. "He's sleeping. He's fine. There's not much more to it," he whispers.

The door creaks open again and Cosette walks in with a little work bag, smiling at Jericho.

"I had some ideas to stop the squeaking noise with your leg," Cosette whispers, looking down to him. "Can I give it a try?"

Jericho meets Cosette's gaze and a familiar light shines in the young man's eyes, the same look Mike used to give Scotty. Cosette and Jericho have spent a lot of time together as she's helped build his leg, and Scotty wonders just how close their bond has become.

"Er, yeah, of course," Jericho says, his cheeks burning red when he looks away to unstrap his leg. Withorn rolls his eyes at Jericho, but Cosette doesn't seem to notice his nervousness, becoming engrossed in her work.

She tinkers with the leg, using some oil and bending some metal pieces with her pliers. Her curly blonde hair is tied back, free from her blue eyes as she works. Scotty can't help but be reminded of her late brother as she watches the quartermaster tinker with the prosthetic. She and Grover would have gotten along well, they could have talked for hours about their handiwork.

Withorn and Jericho place their cards down, the medic growing frustrated as the game goes on. Cosette finishes the prosthetic soon, Jericho sliding it back over his stump.

"Let's go for a walk," Cosette says. "See if the squeak is gone."

"A walk?" Withorn asks. "We're in the middle of a game!"

"It's fine," Jericho says, smirking as he gets up. "You were losing anyway, she's just saving you the humiliation."

Cosette snickers behind him.

"We're about to do a lot of walking, you can test it then," Withorn says.

"You'd really miss me that much?" Jericho teases.

"It's rude to walk away in the middle of a game," Withorn says. "You two can flirt some other time!"

"Flirt?" Jericho blurts out. "It's not like that, she's fixing my leg!"

"I'm the quartermaster," Cosette says, blushing. "It's my job."

A rustling brings their attention to the bed, Connie stirring awake, grumbling something inaudible.

"Well seems you all woke him up," Jean remarks, walking towards them with Aster.

Connie sits upright, rubbing his eyes hard before placing his glasses on the bridge of his nose. He glares at everyone with tired brown and green eyes.

Connie sniffs hard. "Never can get any sleep in this gods forsaken fort anyway. I don't know why I tried."

"We are *so* sorry!" Cosette whispers, clasping her hands over her mouth.

"Good morning," Withorn says. "How are you feeling?"

Connie glowers at him, pushing the light sheets away from his body. He blinks as he looks at the bandages on his arms and Scotty imagines the past few days are rushing back into the dazed man's mind.

He lets out a sigh and then picks at his bandages.

"Hey, don't unravel those!" Withorn says. "I just got you cleaned up before you passed out."

"I'm a medic, and and apostle of Aurthuras, I know what I'm

doing," Connie says. "Hand me that clean rag, will ya?" He doesn't look at Withorn when he barks the demand.

Withorn's nose scrunches up at the mention of Aurthuras, goddess of healing and love. Withorn more recently found his place as an apostle of Nikos, god of plague, and Scotty wonders if he has some resentment towards the rebel for being chosen by Aurthuras. Or perhaps he just doesn't like Connie's tone.

"Well, I'm a medic from Ghent," Withorn says. "There's a reason Ghent got involved in this war — we're a force to be reckoned with because our medicine gets our men back on the field quicker. And if you clean that wound with just that rag, we're going to be working with an infection on this hike of ours. Leave it." The last words come out as a rough demand.

Connie's mismatched eyes stare deep into Withorn's gaze and he gives in with a sigh. "I suppose it's best to not waste supplies if you just dressed it," he mumbles.

Withorn looks satisfied, but still mildly annoyed, and Jean and Aster walk up behind the Raider medic.

"Welcome back, Connie," Jean says, his hand extended to the man. "I'm Jean Kay, commander of the Acros Raiders. Thank you for volunteering to lead us to the investigation."

Connie throws his legs over the side of the cot, responding much more kindly to Jean, shaking the commander's hand.

"Good to meet you, sir. I'm Connie Amsel. Honored to tag along."

Aster, Jericho, and Cosette introduce themselves, Jericho and the quartermaster apologizing profusely for waking him, much to the rebel medic's amusement.

"I'm Scotty," Scotty tells him, Katze nosing her way next to the bed to sniff at the medic. "And that's Katze. Glad you're awake."

A slight smile spreads over his lips when he runs his hands through Katze's blue-grey fur.

"Me too," he says. "The sooner we get out the better. I think I'm ready to get on the road."

Connie gets up and pins his cape around his neck, Withorn's annoyed look not fading as he watches the other medic.

"Can you brief us on what happened?" Jean asks carefully.

Connie frowns, hesitating as he thinks.

"My team..." he begins, his voice trailing. "We are a branch of the Nettlecrest division, we were sent this way since the rebel foothold in the Pinefall Province is heavy. Nettlecrest leadership fully and openly supports the rebellion now, so with the guards and police force of the Pinefall Province's capital on the rebellion's side, we were sent here, to Cannonsburg, to better distribute our forces." Connie frowns, staring at the floor as he recollects his thoughts. "We were supposed to gather intel from the Valkoean forts and settlements around Kip Lake, starting at Fort Kip down south. We had a specific spot picked out for our camp. Far from fort patrols, so far from the lake that we couldn't even smell the ethner on humid days. But two nights into our camp, those Scouts and their fallion had our scent. It was because of those... *things*. The airships. They patrol the Ghentian border. I think our clearing was spotted from the sky and those Scouts were released like hungry hounds to hunt us down. We had no idea."

Scotty grimaces, thinking back to the display the airships made at Vincent, Ghent's capital. They rained ethner bombs on the city as a mere warning. Scotty shudders, recalling the rows of indiscriminate corpses, the bags of remains they collected in the aftermath.

"They're using those airships to patrol now?" Jean asks.

Connie nods. "I was the only one to make it out. We refused to surrender, we refused to be interrogated..." His voice trails and his words come out weaker. "I watched my brother go down. Preston. He's dead."

Jean places his hand on his shoulder. "I'm sorry to hear that," he says, passing him a sympathetic glance.

Connie sniffles and brushes his hand away politely. "I just hope I didn't leave anyone behind that could have been saved. I'm a medic. I should have stayed."

"You would have just died too," Jean tells him. "I can promise you that. The Scouts would not have allowed it."

"It is what it is," Connie says with a defeated sigh, not looking at him. "I don't want to get too caught up on the what-ifs, what could have been. We need to get going."

"Aster and I will go gather the rest of the team," Jean says. "After Withorn looks you over, we'll get going, at your lead, Mr. Amsel. Meet us at the western gate when you're ready."

Connie nods at him, but says nothing as the commander and deputy step out into the fort.

He looks to Withorn, the two medics shooting daggers at each other.

"Well, you gonna give me an exam?" Connie challenges, arms crossed.

Withorn eyes the man up and down and scratches his chin. "Hmm," he mumbles.

"What?" Connie asks.

Withorn shrugs and turns around. "Looks fine to me. Might want to get a second opinion, though. You're a medic, right? You do it." He kneels down to his pack, getting his supplies ready for the road.

Connie sniffles and rolls his eyes.

"Don't mind him," Scotty says. "It took me a while to get used to him when we first met too."

Withorn waves his hand in the air dismissively, but Scotty refuses to acknowledge the cranky medic.

"I'm really sorry about your brother," Scotty tells him. "I lost mine years ago, it's like losing a part of you."

Connie's scowl melts and he slings his backpack over his back. It's not as intricate as Withorn's cabinet, but has the peony symbol on it all the same.

"Preston was my twin," he tells her. "I feel like I lost my better half."

The fire in Scotty's chest grows, hatred for the Valkoeans swirling inside her. She only has herself to blame for Grover's death, but she'd be on a suicide mission if the Valkoeans took Grover from her too.

"We'll make sure they pay for what they did to your team and your brother," she says fiercely. "I promise you that."

Connie gives her a sideways glance.

"I just want to put them to rest properly," he tells her. "I couldn't care less about getting revenge. Their bodies, unblessed by Forez, sitting in the woods, vulnerable to be fodder for the acros..." He shivers.

Scotty can't help the blatant confusion on her face as she listens to Connie. There's no way he isn't angry. There's no way part of him doesn't hunger for revenge.

"I'm an apostle of Aurthuras," Connie continues, "so the least I can do is show them my love through action."

While Mike's soul getting a proper sendoff in Ghent made Scotty feel much better, it hardly made the hatred and grief ebb. It did feel like she finally did something right, like she finally did something good. She shakes the doubt away. She is doing something good by getting revenge and fighting for the rebellion.

Scotty looks for the words to say. "That's noble of you," she remarks. She knows her tone isn't convincing by the confused look on Connie's face.

There's no burning desire for revenge in his mismatched eyes — his gaze cold, washed out, depressed. He will feel differently soon enough. When he puts his teammates' souls to rest, he'll realize it's not enough.

"Right," Connie says. "Well, let's get out of here. The sooner we get there, the better."

"Agreed," Scotty says.

6

LOOMING THREAT

The Raiders set out, Connie taking the lead beside Jean and Aster. Commander Melrose gives them a messenger swift, a copper-colored bird fittingly named Copper, to communicate with Cannonsburg if needed. Copper is without a cage and the hawkish bird seems to favor Aster's metal shoulder, his long, forked tail sweeping down Aster's back.

Melrose bids them farewell, leaving them with a half-hearted "good luck" along the way.

Ren overhears Connie murmuring to Jean. "We'll cut into the woods a ways down the road. From there we should find the telegraph wires connecting Littleton and Fort Kip. We'll follow them south until we hit the Red Forest, then we'll skirt the outside of the forest until we can't smell the ethner from Kip Lake anymore."

"The Red Forest?" Jean asks. "I've heard rumors of that place. I grew up in North Ash when it was part of Ghent."

Connie nods. "So you're aware of its reputation?"

"It's just a superstition," Jean tells him.

Connie shakes his head. "I don't think so. My team avoided it, so I can't attest to the rumors being true, but I'd prefer to stay away from a place deemed as the Holy Ground of Cassius."

Ren scoffs, out of earshot of the two. He's a proud apostle of Forez and rightfully fears the power of the gods, but there are no holy grounds other than their realms. Jean and Connie's conversation fades as Ren loses interest in the talk. It's a ridiculous idea. Holy Ground of Cassius!

Connie and Jean take the group off the dirt road, breaking into the woods on a valen-trodden path. The shade of the trees is welcoming, but the humidity in the summer air chokes at Ren's lungs. Like Connie said, soon enough they find the telegraph wires draped through the trees like grapevines. Usually ran along the roads, Ren learned early on in his time in Valko that the telegraph wires were hastily run between Valkoean forts at the start of the war. It's how most of Valko communicates with each other, weirdly enough. It uses strange noises, sounding like garbled nonsense to Ren. Messenger swifts or the postal service make much more sense. Some roads in Ghent are lined with the unnatural wires, but out in the Tarmigan Mountains where Ren lives, around Sunbell City, everyone relies on swifts.

Ren's legs ache as the sun crawls through the sky, casting dappled shadows throughout the forest. Ren notices Jericho stepping along, watching his leg carefully.

That's all my fault. I ruined him.This walk must be even harder for him than it is me.

The acrid tinge of ethner hits Ren's nose, his senses growing alert. He associates the smell with Valkoeans, with an impending attack.

With the Scouts.

He tenses and prepares for battle, staying calm and assessing his comrades for their reactions to the ethner. They seem to be growing restless from the smell too, except for Jean.

"Smells like home," Jean remarks from the front of the squad, his tone jovial.

"It smells awful," Cosette complains, her voice low. "It smells like Valkoeans."

Jean waves a dismissive hand at her. "The ethner from Kip Lake smells different than weapon discharge. It smells fresh, natural."

Ren's tenseness fades, reassessing the smell. Jean's right, it is slightly different, but Ren can't place how.

"It's as natural as vinegar or turned wine," Farsing grumbles.

"It reminds me of growing up in North Ash," Jean says. "Back before things got so troubling."

"I've always associated the smell with the Valkoean army," Aster says. "It reminds me of things being so troubling!" He lets out a half-hearted laugh.

"Maybe one day after the war's over I can take you to my hometown," Jean tells him. "When it's rightfully Ghent's land again. We can make some good memories there."

Aster smiles at Jean, a longing in his brown gaze. It seems overshadowed with doubt, though.

The valen path comes to a wide ford, a shallow stream bubbling through the forest. It's in a small clearing, lush, trodden grass lining the forest floor. This seems to be a resting spot for wild valen. A good, warm place to relax with a water source nearby. Jean holds his hand up to stop the group.

"Let's take a breather here," Jean says. "Refresh your canteens, eat some trail rations, relax, we'll get going in a few minutes. We have plenty more walking to do before the day's done."

Ren sighs and tosses his backpack in the grass. Exhaustion tugs at him, but he'd prefer to get the walking over with sooner rather than later. He kneels on the stream bank and dips his canteen in to fill it. It's cool and refreshing compared to the soupy summer air.

Splash!

Icy water hits Ren's neck and he gasps and stumbles back, his back thudding on the soft forest floor.

Bubbling laugher makes rage stir in Ren's gut, his gaze locking on Jericho and Katze, the boy splashing at the mutt. Katze chomps at the water in the air, her stupid curved maw snapping around.

"Watch it!" Ren calls. "You're getting me wet!"

Jericho's gaze flickers to Ren, a frown turning to a mischievous grin. He dips both hands in the water and throws them upwards, sending an arc of water towards Ren.

"Go get it, Katze!" he beckons.

"Gah!" Ren hisses, pushing himself to the side as he narrowly misses getting soaked. "What's wrong with you, boy?"

Katze follows the arc of water, landing her stinking, mangy pelt next to Ren and shaking, showering him with filthy water.

"By Forez!" Ren yells. He heaves himself to his feet, brushing water from his arms as Jericho laughs from the stream. "We got a lot more walking to do. I'm not going to dry off easily with this humidity, stop acting like a kid!"

"You two," Jean hisses, walking up from behind Ren. "Quiet down. Valkoeans could be crawling through this forest. Even worse, it could be the Scouts. Jericho, get out of the stream. Ren, you should know better than that."

Embarrassment washes over Ren. Jean is right, he does know better than that. He doesn't apologize, but returns Jean's harsh stare with a knowing nod. The kid just knows how to get under his skin!

"Sorry, sir," Jericho says, his face turning red. He steps out of the stream, Katze racing up to his side once he's on land. His smile returns and he walks over to Ren, his pack on the ground nearby. Ren worries as he kneels down to pick it up, watching his metal leg carefully. Relief washes over him when the boy gets up alright, slinging the pack over his shoulder.

Jericho is young, he should never have had to have dealt with that. Ren thinks back to the raid on Salina Village where he was in charge of the two greenhorns, Scotty and Jericho.

He's lucky they made it out alive.

Some leader he was.

Ren shakes away the doubts, focusing on the crossbow and musket fastened on either side of Jericho's backpack. There's also a rebel-issued revolver on his belt, but Ren has rarely seen him touch it.

"Why do you lug that crossbow around?" Ren asks him, making an effort to move his eyes from his leg to his pack.

Jericho takes a quick glance over his shoulder and shrugs under the pack's weight. "It was a gift from my dad. He showed me how to use it, mainly to hunt. I'm pretty good at shooting it."

"You know that's old school, we don't even use those down in the Tarmigan Mountains," Ren says. "Everyone at least uses powder rifles. They're deadlier than crossbows and not as slow to reload as muskets. Better accuracy too. You should consider trading them out."

Jericho frowns and shakes his head. "They were good enough for dad, they're good enough for me."

Ren wants to bite a remark at the kid. Ren heard that Jericho's dad died in the war, but even he wouldn't shoot for a low blow like that. If anything, that just proves to him that they're ineffective weapons. "I'm just trying to keep you safe, kid. It's a harsh world."

Jericho dips his head. "I'm well aware of that, trust me. I appreciate it, though."

Katze's ears prick, her body language stiffening as her head swivels around. Ren watches her closely, growing alert.

Her eyes point upwards and Ren looks to the sky, a hissing noise flickering on his ears.

"Do you hear that?" Connie asks, panic in his voice.

The rebel medic's wide-eyed gaze snaps around. Ren shudders, its almost like Connie is possessed by something.

"What is it?" Jean asks.

The Raiders have all frozen in place as the hissing grows louder, an ethner smell somehow different from the distant lake's odor, befalling the forest.

A flicker of sparkling metal catches Ren's eye and his gaze drifts upwards, a yellow object appearing beyond the treetops.

"Airship!" Connie howls, panic lacing his tone. "Get to cover! Don't let them see you! We'll all be dead!"

The Raiders scurry out of the clearing, ducking into the cover of the woods. From behind the bole of a tree, Ren peeks out into the clearing. A few backpacks — including his own — are out in the center of the grass.

If spotted by the airship, it'll be a dead giveaway of their location.

"Aurthuras save us!" Connie yells from nearby. "Aurthuras condemn our souls to purgatory! The hounds will be here soon!"

"Connie!" Jean hisses, a few trees down. "Shut it!" His icy gaze turns to Ren as the rebel medic's manic rambling continues. "Ren, shut him up!" he whispers.

Ren steps over to Connie, the medics eyes trained upwards. He doesn't fight as Ren grabs onto him tightly, placing a hand over his mouth.

"Shut it!" Ren whispers through gritted teeth. "If they have trackers out, your annoying voice will be a dead giveaway!"

Connie mumbles into his hand more before giving up, the mania turning to rapid breaths, his eyes still not moving.

The engine hissing grows louder overhead and the metal, winged beast flies further south-east. As the thing looms overhead, the smell of ethner fills Ren's lungs and steam hazes the land. Ren's body locks up, fear possessing him as memories of the bombing of Ghent's capital pour in.

The screams.

The chemical-melted bodies.

Men, women, children.

The indiscriminate murder, a chaos that would sate Cassius's hunger for mayhem.

He watches the bottom housing of the beast, expecting the bombs to drop and steam to smother him. Yet, he can't stop staring.

Connie breaks free from his loosening grasp, gasping as he lands on the forest floor next to Ren.

This airship is unlike the ones that bombed Ghent. Its body is yellow and boasts a symbol all too familiar to him — a red and black coiled snake. Mohkan's symbol animal displayed on their flags.

"A Mohkan airship," he breathes. If Valko is manufacturing them for Mohkan, sharing their technology, then how big is their fleet? How many of these things do they have?

He shudders as he thinks of the ruined capital of Ghent, the warning blow being delivered by just three of the beasts. If they wanted to destroy the city of Vincent that day, they would have.

Something falls from the bottom housing of the airship, Ren's heart leaping in his chest. The little thing falls a bit before spreading wings — a messenger swift. Ren notes that it flies northward, away from Fort Kip, which is to the south. He frowns. Why is it going that way?

"Shit," Connie hisses from the forest's cover. "A messenger swift. They spotted us. We need to go! We need to go *now!*"

"I agree," Jean says. "Grab your gear," he announces. "The breaks over, let's hit the road. Be on alert, they know we are here and will be on the hunt soon."

Ren slings his bag over his back. He grits his teeth as he falls into the march again, an unsettling feeling stirring in his gut.

The Scouts will be here soon, and he has to be ready.

7
A DARK PRESENCE

Scotty sighs as she finishes tying her boots, ready for another walk.

The Valkoeans are hunting them down again. Part of her hopes for a run-in with the Scouts. Maybe she could get one to tell her why Hartwood was their agent. How did they get to him?

She shudders.

Are they trying to get any of the other Raiders to turn?

Paranoia crawls up her spine, her neck tensing as she considers who could be cracked by the Scouts. She watches her comrades, friends she's bonded with since she joined the team in early spring. Could they? Would they?

She pushes the thought aside. That would be nonsense.

Katze stirs at her side, a rustling bringing her attention to Jean. His trench coat hovers over the forest floor, his icy eyes trained on her.

"Scotty," he greets with a nod. "I want you up front on the march, beside me."

Scotty blinks at him, taken aback.

Jean and Scotty have a unique relationship since her secret

mission to find the team's traitor. Sometimes she forgets just how much Jean trusts her.

"Of course," Scotty says with a nod.

"If we do get attacked, it'll be from our back," he says. "The Red Forest should be dead ahead to the south and the messenger swift was deployed to the north. I have Farsing and Aster lingering in the back. With Aster's armor and Farsing's bombs, we should have as much of an advantage as possible. Katze will alert us if anything is nearby." He hesitates before quietly adding. "And if it is the Scouts, I want to make sure I'm next to someone I trust when we engage them."

His comment brings Scotty's mind back to her dreams and doubts about their comrades. Does Jean have the same reservations of the others after Hartwood's betrayal?

"I understand that feeling all too well," Scotty says.

Jean passes her a sympathetic smile and Scotty's tenseness fades. She would trust Jean with her life and she's comforted to be by his side.

A clunking of metal sounds behind Scotty and she turns to see Aster, decked out in his Panzer Suit, behind them. The metal poncho makes him look wide, his armored gloves grasping onto his duck foot pistol, ready for battle. His helmet is like an old bucket with slits and holes in it. Designs are painted over the metal, some old in chipped black paint, others fresher. The Acros Raiders logo, the black bird skull symbol, is the brightest on the shoulders and his forehead. Despite looking old, worn, and chemical-scarred, Aster's armor is bulletproof — it's made of frosted steel. Scotty doesn't know much about the material, but she knows it's expensive.

"We're ready whenever you are, Jean," Aster's voice echoes from under the helmet.

"Thank you, Aster," Jean says with a nod. "Let's get going, Scotty."

The Raiders continue their trek down the valen path, following the telegraph wires snaking through the branches of the trees. Merry-weather is behind Jean and Scotty, and Scotty wonders if that was

Jean's choice. His old friend usually sticks close to him anyway, but maybe he feels like he can trust her.

Scotty keeps a close eye on Katze, each sudden movement sending off buzzing alarms in Scotty's head. She frowns as her energetic companion sniffs around, meandering along the Raiders' trail.

Katze's sleek nose points into the air, her nostrils flaring. Her movement slows, her steps growing more deliberate.

"Jean," Scotty whispers. "She's on alert."

Jean cranes his head over to Scotty and holds his hand up, gesturing for the Raiders to halt.

"What is it?" Merryweather whispers, her brown eyes wide.

Katze's pointy ears flicker and her face swivels around, her beady eyes staring into nothingness as she tries to hone in on something. Jean follows her movements with his eyes, Scotty noticing his hand twitching next to his revolver on his belt.

Katze's gaze points to the north, a low growl bubbling in her chest as her ears flatten back, her legs in position to pounce. The Raiders ready themselves, Scotty growing tense as she waits for the first peppering of bullets. Katze's low growl deepens and with a quiet bark, she tosses herself off the path into the greenery.

"Katze!" Scotty hisses, leaping after her companion, Tex primed and ready in her hand.

Katze's tail is spinning, her snorting nose pressed into the rotten stump of a tree. A quiet squeal cries from the stump and Scotty peers in before letting out a sigh.

It's a lantern-bellied frog, Valko's symbol animal, pinned against the back side, Katze's snout piercing holes into the rotten wood. The frog's slimy skin sparkles and as it squeals, the sac under its chin puffs out and a bioluminescent light twinkles from within.

Scotty cranes her head back around to the team, having let up their guard already.

"Just a lantern-bellied frog," she tells them. Embarrassment washes over her as she joins back up with the march. "Sorry for the false alarm."

Jean shrugs and they continue the walk. "For her limited training,

I won't hold it against her. The frogs are nocturnal, so night will be setting quickly. We should pick up the pace."

The forest's shadows grow longer and the trees stop in an abrupt field. Tall grasses flow like water in the wind, the breeze making Scotty long for her dress again. The pants, while practical for battle, don't allow for as much airflow as her dress.

On the other side of the field, the Red Forest looms eerily. Blood red leaves stand out against pitch black trunks, the forest looking like an endless void.

A strong smell of plant decay overwhelms Scotty. The deep odor mixes with the ever-growing stinging scent of ethner, making for a uniquely disgusting combination.

"Whew!" Farsing exclaims. "I thought we smelled bad after a long hike through the woods. Is this field full of carrion?"

"That's the Red Forest," Connie explains. "The forest is decaying, being eaten by some sort of fungus. That's where the red color comes from."

"It smells as bad as decaying flesh," Farsing says.

Connie nods. "The Red Forest is spreading, or it was at least, that's why this clearcut path has been carved around the forest. It'll spread through the grass, but much slower than if the trees were still here. I suppose it could take over all of Valko if not maintained."

"Bah, I say let it!" Farsing says.

"Oh, it'll just as easily take over Ghent," Connie tells him.

"Harkive would be much better without the two," Farsing remarks.

Connie frowns at him, unwilling to give into Farsing's remarks.

"We're just sitting ducks in this field," Jericho says, his wide eyes sweeping around. "Are we going to take cover in the Red Forest? It stinks, but I'd feel much safer than being out here! What if that *thing* flies overhead again?"

The group comes to a halt where the Red Forest starts, the odor deepening. Here, the tall grasses don't grow, the mossy red ick of the forest crawling outwards like the forest has sentient veins. Where the grass doesn't grow, stumps from the old forest remain.

Her mind flickers back to the tea she had during her training with Ludon's Fang, the rebel faction that worships Ludon, god of beasts and nature. The Red Forest tea sent her into a vivid dream, maybe even a hallucination, she's still not entirely sure. Colborn, the leader of Ludon's Fang, said they use the tea to grow closer with Ludon and strengthen their bonds with their companions. Scotty's vision — more like a nightmare — brought her failures to light, Grover, her brother's death, Mike, her fiancé's death. It ended with a sharfawks showing face before being washed out by storms. Colborn said the sharfawks and the storm could have been Ludon, but doubt tugged at Scotty. It didn't seem right.

After taking the tea, while her senses were still heightened on a patrol, she discovered a secret meeting in the woods between a member of the Raiders — Hartwood — and a member of the Scouts.

Scotty stares into the Red Forest, the black trunks making the shadows look darker. The forest almost seems to stare back, an eerie presence sending goosebumps crawling over her skin. Even among the foul odors, something more sinister seems to lurk within the woods.

"I do agree that we'd be exposed skirting the edge," Jean says. "But my intuition is saying to not go in there."

Ren steps up to the front of the group, scowling.

"I don't think intuition should be our deciding factor," he says. "If the Scouts are coming, we will be easy target practice." He turns to Connie. "What's the quickest route?"

Connie looks to him hesitantly. "Well, through the Red Forest is the quickest, but—"

"There," Ren says. "Why wouldn't we? Because a bad feeling?"

"I hate to say it," Merryweather says, a hand on her hip, "but I have to agree with Ren. If it helps us avoid a fight, might as well go in."

Jean doesn't acknowledge them and stares into the darkness of the forest. He turns back to the group, his icy gaze falling on Scotty. He seems off, like he feels the dark presence too.

"What do you think we should do, Scotty?"

Scotty freezes up. She knows he said he trusts her, but it feels odd being called out as a deciding factor. Her gaze sweeps over the other Raiders, her eyes landing on Aster, Jean's deputy, emotionless behind the slits in his helmet. Copper, the Cannonsburg messenger swift, sits on Aster's shoulder still, preening himself.

She looks back into the forest, this time fear striking her. Katze presses against her leg to comfort her and Scotty hopes she isn't trembling in front of her comrades.

"I... think we should skirt the edge," Scotty says. She looks back to Aster. "But I think you may want to get the input of your deputy first." She feels embarrassed for Jean having to suggest that to him. Maybe Aster feels the darkness too. Maybe the darkness she is feeling is just reminiscent of the stress she felt when exposed to the tea.

Jean frowns, looking lost in front of his men. He seems to be in the same mental state he was when discussing the traitor with Scotty on their meetings, but she's never seen that displayed in front of the others.

"Aster," Jean calls out. "What say you?"

Aster clanks up to the front of the group, pulling his helmet away from his matted red-brown hair.

At first Scotty thinks Aster is angry, his brow slightly furrowed, but his voice is soft and confident when addressing the commander.

"There's nothing odd about this forest besides the smell," Aster assures him. "I spent a lot of my childhood in Littleton, so I'm aware of it's reputation, but it's nothing more than a story my cousins and I told each other around the fire on summer nights. The best choice is to go through, it will keep us the safest."

Jean nods as he considers his deputy's words, Scotty's skin crawling as she and Jean lock eyes again. He is unsure, and Scotty can't help but to share that sentiment. Aster places his armored hand on Jean's shoulder and the commander lightens up.

"You're right, Aster," he says. "We need to do what will keep us the safest."

"This is the Holy Ground of Cassius we are talking about,"

Connie speaks up, anxiety lingering in his tone. "We're all followers of the Soharist Pantheon, right? Do you not fear the gods?"

"We're not *all* followers of the pantheon," Cosette remarks, arms crossed. "I respect that you all are, but I'd rather not risk my skin in fear of something I don't believe!"

Connie scoffs, turning to face the woman. "Don't believe! I've heard the voice of Aurthuras! How could you not believe?"

"Some claim to have heard the voice of Castus too," Cosette says. "In fact, we have a holiday for it — Saint Maxson's Day of Silence. I was raised by my mom to worship Castus," she adds, an edge in her tone. "It's what I have left of her."

Connie's tense stance softens. "Oh."

"Since you're *so* close with Aurthuras, don't you think she'd protect you in there?" Withorn asks. "C'mon, like Aster said, it's just a fireside tale."

Scotty peers into the forest, shivering again at the darkness it exudes. Do the others not feel it? Connie and Jean must. Withorn would even think she's crazy if she argued it further, and the medic has seen the gods before.

"No point arguing," Jean says. "The decision is made. We can make camp in there for tonight and maybe the smell will ward off any tracking fallion if they manage to pick up on us."

"I'll get back to the back of the group," Aster says. "Just let me take a moment to clean out my helmet and we can get going."

The Raiders fall silent as Aster takes his time wiping out his helmet, tossing the rag into the grass. Their march begins again and Scotty's nose scrunches. The odor of decay is overwhelming, the confines of the forest opening like the maw of a hungry beast as they start their walk again.

Scotty lets out a deep breath before moving forward. The shadows of the forest wash over her, and she gives in to the dark presence.

8

THE RED FOREST

S cotty struggles to control her breathing as the forest swallows
the team. She's unsure if it's from her nerves or the mix of
terrible smells. Katze brushes up against her leg and Scotty
relaxes slightly, her breath steadying. She pulls her gaiter over her
nose, but the filter does little to hide the smell.

This forest is odd, not just with the dark presence or smell. The
woody parts of the plants are a deep, unnatural black, appearing to
be made of obsidian. Bright red is washed over what should be greenery, the leaves looking scaled and bloody. Scotty grimaces. From the
outside, it seems like the forest is stuck in autumn, but inside it's
otherworldly. Fallen leaves are scattered over the forest floor, but red
ferns and grasses poke through.

A flutter draws Scotty's attention to the branches above, a black
and blue streak barreling down from the treetops. It crashes into the
ground, Scotty getting a glimpse of the thing. It's an acros, splotched
with the red scale. Its wings flick out oddly, trying, failing to get back
in the air. Scotty cranes her head around as the group passes it. The
red scale is strongest on its blue head, little spores poking out of its
skull. Some of its feathers are falling out and Scotty thinks its eyes are
even gouged, maybe rotted out, but it disappears into a bush. The

sickness in her gut grows and the disgusted looks on her teammates' faces shows they're all thinking the same thing.

By Forez, what was wrong with that bird?

"We need to make camp soon," Jean says bluntly.

"The Valkoeans are after us!" Connie exclaims. "The Black Glove Scouts! We can't, unless you have a death wish."

"We will need a base of operations for scouting Fort Kip," Jean says. "We can't just constantly be on the move. We need rest too."

"Well, I won't be able to rest!" Connie challenges.

"I second that!" Jericho speaks up.

"The forest should throw off their tracking hounds," Jean says. "But we will be ready to engage them. I need two scouts, two fast runners to watch the entrance of the forest."

"I can go," Connie says. "That's one thing I'm confident about, I'm fast. I... ran all the way back to Cannonsburg from here." There's a bit of embarrassment, maybe even guilt in his tone.

"Scotty, you and Katze go with Connie," Jean says.

Scotty nods. She and Connie were the only two to speak out against the forest with Jean, so maybe that's why he's paired the two up. His distrust of the team might also be a factor.

"Watch where we came in at," Jean tells them. "When you see them, be it the Scouts or just some Valkoeans, run back. Do not engage. Get back to us with their movement and we will be ready for the attack. We'll be alert here in the meantime. We cannot lose."

Scotty glances around at her comrades, visibly exhausted from the walk. A dark feeling settles in her gut, doubting the last part of Jean's statement.

"We'll be on it," Scotty assures him, her voice ringing into her ears from the gas gaiter. She turns to Connie, the rebel medic looking to her expectantly.

"Well, let's go," she tells him, slinking into the woods with Katze tailing her. Scotty puts her yellow ethner goggles on when they make some distance from the camp.

She glances around the forest, the dark presence closing in on her. A buzzing noise pierces her ears and she winces, jamming a finger into her ear, trying to shake the buzzing noise away.

"I hope Jean lets us take care of my team first thing in the morning," Connie says. "If we survive tonight."

"Jean's a caring man," Scotty says. "He holds the needs of his men highly. If anyone understands it's him."

Connie sighs. "I hope so."

"And we'll make it through tonight," Scotty assures him. "Jean will come up with a way to shake them if *they're* after us."

Connie looks down to her before looking away. "Aurthuras guide us."

"We beat the Scouts last time we fought them," Scotty says.

"You got lucky," Connie says.

Scotty grimaces. "Our team is skilled." Doubt pricks at her when she remembers the other times they engage the Scouts. "We even had someone relaying information to the Scouts, we still came out on top."

Connie gives her a hesitant glance.

"He's gone now," Scotty says.

Connie nods. "So, how did you all counter *his* steam gun?" he asks.

"What?" Scotty blinks at him. "They all have ethner guns. They're Valkoean."

"No," Connie says. "The blocky looking thing that shoots a stream of steam."

Scotty wonders if it's new technology Connie is talking about. She shivers at the thought of a weapon that shoots straight steam.

"It... it boiled their skin," Connie says. "It boiled them alive. I-I don't know how I evaded him."

Goosebumps crawl over Scotty's skin, but she tries to stay strong. "We will be fine. We *always* find a way to get around the Scouts."

"The gods must have been watching over you on your encounters with the Scouts," Connie says. "The gods do pull some strings, you know." His head swivels around as he looks through the red canopy, somehow made warmer by the colors of the setting sun. "I worry about what gods watch over us here."

Scotty pauses for a moment, silence befalling them. A buzzing rings in her ears and she shakes her head, the noise stopping quickly.

"Do you feel the darkness too?" she asks.

He nods. "This forest," he says quietly, as if the trees are listening, "it holds evil."

They reach the edge of the forest, the clearcut field peeking out from the other side of the black decay bark.

The two recede into the bushes, the smell of decay strong as the red-scaled leaves brush across Scotty's gaiter. Katze doesn't seem to care about the smell, sniffing the leaves curiously before sitting down next to Scotty.

Silver light douses the land as the sun tucks away. The moons are full tonight, Aurthuras and Nikos hanging in the sky, chasing the sun's path. Few stars peek out among their immense light, the moons acting as small suns tonight.

Connie looks up to the moons, eyes locked on Aurthuras, his lips moving in a quiet prayer.

It isn't long before Katze's ears prick, Scotty growing alert, her heart thumping.

Moonlight sparkles on something in the distance, something approaching through the tall grasses along the same path the Raiders took.

Anger overtakes Scotty, her hands tightening on a branch as figures approach, the undeniable armored silhouette of the commander of the Scouts approaching them — Halcy.

The white-and-gold armored man paces through the field, the moonlight flickering on the owl's wingspan symbol hammered into his chest piece. His wide-eyed helmet has owl-like details, horns jutting out of the sides. It has been a while since Scotty has seen the man, but his armor seems to be cleaned and repaired, the joints, especially the elbows, reinforced.

Qailah, the young fallion trainer with a pep in her step, and Arlo, Halcy's second in command, flank his sides. Another Scout is with them. Scotty thinks she has seen him before, but she's unsure. He has soft blond hair and matching whiskers, dyed grey in the moonlight.

Arlo has a wide-barreled ethner gun strapped to his back. With large chemical chambers, hoses, and a boxy steam grate, the weapon is unlike anything Scotty has seen.

"That's it," Connie hisses at Scotty's side. "That's the weapon that took out most of my team." His eyes are wide like a scared cat and Scotty almost thinks she can see his hair standing up on end.

Katze flattens herself into a ready-to-attack position, two figures bounding ahead of the four Scouts.

A quick whistle forces them to stop, two armored fallion breaking through the brushing grass. Scotty's heart sinks a bit when she remembers dealing a fatal blow to one of Qailah's hounds in their last fight. The new fallion is younger and peppier than the other, but he obeys his master's command to halt. He's all black, looking like a shadow in the night.

Connie and Scotty glance at each other for a moment, a silent question flickering between the two: when do we run?

Connie looks like he's about to book it, but Scotty turns her attention back to the Scouts when they reach the two fallion. Their noses are pressed into the ground, the Scouts watching them.

Halcy turns his back to Scotty, the small horns on his helmet glinting, and he leans down to pick something up out of Scotty's view. He looks the thing over.

"Good job, Reese!" Qailah says to her new fallion, rewarding the excited hound with a treat. She turns to the armored man. "What is it, Commander Halcy?"

He tucks it into a field bag on his hip before turning to the forest.

"We should turn around," he says, trying to keep his voice hushed.

Qailah laughs. "What? You're scared of the *Holy Ground of Cassius?*" she teases. "C'mon, it smells, that's the worst thing there is to this place."

Halcy makes some signals to her with his armored hands, Scotty wondering what it means. Qailah's expression changes and she makes some hand signals back.

Arlo and the unnamed Scout make some signals, some of them wide gestures, some with flicks of the fingers. The blond man's face is expressive as he makes the signs, his lips silently moving sometimes. Scotty studies the movements closely. Are they talking to each other with their hands?

Halcy sometimes murmurs something as he signs, his armored gloves not letting his hands get as expressive as the others.

Halcy throws another glance back to the forest and Scotty's heart almost stops in her chest. She's frozen, unmoving. It almost seems like Halcy stares straight at her, like he knows she's hidden among the red foliage.

"It's taken care of for now," Halcy says, his voice hushed.

The four Scouts turn away and head across the field, the shadows of the normal forest on the other side engulfing them.

Connie gasps as he falls back onto the forest floor, his wide eyes staring through thick lenses as his chest heaves. Scotty races over to him, his medic's cape sprawled out under him.

"Are you okay?" she asks.

He puts his hands up to his head.

"By Aurthuras, I thought we were dead!" he whispers. He laughs.

Scotty lets out a sigh. This rebel is dramatic.

"What did he mean?" he whispers. "It's taken care of? The Red Forest? They're godless heathens! Why would they care?"

"I... don't know," Scotty says. What was it that they picked up? Why are the Scouts here? She could throw a million questions back, but she doesn't want to fuel Connie's anxiety further. Enough is swirling inside her as it is.

"Oh, it was a mistake coming out here!" Connie says. "Put a nail in all our coffins!"

"They turned away, we're not dead, and we won't die tonight," Scotty says. "We need to report this to Jean."

9
HIS SECRET

"What could this mean?" Jean grumbles in front of his tent. The large white tent's door flaunts the black Acros Raiders skull logo. Dappled shadows from the moons flicker over the camp, most of the other Raiders eating their rations for the night after getting the news that the Scouts have turned away.

Scotty looks to the commander expectantly. Jean begins pacing, lost in thought. Connie and Katze are on either side of Scotty, Connie having calmed down on the walk back.

Merryweather and Aster watch Jean as he paces, concern flickering in their gazes.

"It's certainly odd," Merryweather says. She steps over to Jean and puts her hand on his shoulder, stopping him. "No sense driving yourself crazy wondering why they turned away." She throws her hands in the air. "Hey! It's a good thing, right? They turned away!"

Jean nods, but doesn't seem comforted by her words.

"Maybe they're scared of the forest," Aster says. "But Merryweather's right. What matters is that they left. They're not our problem tonight."

"Godless heathens scared of the forest?" Connie scoffs.

Aster passes him a frustrated glance. "I don't think there's anything to the forest, but from my time growing up in Littleton, Castists and Soharists alike were scared of it."

"What was really confusing was that they spoke with their hands," Scotty says.

"Well, we have our hand signals too," Merryweather says. "We used them for stealth missions in the Sunbell City Guild."

Scotty shakes her head. "It wasn't like that, it was like they were having a conversation."

"Sign language?" Aster asks amusedly.

Scotty gives him a sideways glance. "You're familiar with it?"

Aster frowns. "You're not?"

Scotty feels her cheeks grow red. "I wasn't exposed to much of the world growing up. How could I know people talk with their hands?"

"I didn't know that either," Connie says quietly.

"Why were they talking in sign language?" Jean asks, a hint of fear twinkling in his eyes. His tone darkens. "Was it because they knew you were there?"

"Maybe they can't hear well," Aster remarks. "Especially Commander Halcy. I'll be the first to tell you, your hearing takes a beating with a metal can on your head all day! Put my helmet on and fire off a gunpowder weapon nearby, tell me when the ringing stops."

The confusion doesn't leave Jean's face. He looks defeated.

Aster must recognize this because he opens his mouth again.

"Don't worry about it too much, Jean. Let's just all get some sleep. Do you want me to assign a night watch?"

Jean shakes his head. "I'll do it." He looks to Scotty and Connie. "Eat your rations and get some rest. We'll take care of your team in the morning, Connie."

Connie smiles and dips his head. "Thank you, sir."

Scotty and the rebel medic part ways, Scotty finding her tent already set up next to Withorn's. The medic sits cross-legged as he chomps on hard tack dipped in water. Jericho's tent is on the other side of Withorn's, the young man already asleep.

"Did you set up my tent?" Scotty asks.

Withorn glances up at her. "Yeah," he says through a mouthful of food. He swallows. "Jericho suggested it, but had a hard time leaning down. I put his tent up too, so don't think you're special."

Scotty laughs and rolls her eyes. "Well, I appreciate it. Don't stay up too late, we're gonna be going to Connie's battleground in the morning."

"Good luck sleeping in this stink," Withorn remarks.

"Goodnight, Withorn," Scotty bids, sneaking into her tent. Katze curls up beside her, the stinking hound heating up the already humid tent. Scotty tosses and turns, and a buzzing rings in her head again, but she eventually drifts off to sleep.

A familiar feeling overtakes Scotty. She's in a voided forest, the ground intangible, the trees dark like shadows. Katze is at her side, standing on the ground that isn't there.

A dark presence weighs heavy on Scotty, her skin pricking with goosebumps. Katze's fur stands on end, as if an electric current is buzzing through the void.

"Do you want to know a secret?" a voice brushes on her ears.

Scotty spins around, trying to find the source of the voice, but nothing is there but darkness.

A pair of amber eyes flicker in a shadow bush. They blink and switch to cerulean, a feminine shadowy figure growing out of the bush. Light passes over the face, revealing snowy skin — it's Cosette.

Like a flash of lightning, her right arm flicks to her side, draws her revolver, and six explosions send six bullets into Scotty's chest.

The force throws Scotty to the ground, grasping at her chest. Her breathing hastens, her lungs sapped of air, but there's no blood, only pain and panic.Katze runs to her side.

Cosette's silhouette walks towards her and Scotty scrambles to her feet, stumbling as she runs away, Katze on her heels.

Explosions and hisses ring out, gunpowder smoke and ethner steam mixing in the air. Bullets pierce around Scotty, black dirt flying into the air.

She scrambles to a halt as two silhouettes step out in front of her:

Farsing and Merryweather. Merryweather swings twin shadow cutlasses and Farsing brandishes a dark dagger, the two lunging at her. The cutlasses swing by Scotty's head and she jumps to the side as Farsing's dagger pierces into the ground.

"Stop!" she begs.

The two rear up for another attack, and Scotty runs.

But I found the traitor!

She rushes past Withorn and Jericho, the two shambling and lashing out at her with shadowy blades. Cuts lick into her skin and she screams and stumbles. She looks up and Ren towers over her, pointing his gun at her.

Scotty rolls and scrambles to her feet as bullets pierce where she was and she runs deeper into the shadow forest.

She cowers behind a large shadow boulder, her heart threatening to jump out of her chest. A shaken Katze presses up against her side.

Scotty almost lets out a yelp when she notices a balled up person next to her — Jean. He's hugging his legs, his eyes wide, possessed by fear.

Scotty opens her mouth to address the commander, but the boulder shifts, the sound of metal slicing through flesh, bone, ribs. Jean convulses as Aster's longsword pierces through his back, through his chest. Jean opens his mouth, his screams a gurgle, blood spurting from his mouth.

Scotty screams and falls back, the shadow boulder standing and morphing, Aster's metal armor now visible. He pulls his longsword from Jean's back, the commander falling to the ground with a thud.

Aster's helmet turns to face Scotty and she runs, the panic and smothering darkness threatening to sap the air from her lungs.

Sinister silhouettes of her teammates descend on her, their hungry eyes staring through her.

Scotty falls to her knees and shuts her eyes.

I found the traitor, I found the traitor.

The dark presence weighs heavy on her and she opens her eyes.

The silhouettes are gone, but she and Katze are not alone.

A sharfawks pads up to her through the shadows, its tail flicking playfully.

"Do you want to know a secret?" the same voice says in her ear.

The voice is childish and trustworthy, yet eccentric and foreboding.

Scotty looks at the sharfawks, its amber eyes familiar.

It cocks its head at her.

"Do you want to know a secret? I can help you."

The sharfawks does not speak physically, the voice is in Scotty's head, but she knows it's from the creature.

"Help me?" she asks.

"Do you want my help? If you accept me, I will give you *everything.*"

The sharfawks blinks at her, its gaze knowing. It waits for an answer.

Lightning crashes overhead, the dream washed out by a sudden deluge.

Scotty can't help but to gasp as she wakes up, the lightning from her dream flashing outside the canvas walls. Water drips from the tarpless tent's roof, Scotty wincing as water drips on her head. She desperately wipes at the water, but her hair is soaked.

"By Ludon," she hisses.

She's thankful for Withorn setting up the tent for her, but he sure half-assed it!

Her heart thumps from the nightmare, but she needs to suck it up and set up her tarp. She digs through her bag, pulling her tarp from the mismanaged mess of supplies. Something clunks out of the tarp and she picks it up without thinking, hesitating when she feels the smooth metal lighter.

The lightning flashes again, revealing the honeycomb symbol etched into the metal.

She lets out a snort. Funny. It's like the gods are mocking her after the nightmare.

She shoves the lighter into her bag and crawls out of the tent, tarp in tow. Once she gets it set up, an oil lantern catches her eye. She sees Jean's tent — the largest with the Acros Raiders skull symbol painted in black on the front. The front flap is open, yellow light pouring out.

Her mind flickers back to Jean in her dream and she decides to see why the commander is up so late, Katze staying at the tent.

She's used to having similar nightmares, but something felt different about this one. The presence, that darkness, was different.

A thin veil of steam fills the forest, but it's not choking like in battle. It has an odd freshness to it mixing with the pure rain.

She passes Farsing, the dewick sitting under a tarp tied between three trees. He's on night watch, bored by the looks of it. He pulls his hand away from his face to wave at Scotty.

Scotty peers into Jean's tent, expecting to see him like he was in the dream. She almost breathes a sigh of relief when she sees him sitting on a small mat reading a book. The image of him skewered with Aster's longsword stays engraved into her mind.

Jean peers up at her. "Scotty, come on in out of the rain," he says with a nod. "You'll catch a cold."

She steps inside the tent. "Thanks, Jean," she says. "I was just seeing if you're alright, it's an odd time to be up."

His tent can fit her standing up, but Jean sets his book aside and unrolls another mat for her to sit on. The oil lantern sits on a wooden plate between the two. The rain is gentler now, pattering on the tarp.

"It *is* an odd time to be up," Jean says. "Is everything alright with you?"

Scotty hesitates before answering. "Just a nightmare is all. And Withorn set up my tent and forgot to put the tarp up. Had to fix that."

Jean snickers. "He chose a good night to forget that."

Scotty rolls her eyes. "Right?"

"I... had a nightmare too," Jean admits.

Scotty frowns. "What about?"

Jean lets out a little laugh. "Just paranoia, I guess. It's funny you came to me tonight because it was... well, it was about the traitor."

"Hartwood?" Scotty asks.

"It wasn't him in the dream. It was... everyone."

Scotty pauses. Did she and Jean have the same dream?

"Everyone except you," Jean adds.

"That's what my dream was too," Scotty says quietly.

Jean hesitates, but laughs. "What a weird coincidence."

Scotty frowns. "Is it, though?"

Jean stares at her for a moment and Scotty feels her cheeks burn red. He must think she's crazy!

Jean sighs. "I like to think so. What else would it be? Is it our doubts? Is it the gods sending us a sign? Why would the gods care? You and I aren't any gods' apostle."

Scotty frowns. "Well, I have been feeling... paranoid around the others lately. Doubts creeping into my dreams makes sense." She shivers thinking back to the dark presence in the dream. She wants it to be true, she wants it to just be her doubts, it certainly makes sense. Guilt burns inside her. She shouldn't feel so paranoid around her comrades. "I love the team," she says, "but sometimes my anxiety from my mission to find the traitor comes back."

"Me too," Jean murmurs, as if he says it any louder the whole sleeping team will hear. "We just need to keep telling ourselves that whole situation is in the past." He smiles and places his hand on Scotty's shoulder. "Because it is."

Scotty smiles back, warmed by her commander's encouragement. Judging by the look in his blue eyes, he doesn't believe his words entirely.

Lightning flashes and the two wince as thunder shakes the forest. Cool air spills into the tent, bringing the sharp smell of ethner along with it.

Jean inhales deeply, a small smile returning.

"Do you smell the ethner in the air?" he asks, a longing in his tone.

"How couldn't I?" Scotty asks, wincing. "I'm not surprised from the rain on Kip Lake."

"Actually, it doesn't rain *on* Kip Lake," Jean tells her. "There's something about the airflow over the lake, something the ethner gives off where clouds cannot form over it. Rainstorms part around it. What you're smelling is the runoff water meeting Kip Lake."

"That's weird," she says. "How do people even figure that out? What does the ethner give off?"

Jean shrugs. "I'm not sure, but the runoff ethner smell... it reminds me of growing up in North Ash. It reminds me of being a kid. It reminds me why I fight." He lets out a sigh. "Sometimes, it's hard to remember what it's all for."

"I can't say I agree," Scotty murmurs. "Not a day goes by where I don't think about Mike, the life we could have together, the life I had ripped away from me."

Jean sympathetically smiles at her. "Maybe things will return to normal for us one day."

Scotty tries to think of the life she and Mike talked about in Ouellette. Having a wedding under Aurthuras's loving eye, raising kids together, the peace they were going to have away from Valko. The rest of the details start to fade. She tries to think about their late night talks about everything the future held. Sadness grips her. She has a hard time placing Mike's voice in her memories.

What else will she forget in the coming years?

Jean lets out a sad laugh as if he's lost in his own depressing thoughts. "What even is normal?"

"I... I don't know," Scotty murmurs. "Is *this* the new normal?"

Jean hesitates, Scotty unable to tell what's going on in his head. He seems to think hard about her remark.

An uncontrollable yawn escapes Scotty's lips, tiredness tugging at her as the adrenaline from the dream drains away.

"Thanks for checking on me, Scotty," Jean says, his tone doleful. "You should really get back to bed. We'll be busy in the morning."

Scotty feels a bit better about their shared paranoia giving them nightmares, but part of her wants to stay back and talk to Jean more. What more is there to say, though? When she can't think of more to say, she speaks up.

"Goodnight, Jean," she bids.

As the darkness of the night and the rain wash over her, she can't help but to latch on to the dream again. She feels like the amber eyes are watching her from the shadows.

The unease, the fear, the doubt, all come creeping back. She grows overly aware of the tents around her, like each hold a monster ready to attack.

Could she and Jean having the same dream really be a coincidence?

10

FOOD FOR ACROS

Ren bites into a chunk of hardtack, grimacing as the crud becomes dust in his mouth. He washes it down with cold brewed tea in an aluminum cup, the meal tasting more like bitter sand.

The rain patters on his tent's tarp, water dripping past the front flap. Some of the Raiders are stepping around, getting ready for the day's mission.

Ren sighs, dreading doing anything today.

He kept waking up last night, probably from the storm. Remnants of a nightmare flicker in the back of his mind, but details are fuzzy, only a lingering sense of doom. He downs the rest of his tea, praying to the gods for the caffeine to kick in.

He packs all his smaller weapons on his body somewhere, tossing his rubbery rain cape over his shoulder and tucking his head into the hood before stepping out into the camp.

Everyone musters around Jean, Ren making his way over to the others. The wet, red leaves overhead remind Ren of fresh blood, the scent of ethner in the air putting his senses on alert for an ambush. While he doesn't think there's anything supernatural about the forest, it's hard to not feel on edge right now.

The other Raiders are exhausted too, especially Jean. It looks like he didn't get a lick of sleep last night.

The only ones who have any energy are Cosette and Jericho. Cosette has been up early passing out cold tea, but she and Jericho are the two youngest members of the Raiders, so that explains their perkiness. Ren envies their youth.

Jean explains how the team is going out to Connie's battle site today, led by the rebel medic. Bringing shovels from their travel gear, Jean instructs them to prepare for an on-site burial.

"We don't know what we will be met with out there," Jean says. "The Scouts are nearby, so we must be alert. Since the battleground still has bodies that need retrieved, the Valkoeans may have trapped the grounds."

"You really think they'd go that low?" Jericho speaks up, anxiety in his tone.

"We've seen them do much worse," Jean says. "Especially the Scouts. They have no honor, it's in their design to be underhanded." He pauses. "Is everyone ready to go?"

Everyone ready, they make their way out of the camp. When they step out of the Red Forest, Ren feels like a weight is lifted off his shoulders. He takes in a deep breath of fresh air, the slight smell of ethner still lingering.

He looks to the sky, letting the cool droplets of rain wash over his face. He closes his eyes and sends a silent prayer to Ludon, thanking the god of nature and storms for the cooling rain to cut through the summer heat. A pang of sadness hits him as he thinks of Ludon — Hartwood was his apostle. One of Ren's few friends, if he'd call their bickering friendship. It still doesn't seem right that Hartwood turned on the Raiders. Eliska was Ren's friend and she liked, maybe even loved Hartwood. She was certainly charmed by him and his rodent — Shako, that stupid thing. Hartwood and Ren were thrown together through their connection with the woman. The idea that Hartwood would help bring about Eliska's death doesn't make sense. It infuriates Ren to even think about.

His nails dig into his palms, a slight pain bringing him back to reality.

The Raiders are silent as they move through the trees beyond the field surrounding the Red Forest. Connie is at the lead with Jean and Scotty, Ren following close behind.

"We're getting close," Connie says to Jean, unable to hide the shakiness in his tone. "It was a small field, at an abandoned farmhouse."

"We'll be ready for anything," Jean assures him.

Soon, Jean gestures for the team to halt, a break in the trees in the distance. They pause by a rotted livestock fence, intermittent posts sticking in the ground.

Cawing of acros echoes through the forest, Ren spotting the black and blue corvids hopping around the rainy canopy. Their curious eyes watch the Raiders.

A familiar odor hits Ren's nose — the stink of death. As an apostle of Forez, he is unbothered by the smell. Forez, the god of life and death, gets one comfortable with mortality. Ren feels too comfortable with death at times.

"This is it," Connie says. "Our camp was just ahead."

"Scotty, Cosette," Jean says. "Sweep the fence line of the farm and secure the perimeter. We'll move forward when everything is clear."

The two women comply, heading in opposite directions through the woods.

"What's that smell?" Jericho murmurs from Ren's side.

Ren gives the boy a sideways glance.

"What?" Ren asks. "It's the corpses. Don't tell me you've never smelled something dead before."

"Corpses?" Jericho asks. "Decomposing people?"

"We're coming up to a battleground. Did you think we were walking into a sunflower field?"

"I didn't expect it, *them*, to smell already," Jericho says.

"In summer, it can happen quickly," Ren tells him.

A few acros flutter from the treetops back into the field, a large flock of the carrion feeders pecking around the tan grasses.

"Doesn't help the acros are speeding it along," Ren says. "Not that the flesh probably wasn't already ripped apart."

Jericho's freckled face looks like it's turning green under his rain cape's hood. "Okay, you can spare me the details," he remarks.

Scotty and Cosette return, reporting that the perimeter is all clear.

Jean moves the group forward, Connie hesitating at the rear. Jean coaxes him along, murmuring something to him and placing his hand on the rebel medic's back. Connie lets out a breath and works up the courage to step forward.

The Raiders step into the overgrown farmland, Ren's gaze sweeping over the land. A ramshackle farmhouse sits at the far side of the field, large trees arching over the building. Ludon is trying to reclaim the building, vines crawling up the side like a leviathan pulling a ship into the sea with its tentacles.

The farmhouse reminds Ren of his homestead in the mountains of Ghent. To think of it turned to a battlefield and abandoned makes his stomach turn.

They reach a patch where the grass and weeds are patted down like where valen had slept, but Ren knows this grass wasn't settled so peacefully. Remnants of trampled tents are scattered around, the fabric corroded by steam. There are spots where the grass is shredded and the stench of decaying flesh grows, and that's when Ren notices the brown blood in the grass, dried and unwashed by the rain.

Caws echo over the battlefield as the acros flush from their feast, startled by the Raiders. Like a massive cloud of black and blue, they take shelter from the rain in the branches of the trees near the house. Their beady eyes watch the Raiders approach, some still chewing on chunks of old meat.

Ren watches the savage things for a moment. Acros are supposed to be clever creatures, which is why their division is named after the bird. After seeing enough of the things eating corpses, no regards or respect for the souls sent to Forez, he wonders if there was ulterior motive to Lady Amala's name choice.

"Spread out and search the field," Jean tells the group, his face hidden behind his rain cape's hood. "We'll gather them for a burial here, let their bodies be respectfully laid to rest. Be on the lookout for traps, scouts in the woods, anything." Ren catches the commander's gaze in the last sentence, Jean's icy blue eyes darting around. If he didn't know Jean better, he'd say Cassius's claws are in the man's head. It's logical to be wary in this situation.

The Raiders fan out, Ren taking no time to find his first body close to the farmhouse. It stinks. The body, a young male, is contorted, lashed and beaten, brown blood stained around it. His eyes have been pecked clean by acros, hollow sockets remaining. Poor bastard doesn't even look at peace in death.

His wounds are brutal, sword lashes deep and many. His uniform is soiled by acros droppings and blood, but near the stomach, the cloth is burnt away by ethner, boils surrounding a gaping stomach wound. Ren feels his heart rate hasten as he studies the wounds.

He wants to think this rebel division is beneath the Acros Raiders in skill and might, but the Black Glove Scouts have beaten the Raiders before when they were out for information, taking them as prisoner or holding back for the sake of intel.

Rain patters against Ren's hood, but blood rushes through his ears as his heart pounds. He can't look away.

Have they really been moments away from being a pile of corpses like this gods forsaken field? Nothing but food for acros?

With Ghent fully and openly in the war now, the Raiders have no special information, nothing of value to the Scouts. Do the Scouts know this? Will they stop holding back now?

A single thought makes Ren's stomach churn.

This could be us.

Ren pushes the fear away. He's an apostle of Forez. Death doesn't bother him. It *shouldn't* bother him. He has a mission to fulfill, the sooner the better.

"I found one!" Ren calls out.

Aster and Connie are soon by Ren's side, the deputy and rebel medic on body collection duty. Aster's metal poncho shows under his rain cape, his helmet dotted with droplets at his side.

Connie halts when faced with his dead comrade.

Ren doesn't say anything as the rebel looks down with wide eyes, his face shadowed by his hood.

"By Aurthuras," Connie breathes. "Preston."

Connie kneels down beside Preston's body. This must be his brother.

Connie's hand hovers over his brother's corpse and he recoils from touching him. His gaze seems to be lost in the empty sockets where his brother's eyes used to be.

"His... his eyes were like mine," Connie says calmly after a moment. "It's the only thing we shared as twins." He trembles, tears mixing with rain behind his glasses. "He always had a better outlook than me. Preston was my better half." He turns to look to Aster and Ren, his face tear-stained. "Could you give us some space? I-I need extra time with my brother... to say goodbye."

"Of course," Aster says. "Let me know when you're ready to bring him to the burial site."

The two step away from the grieving man. Ren has no siblings, so he can't understand Connie's loss, but Ren always describes his wife as his better half.

The thought leaves a hollow feeling in his chest, so he forces himself forward. He'll be more help the more bodies he finds.

He approaches the farmhouse and notices a flick of black as an acros dives into the nearby grass. Ren makes his way towards the carrion-eating bird, and it flies into the air again, startled.

The smell of death is faint here, but another flattened area of grass reveals another body in the muck. She's a clansman, her visible skin pale-grey like Scotty but with dark patches, and her dark brown hair is shorter than most men. The patched skin tells Ren that she was a Camdian, different than whatever Clanland Scotty's family is from.

She looks more at peace than Connie's brother, less brutalized.

She has those same ethner burns as Preston, but only her flank got the blow. The burnt cloth, the boils, it's like she was shot with a stream of ethner steam. Ren wonders what kind of weapon could do such a thing.

75

As Ren stares at her side, he notices a slight rise and fall of her chest and his eyes widen.

She's alive.

"Withorn!" he hollers. "We have an alive one!"

His ringing voice is echoed by the caws of startled acros.

Connie pushes his way through the grass frantically, mouth agape, a crazed look in his gaze.

"Who is it?" he gasps. "Alive? Are you sure?"

Aster tails Connie, reaching out to the man as he throws himself next to the woman.

"By Aurthuras! By Aurthuras! Bless Yuna!" he says, trembling. "Rea! Rea! Can you hear me?"

Withorn finds his way to them soon, throwing his medicine cabinet on the ground next to Connie. Jean is close behind the Raider medic.

Connie grabs onto the woman's shoulder and gives her a shake, giving in to his panicked state. "Reagan!" he hollers.

Withorn grabs onto Connie's shoulder and throws him back into the mud with force.

"Hey!" Connie bellows.

"You'll kill her, you idiot!" Withorn hisses. "Get out of my way!"

"Let me save her!" Connie demands. "I-I need to!" He reaches out to Withorn's cabinet, but Aster grabs onto his arm.

"Let go!" Connie yells. "Let go of me!"

"Connie, you're acting erratically," Aster says. "Withorn can treat her better in his state. Let him take care of her."

"I couldn't save anyone," Connie breathes.

"If you didn't run, we wouldn't be here to give her a chance," Aster says.

That shuts Connie up, the rebel medic watching Withorn clean up his comrade. Connie looks like he's in shock now, unmoving.

The terror in his gaze is disturbing and Ren can't tell if he's crying or if the rain is staining his face.

"He's buckling under pressure," Ren remarks to Jean. "No wonder the rebellion's in the state they're in." Ren doesn't even think Withorn's a great medic, he acts out in stupid ways, but compared to Connie right now, Withorn seems like a accomplished doctor.

"Have some compassion, Reiner," Jean says. "How do you think he feels right now, surrounded by the corpses of his friends and family? We were lucky our comrades got hanged and we didn't have to see them like this."

Ren looks to the rebel woman and thinks of Eliska, pushing that thought aside quickly, not wanting to humor the idea. He looks back to Connie, the weakness he's displaying disturbing Ren to his core.

Surely, Ren couldn't react that way.

He wouldn't.

Would he?

Ren turns away. "I'm going to search for more bodies. I'm not much use here."

Ren scours the field for a while, teaming up with Aster to haul bodies to the grave site. Farsing and Jericho dug a majority of the shallow graves, the two enjoying a smoke break since the rain disappeared.

The bodies rest in the shallow holes, though Ren wouldn't say they look at rest. The grass is trampled here to mark the gravesite, Ren standing on the edge of the area, his rain cape's hood still draped over his head.

Footsteps sound to his right, so he cranes his head over, Jean and Connie approaching.

"Was that all of them?" Ren asks, turning to Connie.

Connie nods. "Yeah. All twenty of my comrades are accounted for." His mismatched gaze meets Ren's. "Thanks for taking over carrying them."

Ren frowns and hesitates. "You're welcome."

"Ren," Jean says. "How about you say a blessing for the bodies? You are an apostle of Forez, after all. Can you help guide them to purgatory?"

Ren shakes his head. "I may have been chosen by the god of death, but the connection one had to the deceased is what matters when blessing the dead. Connie should bless them." Ren thinks about how pathetic Connie looked when he couldn't help Withorn with Reagan. How disturbing that was. "I... think he needs to."

Jean dips his head. "Understood. Connie, what do you think of that?"

"Do you really think it will be enough?" Connie asks.

"Well, yeah," Ren says. "I'm not just making something up. Their souls will get safely to Forez regardless. Blessing helps guide them. Best to be guided by a loved one than a random apostle."

Connie and Jean make their way to Jericho and Farsing, prompting the two to get back to work with their shovels.

Ren notices Withorn and Scotty at the far side of the grave site, watching over Reagan, the clansman resting on a makeshift cot. He walks over to them, not wanting to watch Connie get emotional wishing his comrades a safe trip to purgatory.

He gets up to the three, Katze stirring at Scotty's side at his arrival.

"How's she doing?" Ren asks, shooing Scotty's fallion away with the wave of his hand.

"Breathing," Withorn says. "I want to call it stable."

Reagan mumbles, Withorn and Scotty not reacting to the noise.

"She said something!" Ren exclaims.

"She's been mumbling for a bit now," Withorn says. "Could be dreams, maybe pain, I'm not sure. We're keeping a close eye on her if it changes."

"Did you give her something for pain?" Ren presses.

"No, why would I do that?" Withorn asks sarcastically. "Of course I gave her something for pain!"

"Can't you take this seriously?" Ren asks, frustration whelming inside him. "It was an honest question."

Withorn just stares at him with tired eyes.

A louder mumble forces their attention back to Reagan.

"Help... help..." she grumbles.

"Words," Withorn whispers. "That's new."

Her face scrunches up and her eyelids flicker open a few times. She has soft grey eyes, like Scotty's, but they're hidden quickly as they settle shut.

Ren watches her carefully.

Forez, please let her live.

She rustles around for a few minutes before her eyes open again, staring right at Withorn.

She blinks a few times. She looks confused, but not surprised.

She takes in a deep breath, her face contorting from pain. "Who," she breathes. "Who are you?"

"We're on your side," Withorn assures her.

She blinks at him slowly a few times.

"Ren, go get Connie," Withorn says. "Familiarity might comfort her more."

Ren nods and complies, pulling the rebel medic away from his blessings, Jean following the two. By the time they get back, Reagan is already drinking water from Withorn's canteen, the man supporting her head and neck as she sits upwards.

Connie trembles as he approaches.

"Rea," he murmurs.

She turns her head after taking a few gulps from the canteen. Withorn rests her head back down and her eyes stay locked on Connie, her mouth agape as she breathes.

"Connie," she rasps.

Her lips twist into a small smile.

"Who else... made it?" she asks, her words strained.

"No one," Connie says.

Her smile fades and she slowly adjusts her head to look at the sky.

Connie kneels down next to her.

"We're working on putting the others to rest," he tells her. "The Acros Raiders, a Ghentian division, are here to help."

Reagan's eyes sweep around the Raiders around her.

"We need... to leave," she says.

"We'll leave after the team's fully buried," Connie says.

"Valkoeans," she breathes. "Troops moving north. Through here. We *need* to leave."

Jean butts into the pair's reunion, kneeling down next to Connie. "You've seen Valkoeans come through here?" he asks.

Reagan gives a slight nod. "Before I passed out," she pauses, "I saw two sections. Moving that way." She weakly tilts her head northward.

"Were the Black Glove Scouts one of them?" Connie asks.

Reagan takes in a deep breath. "No."

"That's not good," Jean remarks. "We will investigate this after I send an update to Commander Melrose." He stands up, looking around the field. He hesitates, as if expecting to be jumped by a Valkoean unit at any moment.

"We'll finish the burial and blessings, but we need to make it quick," Jean says. "We need to get back to camp as soon as possible so we can plan our next move. Fort Kip is to the south, there's no reason for Valkoeans to be moving north unless they're planning something — something that will happen soon."

Ren frowns. With the Scouts involved, there's no doubt in his mind that the Valkoeans are planning a serious takeover of Cannonsburg. The Raiders need to wrap it up here before it's too late.

11

HIS OMEN

T he Red Forest stretches above Scotty's head once more, the dark, suffocating feeling settling back in now that the Raiders are back at camp.

The sky is still grey, humidity and steam hovering through the forest, but at least the rain is gone. Jean gave up his large tent for Withorn and Reagan, the woman resting on some dry sleeping bags. Connie fawns over her still, pestering Withorn in the process. Withorn must feel bad for him or something, he stopped reacting negatively to the rebel medic's annoyances. Still, he isn't letting Connie assist besides fetching boiled water from Cosette.

Jean sent out Copper, Melrose's messenger swift, to report the news to Cannonsburg's commander. It's been almost a half an hour since then, the group waiting with baited breath as Aster and Jean discuss tactics.

Scotty glances around the camp, anxiety buzzing in her head. She hates waiting.

Her ears ring and she winces, a dark presence forcing her attention behind her. She spins, her eyes snapping around the forest.

Is something there?

Scotty looks at Katze, the fallion's pointed ears pricked in the direction the presence is coming from. Scotty gives a hesitant glance back to her comrades before stepping out of the campsite into the woods, Katze on her heels.

The buzzing in her head grows, keeping her honed on a specific path, just out of earshot of the camp. She feels a pop in her head, and the darkness washes away and her senses clear, like the steam and humidity have blown away from this part of the Red Forest.

She stops, a little rusty figure sitting among the red leaves, its back turned to her, antlers pointing towards the treetops. It's a sharfawks. Scotty hesitates as she studies it, the little animal staying uncharacteristically still as it keeps its back turned to the two.

Is this the same sharfawks from her dream?

The same sharfawks she saw during her Bond of Beasts ceremony to receive Ludon's blessing?

Scotty wants to laugh at the ridiculous notion, but a certain familiarity tells her she is right, but she can't explain it. She can't explain the feeling overtaking her.

A low growl emits from Katze's throat, but the fallion doesn't dare lunge at it.

Scotty hesitates, her interaction with the sharfawks from her most recent dream flickering in her head. Her body is frozen in place as a voice rings in her mind, a head-splitting migraine pounding through her skull.

"My summon worked. You're smarter than I thought. Have you come to take up my request for help?"

She winces and yowls, falling to the ground, her hands clasped around her head. It's not a talking sharfawks. The voice is divine; the voice is part of Scotty, like in her dream. Is this a vessel of a god? Of Ludon?

Or is she crazy?

Her heart thumps hard as the pain settles to a tolerable throb.

The sharfawks doesn't turn around, Scotty's eyes wide as she stares at the creature.

"What are you?" she demands.

The sharfawks flicks its tail, but still faces away from her.

"Do not ask questions you know the answer to! Do you accept my help?"

The voice pounds in her head again and the pain strengthens and ebbs.

"Help for what?" she asks. "Are you Ludon?"

The sharfawks turns around, its head low as its amber eyes pierce into Scotty's soul. It's as if it can read her thoughts. The voice speaks again, the pain sharp, but Scotty numbs as she stays in the shar-fawks's gaze. It studies her.

"I see I need to earn your trust," it says. "I will give you this: Go as the acros flies."

Scotty blinks.

Is this really Ludon, god of beasts and storms?

The same god Hartwood is an apostle of?

"As the acros flies?" she echoes.

"When you need more, just accept me. I can give you everything you seek, my child."

Time seems to pause as Scotty tries to understand what that means, what just happened, and why Ludon is drawn to her.

"Scotty!" a familiar voice calls.

Scotty snaps around, fear surging through her. Something feels wrong about someone seeing her with this sharfawks. Jericho approaches through the red brush and her heart thumps in panic.

She turns to face Ludon again, but the sharfawks is gone.

She blinks at the empty space, wondering if all of that really happened or if she hallucinated it.

"Scotty!" Jericho says again, looming behind her. "Are you okay? I heard a scream."

Scotty turns back around, she must look some sort of way because Jericho's expression is more panicked now.

"Are you okay?" he repeats.

He tries to kneel down to help her up, but she puts her hand up to stop him.

"Sorry to have startled you," she says, rubbing the back of her head nervously, on her feet now. How can she even begin to explain what happened? Did that even happen? He'd think she is crazy. "I tripped while taking Katze out to do her business," she says. "The damned forest floor is all red, hard to tell where you're placing your feet." She is taken aback by how fluently the lie comes out.

"Well, I'm glad it's not just me having trouble walking in this forest then," Jericho says with a laugh. "Glad you're okay."

A flicker of feathers and distressed squawking draws their attention to the canopy. Copper flies towards the camp in a frenzy, Scotty and Jericho putting their conversation on pause to follow him back.

The Raiders' attention turns to the messenger swift returning, Jean catching him on his arm. Copper looks flustered, his feathers awry, blood on his talons.

"You sure look beat," Jean says. Cawing makes Copper look to the trees, a flock of acros beyond the treetops heading north. "Must have gotten into a fight with the acros littering this area. You're a fighter, aren't ya?"

Copper preens himself, Jean pulling the message from the cylinder on his back.

Scotty's gaze focuses on the large flock of acros overhead. They must be moving since the Raiders buried their food at the farmhouse. She notices the direction they're going, northward, thinking of Ludon's omen.

Go as the acros flies.

Did he want her to literally follow acros?

Confusion overwhelms her.

Did that really even happen?

Surely this forest is just getting to her.

Jean blinks in disbelief as he reads over the order. "Melrose still wants us to investigate Fort Kip," he remarks. "He doesn't think the Valkoean movement is a threat."

"He knows this area well," Aster says. "Maybe it's something he has seen before. Does he give reasoning?"

Jean shakes his head and passes the parchment to his deputy. Aster looks it over and Jean turns to face the Raiders.

Scotty watches the acros in the sky, the flock still intermittently peeking through the canopy.

Her heart thumps hard as she thinks of the omen.

She needs to know if that was real.

Maybe she is going crazy.

"Since Reagan saw the troops moving recently, shouldn't we investigate to the north sooner rather than later?" Scotty speaks up.

Murmurs of agreement wash over the Raiders.

"Melrose must have his reasoning," Aster remarks. "It's not smart to stray from orders."

"What's got you so agreeable with Cannonsburg?" Ren asks. Aster's face twists into a scowl, but Ren speaks up again before the deputy can bite back. "Can we divide up the team?" he suggests. "It's just reconnaissance. Smaller units will be less detectable, we can kill two birds with one stone."

"I like that idea," Cosette says. Most of the other Raiders speak up in support.

"We will be safer together," Aster argues. "We can go north later."

"I like the idea of safety in numbers," Jericho says hesitantly.

"We will split up," Jean says. "We are more than capable of tackling two reconnaissance missions at once."

Aster frowns, but doesn't argue once Jean's decision is set. "If that's what you think is best," he says.

"Aster, you can lead the team to the south," Jean says. "Take Ren, Jericho, and Merryweather with you. I'll take Scotty, Cosette, and Farsing to the north. Withorn, Connie, and Reagan will stay back at camp."

Connie scowls at Withorn. "I know Reagan needs looked after," he says, "but do you think have two teams without medics is a good idea?"

"Jericho and Cosette can act as medics in a pinch," Jean says. "I'm confident in their skills, I'd trust them with my life as much as I would with Withorn." Jean's eyes land on Withorn. "And Withorn, please behave while we're gone."

Withorn gives Jean a thumbs up signal, too tired to argue with the commander. Scotty doesn't believe that he will behave, but at least she will be far from his bickering.

"If the situation gets too dire, retreat back to the Red Forest camp," Jean says. "Does anyone have any qualms before we head out?"

Aster and Jericho look like they want to argue, Aster still frowning, and Jericho fidgeting, but they stay silent.

"Alright, let's move out then," Jean says.

12

AS THE ACROS FLIES

J ean's team heads to the north, Scotty at the commander's side
with Katze. Cosette and Farsing walk with them, keeping silent.
Acros dot the lush branches overhead, their blue heads pointed
towards the small group of Raiders.

Scotty is thankful to be out of the Red Forest again, the dark presence having lifted since they made it back under the cover of normal
trees. The acros flush from the trees, fluttering northward, the group
staying under their flight path.

The Raiders keep an eye out for signs of troop movement, Scotty's
senses on alert. Katze doesn't seem to be wary of anything, padding
slowly beside Scotty like any normal walk.

Caw!

Scotty doesn't need to look up to know those damned birds are
watching them. The words of Ludon ring in her ears.

Go as the acros flies.

She almost feels laughter bubbling in her chest. That couldn't
have happened.

The amusement turns to a looming darkness in her mind.

"Scotty, are you okay?" Cosette asks.

Scotty is pulled from the darkness of her mind, turning to the quartermaster.

"Er, yeah," she says.

"You're looking different today," she remarks. "Didn't sleep well?"

Scotty glances over at Jean, the two sharing knowing glances. They say nothing, though.

"I think that Red Forest is just getting to me," she tells Cosette.

"Bah, don't listen to what people say about that forest," Farsing speaks up, speeding up to walk in line with the two. "It's just paranoia, it's just the rumors getting in your head." He prods his finger into his head, just shy of his ground-down horns. "Maybe it's that gods forsaken smell. Who knows! Smell's been giving me some nightmares, that's for sure."

Scotty blinks at Farsing and opens her mouth to speak, but Jean speaks up first.

"You're having nightmares too, Farsing?"

Farsing hesitates and nods. "Well, yeah, I have nightmares sometimes. Been just about every night in that forest, though."

Jean frowns. "Interesting."

"How about you, Cosette?" Scotty asks.

"What?" she asks. "Nightmares? No, none I can recall."

"It's normal in our trade," Farsing remarks. "Can hardly tell a dream from a nightmare anymore. Eh, I'm used to it, honestly."

"Well, it's certainly not normal for me," Cosette remarks.

"Maybe when you're older, they'll hit ya," Farsing says with a snort. Cosette fumes at Farsing

"Cosette and I are just about the same age," Scotty says, an edge in her tone. "I've been having nightmares too."

Cosette glares at Farsing, but calms after Scotty speaks. "That's weird that you all have been having nightmares. I wonder if there's something to it."

Farsing shrugs. "Maybe you got it right and Castus is the true god."

Cosette chuckles. "Well, I know I'm right," she says with a smug smile.

Jean halts, the rest of the crew following suit.

"I think we need to split up," he says. "We need to cover more ground if we want to find any sign of troop movement. From what Reagan said, there were a lot of men marching, so it should be obvious. Cosette and Farsing, go to the west and northwest respectively. Scotty and I will got east and northeast. We'll meet back here in twenty minutes, that should keep us all within earshot of each other in case we run into any trouble."

They pair up and split from each other, Scotty and Jean walking together.

Scotty looks for the words to say and finally breaks the silence, the two alone.

"Do you... think that forest is giving us nightmares?" she asks.

Jean laughs. "No, of course not."

"It's a weird coincidence, then," she says, a bit irritated that Jean laughed at the idea. She frowns. It *is* a silly idea, but she can't help but to feel it's a serious issue.

"Cosette said she isn't having the nightmares," Jean remarks. "So I think it's hardly a coincidence. Farsing is right, we are... troubled people. Nightmares are normal. This is a high stress situation."

"I suppose you're right," Scotty says.

Could that aspect of Ludon been from stress?

Caw, caw!

Scotty winces as the acros fly and cheer overhead, almost as if to mock her, to remind her of the omen.

"Head to the northeast," Jean says. "I'll go east, report to me if you find anything."

Scotty nods. "Got it."

They break away, Scotty and Katze pacing slowly through the forest. Scotty watches the acros overhead. She needs to know if that omen meant anything, she needs to know she actually saw something meaningful.

It's a deviation from Jean's order, but she follows the birds' flight-path. Every so often, she loses them from her view, but she presses forward.

89

She steps carefully over the forest floor, keeping her footfalls on the soft moss. A flash of copper on the ground catches her eye, a stark contrast to the muted greens and browns.

She kneels down in the soft moss, a distinct copper flight feather laying on the ground. It looks like one of Copper's feathers covered in blood.

Upon closer inspection, smaller down feathers are peppered over the forest floor.

She remembers Copper returned looking like he got in a scuffle. This must be where he fought the acros. It's interesting, but not helpful.

She stands up and looks to the canopy, the trees a bit more sparse here, the sky opened up. Some acros rest in the trees, a pair fighting over a flashy object hanging from a branch. It looks like two metal balls connected by a rope.

Scotty studies the object for a moment before a rustling brings her attention back to the forest floor. She snaps around, the figure of a man startling her, throwing her to the ground.

"Gah!" she spits.

Jean laughs, the commander standing over her.

"We're supposed to be on alert," he tells her.

Scotty feels her cheeks grow red. She'd be dead if that was a Scout. Jean extends an arm to her and helps her up.

"This isn't where I told you to scout," he says. "This is my section."

"Er, sorry," she says, rubbing the back of her neck. "I got... distracted."

Jean gives her a sideways glance, but Scotty talks before he can question her further.

"But look," she says, pointing into the canopy. "There are some weird metal ball things in the trees."

Jean cranes his head upward, narrowing his eyes when he spots them.

"Those are bolas," he tells her.

Scotty frowns. "What are those? I've never heard of them before."

Jean looks like panic is starting to settle in, his stance less strong, his eyes wide.

"They're used to capture animals alive," he says. "Valko uses them to intercept our messenger swifts."

Scotty leans down and grabs the bloody copper feather. She and Jean remain silent as she holds it up between them.

"It's a trap!" he hisses. "We need to go back!"

Caw! Caw!

Scotty looks upwards, the acros starting to fly to the north again.

Go as the acros flies. Was I meant to find this? Or is there more?

Anxiety swirls inside her. Ren, Jericho, and the others could be in trouble. But there could be more ahead. The Valkoeans could be trying to keep them from the north, trying to keep them from learning the truth. What is the right thing to do?

Caw! Caw!

The birds' calls ring in her head.

"C'mon, Scotty!" Jean says, grabbing her arm. "Aster and the others are in trouble! Melrose's order was forged, they've been led into certain ambush!"

She pulls her arm back, Jean turning back to her, a surprised look in his eyes.

"What are you doing?" he asks.

She leans down and grabs a rock, tossing it at the bolas. The weak branch breaks, the balls tumbling to the forest floor, and Scotty snatches them up.

"These came from somewhere," Scotty tells him. "Katze and I are the only ones who can find where they came from." Her gaze points to the north. "Let me find out where." Her words are demanding but her tone begs. She turns back to Jean. "Please, Jean. Something is going on to the north. We need to know what."

"We can go later!" Jean insists.

"The scent on the bolas won't last forever!" she argues. "The Valkoeans are moving, we need to know what they're up to before it's too late."

"What, you just want me to send you there alone?" Jean asks.

"Yes!" Scotty says. "I can run if needed! Aster, Ren, and Merry-weather are our strongest fighters. If Aster wasn't there, I'd be more worried. The information I get from scouting could be more life-saving than intercepting a possible fight. The forged note was telling us specifically not to scout out the north. The Valkoeans want to keep us away from here. They know we are going to investigate Fort Kip, that's it, but Aster's team is staying on alert anyway."

Jean looks like he's about to argue further.

"If you feel so strongly about it, go," he decides.

He turns away. "I'm pulling Farsing and Cosette off this mission to come with me. You're on your own. Good luck, Scotty." He disappears into the forest, Scotty left standing still, bolas in hand.

Her heart thumps as she considers chasing after him.

Guilt claws at her. Is this the right thing to do?

Caw!

She snaps around to look at the flying acros again.

She has to know. Something is going on to the north. Disre-garding the omen, disregarding what Reagan said, these bolas are a telltale sign of Valkoeans in the north.

She puts the bolas in front of Katze's muzzle, the fallion's nose twitching as she sniffs it.

Katze's head cranes around before stuffing her nose to the ground, padding northward.

"Let's go, girl," Scotty says.

As Katze leads Scotty along, the acros disappear from the sky. No sign of the black and blue birds lingers in the trees, their distant caws having vanished. Anxiety pricks at Scotty. Does this mean she's making the wrong choice?

She focuses on Katze and the bolas in her hand. Of course not. She has physical evidence of Valkoeans in the area and she trusts Katze to take her to them.

If the acros meant anything or not, it doesn't matter now.

Songbirds sing out as they make their trek through the woods, a slight breeze ruffling the treetops. Katze's attention wanders occasion-ally, but Scotty gets her back on track with a sniff of the bolas.

Katze's movements become more cautious and a short break in the trees ahead grabs Scotty's attention. Her hands hover over her belt, checking for Tex and her twin daggers, her eyes still stuck on the clearing.

"Katze," she whispers. "Hold up."

Katze looks to her hesitantly, Scotty's voice bringing her off the scent trail.

Careful with her foot placement, Scotty closes the gap to the clearing, keeping hidden among the brush as she peers ahead.

The land slopes down, a massive Valkoean encampment sprawled out in front of her. The trees from the clearing have been used to construct new buildings and a thick wood fence — this isn't just a temporary camp.

Scotty produces her scope from her field bag, bringing it to her eye to inspect the camp closer.

Buildings, tents, and cannons are in Scotty's sight, anger coursing through her veins when she sees the Black Glove Scouts symbol posted on a tent. Their rival team is nowhere to be seen, though.

Valen huddle under a makeshift stable, and Valkoean and Mohkan soldiers carry supplies around. Scotty shivers — they're preparing. No doubt for a takeover of Cannonsburg. Scotty isn't sure if it's close enough for the cannons to reach the rebel fort from here, but either way, it's certainly an easier spot to launch an attack from.

They have the manpower to protect a small city, and diverse divisions are in the camp's ranks. Cavalry, fallion units, foot soldiers, cannoneers — it is clear to Scotty that this has been months in the making. No wonder they have been protecting this area with the airships.

A roaring, hissing noise makes Scotty's heart stop in her chest and she pulls her scope away. Beyond her cover, she catches a glimpse of a massive, bright yellow airship starting to hover. She moves her position slightly, the large yellow beast coming fully into view, boasting Mohkan's red and black coiled snake symbol. Horned Mohkan soldiers are giving the ship space, shouting and hollering as the thing levitates into the sky.

The undercarriage looks like a windowed boat hull, a mix of Mohkan and Valkoean soldiers in its belly, presumably captaining the thing.

Still far from the airship, the size freezes Scotty in a state of awe. Its sail-wings heave up and down as engines pump ethner steam into the sails. The steam lifts it, some of the steam rolling gracefully away from the wings as it raises into the clouds.

Scotty's gaze lingers a bit too long on it, wondering where it is going. It heads northeast — not towards Valkoean controlled Littleton, but also not towards Cannonsburg.

She looks back down to the crew, her heart sinking when two other airships are revealed behind it, these painted red, but sporting a blocky yellow sun logo. Scotty recognizes the symbol from Ghent's bombing, she assumes it's the symbol for all Valkoean airships.

Are these the same airships that dropped the bombs that leveled part of Ghent's capital, Vincent?

Her mind flickers back to that day. All the bodies they retrieved, the indiscriminate killings — the mayhem rivaled the destructive power of Cassius, god of chaos.

Scotty shakes herself out of the past.

Without a word to Katze, she breaks off in a mad dash back to the Red Forest camp.

The sooner she reports this to Jean, the better.

It may already be too late.

13

THE GEYSER FIELD

The grassy area alongside the Red Forest becomes bleak stone land as Ren's group travels south along Kip Lake's coast. Boulders and rubble dot the ground, blown from ethner geysers on the shoreline. Steam hisses from fissures in the ground and the coast fizzes as runoff from the summer rains meets Kip Lake. The ethner lake shimmers in an iridescent purple, a fog-like steam swirling around it. Ren keeps his attention on the land around him, ethner geysers hissing from the ground as tall, toxic columns.

He's been to the lake's shore a handful of times in his life, but he still finds it fascinating. It's like a lake of poison. No one knows how deep it is, but the Valkoeans keep sucking all the resources they can from it.

Ren's team is donned in small masks and goggles, the mask filters looking like chopped off boar tusks. The masks and goggles were taken from Connie's teammates. Melrose thought to prepare Connie's team for being so close to Kip Lake, but he hardly gave the Raiders' safety a second thought. Typical Valkoeans.

Jericho limps along with Merryweather, the two making smalltalk. Aster has been nearly silent the whole time, but Ren can't blame him. He has to be hot in that armor. The deputy chose to keep his helmet on — it has a built in gas mask.

Despite the mask, the acrid odor breaks through and Ren feels the choking effects of the ethner steam. He's at least thankful for the steam's cover, he doesn't think the boulders would hide them much from Valkoean scouts.

A large, boxy shadow towers over them in the steam, the team halting at its presence. The sun sparkles behind it through the white haze.

"What is that?" Jericho breathes in awe, his mask hissing.

"Red Level Ethner," Aster says, his voice echoing in his helmet. "One of the many facilities that harvest ethner from Kip Lake. Red Level is the biggest provider for Valko's military ethner supply. They're in the pockets of the government officials. It's why Fort Kip is so close to it."

"I've heard of Red Level," Jericho says. "Do you think the rebellion will target it?"

Aster shakes his head. "No. If this facility was destroyed, the government would just find another one. Ethner harvesting facilities are a mensin a dozen here. It's not worth the rebellion's resources to destroy."

Aster turns away from the coast and starts walking again, the team following suit.

"All this place is to us is a marker," Aster says. "We're close to Fort Kip and thanks to the rain and these geysers, we have the cover of the steam."

The three Raiders follow the deputy as he leads them through the hissing geyser field towards Fort Kip. A little flash catches Ren's eyes.

Clunk! Clunk, clunk...

A canister bounces towards him, his eyes widening.

Hissss!

Purple steam rises from a valve on it and Ren gets a whiff of a sweet ethner smell, something he's familiar with from his time in the guild. Tiredness tugs at him, Ren struggling to keep his eyes open.

"Ethosom gas!" Ren exclaims, jumping back. "Don't breathe it in, you'll pass out!" Without the mask, Ren would already be unconscious on the ground.

More canisters bounce through the rocky geyser field and the Raiders shout and jump back. The team retreats behind some of the large boulders, coughing through their gas masks.

"You're outnumbered!" an echoed voice calls. It is familiar, but Ren can't quite place it. "Surrender! We can do this peacefully."

"How'd they know we were here in the steam?" Ren asks. "There's no way they just happened to get the jump on us!"

"They seemed all too prepared to capture us," Merryweather remarks from another boulder.

"Did they know we were coming?" Ren asks.

"Does it matter?" Aster asks. "We need to deal with the situation now."

"Come out, now!" the Valkoean calls. "We don't want to harm you."

Ren grits his teeth. Aster's right. "Let's engage them," he says, readying his revolver.

Aster shouts something, but it's drown out with gunpowder booms.

Silhouettes dive to cover in the haze, shouts erupting. Ren empties his cylinder and snaps back behind the boulder as ethner bullets hiss out.

"What are you doing?" Aster booms. "There's twice as many of them as us!"

"What?" Ren asks, reloading. "We are dealing with the situation. You want to get captured?"

Gunpowder booms out and Jericho falls behind his rock, his musket smoking. "There's way too many! It-it's the Scouts!"

Ren freezes. The Scouts? *Were* they expecting them?

Clunk! Clunk! Clunk!

Three ethosom canisters bounce between the boulders, hissing as ethner bullets pepper the ground.

"Fall back!" Ren hollers.

"*I'm* the deputy here!" Aster bites. "Hey!"

Merryweather and Jericho are smart enough to fall back with Ren, Aster racing after them, bullets clunking off his armor as he covers them.

Hiss!

Ren skids over the ground as a geyser erupts in front of him, narrowly missing the toxic wall. He scrambles to the side and snaps behind another boulder, heart thumping hard.

"Watch your step!" he hollers. "Geysers!"

"We have other stuff to worry about now!" Jericho calls.

Ren peeks out and the Scouts flank the ethosom cloud, their bug-like gas masks trained on the Raiders. Ren fires and takes one out, his aim sloppy. His targets move in low visibility, their guns hissing in retaliation.

Ren snaps back to reload, but scuffling feet round the boulder. He stares down the barrel of an ethner pistol and yells as he ducks to the side.

Hiss! Hiss! Hiss!

A bullet tears through Ren's bicep and he yells. Adrenaline rushes through his veins as he lunges forward, barreling into the Valkoean's stomach, taking him to the ground.

"Gah!" the Scout yells, his gun bouncing over the geyser land.

Ren and the man tussle on the ground, rolling over and exchanging punches. Nails dig into Ren's bullet wound and he hisses, grunting as he pries the Scout's fingers free. Ren hears a snap and the man yells, pushing back and grabbing his broken fingers.

"You bastard!" the Scout hisses.

He punches forward with his good hand and Ren dodges, throwing a punch into his gut. The Valkoean coughs and lunges at Ren. They punch and grab at each other, their gas masks and goggles flying off. Ren spits out a tooth and his lungs tighten as he gasps, the ethner suffocating here. His opponent also struggles, gasping as he reaches out at Ren.

Ren weakens from the steam, grabbing at the man's arms as they tighten around Ren's throat. Ren tries to wheeze, panic surging when he can't take a breath.

The man steps forward, angry brown eyes tearing into Ren as he is forced backwards. Ren sets his feet solid like the boulders around them, refusing to let the man move him.

HISS!

Ren feels the wall of a geyser brush his back, his neck stinging.

He's trying to push me into the geyser!

A new wave of adrenaline overtakes him and Ren's nails draw blood against the Scout's arms. He jerks his head, breaking free under the man's broken hand. He grabs and squeezes the broken fingers, the Valkoean shouting out in pain, being caught off guard.

Ren steps to the side and yanks forward with a mighty howl, sending the Scout flying behind him.

HISS!

The roaring geyser rises again, the Scout yelling as he falls into its embrace. His body contorts into a mass of boils, the yelling and gurgling and cutting short as the man dies.

Ren falls to the ground as the ethner grabs at his lungs, crawling over to his mask and goggles on the ground. He puts them on and gasps as he drinks in cleaner air. He barely has time to adjust when he sees Jericho pushed to the ground, a Scout swinging a sword towards him.

"Jericho!" Ren hollers.

His feet move fast and his hand tightens around his bayonet's handle. He jumps and sends his boot into Jericho's attacker, the sword flying over the ground. The Valkoean yells as he thuds to the ground, Ren stabbing his bayonet through through the man's chest.

"Jericho!" Ren spits, turning around.

Jericho struggles to his feet, shaken and staring at the fallen Scout.

"What were you doing?" Ren demands.

"He knocked me down, I—"

"You were going to die! You need to be more careful!"

"I-I couldn't help it! I— You— Ren, thank you for—"

"Thank me by getting out of here!" Ren shouts. "You're useless in battle, I won't always been here to save you. Just go!"

Ren can't see Jericho's expression behind his mask, but the boy hesitates before complying, running off with a limp.

Anger swell inside Ren, but he can't tell if its anger at Jericho for being a burden or if its because Ren made him a burden.

A yowl makes Ren spin, shocked to see the Scout he felled standing, blood swelling from his chest. He swishes a sword towards Ren, Ren parrying the blow. His strength is astounding, the Scout must be running off pure adrenaline.

Ren parries more blows, stepping back as the wounded man lashes at him, overpowering him.

He's strong!

Their feet move over the rocky ground, Ren's ankles twisting on the uneven stones. Blocking a two-handed blow sends shivers up Ren's arms, his body jolting. Ren yells and steps forward, lashing harder and stronger, but the man is quick to overpower him. A poor block sends a blade licking across Ren's shoulder and he winces. His bullet wound screams and his shoulder drips with blood and Ren's first instinct is to run.

He doesn't have time to consider it as he steps back, tripping over the uneven stones. He falls on his back and yells when the flash of a blade comes down on him.

Ren winces.

Forez, make it quick!

Clink!

An immense pressure hits Ren's chest and he grunts, the man's body toppling on top of him. Ren yells and pushes him away, the Scout's chest wound spilling blood over Ren's shirt.

Did he bleed out?

Ren blinks when he sees a single cross-bow bolt sticking from the man's forehead.

He almost can't believe it, his eyes snapping around to see where it came from.

Did Jericho just save me?

"Fall back, fall back!" Aster's voice booms.

Ren's feet scramble under him and he chases after his fleeing comrades. He turns his head to see more silhouettes racing towards them — more than what they started the battle with. The Scouts must have reinforcements from Fort Kip. They are outnumbered again.

They race over the geyser land, Ren zig-zagging as the ground explodes with toxic columns. His wounds sting from the ethner in the air, exhaustion tugging at him.

Plunk, clunk! Plunk, clunk!

Canisters fly overhead and walls of ethosom explode in front of them, the three skidding to a halt.

"Halt!" a voice hollers. Ren now recognizes it as Commander Halcy's.

The three spin around and Ren's heart sinks when he sees ten Valkoeans in their otherworldly gas masks facing them from a distance. Some he recognizes as Scouts, some just normal Valkoean lackeys from Fort Kip. Commander Halcy stands in the front, his horned helmet devilish. Arlo flanks him, holding a strange weapon in his gloved hands with a wide barrel, boxy steam grate, and twisting hoses.

"Don't do anything stupid and you'll come out of this with your lives," Halcy.

"Bullshit!" Merryweather hisses. "You've never shown mercy!"

"Typical hot-headed Raiders," Halcy says. He gestures for someone behind him to come forward. "How's this for incentive to not do anything stupid?"

Ren's chest lurches when he sees the team split and a blond Scout steps forward, kicking Jericho along with a gun pointed to his head. Jericho trembles, his gas mask removed. He gasps for air, his eyes terrified.

"Don't hurt him!" Ren spits.

"Then come with us," Halcy says.

"We don't have much of a choice," Aster murmurs at Ren's side.

Ren's eyes snap around.

The impossible amount of Scouts, the gun against Jericho's head, his stinging wounds bleeding.

Aster's right.

"Hands up as we approach," Halcy says. "Don't try any dumb tricks."

The three raise their hands in defeat, a hollow feeling sinking into Ren's chest.

What happens now?

He grimaces. He's weak and helpless.

Three Valkoeans walk towards them and Ren hears a slight clunk.

Hiss-BOOM!

Shouts erupt as a grenade takes out the three Valkoeans between the two teams. Everyone falls back behind the boulders, Ren's heart thumping hard.

"What just happened?" he shouts.

Farsing's crazed laughter echoes behind them, Jean, Cosette, and Connie opening fire as they snake through the boulders towards them. They've donned gas masks, their yellow eyes assessing the battlefield.

"Jean!" Aster exclaims. Ren almost thinks Aster sounds terrified.

Jean presses into the boulder at his deputy's side.

"Aster," Jean says. "Be my shield. Let's go get Jericho." Jean turns to the others. "Press forward!" he howls. "Cover Aster and me! No mercy!"

Ren's comrades cry around him as they press forward, guns blazing. Aster stomps forward, duck foot pistol booming. Jean follows behind him, shooting his revolver with terrifying accuracy.

Ren's heart races, his wounds numbing as bullets expend. They move forward, leaping from boulder to boulder, avoiding columns of steam and bullets. The Scouts fall back, some retreating to lick their wounds from Farsing's surprise attack. Scout bullets halt, the battlefield growing eerily quiet.

Aster and Jean pull Jericho from where he cowers behind a boulder, the boy beaten and shaken.

"Go!" Jean calls. "Retreat back to the Red Forest! We'll cover you."

Jericho doesn't argue, weaving through the geysers to retreat.

"Raiders!" Jean bellows. "Retreat!"

"Cowards!" a voice calls from cover. Ren thinks it's the voice of Arlo, though he's not sure.

"Ironic," Jean mocks over hissing geysers. "Spoken by someone hiding in fear."

"Not fear," Arlo says. "Preparation. You're fighting for the wrong god, the wrong side. I'll show you who the real god is! I'll take you to him myself!"

"Show yourself and we'll settle this now," Jean says.

"My pleasure."

"Run!" Connie booms. "He'll kill us all!" Ren turns to see Connie already retreating.

Arlo steps from behind the cover, his blocky gun in hand. In a flash, his weapon blasts out a wall of steam. Aster steps to cover Jean, but the wall hits both of them.

Ren looks on in terror as screams of pain erupt from Jean. Aster's cover would be enough to stop bullets, but the steam warps around him and consumes the commander.

Ren's stomach tightens.

Arlo doesn't stop at them, his weapon sweeping wide as steam engulfs the battlefield. Jean's horrified screams chill Ren to the bone and he feels frozen in place.

What is that weapon? It's like a portable geyser!

Aster bursts through the steam, Jean draped over his shoulder.

"Retreat!" Aster booms. "Retreat!"

Ren turns and runs, narrowly missing the sweeping wall of steam. Adrenaline and fear fuel him, his aches from the battle numbed.

Aster run with the commander ahead of Ren, the sickness not fading from his gut. Jean is paler than usual, moaning in agony. As Ren looks at the commander, he can't help but to think he already looks like a corpse.

14
THE FIRST DOMINO

Scotty's heart races as the Red Forest wraps around her once more. Her chest heaves as her lungs grasp for air, panic surging through her at the air of anxiety when she's back in camp, her comrades distressed and wounded. Connie and Cosette are tending to the injured, Scotty's head spinning around the camp.

Aster's hysteric voice brings her to Withorn's tent, the sight cutting her like a knife in the chest, deeper than any battle wound. Jean lays on the floor, his chest a gaping wound. The commander heaves pained shallow breathes. His eyes are wide and unblinking, but holding onto life. Withorn searches through his cabinet, the medic in a frenzy. Aster is next to him, shouting demands.

"Save him, dammit!"

Aster's voice holds a certain desperation that shakes Scotty to her core. Is Jean going to die? Guilt pangs in her chest. If she was there to help, would Jean still be like this?

"What happened?" Scotty blurts out.

"Arlo happened!" Aster spits. "Arlo shot him with his geyser gun!"

"Geyser gun?" Scotty says. That must be the weapon Arlo carried when she saw him. She knew what it did to Connie's team, but seeing Jean in this state brings it to a new, personal perspective.

"Luckily Aster was shielding Jean," Ren says, Scotty not having noticed the man's presence. "It... it wasn't even a direct hit."

Scotty looks at the gaping wound in disbelief. "The Scouts were at Fort Kip?" she asks.

"Around the perimeter," Ren says. "We didn't get close to the fort."

Scotty frowns, thinking about the Scouts' tents she spotted at the massive Valkoean encampment. They must have been responsible for Melrose's forged message. It was a trap.

"If Jean didn't get there when he did, the rest of us wouldn't have made it," Ren remarks. "I just wish Jean didn't have to sacrifice himself."

"He's still alive!" Aster exclaims. He turns to Withorn. "Withorn, is there *anything* you can do?"

Withorn ignores him at first, hands fumbling through his cabinet.

"Withorn!" Aster presses.

"Aster, now's not the time to harass the medic," Ren says.

Scotty feels herself go numb, eyes wide as she watches Jean in his pained state. None of the Raiders have died since she joined, can she really go through this again? The familiar darkness of grief starts to fill her chest.

Jean's head turns, his mouth parted as he looks to Aster, and then Scotty.

"Jean," Aster's trembling voice whispers.

Jean's lips press together and it looks like he's trying to make words, but nothing comes out. He winces and turns his head back.

"Take it easy," Withorn tells Jean. "Whatever you want to tell them, you can say it later."

Withorn pulls a vial out of the cabinet and Scotty thinks she hears him manically laugh for a moment, murmuring thanks to Nikos. When he turns back, he pops the vial open, the swirling liquid mesmerizing to Scotty.

"Kavio salve!" Withorn shouts.

"Will that help?" Scotty asks hopefully.

"This is the only thing that can help!" he cheers. "This is our only hope! This is kavio salve, it was made by the doctors in Vincent to combat the corrosive abilities of ethner."

"It looks like the damage is already done," Ren remarks.

"Ethner will continue to do damage unless neutralized," Scotty tells Ren. "So this will neutralize it?"

Withorn nods, pouring the salve onto the wound. "Even more, it should start the healing process. We aren't out of the water yet. If this doesn't work, then... well, Forez guide his soul."

"Don't say that!" Aster bites.

"You're the deputy, keep your damned composure!" Ren says.

"Don't tell me what to do," Aster bites back. "Jean's my commander, my best friend!"

"As deputy, you're acting commander right now," Ren reminds him. "You should probably rally the men, make sure medical attention is being carried out, you should be doing anything but this."

"My first demand is you shut the hell up," Aster says, a darkness in his eyes.

Ren narrows his eyes at Aster. He looks like he's contemplating arguing, but decides to keep his mouth shut.

Aster stands up, eyes wide as he looks around the camp at the wounded Raiders. Scotty imagines the world swirling around Aster at the new responsibly. He has a tremendous weight on his shoulders right now, and Scotty is not envious of him.

Anger overtakes the deputy, his brow furrowing.

"Arlo did this," he grumbles. "That damned Arlo!" He spins on the ball of his heel to face Scotty. "And where were *you* during all this?"

Scotty scowls at him, but feels the same anger at herself for not being at the battle to help.

"I was doing reconnaissance," Scotty says, mirroring his tone. "It wasn't in vain, either. I found a massive camp."

She explains what she saw and stresses the size of it, Aster unmoved by her report. Ren listens behind the deputy, his face twisting at the news.

"We need to get a report to Melrose now," Ren says. "That can't be good."

"I don't care about Melrose or Cannonsburg right now!" Aster exclaims. "I only care about Jean healing!"

"You need to be our leader right now," Ren sneers.

"Ren's right," Scotty adds, more calmly. "Aster, we need to do *something*. The camp has those patrolling airships, some structures are even permanent. This is going to be a serious attempt at taking Cannonsburg and it's going to be *soon*."

"I'll use Copper to send a message to Melrose," Aster says.

"The Valkoeans are intercepting messages, that's what they did with our first one," Scotty says. "It's too risky. If they know we know about their camp, we lose our upper hand."

Aster sighs. "So, what? Are we supposed to walk all the way back to Cannonsburg with Reagan and Jean in the condition they are?"

Scotty's eyes point to Withorn, the medic finishing dressing Jean's wound. Jean is resting, his eyes shut, but his face twists in pain.

Withorn frowns. "It wouldn't be ideal, but I think it's the best choice. The medics in Cannonsburg can do more with their supplies than I can here. Plus, I don't want to divide up the team right now. The Scouts are out there, it's best to have everyone together."

Aster frowns and sighs. "You're probably right. We'll go back and let Melrose know the Valkoeans are preparing for a full westward attack." He looks to Scotty. "Maybe Cannonsburg can get the jump on them and send their troops there first."

Scotty nods. Aster and Jean are close, she can't blame him for being so brash right now. He seems to be coming out of his shock at least.

"Good job on your reconnaissance, Scotty," Aster says. "This information could be setting up the dominos for this war to finally be over."

Scotty smiles, pride whelming in her chest over the pang of grief for Jean. They aren't out of the water yet, but she grows excited at the thought of her information possibly having a huge impact on the war.

Aster composes himself more, addressing the team with a shout.

"Raiders!" he calls. "We will start traveling back to Cannonsburg soon. Get ready for a march!"

15

HUNGER FOR MORE

Leaving the Red Forest behind, Scotty is thankful to be free of the stench and anxiety. A weight lifts off her shoulders when they're out of the blood red canopy, but a darkness still lingers inside her. With the state the team is now in, she can say with certainty there is evil in that forest.

They travel slowly, Ren and Aster carrying Jean's stretcher as the rest of the team limps after them. Connie and Farsing carry Reagan on another stretcher, the clansman still in no shape to travel. They take breaks through the walk for the injured to recoup their strength and for Cosette and Jericho to make hot meals.

The sun sets and an hour later they find themselves collapsing at Cannonsburg's front gate, sentries swarming to check on them.

The shouts and frantic medics all seem to be quiet and in slow motion for Scotty, watching as they whisk Jean and Reagan away to their infirmary on real stretchers. Exhaustion tugs at her, and her heart is heavy as she thinks of losing their commander. Jean is why she is a Raider, he's why she has this opportunity to get revenge for Mike's death. He believed in her and made her feel like she had worth, rather than just being a lowly hitman. He brought her into this family.

Anger swells inside her.

If he doesn't make it, she'll personally see to Arlo's death herself!

A hand on her shoulder brings her mind away from revenge, looking over and up to see Aster staring at her, bags under his eyes outlined in the yellow lantern light. He is already free of his armor, looking smaller in his plain clothes.

"We need to give a report to Melrose and Bramblewood," Aster says. "I need your details on the camp. Let's get it over with."

Scotty nods, tiredness tugging her towards the barracks. This is far more important than a good night's rest.

"How are you holding up?" Scotty asks as they walk across the fort's grounds.

Aster looks down to her before his eyes point forward again, his shoulders tense as he stuffs his hands into his pockets. He considers her question and Scotty almost regrets asking as his face twists into a frown.

"I should have never joined the Raiders," he tells her.

A jolt of surprise shoots through Scotty and she turns to face him.

"What?" she blurts out, stopping.

Aster stops and turns around, his eyes scanning around the dark fort with disdain.

"My life would be a lot easier if I'd never set foot in this damned fort! My life has been nothing but hell since that day."

Scotty gives him an odd glance, Aster's expression softening.

He sighs. "I'm sorry, I shouldn't be saying this. It's just been rough."

"You're the deputy," Scotty tells him. "Of course your life got harder."

He sighs again and Scotty thinks he's about to lash out, but the quietness in his tone takes her aback.

"I just feel like I always make the wrong choices," he murmurs. "I—" he stops himself. "I really shouldn't be talking to you about this." He sounds so defeated.

"I understand how you feel," she says.

Aster shakes his head. "You really can't."

"You're afraid of making the wrong choices," Scotty pauses as she considers the weight of her next words, "if you have to become leader."

"You just struck a nerve when you asked how I was holding up," Aster says. "It's just..." his words trail off.

"You don't have to say any more," Scotty says.

They make their way to Melrose and Bramblewood near the barracks entrance, the two awake from the news of the Raiders' return.

They look tired and if they're concerned about Jean's condition, they don't do a good job of showing it. Aster greets them and delves into the details of the mission. He explains Arlo's weapon, finding Connie and Reagan's team, and how the Valkoeans are using their airships to stalk the land.

Scotty tells them about the encampment west of Cannonsburg. She goes on about the fleet of airships and tries to stress the immense size and diversity of troops of the Valkoean post.

"We will make sure our cannoneers are ready on the western bulwark," Melrose says after considering her story. "Thank you for your bravery and your report, Miss Scotty."

Scotty hesitates on his gratitude, but decides to respond with a curt nod.

"We didn't find any evidence of a multi-pronged attack," Aster speaks up. "I think it's safest to prepare for a full westward attack. However, we have the airships to contend with. Do you have anything that can take them down?"

Melrose frowns. "We don't know anything about the airships. The Valkoeans are doing a great job keeping information about them safe from our intelligence agents." Melrose sighs. "As spread thin as our intelligence is anymore, it's not hard to keep them in the dark."

"With that in mind, may I offer a suggestion?" Aster asks with a respectful nod.

"Of course," Melrose says.

"Cannonsburg could go on the offensive. Based on Scotty's report, we have enough men stationed here to equal their manpower." He turns to Scotty. "Am I wrong?"

Scotty shakes her head. "There are plenty men here, but with the destructive power of the airships, I don't think it'd be possible."

"The airships won't be bombing the Valkoean encampment with Valkoean soldiers in it," Aster points out. "The path to the encampment is wooded, so we'd have plenty of cover to move troops there. Fall is nearing, so we have a small window where this could work. The camp is established, we have no idea for how long it's been there, so who knows when they plan to attack."

A small smile spreads over Melrose's lips. "You've thought this through, it seems. Great insight, Aster. I wouldn't expect less from a former Cannonsburg soldier."

Aster only reacts with a nod.

"I'll get our best scouts to the encampment first thing in the morning," Melrose says "The leaves will be changing and falling soon, we have limited time for this to work. This information you brought back is valuable to us. Bramblewood and I will plan the attack, but I'd like your team to sit out for it. With your team's injuries, you've earned a rest."

Scotty and Aster step into the barracks, Scotty excited about her intel. Her brain still buzzes from everything that happened. Ludon speaking to her, following the omen, finding the encampment. Ludon said she could have more, and Scotty hungers for more knowledge. Information like that could help the rebellion win the war.

16

THE GOOD BOOK

The next morning, Scotty can't get her mind off of what happened on their mission. Jean's injuries, the Scouts intercepting their messages, Ludon speaking to her. Sadness and anger swirl inside her. The information Ludon gave her could help her get revenge. Jean isn't dead yet, but she wants to drown that Arlo in his own steam for what he has done.

Ludon helped her and the rebellion already, and he said he would help again. She needs to find out how to speak with the god of beasts and storms again. She hoped he would come to her in a dream last night, but she had another typical nightmare.

Maybe Ludon will be able to ease my nerves about the others. Hartwood was the traitor, I need to come to terms with this.

As her mind obsesses over it, part of her also thinks she might be crazy.

I talked to a sharfawks who said he was a god! Did I make it all up?

She recalls Withorn having a run in with Nikos, the god of plague. He communicated with him, got guidance from him, and is now the plague god's apostle. Withorn studied the Good Book to make sense of it. Maybe he can help her learn about Ludon, maybe he can tell her how she can get more from the god of beasts.

She steps into Cannonsburg's infirmary, the dank grey walls surrounding her. The bulwark ceiling is high, barred windows letting in the summer air. Both Ghentian and rebel medics look over the sick and injured in the room. Trays of medical tools sit on wheeled carts, the scent of alcohol strong in the sterile place. Wood cabinets of varying sizes are pressed along the walls, holding weird vials unfamiliar to Scotty.

Scotty carries four bowls of bean stew, Katze padding beside her. She steps among cots of healing rebels, finding her way to Jean and Reagan's resting spots. Aster sits in a chair next to Jean, the deputy sleeping. Scotty figures he hasn't left his friend's side.

Merryweather is also in there, recovering from a nasty slice from their battle in the geyser field. She smiles and nods at Scotty when she walks by.

Connie is glued to Reagan's side, the two quietly taking in the familiar comfort. Withorn cleans Reagan's wound, the clansman wincing as he works. She looks much better than when they first found her, but still has much healing to go.

"Breakfast time," Scotty says. "Hope you're hungry."

"I feel like I could eat a whole feast," Reagan says, her voice still weak.

Withorn finishes wrapping her wound and Scotty passes a bowl to Reagan first, Withorn grabbing his own from her arm. Connie doesn't address Scotty until she sits and hands him a bowl. He shakes his head and blinks at the bowl, as if it materialized in his hands.

He looks over to Scotty. "Oh, thank you," he says.

Scotty smiles and nods. The grief must be fully settling in.

She doesn't know what to say to him, so she stays silent as he and Reagan eat. Scotty and Withorn shovel their own food into their mouths, Katze having given up begging, laying quietly at Scotty's side.

"Thank you for the meal," Reagan says.

Scotty swallows a spoonful of the slop. "Of course," she says. "You're not gonna heal from Withorn's medicine alone."

"We haven't formally met. I'm Reagan," she says, weakly reaching a blotched arm out to Scotty. Her voice has the slightest hint of an accent, one that is reminiscent of Scotty's parents' accent.

Scotty gives her hand a shake, the woman's hands cold.

"My name's Scotty," she greets. "And this is Katze." She nods to her companion, Katze's ears flickering upon hearing her name. "I'm glad you're pulling through. The gods must favor you." Scotty's gaze drifts to Jean, fear overtaking her. *Hopefully the gods spare Jean too.*

Reagan takes another bite, slowly chewing and swallowing.

"Yuna must have convinced Forez to free me from death," Reagan says. "I was the only apostle of Yuna in the unit. I must bring the Castists to justice for what they have done as soon as I'm better."

Scotty lowers her bowl to her crossed legs. "Revenge is a strong motive," she says. "That's why I'm here."

Reagan shakes her head, bringing her own bowl to the ground. "Not revenge," she says. "Justice."

"What's the difference?" Scotty asks.

"Revenge is a foul, violence-driven act," Reagan tells her. "Revenge is selfish, it is drawn from your wants." She pauses to take a breath. "Justice does not always involve violence. Justice is carried out with good intentions, not bad. As Yuna intended."

Scotty's nose scrunches at her words. "What does it matter if we're both fighting for the same goal?" She stuffs a spoonful of slop into her mouth to hide her frown.

"There's a very thin line," Reagan says. "Revenge will corrupt your soul. Revenge you will do anything for. Justice is doing things right to get to the right goal."

Scotty swallows. This talk of soul corruption — Reagan must be delusional. She's been through a lot the past few day's, so Scotty doesn't blame her. There's no way apostles of Yuna believe that. Withorn is trying his best to ignore the two women and Connie listens in, almost done with his bowl of food.

Scotty must be looking at Reagan some sort of way because she speaks up again.

"What are you getting revenge for?" Reagan asks.

Scotty puts her bowl down and wipes her mouth with her forearm, making sure to keep the bowl out of Katze's reach.

"My fiancé was killed by the government for being an apostle of Forez," Scotty tells her, rage blooming in her tone. "I'll help destroy them for what they've done — I'll bring them to justice." She recalls the hanging, so many months ago. She was helpless as her fiancé was dropped from the platform. Anger whelms in her chest at the thought. The Valkoean government, Mike's family — the Brunswicks, they're all to blame. They all deserve to die to pay for what they did to him.

That is justice, Scotty is certain, no matter what this woman says.

"I'm sorry to hear that," Reagan says with a dip of her head. "With Yuna's guidance, you can bring those who did wrong to justice." She looks like she wants to say more, but picks up her bowl and continues eating.

"Justice or revenge," Connie speaks up. "I think honoring the dead is the best."

Scotty grows irritated at Connie butting in, her nose twitching. "It doesn't really matter," she insists. "We all have our own ways to grieve."

She turns to Withorn, grabbing the three empty bowls.

"Withorn, can you take a walk with me?" she asks.

He looks to Connie and Reagan hesitantly, and back to Scotty, obviously interested in why she is asking. He nods.

"Connie, keep an eye on Reagan and Jean," he says. "We'll only be a minute. If Jean wakes up, come find me."

"Mmhmm," Connie mumbles with a nod.

Withorn and Scotty slink out of the infirmary, returning the empty bowls to the kitchen. The two walk across the fort, Scotty hesitating on where to start.

"So, what's going on?" Withorn asks, hands stuffed in his overalls pockets. "Can't imagine you want my company in silence."

"Well," Scotty begins. She presses her lips together and lets out a nervous laugh. "By Forez, there's no way to say this without sounding crazy."

"If it makes you feel any better, I already think you're crazy," Withorn says. He frowns at her when she doesn't react. "What is it?"

"I saw... a sharfawks," she tells him, her voice hushed. "He... spoke to me."

Withorn halts, the two far out of earshot of the others, Scotty following suit. Her heart thumps as Withorn studies her. When he doesn't speak, Scotty continues.

"I think it was Ludon," Scotty murmurs. "I think I'm his apostle. He gave me an omen. He told me to go as the acros flies, and when I followed the acros, they led me to the Valkoean encampment."

"You've done a ceremony for Ludon before," Withorn tells her. "It makes sense."

Relief floods over her. "So you don't think I'm losing my mind?"

"No, you're not," he says with a laugh. "You know I've had my fair share of encounters with a god."

"Since you're a bit familiar with the gods communicating with you, do you think there's anything I can do to make more sense of it?" Scotty asks. "I want to get more omens to help end this war."

"Well, as far as I know, omens about such trivial things to the gods are a bit unheard of," Withorn says. "Nikos has guided me, but he's never given me an omen."

"Ludon said I could have more," Scotty says. "I just need to accept him."

"That seems odd," Withorn says. "What does Ludon have to gain?"

"I don't really know," Scotty admits. "Is there anything a god can gain?"

"Lets check out the Good Book," Withorn says. "Maybe it'll have your answers."

Scotty and Withorn head to the barracks, tucking away in the corner reserved for the Raiders. The Good Book, a thousand page brick of a tome, is open between them, doused in the warm yellow light.

Withorn flips through the pages, searching for something. He seems to know the pages well as the paper flickers under his thumb.

"I don't know if I've ever sat down to read the Good Book," Scotty admits.

Withorn raises a brow at her, sticking his finger in the page to stop the pages from turning. "You're a Soharist, surely you've read from it at one point."

Scotty shakes her head. "The only books I was able to read were ones taken from the Brunswicks without their knowledge. The Brunswicks' Good Book was a family heirloom, so it wouldn't have been in our best interest to take it."

"It's an interesting read," Withorn says. "You can borrow this any time if you're interested. It was a gift from Civran early into my apprenticeship because she wanted me to learn all about her god, Aurthuras. It's not exactly a family heirloom, but it's important to me. Doesn't mean I won't share if it can help you, though."

He continues flipping through the pages.

"What Civran taught me is that the Good Book is a tool to study the gods. Some of it is up to interpretation, some of it is supposed to be the words from the gods themselves, and some is speculation. There are a lot of grey areas on which is which, though."

"That's confusing," Scotty says.

Withorn nods. "It triggers a lot of debates among Soharist scholars. And fuels the Castists' arguments against Soharism as a legitimate religion."

"How can they argue against Soharism when people like you and me have actually seen the gods?" Scotty asks.

"I get the feeling that people like you and me are hard to come by," Withorn says, his voice hushed. "Most of the Soharists in this fort would probably think we're crazy. And some Castists claim to have seen and heard Castus. It's why his face is plastered everywhere in their churches and homes."

Scotty frowns, thinking back to the barracks in Salina Village, images of Castus proudly displayed as shrines on the tables. If Ludon is truly speaking to her, that would mean Castus isn't real. So who is the man in the paintings? She opens her mouth to pose the question to Withorn, but he's quick to move the conversation back on track.

"The Good Book is easy to navigate," he says. "There are nine sections: a foreword, a chapter for each god, and an afterword. Each of the gods' chapters vary in length — some gods are more popular and have more followers than others. Regardless of length, each chapter is split up into five subsections: Teachings and Commandments, Trespasses, Rituals, Realm, and Instances and Omens."

Scotty shakes away the thoughts of Castus, the last item on the list sticking out to her. "Instances and Omens of Ludon sounds like a good place to start," she says.

Withorn nods, stopping on the section to read aloud. "Instances and Omens of Ludon." He skims through lesser important material. As Withorn reads out loud, he speaks of things Scotty knows: Ludon doesn't come in the form of beasts and storms at the same time, he speaks through nature, he watches Harkive through "Ludon's Eyes" in the bark of birch trees.

The hope in Scotty's heart dwindles as their research continues. Withorn reads some other parts about Ludon speaking in the wind, his voice in thunder, and that sometimes he gives omens in bones of carrion. Nothing about a talking animal, but Scotty thinks it makes sense for the god of beasts.

The hope is squashed fully when Withorn flips the last page of Ludon's Instances and Omens. It has a guide of interpreting Ludon's messages, but it mentions nothing of what Scotty experienced.

Scotty takes the book from Withorn and fingers through the section once more, the last page of Ludon's section giving way to the last chapter of the book. It surprises Scotty, she figured Ludon's was the last. There are maybe twenty pages left in this thousand-page tome. Her finger sits on the Teachings and Commandments page for Cassius, boasting a flame symbol on the page for destruction.

"Cassius's section," Scotty murmurs. "It's so short."

"Oh yeah, don't waste your time reading that," Withorn tells her, grabbing and shutting the book. "It's all gibberish or poetry, it really doesn't make sense. It's like looking into the mind of a madman. It's evil."

"People always fear what they don't understand, maybe that's why Cassius is seen as evil," Scotty says.

Withorn grits his teeth. "As an apostle of Nikos, I feel compelled to agree, but as a person with common sense, I have to say I wouldn't trust the god of chaos and lies."

Scotty frowns, feeling an odd longing to learn what the section of the dark god says.

"It sure didn't do my old comrade Storn any good," Withorn mumbles.

"Storn?" Scotty asks.

"He was one of the Raiders who died in the hanging," Withorn says. "He had a few screws loose, and not in the same way as Farsing. He was... disturbed."

"Was he a bad person?" Scotty asks.

"Nikos, no!" Withorn exclaims. "Just... lost. Unpredictable."

Scotty frowns. How could an apostle of Cassius not be evil?

"I know the book had no answers, but I think you should try Ludon's lavender burning ritual tonight," Withorn says. "I'll get some dried lavender." He frowns. "I... have some left over from Hartwood's stock."

Scotty nods, shaking the odd pulling feeling away. "Thanks, Withorn. I appreciate you helping me with this tonight."

At the mention of Hartwood, Scotty wishes the traitorous tracker was back. If only she could ask him about Ludon. He said a lot of lies, but she believes he was truly an apostle of Ludon.

The day soon comes to an end, each anxious hour spent watching over Jean and Reagan. The Raiders don't help around the fort much, awaiting an all-clear report from Withorn. Today, that report doesn't come.

As the sun sinks behind the mountains, Scotty retreats back to the barracks again. She hovers the flame of her lighter underneath a scorched bundle of lavender. The sweet, smoky scent wafts around her as the bundle burns. Katze is already sound asleep in the hay.

Before the smell gets overwhelming, Scotty dabs out the light ember and tucks herself into her bedroll, careful to not stir her fallion awake. She's all too aware of her comrades around her, being over-taken with a sense of dread in anticipation of the repetitive nightmare.

Scotty is barely asleep when the dream starts. She winces, but a calm rain starts. She opens her eyes, looking over her arms as warm, comforting drops splash over her. The rain hastens, the warmth wrapping around her like a cozy blanket. Scotty figured the feeling of heated water would be off-putting and uncomfortable, but this feels healing and nurturing.

The storm creates a veil around Scotty. Thunder booms and light-ning strikes, energizing Scotty. The roar of thunder reverberates in her chest like a battle cry and the electric flashes through her veins.

A dark presence invades the dream and Scotty pivots until she can make out the intruder, the familiar pair of amber eyes glowing at her through the wall of water. She can only make out the sharfawks's eyes, but she imagines its pointed ears and twisting antlers behind the gaze. It looks as if it is hunting her. It studies the water veil before the rain grows stronger, washing its presence away entirely. It's like the wall warded it off.

The water continues to cascade over Scotty.

She finally feels safe.

Scotty shuts her eyes and lets herself relax into the most comforting sleep she's had since Mike's passing, giving in to the embrace of the water.

17
LOYALTY

Scotty returns to the infirmary when she wakes up, finally refreshed after a good sleep. The happiness from the dream is quickly washed away when the reality of Jean's condition comes crashing back in.

Withorn is glued to Jean's side, watching over the commander. To Scotty's relief, Jean's eyes are open and focused, and he quietly murmurs to Withorn. He's still laying on his back and looks weak, but it's an improvement.

The wound is still in a pretty awful state, but that's expected after a day. It looks newly cleaned with another thin layer of kavio salve. Aster steps through the infirmary door soon after Scotty, walking up behind her.

The commander turns to face the two, stopping his conversation with Withorn. Withorn glances at them, staying quiet.

"This damned place is depressing," Jean tells Aster tiredly.

"Jean," Aster blurts out. "How are you feeling?"

"Great," Jean says sarcastically. He laughs before moaning in pain, his face convulsing. "Oh, I shouldn't make myself laugh."

"Don't do that, then!" Aster says, frustrated. "You need to heal, don't make it worse!"

Jean just smiles at his deputy, Aster's frustrated frown turning to a small smile.

"I'm glad you're awake," Aster tells him. "I'm really worried about you."

Jean looks at Aster, then to Scotty. "It's a coincidence you two are here right now, you're just who I wanted to talk to."

Aster blinks at him. "Both of us?"

Jean nods. "Yes, both of you. But first, have you given a report to Milos?"

"We have," Aster says. He tells Jean about the camp Scotty found. "Thanks to Scotty's scouting, Melrose is going to launch an attack to squash the Valkoean camp before it can become a problem."

"That's wonderful," Jean says. "I'm very proud of you, Scotty. You're a fine soldier and a valued member of the Raiders. You have good judgement, I'm glad you continued scouting."

Scotty can't keep herself from smiling, pride swelling in her chest. Without the omen from Ludon, she wouldn't have been able to find the bolas that led her to the camp. For once, she feels important. She almost feels laughter bubbling in her chest. At the start of the year, she was just a lowly hitman.

The good thoughts are swept away quickly. At the start of the year, Mike was still alive. She was engaged.

As she looks at Jean, filled with worry and fear, she longs for her time with Mike again. They were still in danger, but the nostalgia tugs at her.

"Withorn." Jean's voice brings Scotty back to reality. "Can you give us some space? I'd like to talk to these two alone."

Withorn gives them a hesitant glance, making eye contact with Scotty for a long moment. His gaze is inquisitive and his brow raises, as if he's asking Scotty to tell him what Jean says anyway afterwards.

"Of course," Withorn says, getting up and stepping over to assist the other medics in the room.

Scotty and Aster kneel next to their injured commander.

"You are my two most trusted men," Jean tells them. "Without both of you, this team would have fallen apart long ago."

Aster gives Scotty a sideways glance, but doesn't argue the statement.

"Aster, if I die, I think Scotty would make a fine choice as your deputy," Jean says.

Scotty feels her heart start to race, the looming threat of responsibility weighing on her.

"I-I've done nothing to deserve it!" Scotty blurts out. "I couldn't!"

Aster looks in shock, a mix of fear and sorrow in his eyes at Jean's admittance that death may be near. He clears his throat, trying to regain his composure. "With all due respect, Scotty is one of our newest members so—"

"Were you not the newest member when I made you deputy, Aster?" Jean asks slowly.

Aster frowns. "Well, I was, but—"

Scotty's not even offended and interrupts the deputy to support him. "I'm just a hitman!" she says. "I'm nothing special. I just learned how to work in a team and, and—" *I'm still paranoid about a traitor when there is none!* She is careful to keep that in her head around Aster. "I couldn't lead if it came down to it!"

"I think your passion could help lead this team to great success," Jean says.

"You're just wrong!" she says, not meaning to yell.

"I don't think it's a bad choice," Aster speaks up. "Scotty, the anxiety is normal, the responsibility is great, so I don't blame you." He turns to Jean. "But I want to know why you trust her so much when you've know the rest of the team for much longer."

Jean lets out a pained sigh. "Aster, I've been wanting to tell you this for a while. I never knew how to say it, but I suppose I should find the words now."

Aster starts to break down, the deputy struggling to hold back tears. "Tell me when you're better, then," he begs. "We don't have to do this now. You have time."

"Aster, I'm being realistic. I might not make it. I feel like Forez is pulling at me already, and I don't know how much fight I have left in me."

Scotty shivers at the darkness in Jean's last sentence. It's almost like he is welcoming death. Although in pain, Scotty has to admit, he looks at peace and unafraid.

She feels herself start to tremble, but she's not sure if it's from anxiety, grief, fear, or a mix of them all.

"Aster, ever since the disaster at Fort Vail, there has been evidence of a traitor in the group."

"Hartwood?" Aster asks.

Jean nods. "I didn't know who it was, but I knew that it couldn't be Scotty because it started at Vail. We had that mission planned to the second, the information was leaked and that's why the team was nearly wiped out."

Aster just stares at Jean, his face flushed as if he saw a ghost.

"After more evidence came up, I put Scotty on the mission to find out who it was," Jean continues. "I trust her with my life after that. If she didn't find that it was Hartwood in time, I suspect the team would be gone by now."

"You didn't trust me with that mission?" Aster asks, his voice quiet, but hurt.

"If Scotty wasn't our newest, unbiased member, you would have been the man for the mission, Aster. It would have been a lot to put on you, sneakily interrogating our friends like that."

Aster nods. "I understand."

Aster frowns, so Scotty thinks he doesn't fully understand and some underlying feelings remain, but she isn't going to make a comment on it.

"I certainly didn't know you were interrogating anyone," Aster tells Scotty. "Great work. You were a good match for the mission. Hartwood almost killed me when he was planting those bombs in Salina Village, so I'm glad you were there to keep him from hurting anyone else."

"That's why I think she would make a fine deputy," Jean says.

"Just get better so we don't have to worry about that for a while," Scotty says, nervously rubbing the back of her neck.

Scotty glances over to Aster, the deputy starting to tremble over Jean.

"Yeah," Aster says, trying to keep his tone positive. "Just get better."

He smiles through the pain, Scotty observing him closely.

She thinks back to Aster's outburst about how he should never have become a Raider. She wants to know what he's thinking now with the impending threat of leadership weighing on him. He seems clouded by his grief for Jean.

"I *know* you'll get better," Aster tells him. "You have to."

"I've always appreciated your loyalty, Aster," Jean says. "When I'm not sure of myself, you always seem to be. I sometimes think that faith keeps me going."

Aster smiles, but the smile can't hide the complicated emotions in his brown eyes.

Anxiety pricks at Scotty at the idea of leading the team alongside Aster.

Buzzing starts in Scotty's ears, her face scrunching up. A fuzzy bee hovers nearby, having come in through the infirmary's open barred windows. She swats the thing away, but the distant buzzing noise sounds loud against the quiet room.

Bzzzzzzzz.

She's sure Aster will be a fine leader, but she doubts herself as a deputy. She couldn't do it! Jean must be losing his mind!

BZZZZZZZ!

The buzzing grows louder as Scotty lets the fear take over as tears fall from her eyes.

Fear for herself, for Jean, and for the future of the Acros Raiders.

18
THE APPRENTICE

Ren meets Jericho in the infirmary, the boy patching Ren's arm. Withorn put Jericho on Ren's wounds for whatever reason. Probably wanted to make Jericho feel useful after almost getting Jean killed because he got captured by Fort Kip. It's been a few days since then, the whole team on edge waiting to see how Jean's healing goes.

Ren's bullet wound in his bicep still stings, but it's not the first time he has had to heal from a bullet. He hisses when Jericho pulls the bandage too tight.

"Hey!" Ren says.

"Sorry, too tight?" Jericho says, loosening the wrap.

Ren stretches his arm around when Jericho pulls away to gather his supplies up to take back to Withorn. Footfalls bring the two's attention up, Aster looming over the two.

"Jericho, are you done here?" Aster asks, eying Ren's bandage.

"Er, yeah, I just finished up," Jericho says, concern lingering in his tone. "Is something wrong?"

"Come with me," Aster says, putting his hand on the boy's shoulder. "Jean wants to speak with you."

Jericho gives Ren a hesitant glance before being whisked away to the commander's cot. Ren frowns, curiosity getting the better of him. What could Jean want with the boy?

He gets up and moves to where some bowls were left from the last meal, slowly picking them up to take them back to the cafeteria. He takes his time, moving close to where Jean's cot is, his senses honing in on the commander. Jean sits in the bed, exhaustion tugging at her face.

"Jean, is everything alright, sir?" Jericho asks.

"We need to talk about your performance," Jean says.

"Er, what about it?" Jericho asks.

"Jericho," Jean begins carefully. "Aster gave me a full report of the battle. He said you needed saved another time before you got captured. You could have compromised the whole mission. While... I do think there were other forces at play for why your team was ambushed, the others handled it much better. I think you're lucky to be alive." Jean's words are strained as he heals.

"I-I, well, yeah," Jericho stammers, searching for words. "We weren't exactly in the best situation. You can't blame me for that!"

"Regardless, everyone else was able to improvise and thrive," Jean says. "They... Jericho, you held them back, and made a difficult situation."

"Jean, sir," Jericho says. "It-it was the Scouts for Gadias's sake!"

"We seem to run into them a lot," Jean says. "What happens next time?"

"I'll handle it," Jericho says. "We all have our bad days!"

"Jericho, I think you should go home," Jean asserts. "Leave the fighting to us. You're... a bright kid."

Ren feels his heart drop. He's failed the boy. This is all his fault.

"I'm not a kid!" Jericho exclaims. "Give me more time to prove myself! You said I can be a Raider if I prove it! And by Gadias, I'll prove it!"

"You are going to get yourself killed!" Jean says, an edge to his tone. He hisses in pain, his next words bitten out through gritted teeth. "A boy shouldn't have to give up his life before he's had a chance to even live."

Jean's tone shift shocks Ren, it's almost like he's possessed by something. Ren places more dirty bowls on his stack, focusing on the talk.

"If I can't fight for the rebellion, I'd rather be dead," Jericho says darkly. "Okay? I've given my leg for this team, I'll give even more. Give me more time, Jean. If I don't do well enough, give me a good burial at the end."

"You need to live your life, Jericho," Jean says, more softly now. "A lot of us have nothing to live for and nothing to die for. You have plenty of both. Please, leave it to us." Jean pauses, choosing his next words carefully. "I'd rather die in your place."

Ren grits his teeth and tightens his hands on the bottom bowl, the things slipping from his grasp, clunking onto the floor. Ren snaps around.

"Jean!" Ren shouts, stepping over to the three. "Give him another chance."

"You were eavesdropping?" Aster asks.

"I was trying to tidy up. You're not exactly being quiet over here," Ren lies.

"He's going to get himself or his teammates killed," Jean says.

"Jericho saved my life," Ren tells Jean.

Aster and Jean's body language softens, their hostility seeping away.

"With his crossbow," Ren explains. "The boy's a good shot. He may not be the most agile on his feet anymore, but he can lay low in battle and assist from afar. He's responsible, he can help Cosette with quartermaster duties and has the intelligence to assist Withorn. He's much more than a fumbling kid. He *has* something to fight for. That drive is stronger than you think, Jean."

Jean frowns as he considers Ren's words.

"We get ambushed and thrown into sword battles often, it's the nature of this war," Aster tells Ren. "His inability to fight in those battles will get him killed. I know he's smart and responsible, but being smart, responsible, and dead is useless."

"Jericho would do a lot better with sword fights if he improved his core strength," Ren says. "He can pivot quickly, he can swing, he just needs to take blows better with his limited mobility. Besides, his mobility is *limited*, not gone. At first, I bet you felt limited by your armor, Aster."

"It's *armor*, Ren," Aster says. "I could afford the time to be limited."

Ren frowns. He's right.

"Just let me train the boy," Ren says through gritted teeth. "I'll help get his core strength up, but he's an asset to this team as a sharpshooter."

And if he's not an asset, then he's my failure. Ren doesn't want to speak that part out loud.

Jericho looks at Ren with wide eyes, but remains silent.

"You want to help?" Jean asks.

"I want what's best for the team, Jean. I always have. Aster had to whip Scotty into shape when she joined. It's not a big deal," Ren says.

"If you feel so strongly about this, then I'll allow it," Jean says.

A smile beams over Jericho's face. "Thank you, sir! I won't let you down!" He turns to Ren. "Thanks, Ren."

Ren nods. "Of course. I... know you're fighting for your family. It's what keeps me going too."

"That can be dangerous," Aster says darkly. "It makes fighting more emotional than needed."

"I just want to honor my dad," Jericho tells him.

Aster hesitates at the mention of Jericho's dad.

"I look up to my father a lot," Aster tells him. "He's like a hero to me. In fact, he's why I'm here." A slight smile spreads over his lips.

Jericho nods. "Me too."

"Take it from me," Aster says, the smile fading. "Don't let that consume you. The need to please can make you a different man, it can make you do things you never thought you would, it makes you desperate. And I don't think any father wants a dead son."

"I don't have anything to prove to my dad," Jericho says. "The Valkoeans sent him to his death in the first draft."

Aster pauses, he looks conflicted.

"That's really awful," Aster says. "I... can't even imagine."

"You have two months," Jean tells Ren, his voice growing tired. "Whip him into shape and he and Aster will duel at the end."

Ren wants to bite back at Jean — it's an impossible task! Ren doubts even he could beat Aster if he prepared for two months.

"I'll give it my best!" Jericho asserts. He dips his head at the commander and deputy. "Thank you for giving me another chance. I will not let you down."

19
ON SUNSET LEDGE

The sun casts long shadows across the rocky mountains around Cannonsburg, the fresh scent of the distant Mayhew Lake filling the valleys. Scotty walks along a stony path, the beiges of the mountains standing out against the summer greenery drowning the rest of the land.

Aster walks next to Scotty, the deputy quiet. Withorn, Connie, and Reagan walk far ahead of them, the two medics watching Reagan closely. Withorn and Connie's short capes bounce behind them as they walk, their steps getting more exaggerated as they grow frustrated spending more time together. Withorn insisted Reagan get some exercise and fresh air since her recovery is going well and Connie pretty much demanded he come along. While still protective of his comrade, he was very persistent about coming to watch the sunset.

Of course, Withorn didn't trust Connie to look after Reagan alone, but he trusted Cosette and Jericho to watch over Jean in Withorn's absence. He said Jean's health is in Aurthuras's hands now.

Scotty and Aster needed some fresh air and time away from the fort, and Aster still knows the land well, so they followed the group. Katze pads after them, her tail pointed high as she trots.

The moons hang high in the evening sky, ready to shed some light on the night when the sun sets, which should be soon.

"There's a ledge up ahead," Aster says, breaking the silence. "It's a good spot to watch the sunset on Mayhew Lake without going all the way to the peak."

Connie looks up at Aster when he mentions the sunset, Scotty noting a hint of excitement behind his round glasses.

At Aster's direction, they come to a halt on the stone ledge, Mayhew Lake twinkling in the distance as promised. Shimmering stars dance on the waves, the far-off silhouette of Hightower Harbor's chain of islands standing out against the bright water. Even from here, the rebellion's Navy is brilliant in all its might. The tower on the main island is dwarfed by the massive landscape, looking like nothing more than a toothpick in the ground.

"We didn't walk very far at all," Scotty says. "I see why Cannons- burg is so important to the rebellion. Hightower Harbor is right there."

Aster nods. "It's still miles away, but Cannonsburg being in Valkoean hands for too long could be devastating for the rebellion."

They all take a quiet pause, the sun rushing towards the horizon.

"I'm finally feeling better, but I can't help but to feel lost without the team," Reagan says to Connie. "It feels like we're the only two people left on all of Harkive. We've had loss, but it's never felt this... empty."

Connie nods. "I know what you mean."

They get lost watching the sunset.

"What do we do now?" Reagan asks.

A pause hangs over the group, Scotty speaking up.

"The Acros Raiders always need more members," she says, the rebels turning to face her. From their reaction, Scotty is convinced they actually forgot the Raiders were there, like they really were the only two people left on Harkive. Scotty turns to Aster to gauge his reaction. He's nodding, but Withorn's face is twisted in a scowl behind him.

"We don't need another medic," Withorn says.

"We could always use the help," Aster says to Connie and Reagan. "We will have to see what Jean says when he recovers, but we do need more members. We'd be honored to have you."

Connie looks hesitant, but Reagan is beaming.

"If Commander Jean will have us, I'd love to join," Reagan says. "You saved my life, I couldn't think of a better team to aid."

Connie sighs. "I'll follow Reagan wherever she goes," he says. "Even if you are a Ghentian team."

"You'll get used to it," Aster says with a smile. "They can be a bit rough around the edges, though. We almost take pride in that."

"Sounds like there's never a boring day," Reagan says. Connie doesn't seem as convinced as she does, but remains silent, his eyes pointed at the horizon as the sky glows orange.

A small smile forms on Reagan's lips as she watches her comrade.

Scotty senses some kind of understanding between the two, but she can't place it.

Scotty turns her attention to the sunset, letting out a sigh. Katze lays at her feet, deciding to snooze while everyone else takes in the view. The few clouds on the horizon shine pink before the night takes over, the land going silent. Aurthuras and Nikos glow in the sky, the moons' silvery light replacing the orange haze. Scotty looks to Aster, the deputy looking tiredly at the lake. His gaze shifts to the silhouetted islands of Hightower Harbor, lights glowing from the walls and towers. Scotty cocks her head at the deputy, wondering what he is thinking.

All she knows is the future of the Raiders weights heavily on him. Maybe even on *both* of them. A slight breeze wafts from the lake and she shivers at the thought of the responsibility of being deputy.

"Yeah," Withorn says, nudging her. "It's getting a bit cold isn't it? Let's get back to Cannonsburg, the moons are bright but I don't need anyone tripping and hurting themselves."

The others turn to walk away, Katze getting up and giving herself a good shake at the motion. Scotty watches Aster as he walks, the thought of deputyship swirling in her mind.

A buzzing sound grows in her ears as her thoughts darken before she realizes a bee is hovering, swatting the annoying thing away from her face. It swings back around, and the buzzing seems to grow louder, Scotty's anxieties and doubts growing with the noise. Frustration swelling, Scotty swats harder, the bee finally giving up and flying away.

As she looks at Aster, she almost thinks she can still hear the persistent, irksome buzzing.

"Aster," she says. "Want to stay and talk for a bit?"

Everyone turns to look at her, Connie and Reagan the first to turn away. Withorn gives her a questioning glance before turning around to follow them.

"Of course, Scotty," Aster says with a respectful nod.

They walk to the edge of the ledge and sit down, their feet dangling. Katze lays down again, stuffing her chin onto her paws and letting out a huff.

The ledge beneath Scotty leads to a gentle slope of the mountain, the land below melting together in the darkness. Scotty hesitates for a bit too long, looking for the words to say. She and Aster haven't talked about what Jean said, but they both needed some time to let the commander's words sink in.

"Don't pick me as deputy if you think I wouldn't be a good choice," she finally says. "I don't think I would be. When I first joined the Raiders, I couldn't even work as a team."

"And look at you now," he says, nudging her. "You've grown so much. You fully put your trust into Katze in battle now. And you're fine fighting alongside and supporting your teammates."

"I've grown," Scotty admits. "But that doesn't make me ready to be the deputy."

"I understand the fear," Aster says. "I felt... something similar when Jean first made me his deputy."

"What were you worried about?" Scotty asks. "I think you're a great deputy."

Aster laughs. "Oh, I was worried about more than you could imagine. I was the only Valkoean on the team, you have no idea how much pressure I was under." He flashes her a toothy smile before turning back to the dark horizon and letting out a sigh.

"Since we are here alone, I want to ask you," Aster says, hanging on his words. "About the mission Jean put you on to find the traitor..."

Scotty pauses as she waits for Aster to find the words, confused by the topic change. Her brow furrows when he stays quiet for too long. "What about it?"

"Was... anyone else suspicious to you?" he asks.

Scotty considers this for a moment. "Well, I was suspicious of Ren at a point. Farsing for a bit, but he's got one too many screws loose. But it felt like I was constantly hitting dead ends until I found Hardwood's lighter, the one he used to give away our position in Little Bay Pass."

"His lighter?" Aster asks.

Scotty nods. "A little metal lighter with a honeycomb symbol on it. It was really the only lead I had." As she talks, it feels like a weight comes off her shoulders. It feels good to talk about it with someone.

"Interesting," Aster says, lingering on her words for a moment. He stares at her as if he could get more of an answer from her expression alone. "That sounds tough. He really hid his tracks well. Fitting for the team's tracker."

Scotty frowns. "I should have done my job better and figured it out sooner. You should have never had that broken arm."

Aster snickers. "I pulled through. Don't feel bad about it." He laughs a little longer before falling silent. A slight buzzing sound starts and Scotty grimaces, expecting more bees to show up. She doesn't remember seeing so many bees, even in the summer time!

She looks around and notices Aster's attention is piqued, the deputy standing up, his attention pointing north.

Scotty stands up too, Katze stirring from her rest. The mountains stretch far into the sky around them, but Scotty realizes the buzzing is a humming motor and the silver moonlight washes over some figures in the sky. They almost look like clouds in the night sky, but even the silver light can't drown out the unmistakable yellow and red of the airships.

"More airships," Scotty says.

"They're doing night maneuvers," Aster tells her. "And this close to Cannonsburg and Hightower too."

The ships take a slight turn and are hidden behind the mountains again.

Scotty thinks back to the destruction from the airships' bombing of Ghent and she turns to face Hightower Harbor, the islands just a line of lights in the dark.

"That's not good," she says.

Aster lets out a sigh. "Melrose will have to act fast or else there may be dark days ahead for this war."

20
A BIT OF COMPASSION

A slight chill hangs in the summer air as Ren and Jericho train among the rubble of Cannonsburg. Ren plans to start the day with stretches, then sparring to test Jericho's new style, then muscle building.

Ren watches Jericho finish up his stretches, paying close attention to his prosthetic.

"You have great balance," Ren tells him, grabbing his sheathed bayonet. "It would be great to play off that with a faster fighting style, but it can benefit you when we build up your core strength too. Now let's spar."

Jericho faintly smiles at the compliment. He nods and picks up his own sheathed bayonet, taking a defensive stance towards Ren.

"You have the initial stance down for your style," Ren tells him, holding his bayonet up. "But you lack the confidence. We can build your core strength for years, but if you second guess yourself in battle, if you're not fully confident in your ability to take on an enemy, you will fall. You're always ready to run in the back of your mind, and I can see it."

"Just by my stance?" Jericho asks. "Are you serious?"

Ren just glares at him and Jericho's brow furrows as he tightens his grip on his bayonet.

Ren lets out a yowl as he rushes forward, slicing his blunt blade towards Jericho. Jericho brings up his blade in a strong block, but he flinches.

Ren grits his teeth as Jericho pushes him away.

"Not good enough!" Ren says.

Ren lunges forward again, swinging his blade at Jericho's side. The boy pivots and brings his blade down to block it. The force pushes his own blunt blade into his flank and his stance falters as he takes a step back.

"No, no!" Ren hisses. "Don't falter! That's from your lack of confidence."

Jericho's nose scrunches, but he nods. They exchange blows, the sheathes clunking as leather meets leather. Jericho seems to be coming around at first, his feet moving occasionally — sometimes in retreat, which Ren scolds, and sometimes powerfully moving forward, which Ren rewards him for. Exhaustion overtakes the boy long before it effects Ren. They're both sweating and breathing heavily towards the end, but the little confidence Jericho did have has waned.

Ren sends one carefully placed blow into Jericho's flank, dodging his block with ease. The impact knocks Jericho to the ground, the boy spitting out a curse when he hits the ground.

"C'mon," Ren says, his chest heaving. "I've got a good decade on you! Why are you running out of energy quicker?"

Jericho is laying on the ground now, hands over his face, bayonet tossed to the side.

Once he catches his breath, he sits up. Ren offers him his hand, but Jericho declines and forces himself to his feet himself.

"It's a new style," Jericho tells him. "I'll get better, it just takes time."

"We hardly have time," Ren says.

Jericho's blond brow furrows. "Well, I don't know what to do. Push myself until I die?"

Ren sighs, ignoring his remark as he tosses a canteen to the boy. "Drink some water and take a short break. Focus on your core today for strength building. I'll watch your form."

Jericho listens, getting into their core building technique. He already has decent muscle mass, it came naturally after working in the rebellion for some months now. He's anxious, skittish, and a bit lanky, so his strength impresses Ren, but it could be better.

Jericho gets most of the core workouts down, but struggles with the planks, keeping his rear too high.

"Move your butt down," Ren says, pressing Jericho's back. "Your body needs to be straight."

Jericho winces at Ren's push and his metal foot slides out from underneath him.

"Gah!" Jericho says, flattened on the ground.

"C'mon, boy!" Ren exclaims. "You need proper form to make any progress. Get back up, I want to see it done right."

"Why do I have to do it like that?" Jericho asks, sitting on his rump and massaging his left thigh. "It feels better when I'm doing it the other way."

"Why's it matter? Just do what I say," Ren says. "You have two months to work up the strength to beat Aster."

"My stub's starting to ache," Jericho says, getting up carefully. "I think we should call it."

Ren frowns. He's never going to be able to whip this kid in shape at this rate! He's going to fail.

"Don't you want to get better?" Ren asks.

Jericho turns to him. "Get better?" he echoes.

"You almost died in that battle!"

"You did too!" Jericho says. "And *I'm* the one that saved you. I don't care what Jean or Aster think. I'm a damn fine soldier and my dad would be proud!"

"Being cocky like that will get you killed, don't be too sure of yourself," Ren says.

"I'm not as weak and pathetic as you think," Jericho says. "I'll keep sparring with you and keep working out to get my strength up, but

I'm not going to kill myself doing it. It's lunch time, I'm done for the day."

"Whatever, take a break," Ren says. "We'll pick back up tomorrow."

Jericho storms off to the bulwark's kitchen.

"Kids," Ren scoffs.

"He's not a kid, Ren."

Cosette's voice makes Ren turn around, his brow furrowing at the cross-armed woman shooting daggers at him.

"He's close enough," Ren says. "Why were you watching us? Don't you have anything better to do?"

"I heard you two bickering, I came over to see what was up." She sighs and her posture relaxes. "Have you ever once in your life been compassionate?"

"I'm helping Jericho get stronger," Ren says. "That's compassion."

Cosette shakes her head. "Sure doesn't look like compassion to me."

"It's how men show compassion, you wouldn't get it."

Cosette rolls her eyes and steps closer to Ren. "You're not doing this for him, are you?"

Ren feels his face contort at her accusation. "What? Of course I'm doing it for him. He's injured because of me, he's my failure and I need to take responsibility for it."

"There it is!" Cosette exclaims. "Do you even hear yourself?"

"What?" Ren asks.

"He's *your* failure. *You* need to take responsibility for it. Me, me, me! It's not about Jericho."

"What's it even matter why I'm doing it?" Ren says. He turns and starts to walk away. This conversation's just a waste of time. He hears Cosette's footfalls behind him, suppressing a sigh when he realizes he's not escaping that easily.

"Ren, that's awful," she says, chasing after him. "Help him from the goodness of your heart — if that's something your capable of. Don't help him because you feel guilty, because you want to *fix your failure*." The anger in her tone grows, and Ren imagines her arms

141

gesturing around as she chastises him. "He's not *your* anything! Certainly not a failure! Jericho is an adult who knew what he was doing when he joined. He's seen the price paid for being a soldier."

"Jean almost kicked the brat off the team, okay?" Ren tells her, still walking, refusing to face her. "I'd feel bad if my inadequacy at Salina Village led to the boy failing his dad."

"If you're really trying to help him, try being nicer to him when his form is off," Cosette says. "Try being constructive when you help, in a nice way — see how much quicker he makes progress. He's a sensitive guy, he responds well to kindness."

Ren feels his blood pressure rise as she nags him and he stops and pivots to face her, frowning. He considers her words for a moment, but they only make him angrier.

"What would you know about the proper way to teach someone?" he asks. "You're basically a child too. I don't need someone I have over ten years on preaching to me."

Cosette just frowns at Ren and shakes her head. Her hands ball into fists, but she quickly relaxes.

"Whatever, Ren," she says. "I'm just trying to help. There's nothing more immature than someone who doesn't listen. Our age doesn't matter, our maturity does."

With that, she steps away, part of Ren happy to finally be rid of her nagging. Her words tug at him still, and he grows frustrated that he let her get to him. She didn't have any business butting in like she did!

A quietness settles over him, an odd loneliness inviting its way in. Cosette and Jericho are just dramatic, there's nothing more to it.

21

DEVASTATING BLOW

A week passes, dark clouds blotching the sky above Cannonsburg. Summer's humidity is gone, the chill of fall stronger than the heat now.

The fort is a ghost town today, over half of Cannonsburg's men are out getting ready to ambush the Valkoean encampment. Melrose is leading the ambush team, leaving Bramblewood in charge of Cannonsburg. Less people are scattered around the grounds, Ghentians and rebels working together to reinforce the bulwark.

Scotty finishes pounding a nail into a board, taking a step back to assess the makeshift reinforcement. Aster and Farsing step away from holding the board in place, looking over the half-finished project. Some of the wood was processed at a mill, but most of it is poorly chopped wood the soldiers collected from the nearby woods.

Farsing's lighter clicks and the odor of smoke washes over Scotty.

"Break time," Farsing announces, taking another long drag from his cigarette. He blows out smoke, still looking at the wall. "Why in the name of Cassius do they got us building wooden reinforcements for a stone wall?"

Aster and Scotty relax, leaning up against the bulwark. Scotty loosens her grip on the hammer's wooden handle, side-eying their work. Wood definitely isn't an ideal material to patch the stone.

"It's what we have," Aster tells Farsing. "With the Valkoeans around, it doesn't hurt to have the walls built up."

"With those airships we saw flying around, I don't think this will do anything besides waste our time right now," Scotty says.

Aster looks to Scotty hesitantly, hanging his head. "I agree," he says. "But we should follow orders while we are here."

Farsing scoffs. "Following orders, spoken like a true Valkoean."

Aster glances up at Farsing, raising a brow at the dewick.

"What do you mean by that?" he challenges.

Farsing swishes his cigarette through the air before tossing it into the dirt. "You know what I mean," he retorts. "You're a rebel, you'll always be a rebel, and when Jean kicks the bucket, you're gonna be our gods forsaken leader! We're a Ghentian division!"

"Farsing!" Scotty exclaims.

Farsing turns to face her. "Listen, Scotty, I respect you, but you're from Valko too. Don't be blinded by this guy, we need to be led by a guild member."

"You saw what the guild did to us," Scotty challenges, her blood boiling. Regardless of any of the Raiders' pasts, the Sunbell City Guild tried to kill them. "I don't give a damn who leads us so long as I can see Hayward City burn at the end of all of this."

Scotty feels a hand on her shoulder, her anger fleeing from the surprise. She turns to see Aster staring at Farsing. There's a darkness in his eyes, like he's holding something back. She sees his free hand flex and ball into a fist.

"You won't have to worry about me being leader," Aster says to Farsing. "Withorn said he's giving Jean a final assessment today to see if he can be transported to Hightower Harbor. I already told Melrose we won't be here when he returns. Once we get Jean to Hightower, we can get better medicine and you don't have to worry about a *Valkoean* running this circus."

Farsing's brow furrows at the circus comment, the dewick opening his mouth to protest it. Aster is quick to get the next word in, asserting himself.

"You want a damn break, well go," Aster says, gesturing to the fort's grounds. "You're dismissed."

Farsing eyes him hesitantly, not knowing how to react. He grumbles as he grabs another cigarette from his carton, hunching his back as he steps away puffing smoke.

Aster lets out a quiet huff. "Funny. The Ghentian criminal will take orders from a Valkoean if it's to slack off."

"Isn't calling him a criminal a bit harsh?" Scotty asks, taken aback by Aster's remark. It is true, Farsing *is* a Ghentian criminal, but it just seems off for the deputy.

Aster sighs. "Sorry. He just got on my nerves."

"I think we are all just nervous to see how Jean's assessment goes," Scotty says. "And I think most things Farsing says should be taken with a grain of salt."

"Yeah, you're probably right," Aster says. He looks to their half-assed reinforcement and turns to look at the rebels and Ghentians working in the fort. "Screw this," he mumbles. "Let's go check on Withorn and Jean. We need to get out of here for everyone's sake..." His words trail off as he looks at Scotty. "If we get Jean on the road, that might raise morale."

"That makes sense," Scotty says. "I know I'll be feeling a lot better when we can see Jean making some forward momentum on recovery."

As they walk over to the infirmary, they're intercepted by Bramblewood, the clansman cross-armed as she stares down Aster.

"Taking a break?" she asks.

Aster narrows his eyes at her. "We are just checking on Jean," he says. "We are going to be leaving as soon as our medic okays it." He turns his attention to the sky. "It will be before the end of the day."

Bramblewood sighs. "We could really use the help before Melrose gets back, you know."

"Our priority is Jean right now," Aster says sternly. "I'm sorry, I hope you would understand if Melrose was the one in that infirmary with a hole in his chest."

Bramblewood considers his words and Scotty sees her expression melt as she gives into it, her arms falling to her side.

"I'll come with you to check on him," Bramblewood says. "If you don't mind. Neither Melrose nor I have thanked him for his sacrifice yet. If he's still conscious, I'll say it on Melrose's behalf since you'll be gone before he returns."

"Of course," Aster says. "Come on."

The three step into the infirmary, the meager bit of light cutting through the high windows in the stone walls. The smell of cleaning alcohol hits Scotty's nose, her eyes falling on the part of the room Withorn and Jean are posted up in. Jean is standing, talking to Withorn.

"Jean!" Aster exclaims, hurrying over to the commander's cot. "You're up! You're standing!"

Scotty and Bramblewood follow the deputy closely, a smile spreading over Scotty's face as relief swells through her. Jean is getting better, she doesn't have to worry about her friend.

A second wave of peace hits her.

She doesn't have to worry about being deputy.

Aster throws himself onto Jean, giving the commander a hug.

Withorn shouts at Aster, but his chastising goes ignored.

Jean hisses in pain from the armored man's embrace, his eyes widening for a moment before he smiles and weakly wraps his arms around his deputy.

"Thanks for your constant faith, Aster," Jean says, his voice still shaky.

Aster finally pulls away, beaming.

Scotty steps to Jean's side. "How are you feeling?" she asks.

Jean smiles at her. "Rough," he says. "But I can make it to Hightower Harbor."

Withorn pushes his way into the talk. "I think you could benefit from more rest—"

"I can rest in Hightower," Jean asserts quickly.

Withorn sighs. "If anything takes a turn for the worse, being in Hightower *would* be best. Since you two are both so persistent about getting out of here, if you think it's worth the risk, then so be it."

"It's not horribly far away," Aster says.

Bramblewood steps up besides Scotty, nodding in greeting to Jean.

"Glad to see you're doing better, Jean," she says.

"I don't think I've been in this rough of a shape in my whole life," Jean tells her. "I'm lucky I'm still here."

"I want to thank you for your sacrifice," Bramblewood says. "You almost lost your life to our cause. What you have done will keep Cannonsburg alive for a bit longer, it could be what we need to catch the Valkoean troops off guard."

Jean smiles and opens his mouth to say something but everyone freezes at the sounds of gunshots popping outside. Scotty hears her heart beating in her chest at the stark silence, honing in on the noise outside. The shots are more frantic than target training gunfire, and yelling rings out beyond the infirmary's door.

The acrid odor of ethner wafts in through the infirmary's window, Scotty's stomach churning.

Aster stands upright with wide eyes, looking around in a panic.

Bramblewood grabs at her gun and suddenly the bulwark and ground shake, a cacophony of explosions ringing outside.

"No, no, no!" Aster spits.

Scotty's heart races, images of those airships flashing in her mind. Are they about to be flattened like Ghent's capital?

Aster kneels down and sweeps his helmet up, quickly covering his head.

The infirmary door slams open, Merryweather hurrying inside, her chest heaving.

"We are being attacked!" she announces, racing over to her comrades. Her eyes are pointed at Jean, concern for her friend plain as day on her face.

"What?" Bramblewood shouts. "That's impossible! Melrose just left, there shouldn't have been any way his party missed them!"

A boom rings out and the bulwark shakes again, debris falling from the high ceiling.

Scotty winces and holds her arm over her head as the flecks tangle with her short hair. Her breaths grow shallow. Is this wall going to fall on them?

"Cannoneers are to the north and south," Merryweather reports. "Rebels are holding off attackers from the west, but the walls are about to be compromised near the eastern gate."

"What?" Bramblewood says. "There must have been more Valkoean encampments for this ambush. Dammit! We should have sent more scouting parties out! Dammit!"

"We should evacuate," Aster says. "The fort might as well be lost."

"I'll die to protect this fort!" Bramblewood says. "It won't fall under my watch!"

Scotty's mind swirls at the news.

She thinks back to seeing the airships in the northern mountains with Aster. Could there have been more camps preparing for this day?

Has her intel sentenced this fort to certain death?

Guilt courses through her. Did they jump the gun assuming that was the only camp? Why didn't Ludon tell her more?

Another nagging question tugs at her: Why today? Why when half the fort is out?

The Valkoeans must have known.

Bramblewood grits her teeth. "Aster, I need your team. We need all the help we can get."

Aster just stares back blankly, looking to Merryweather, then Scotty, and then to Jean.

He hesitates before his voice echoes out, "We'll fight alongside you, but if things go south, our focus will be to save ourselves."

Bramblewood's face twists in frustration. "If things go south, we will need a group of runners to warn Hightower Harbor. Can your team handle that?" Her tone is almost mocking, her eyes pointing at Jean almost as if to say it is impossible.

"Of course we can," Jean retorts, shifting from where he leans against the wall. He winces in pain, but glowers at Bramblewood.

"Come with me to defend the northeastern wall," Bramblewood demands to Aster.

Aster nods, gesturing for Scotty to follow.

"Merryweather," he says. "Stay back with Jean, make sure he and Withorn are safe." His eyes sparkle with concern as he look to his commander. "And Jean, please, *please* take it easy. We'll handle this."

"Of course," Merryweather says. "Don't worry, Aster, I'll keep him in line." She flashes him a smile.

Aster, Scotty, and Bramblewood stomp out of the infirmary with Katze on their tail, Bramblewood parting to rally her men in Melrose's absence.

Scotty passes a hesitant glance to the infirmary as they exit, her heart heavy knowing she's leaving Jean and Withorn in there. Aster telling Merryweather to stay behind was a good idea. If Valkoeans get in there, Merryweather will stand strong to defend Jean. Their friendship goes way back, the two care for each other deeply.

Scotty glances around the battlefield, gunpowder explosions ringing out, the blasts of cannon shots thumping in her bones. Smoke twists atop the bulwark where rebel cannoneers are posted, the sweet scent mixing with ethner odor, making adrenaline rush through Scotty's veins.

Men have congregated at the eastern and western gates, some posted atop the bulwark. Gunshots ring out against the hissing ethner and booming cannons, Ghentian and rebel soldiers falling from the wall as bullets pierce them.

Faint shouts and sword clashes erupt at the western wall, but Scotty's attention swoops back to Aster when she notices the rest of the Raiders swarming to them, shouting out a volley of questions.

"What are we doing?"

"Is Jean okay?"

"There's too many of them coming!"

"Quiet!" Aster hollers, his voice booming under his helmet.

When they go hushed, he speaks up again.

"We need to protect Jean," he says. "He's not in the best condition to move right now, so if the infirmary is taken, he's done."

Reagan has even joined, Connie close by to her. The clansman is ready for orders, Connie looking more hesitant, the medic wide eyed behind his glasses.

"Connie!" Aster demands.

Connie snaps to look at Aster, the deputy shouting out an order before he can say anything.

"Into the infirmary! Defend Jean and help with medical assistance if needed."

Connie nods and disappears behind the wooden door.

"Jericho, to the top of the wall with the cannoneers! Defend the wall. Once it's breached, focus on covering us."

Jericho nods, but a harsh voice speaks up.

"If the wall falls, he dies," Ren argues. "No way he's going up there!"

"I can assist better up there," Jericho says, clutching his crossbow.

"He's going," Aster tells Ren. He turns back to Jericho. "We'll call a retreat and run to Hightower if needed to report the news. Keep an eye on me and Scotty if things get hectic."

"Why Scotty?" Ren challenges.

Scotty glances at the Raiders nervously, wanting to shout out at Aster too. Ren is right, why her? Jean is okay!

"Now's not the time to argue!" Aster yells.

Cannon blasts sound out again, the impact on the northeastern wall shaking the ground. Aster stumbles, freezing as he looks to the wall as if expecting it to break in front of them and crush them. When he doesn't say anything else, Scotty shouts out.

"Aster?"

The deputy just stares at the wall, and she imagines wide eyes behind the helmet.

Scotty grits her teeth and turns back to the Raiders.

"Farsing, can you go with Jericho?" she asks. "Your grenades will be good defense."

Farsing nods and salutes her. "Sure thing!"

Jericho and Farsing break off from the group, disappearing into the staircase within the wall.

Aster regains his composure, his voice ringing out. "The rest of us, to the northeastern wall! We fight with Bramblewood!"

Scotty grimaces as she dons her goggles and steam gaiter.

The Raiders race to Bramblewood's party and the fort shakes as cannons boom out. Scotty stumbles as a cannonball breaks through the wall, debris flying over the fort's ground.

Scotty skids to a halt, narrowly missing a piece of the bulwark's wall, her heart racing. She throws herself behind it, priming Tex for battle. She peeks out, rebels falling as Valkoean and Mohkan soldiers stomp through the breach and open fire. Scotty shoots at the intruders, snapping back as fire focuses in her direction. The frontline Valkoeans fall in a bloodied mess, their comrades stepping over their bodies, two taking their place for each one that falls.

The fort shakes as the walls' cannoneers fend off other soldiers, sounds of battle engulfing Scotty.

She peeks out and fires more, wincing at the sight of more Valkoeans pouring in. Rebels fall back as Valkoeans overtake their cover, the Valkoeans howling a mighty battlecry, sending chills over Scotty's spine.

"They're pressing forward too fast!" Ren bellows.

"Fall back!" Aster calls. "Fall back to the in—"

A panicked voice overtakes Aster's howl. "Cavalry!"

Scotty spins — a breach in the western gate. Valen mounted soldiers careen through the fort, trigger-happy with their ethner rifles. Scotty leaps and ducks as a rifle points her way, all too aware of her back open to the Valkoeans behind her.

Scotty peeks up and fires, a solider falling from his mount, limp. Her gun clicks empty and she snaps back behind cover, moving further back as the cavalry descends on them.

She winces as the ground shakes, grenades hissing and booming all too close. Her heart races. Even Farsing is desperate.

She reloads and turns the corner, howling as flailing hooves barrel towards her. She narrowly misses them caving in her skull, ducking and rolling away. Her feet scramble under her as she presses forward, the Valkoean ethner rifle hissing as a bullet grazes Scotty's left arm. She winces.

Her heart thumps as she knocks into cover, scraping her arm as she spins around to face the valen mountie. The cavalryman reloads and Scotty lifts her gun, firing a shot to the valen's rear. It wails in pain, throwing its antlered head back, knocking the cavalryman in the head. He shouts and the valen races forward, the cavalryman jerking and falling off. Scotty turns and runs, tripping and falling over the new debris, her heart racing when she turns to her back.

The sun glares in Scotty's face and she lets out a scream as a silhouette descends on her. She winces, but Aster's echoed voice hollers out. "This isn't looking good!"

She opens her eyes to see the deputy reaching an arm down to her, his armor licked with blood. He helps Scotty to her feet and she glances around the battlefield, the rebels falling as more Valkoeans and Mohkans storm the walls.

"No, it's not," Scotty says.

A humming noise grows in the air and a massive shadow looms over Cannonsburg. Scotty and Aster turn their heads to the sky, a mighty red airship buzzing overhead. It has five others in tow, the fleet hovering menacingly over the rebel fort. Two of the ships are red with Valko's fleet symbol, the other three with Mohkan's colors.

Scotty trembles. Surely they won't bomb the fort with their own soldiers here?

"We're getting out of here," Aster tells Scotty. "I'm going to the infirmary to make sure Jean is okay. Call a retreat, rally up the Raiders and bring them to me. We'll get out from there."

They part from each other and Scotty musters up all her might to holler from deep within, "Acros Raiders! Retreat!"

"No!" Bramblewood calls out.

Scotty hadn't realized the fort's second in command was so close by, spinning on her heel to face the other clansman.

"The battle isn't lost yet!" Bramblewood yowls, a gun with a bloodied bayonet in her hands.

"This fort's done for!" Scotty says. "You have not seen what those airships are capable of!" Her tone grows desperate. "Trust me! Pull your men out, they will die."

"I'll gladly die for Cannonsburg," Bramblewood snaps.

"You'd die for the fort, but would you live to save your men?" Scotty challenges. "Do you think *they* want to die? Is it worth it for your damned pride?"

Bramblewood grits her teeth and looks like she wants to argue, but the Raiders have all gathered around Scotty, Farsing and Jericho the last stragglers.

"Get your team to Hightower," Bramblewood says, defeated. "With any luck, the survivors will be close behind."

Scotty nods and leads the Raiders through the rubble into the infirmary, Farsing and Ren pushing a large wooden cabinet against the door to buy some time before the Valkoeans get in.

The battle thunders outside, the infirmary covered in dust and debris from the unstable ceiling. The rest of the patients have evacuated, none were in too serious of a condition, so Scotty assumes they joined the battle with the rest.

Scotty's attention snaps to where Jean is usually at, her heart racing when she sees he isn't there either. A few Valkoean corpses are on the ground, the smell of blood strong.

A shout behind them calms her nerves, turning to see Aster in a dark nook swinging something into the wall. Withorn supports Jean and Merryweather pants next to him. Her arms are bandaged and blood is on her side — she must have fought off some invading Valkoeans.

Connie gestures the Raiders over.

"We need help!" Connie says.

"I got it!" Aster tells him.

Aster swings the back of his pack axe into the wall. The corner is dark, some daylight showing through cracks in the wall. It looks like a section was carved out and rocks were stacked up there long ago, solidifying into place as seasons passed. A small cabinet was moved to reveal the spot.

"What are you doing?" Scotty asks.

"Getting us out of here!" Aster's echoed voice bites back.

Scotty wants to ask why this weak spot is here and how he knows, but decides now isn't the time. He spent a lot of time here as a rebel.

"Won't there just be Valkoeans on the other side?" Ren argues. "This fort's surrounded!"

Aster ignores Ren's remark, continuing his hammering before he lets out a frustrated yowl and rips his helmet off, revealing his sweat-slicked hair. He turns to Farsing, his brown eyes shooting daggers.

"Farsing, grenade, here," he demands.

Farsing steps forward, rustling in his field pack. Aster stands cross-armed over the explosives expert, watching him impatiently.

"A grenade would reduce us all to mush in this room, but I got something that'll do the trick," Farsing says, producing a couple vials of chemicals from his pack, Scotty recognizing an ethner vial. "Unstable dynamis," he says, carefully mixing the chemicals on the ground next to the wall. "Not as immediate as the reaction between ethner and water—" He puts away the vials and pulls his lighter from the pack. "—but when mixed and disturbed, say with a spark or flame—" He gestures to the Raiders to move back, stepping back himself. "—produces a smaller explosion, mainly used for mining." Once behind the cover of some cots a safe distance away, he flicks the lighter and tosses the flame into the chemical mix.

Scotty winces and pushes herself further into the cover of a cot as the explosion rings out, her chest reverberating at the nearby boom. The Raiders pop out from cover and race over to the wall. Half of the cabinet is splintered and the weak spot in the wall has been shattered with a new dip formed in the floor. Aster grabs at the stones and pulls them away with his gloved hands, widening the hole.

"C'mon," he says, gesturing for the Raiders. "Go, go! We'll be safe on the other side! Trust me!"

Scotty is one of the first to squeeze through the hole, her eyes taking a moment to adjust to the bright sun. She looks around, shocked to see that they're in a natural trench carved into the rocky ground, the trench leading towards the mountains. The walls are about four feet high and there's enough room for two people to stand comfortably. Scotty peeks out for a moment, noting the rocky terrain hiding them from Valkoean eyes.

She and the rest of the Raiders duck, careful to keep their heads below the trench's top. Katze stands at Scotty's feet, her ears pricked at the sounds of distant battle.

Jean and Aster are the last to come through, Withorn carefully urging the injured commander through the hole. Jean winces as he hobbles forward, supported by Withorn. The commander's shirt is removed to reveal stained bandages.

Aster builds up a wall of rocks to cover their trail, the Raiders slipping away from the fort as booms and howls ring out from the walls. Scotty glances up at the hovering airships, expecting destruction to rain down from them like in Vincent. Eventually, once the mountains wrap around them in a safe embrace, they pause for a briefing. Withorn and Connie look everyone over, patching up wounds. Connie wraps Scotty's arm with a salve and bandage from Withorn's cabinet.

Withorn looks Merryweather over again, the woman exhausted from defending the infirmary. Bags line her eyes, but she tries to stay strong.

"Reagan and Connie," Jean says eventually. "You're joining us?"

Reagan steps forward to him. "I'd be honored to stay if you allow it, sir. I owe the Raiders my life."

Jean smiles through the pain. "Of course. I now understand what you've been through. You ought to share the blood of Gadias to power through a wound like this as quickly as you did."

Reagan laughs and Jean turns to Connie to hear him out.

"I don't have a choice," Connie says, finishing a checkup on Farsing. "I'm not ready to see my brother again." He looks to Reagan. "And I'm not about to abandon what's left of my team."

Jean dips his head, his face scrunching at the pain. "You two are more than welcomed on our team. Thank you. The knowledge of a medic is invaluable."

Withorn frowns next to Jean, but thankfully he doesn't argue.

"We need to get the news about the loss of Cannonsburg to Milos," Aster says. "I'm sure Milos has seen the airships beyond the mountains from his tower, but a detailed report will help him plan his next move. Jean's not much to be a runner right now, so Withorn and I will help support him, but you all need to go ahead. Scotty's in charge until we get to Hightower. We shouldn't't be far behind."

Scotty grits her teeth, but decides to not argue. With any luck, nothing will happen. All she needs to do is lead them east. Scotty catches Ren's gaze as she looks over to the Raiders, the man scowling at her. Thankfully, he knows to keep his mouth shut now. The others look a bit confused at the choice, but they're ready to respect Aster's command.

"Alright," Scotty speaks up. "Let's go."

"Wait!"

Scotty spins around, getting ready to defend herself.

She realizes it was Jericho, the young man standing between the runners and Jean's escort party.

"I'm not as fast as the others," Jericho says. "I know this is true, and it may always be true, but I want to help escort Jean. With Withorn and Aster being your crutch, you'll need defense, and I've got a keen eye." His blue eyes shine as he stares down Jean.

"Good idea," Jean says. "Stay back with us and keep an eye out."

Jericho smiles and nods, taking his place beside them, clutching his musket tight.

Scotty lets out a breath and turns to the mountain path winding down the rocky slope. Green forests below give way to the waving grasses of the plains. The crescent moon island of Hightower Harbor is far in the distance, Scotty feeling a lump in her throat. She swallows hard and anxiety pricks at her at the looming responsibility.

She turns back to the group, gesturing for them to follow. "Let's head out," she says.

I just need to lead them there safely.

22
TO HIGHTOWER

S cotty's group makes their way down the winding mountain path, the warmth of the sun disappearing as the forest engulfs them. The path disappears a little ways into the woods, the Raiders trudging through thick undergrowth as thorns tear at their legs.

Scotty's mind wanders as she leads the Raiders along.

Guilt swells through her still. She can't help but think the intel directly led to Cannonsburg's fall. They told Melrose to prepare for a westward attack, they never even considered other encampments. The fort was attacked from nearly every side.

But how did the Valkoeans know exactly when to attack? Did intel get leaked? Scotty is all too aware of her comrades around her. Was it one of them? Can she trust anyone right now?

As her gaze sweeps over the others, Cosette flashes a smile at Scotty. Merryweather walks slowly in the back with Reagan and Connie, and Scotty grows uneasy when she notices Farsing and Ren glaring at her.

You can trust them, stop being so paranoid.

Lost in her thoughts, Scotty finds herself getting turned around, carefully stepping over the briars and vines. She pauses and looks around for a moment, Farsing speaking up behind her.

"A bit lost?" he asks.

Scotty feels her cheeks grow red as she looks over the rest of the Raiders, feeling stupid at the accusation. "No!" she exclaims. "Er, I'm not sure which direction to go. The damned bushes got me turned around!"

Farsing gives her a blank stare. "So, lost?"

Scotty turns around to face the stretch of woods they arrived from. "I'm going to go back to the start of the woods where we last saw the islands, I'll get the bearing on my compass and get us through the woods."

"A massive waste of time!" Ren says. "We're supposed to be runners!"

Scotty's cheeks burn. *He's right.* "I'll be quick!" Scotty assures him. "We'll waste more time if I lead us wrong through the woods." She catches Cosette's sympathetic gaze before turning away from the Raiders, trudging away through the woods with Katze on her tail.

Gods, what a greenhorn move! I know how to navigate! I'm just under too much pressure. Aster and Jean were stupid to trust me!

It doesn't take long for Scotty to pop out of the forest, seeing the sun diving towards the horizon. She grits her teeth. They have to hurry to make it to Hightower before sundown.

She makes it back to the Raiders with a solid bearing towards Hightower, stepping to the front of the group, compass in her palm.

"We gotta hurry now," Ren tells everyone. It doesn't seem angry or malicious, but it annoys Scotty because it's downright obvious. She glances back and shoots daggers at him, not catching his gaze in the process.

As they walk, Cosette makes her way to Scotty's side. "You know to not let Ren get to you, right?" she says, staying out of earshot of the man.

"I know," Scotty says. "It's just annoying that he's right."

Cosette frowns. "We're all a bit off and injured right now. Don't beat yourself up over it."

Scotty lets out a breath, surprised to find herself comforted by Cosette's politeness.

"Thanks, Cosette," she says. "I just feel like I'm letting Jean and Aster down by not doing things perfectly. It's such an easy thing to do, get the team to Hightower, but the pressure made me miss an important step."

"We're all in this together," Cosette says. "If anyone has an idea that can save us time, we'll speak up. It was no more than ten minutes lost, so just don't worry too much."

Scotty smiles at Cosette, thankful for her support. They fall silent as the walk continues, Scotty's spirits raised, urging her forward quicker. She finds some wild valen paths that lead them eastward, noticing the rest of the team is falling behind as the walk continues. Her own legs ache and her wound throbs under its bandages, but she continues forward.

The woods grow sparse and they're faced with the last stretch of grassy field before they can get to the road leading them to Hightower Harbor.

Farsing grumbles. "I got enough ticks from that Red Forest," he complains. "I just see a field of disease."

"It's an excuse to get a good bath in Hightower," Cosette remarks, wincing next to Farsing. "You could probably use one anyway."

"Dewick are hairy, Cosette," Farsing says. "I get more ticks than you all!"

Scotty hesitates as she assesses the team. Merryweather is near the back of the group, struggling with exhaustion as the worst wounded of the group. Reagan and Connie are close to her, both trying to hide their tiredness.

"Let's take a little break before continuing forward," Scotty says. "Drink up, rest your legs, and we'll get going soon."

"Scotty, we can't afford a break," Ren says. Farsing nods behind him.

"Best to get there sooner rather than later," Farsing adds.

"We're all wounded," Scotty says. "A small break can save us time."

"The sun will set soon," Ren says, walking past Scotty. "No chance."

"Ren!" Scotty calls. She grits her teeth watching him go, Farsing following him closely. "Guys!"

She passes a glance back to the more heavily injured. "Are you guys good to move forward?" she asks.

"Of course," Reagan says, Connie nodding next to her.

Merryweather gives her a thumbs up with an unconvincing smile.

Scotty knows it's a bad idea, but continues forward, chasing after the two men.

We're almost there, what's the worst that could happen?

The field wraps around them, Scotty unable to see over the tall grasses unlike the others. Ren trudges forward, Scotty giving in and letting him take the lead. He steps arrogantly ahead, Scotty's blood boiling as she watches him.

They near Hightower Harbor, the winds blowing the grasses over so Scotty can see the rebel city growing closer and closer.

Her aching legs struggle to keep moving forward, the entire team slowing down, even Ren. Everyones' canteens drain and stomachs rumble, no time to break to get rations out of their packs.

Merryweather lingers further and further behind, beckoning Ren to slow down every once in a while. He slows down for a bit before his determination takes back over and he forgets about his comrades' conditions.

Scotty's irritation with Ren grows and a buzzing noise sounds in her ear. She sees a bee taunting her out of the corner of her eye, swatting at the thing.

Gods forsaken bees!

The buzzing grows and immediately ceases, the bee fleeing as a thud sounds behind Scotty. Reagan lets out a weak holler, Scotty snapping around to see Merryweather toppled over, Reagan and Connie kneeling over her. Connie checks her vitals, Reagan waving to the rest to slow down.

"Ren!" Scotty hollers. "Farsing, stop!"

"There's no time!" Ren says, spinning around. His jaw stays

dropped when he notices Merryweather, his eyes widening at the realization of what has happened.

"Merryweather!" he shouts, loping back to her.

The team surrounds her, throwing out prodding questions.

"Everyone back but Connie!" Scotty announces. She wouldn't want everyone hovering over her if she were on the ground like that, and Connie doesn't need the pressure.

"I'm fine," Merryweather chokes out. "Keep going."

"You're obviously not fine!" Scotty exclaims. "Connie, what's going on?"

"Exhaustion," Connie says. "She just needs a break and probably some water."

"We can't afford a break," Ren says.

Scotty's blood boils, the buzzing in her ear returning as she snaps on Ren.

"Do you see why you're a dumbass, Reiner?" she shouts. "We are weak from battle, we need breaks! We are not steam engines that keep running so long as you have ethner, we need rest! If you didn't push us so hard, this wouldn't have happened!"

Ren blinks at her for a moment, taken aback. His brow furrows and he quips back, "Now's not the time to lose our cool and point fingers, this could have happened regardless."

Scotty's about to shout back, but Connie speaks up.

"Does anyone have extra water? Her canteen is drained."

Scotty shoots daggers at Ren before turning to what's more important. The Raiders pass their canteens to Connie, the medic filling Merryweather's canteens with the others' water rations.

"Do you know how long until it'll be safe for her to walk again?" Scotty asks.

Connie shakes his head. "Only time will tell."

Ren turns to Scotty. "Keep going forward," he tells her. "I'll stay back with her."

Scotty feels the rage bubble in her chest again. "No!" she exclaims. "I don't trust you!"

"Yeah, it was a stupid choice in hindsight to push us," Ren says.

"Don't get so hung up on it. There's a more important mission at hand, you need to get to Hightower."

"I'm not leaving Merryweather behind," Scotty says. "I'm not breaking up the team more."

Merryweather is sitting up now, carefully drinking from her canteen.

"Scotty," she says carefully. "Please go, I'll be fine."

Scotty lets out a sigh. She should have had Merryweather weigh in earlier. She's not helpless, she just needs rest.

"Connie, Ren, please stay back with her," Scotty says. She meets Ren's tense gaze. "And Ren, get them back to Hightower safely."

Ren nods at her.

With that, they wish Merryweather luck, the remaining team breaking off to Hightower.

Guilt churns in Scotty's stomach as they walk away. She had Jean and Aster's trust and she already let Ren take over and put Merryweather in harm's way.

Now the team is split and she has a small group to follow her back to Hightower Harbor.

The grasses are shorter here, the setting sun bright as Scotty faces the silhouette of Hightower Harbor. Without a word, she and Katze step forward, Cosette, Reagan, and Farsing close behind.

———

Ren watches Scotty and the team step off, the grasses eventually hiding them from view as the sun heads towards the horizon.

He turns back to Merryweather, Scotty's words swirling in his mind. Merryweather is tired, sipping at the canteen every once in a while, Connie sitting cross-legged next to her. He can't help but feel like a bit of an idiot, a *dumbass* as Scotty said, for potentially causing this. That clansman has a good head on her shoulders. Maybe Jean and Aster were right to trust her with leading.

Ren frowns and takes a seat in the grass next to Merryweather.

Connie watches the setting sun, his gaze lost in the mixing of beautiful colors in the sky.

Ren sighs, hesitating before speaking up. "I didn't realize you needed a break. You should have told me."

"Scotty tried to," Merryweather says. "Aster and Jean trusted her to be in charge for a reason, you know."

"I know," Ren says. Envy flares inside him. Why Scotty and not him? Ren's been a Raider much longer.

"You don't have to argue with every choice the man in charge makes," Merryweather tells him. She laughs. "Funny how you have that fire red hair and you're equally as hot-headed."

"I want the best decisions to be made for the Raiders," Ren says. "I respect Scotty, I do. I just want to feel confident the best choice is made. Testing their confidence in their own ideas is important."

"That can be true and constructive to a point," Merryweather admits. "But let's be honest, you do it *way* too much. You end up being more destructive than you think, instilling doubt in the others. Maybe, just maybe you should try to *listen* for once." The growing frustration in her tone takes Ren aback. He's used to making people angry, but seeing Merryweather chastising him while heaved over from exhaustion hits him differently.

"I can't stop questioning their choices," Ren says.

"You're already not listening to me," Merryweather says.

"I get what you're saying, I just—" Ren pauses, holding back his argument. He quiets down as her words settle with him, frowning at his choices today.

A breeze ruffles through the grasses, the orange rays of the setting sun casting deep shadows over the three Raiders.

After a moment, Merryweather chuckles. "Maybe you do get it a bit." She takes a sip from her canteen.

Ren always questions Jean's leadership, but he has to admit, at least Jean thinks about how his men feel. Scotty was thinking the same way too. Maybe there is more to leadership than being smart and strong. It's hard for Ren to imagine how others feel, but deep down, it bothers him to think about the ones he loves hurting.

"Let me know when you're ready to head out," Ren says. "Take all the time you need."

Merryweather flashes a smile at him. "Will do. Thanks, Ren."

23
MORNING OUT

Aurthuras and Nikos bathe the land in silver light, Scotty and Katze leading Cosette, Reagan, and Farsing into Hightower Harbor.

With news of the loss of Cannonsburg, the one sentry leads them over the bridges to the main island. The rebels are alert, the wall around the main island crawling with more lantern-wielding patrols. Scotty notices extra reinforcements and cannons perched atop the walls as well.

Milos is posted atop the front gate, greeting the team when the sentry brings them inside and up the wall. An older woman with a freckled face stands next to Milos, Scotty recognizing her as Newt, Milos's advisor.

"I saw the airships," Milos says. "I can't imagine you bear good news."

Scotty shakes her head. "Cannonsburg is in Valkoean hands again."

She winces as she expects Milos to explode with questions about how or why it happened, but he just nods. He narrows his eyes at the team and sudden realization crawls over his face.

"The Acros Raiders," he says, eyes wide. "Is this what's left of your team?"

Scotty shakes her head. "Jean and some others were injured. Bramblewood wanted us to be runners with the news, so we came ahead. We luckily had no casualties."

Milos lets out a sigh of relief.

"Bramblewood..." Newt says, her voice trailing off. "Commander Melrose didn't make it?"

"We aren't sure," Scotty says. Knowing his mission and that the Valkoeans were expecting him, she doubts any of them survived. "Bramblewood was calling a retreat when we left, so with any luck they'll at least be back here soon." Scotty recalls the battle, thinking back to all the rebel blood spilled. "There will be plenty of injured coming back here."

"A retreat?" Newt asks. "Shocking coming from Bramblewood. Cannonsburg sure has a way of crushing peoples' spirits."

Scotty frowns, thinking about how Aster has been since they got to the fort. "Yeah... it sure does," she says dolefully.

They turn to face the west, the night sky dark, but the silhouettes of the airships are just beyond the mountains like small pebbles in the moonlit sky. Guilt pricks at Scotty as she thinks to her bad intel — if only she had the foresight to check for more camps. If she didn't jump to conclusions about the camp she found, could all of this have been avoided?

If Ludon led her to the camp, why didn't he give her more information? Either way, with or without Ludon, the weight falls on Scotty's shoulders.

"The airships look so small from here," Milos says. "Almost funny when you know what they're capable of." He sighs. "When Commander Jean gets back, we will start planning our next move. We need to take out these airships, and I think I have an opportunity your team can help us with."

Scotty frowns, her heart sinking as she thinks of the safety of the others. "We're in pretty tough shape."

"The mission would be a while out," Milos tells her. "On the autumnal equinox."

The mention of the equinox brings Scotty's mind back to the spring equinox, the celebration that ultimately sentenced Mike to his death. Her tired hands ball into fists. "I'm sure we'll be good to go by then." *This is just another step to get us to taking down Hayward City.* The reminder makes her relax, her sights set back on her goal, *her* mission.

"Granted we aren't attacked before then," Milos adds, smiling at his sick joke. "I'll... get more details when your commander is back."

Scotty dips her head respectfully. "Thank you, Milos."

"For now, get some rest," Milos says. "Your team deserves it."

The four head to the barracks closest to the base's tower. Scotty takes a detour to the bathhouse, getting herself washed off in some filthy communal water. The rebels at least keep it warm, and as the summer nights grow chilly as fall approaches, she appreciates it. It's much better than the cold rivers and streams she's become accustomed to using.

She has a medic patch up her wound after the bath, noticing the rebel's work is not as neat or clean as Withorn's.

Ren, Merryweather, and Connie return soon enough, meeting with the rest of the Raiders in the barracks. They're not in some filthy transient room, but instead Milos insisted they take the cushier beds by his tower. The room is connected to the fort's namesake tower, furnished with dressers and rugs unlike most of the rebel barracks. Scotty is quick to wrap herself up in the clean blankets. Katze curls up with her, Scotty thankful for her companion's warmth as she dozes off.

Her sleep is restless, anxiety for Jean's safe return tugging at her. She is confident in Aster and Jericho's abilities to protect them, but she finds herself worrying about and missing Withorn too, feeling lonely among the rest of the Raiders. Her dreams are black nothingness, accompanied with the damned buzzing noise, refusing to let her get a good night's sleep.

The sun doesn't even break the horizon as Scotty stirs out of bed, giving up on her attempt to rest. Katze leaps off the bed and gives herself a good shake and an exaggerated stretch, Scotty jealous of her renewed energy. Scotty's arm aches under the bandages, and she gets dressed for the day. She gives her shirts a good sniff, trying to find the cleanest one, her face contorting at the smells.

"Good day for a laundry day, huh?" Cosette asks.

Scotty lets out a surprised shout, looking around embarrassedly to make sure she didn't wake anyone.

Cosette puts her hand over her mouth and giggles. "Sorry, didn't mean to startle you," she whispers.

"It's okay," Scotty says, finishing getting dressed. "What are you doing up so early?"

"I always get up before dawn," Cosette says. "Usually to prep breakfast for the early risers. Kinda weird not having to do that here. I'm excited for a hot meal, not made by me."

"Want to get breakfast together?" Scotty asks. Her stomach growls and she realizes they missed supper last night. Some food and tea would be a good way to fight her tugging exhaustion.

"Of course," Cosette says.

"Care for another to tag on?"

The two turn to Merryweather, sitting on her cot. Scotty doesn't need light in the dark room to see that she is exhausted. Merryweather stands up, towering over the two women.

Scotty looks to Cosette to answer, Cosette nodding. "Sure," she says blandly.

"Can't sleep either?" Scotty asks, trying to be more sympathetic towards Merryweather.

Merryweather shakes her head and opens her mouth wide in a yawn.

"I'm just a bit worried about Jean. Weird that they're not back yet," she says. "I won't be able to sleep until I know my old friend's back and safe. I also won't be able to sleep with my stomach this hollow."

They head out into the cool morning air with Katze, the silver light from the moons shimmering off the roofs of the buildings at Hightower's square. The city is quiet at this hour, the streets lined with shops having very few windows lit with lanterns. Rebels and Ghentians are posted on patrol, quietly nodding in greeting to the three women as they pass.

"The cool thing is that we actually have options for food for once," Cosette says. "I feel spoiled here. Sometimes I forget it's an actual city."

"Me too," Scotty says, glancing around at the alleys that lead away from the square into the residential parts of the island. Residents, civilians, innocent people, children. She looks to Cosette. "They say this is supposed to be the safest area in Valko for rebels, but you and I both know this is just a big target to those airships."

"Milos knows it too," Cosette says. "It sounds like he has a plan to try to prevent the inevitable."

Scotty shivers. "I wonder why they haven't done it yet."

"I wonder that too," Cosette says. "Since Cannonsburg is taken, what will stop them now?"

"What stopped them before Cannonsburg?" Scotty adds grimly.

"There must be something," Cosette says. "Ethner engineering isn't cheap and it's a lot of work. Valko has the money, they have the hands and the minds to make that terrible stuff, but maybe they have limits."

Scotty recalls how long her brother tinkered on his inventions — it took him a year to perfect Tex. Surely Valko isn't held back by the same setbacks? She frowns. She wonders how much Hayward City Steel put into the creation of those bombs. She wouldn't put it against the Brunswicks to help make them without a hint of guilt, but it's not like they would have a choice anyway. They have to make what the Valkoeans demand or they'll be killed as Soharists. Scotty feels a smile spread over her lips at the idea, but a thought hits her.

I almost feel bad for them...

She frowns at the intrusive thought, brushing it away. If they died, it'd be a good thing. She wouldn't care.

"I didn't see the destruction Valko is capable of," Merryweather says, pulling Scotty out of her head. "It's hard to fathom that level of damage. Did part of Ghent's capital really get flattened?"

Scotty nods. "They just... *removed* a section of the city."

Merryweather grimaces, turning her disturbed face away from the two. "I heard there's a good Ghentian restaurant here," she says, making no effort to smoothly change the subject. Her tone perks up. "The rebels said there are table games there too."

"Is it really that hard for you to stop gambling?" Cosette asks, not trying to hide the judgement in her tone.

"Hey," Merryweather says, shrugging. "I'm on edge, it takes my mind away from everything. What's the harm, huh? Everyone has their vices."

Cosette lets out an impatient huff. "I've been dying for a traditional Ghentian meal, so I'm fine with going there, so long as you don't drain our team's budget."

"Bah, I won't!" Merryweather says playfully. "I'm over twice your age, get off my back."

Cosette rolls her eyes. "What do you think about Ghentian food, Scotty? Missing a taste of home?"

"Not particularly," Scotty says, rubbing the back of her neck awkwardly. "We've been eating enough Valkoean food. I could go for some Ghentian food, though."

Cosette's eyes widen. "Oh by Castus, I'm sorry! I always forget you're not one of us. Er, not from Ghent, I mean."

Scotty laughs. "It's okay. I always forget that you're a Castist, if it makes you feel better."

Cosette smiles. "Funny how we are all so similar yet wars are fought over the borders or religions."

Merryweather scoffs. "If the Sunbell City Guild's taught me anything, it's that people will fight over everything. It's why I stopped taking hit jobs and joined up with Oliver." She sighs. "Back to fighting anyway... If it's something Jean believes in, it must be good."

They make their way to one of the main roads, gothic spires lit by the silver moonlight at the city's center in the distance. The stretch of road lined with tight storefronts is quiet at this hour, lanterns making shadows dance in the window of one building. The wooden door has a novak's head on it, the restaurant's name plastered between its horns: The Hungry Novak.

"Heh, that's a Ghentian restaurant alright," Merryweather says. "Hope the food's good."

The three women step inside, Katze tailing them, her nose twisting up at the new sweet and savory smells. The inside is rustic, adorned with soft blue curtains. A novak pelt sits on the floor as a rug, a taxidermy head above the slate counter. A few patrons drink and eat, a bit too cheery for Scotty this early in the morning.

They step up to the counter, a quiet man pulling a pan of fresh pastries out of a brick oven. The expression on his steam-scarred face is solemn, and he's missing half an arm, using his right elbow as leverage.

"Oh!" Cosette exclaims. "Fresh pastries! What are they? Fruit? Goose pies?"

A shy smile spreads over the man's lips. "These are blooddew pies, the fresh ones. We have meat pies and sweet breads already made too." He gestures to the rack displaying the treats, Cosette turning her sparkling eyes towards them.

"Oh, I can't decide!" she exclaims. "Meat is best for breakfast, but... I can't pass up sweets!" She starts pointing to the different pies and breads, the man having a hard time keeping up with her order. Scotty settles on a meat pie, make it two, one for Katze. Katze is pawing up at the counter, tongue lolling at the pies as the man hands them the plates.

Merryweather orders a sweet bread, ham, and jam sandwich, eying the other patrons in the restaurant, specifically the louder ones in the corner.

"I hear you got table games here," Merryweather says. "Is it those saps?"

The man sighs and nods. "The rebels need something to keep

spirits up. Back in Ghent, I'd mind it, but here... I try to be more lenient."

Merryweather doesn't need to hear anymore, twisting around to the gamblers, sandwich in her mouth. A woman and a man sit across from each other, snapping their hands into a flaming bowl of something, their comrades cheering them along. A few fallion lay on the ground next to them, their chests heaving as they nap.

Cosette gets them a flagon of tea, Scotty ordering a glass of hard blooddew cider with it. Maybe that'll help her take a somewhat calm nap.

"Hard cider in the morning," the man remarks. "You ladies are with the rebels?"

"Who isn't in this town?" Cosette asks. "We're a Ghentian division."

"I'm not a rebel," the man remarks. "I'm Ghentian, but I'm not fighting."

"Well, the homeland food is welcomed," Cosette says. "Your service is giving me a major boost, I really needed it. What brought you to the rebel capital if you're not fighting, then?"

"You sure look like a fighter," Scotty remarks, noting his face and arm. Cosette nudges her slightly and Scotty realizes that was probably inappropriate. "Er, sorry, I didn't mean—"

"It's fine," the man says, flashing her a smile. "My wife's fighting. We lived in Vincent when the bombs fell... We lost our son in the destruction. We were about to retire and pass our restaurant in Vincent to him, but well, the gods had other plans for us. They led us here to help."

Guilt pricks in Scotty's gut. Vincent was bombed because of the Raiders intervening in the rebellion.

"I'm sorry to hear that," Scotty says.

"Eh, the past is the past," the man says. "All we can do is move forward." He produces a rag from under the counter, starting to wipe down the countertop. "You ladies enjoy."

"Thank you," Cosette says with a nod.

The two take a seat at a table butted up against a dark window. A candle sits between them, Cosette getting a dancing flame going on them with her lighter. Scotty puts a meat pie on the floor, Katze inhaling it. Scotty takes her time eating hers, Cosette chowing down on the sweets.

Scotty sips at her blooddew cider, savoring the fruity alcohol.

"I know we've been through it the past few days," Cosette says, swallowing hard. "But really? Hard cider with breakfast?"

"I need something to calm me down so I can sleep," Scotty says.

Cosette pulls the flagon of tea away from her. "Well, nix the caffeine then!"

A ruckus draws the two's attention to the table games corner, Merryweather and a handsome man snapping at the flaming bowl in the center of the table, a pile of coins next to it. Between each turn, the two seem to quip at each other, Merryweather flirty as she bats her eyelashes at the man. He seems to love the attention. Scotty rolls her eyes. When Merryweather joined the Raiders, everyone thought she was into Jean, but she just has a flirty personality that men eat up.

The group laughs and cheers the two on. A large grey fallion stands next to the handsome man, ears pricked at the noise.

Cosette shakes her head as she watches them.

Katze stands up, her attention pointed towards the grey fallion.

"Katze," Scotty says cautiously.

Katze licks her maw and a low growl rumbles from her throat.

"Katze, don't," Scotty urges sternly.

Katze ignores her, stepping towards the fallion, growling.

Scotty shoots up from her seat and reaches after Katze, her arm stinging under her bandage. She dashes towards them but halts when Katze reaches the other grey fallion, the two perked up as they look each other over. They sniff each other and start wagging their tails, Scotty letting out a sigh of relief when Katze doesn't attack.

The man looks to the side hesitantly, letting out a confused, "huh?"

Merryweather snatches into the bowl a few times, putting the flaming things into her mouth and shouting out valiantly. The people surrounding the table cheer for her, apparently she won.

"Hey!" the man exclaims. "This stupid fallion distracted me!"

"I think I saw them walk in together," another patron says.

The man stands up, towering over Scotty. "Are you sabotaging our game?" he asks.

Scotty grimaces. "No, my fallion was just interested in yours. I don't care if Merryweather wins or not."

Merryweather scoffs, piling coins into her coin purse. "Thanks, Scotty, I thought we were friends!"

"Keep that thing under control," the man says. He shoos at Katze with his hand.

"Hey, watch it," Scotty says. "She's not a great hound and I'm not a great trainer, I haven't had much time to get good at it. I don't think she'd even listen if I *was* good at it!"

"Well, you should try to learn," the man says, an edge to his voice.

Cosette presses between them.

"Alright, let's not do this," she says. "C'mon, Scotty, let's just get back to the other Raiders. We—"

"Raiders?" the man echoes.

"Er, yeah," Scotty says.

"Hey, you wouldn't happen to be the Acros Raiders, would ya?"

Scotty frowns at the man's sudden demeanor change.

"That's us," Merryweather says, elbows propped up on the table across from him. She seems to be admiring the younger man's muscles under his tight shirt, but he doesn't notice.

The man sits back down and laughs.

"What?" Cosette asks.

"I've been wondering about you all," he says.

"Uh, what about us?" Scotty asks.

"I'm one of the wardens at the prison here," he says. "One of our prisoners rants about you all."

Scotty's heart lurches.

"Hartwood?" Scotty asks.

The warden laughs. "Yeah! Crazy guy. The one with that lil rodent thing."

"Shako," Scotty murmurs, thinking about the team's previous tracker.

She longs to get answers about Ludon. She needs to connect with the god of beasts again, she needs more of his omens, more of his help to avoid another disaster like Cannonsburg. If only Scotty had more guidance, the rebellion wouldn't be so troubled.

Would Hartwood help her? He doesn't have to know it's to aid the rebellion.

"He's a tough nut to crack," the warden says. "He just keeps yelling about how he's innocent. Still so convinced after all this time. Usually they break by now."

Scotty winces at the words.

"He caused our team a lot of distress," Cosette says, an edge to her tone. "We really don't want to discuss it."

The warden shrugs.

"Where's the prison at here anyway?" Scotty asks.

"Oh, it's that gothic building tucked among the trees near the island's center," the warden says. "It's dressed up with barbed wire and guards. Not too far from here, actually."

Scotty nods, the hunger for answers growing. Maybe this is her ticket to get an explanation.

"Hey," Merryweather butts in, her tone teasing.

The man turns to face her. "What?"

"Since you think Scotty sabotaged our game, how about double or nothing?" Merryweather raises a brow at him, wearing a mischievous grin. "I'm a gambling woman, but I'm an honest one."

Scotty eyes the now extinguished liquid between the two, recognizing a strong alcohol smell. Raisins and nuts float around the bowl's rim, having a slight char to them.

A smile spreads over the man's lips at Merryweather's challenge. "Alright, you got a deal! Double or nothing!"

One of the warden's friends clicks a lighter over the bowl, setting it ablaze again. On a cue, they take turns snatching the flaming fruits and nuts out of the bowl, Scotty wondering how they're even gambling over this game.

Scotty lets out a sigh as the morning light cuts in the restaurant's windows.

She's still anxious for Jean's safe return, and exhaustion tugs at her, her eyelids heavy. Knowing Hartwood is nearby where this warden works makes Scotty's brain buzz. The team's former tracker could have answers for her about Ludon or about another traitor.

24
THE NEXT STEP

Merryweather ended up losing everything in her bet against the warden.

They return to the barracks, Merryweather a bit tipsy and whining about her loss, Cosette not hiding her frustration with the woman. In all her tiredness, Scotty can't help but to laugh at them, receiving daggers from Cosette.

"By Aurthuras, he was cute though!" Merryweather exclaims. "I hope we run into him again."

"I think you need to run into your bed and get some sleep," Cosette remarks.

"I wanna sleep with him," Merryweather says and giggles.

Cosette glances at Scotty as Merryweather crawls into bed. "I get a lot of flack for my age here, but sometimes I think *I'm* mentally older than everyone."

They bid each other good rest and Scotty makes her way to her bed. As she settles into the sheets, she remembers the bundle of lavender Withorn gave her. She burns the charred end of it, breathing in the sweet smoke.

Please Ludon, I need answers.

Blackness takes over and she's pulled into the dream world where she's in the dark woods again. A storm howls around her, the warm embrace of the rain having returned. She spins around and sees the amber gaze of the sharfawks beyond the veil of the rain again.

"I want to know more!" she hollers. "I *need* to know more!"

It just watches her, its voice not reaching her from this distance.

"Ludon, please! The rebellion depends on it!" Scotty can't help the desperation in her tone. "Why didn't you tell me there were more camps?"

The sharfawks stares at her through the veil, but stays silent. It tries to step forward, but it can't seem to get past the water.

As soon as the dream started, she finds herself being jolted awake by large hands.

Her heart races and she shoots up, arms flailing at her attacker. Her eyes snap open to Withorn kneeling in front of her, laughing.

"I just fell asleep!" Scotty snaps. "What's the matter with—" She freezes, the events from the past few days rushing back to her. "Withorn! You made it back safely!" She hugs him, taking in the warmth of her friend's embrace.

"That's more like it," Withorn says, his voice taunting yet tired. Scotty notices bags under his eyes as he pulls away. "I thought you'd like to know Jean is back and in the infirmary."

"Is he going to be okay?" Scotty blurts out.

Withorn nods. "Yes, I'm certain of that now. He handled the trip very well."

Scotty lets out a sigh of relief, unable to hold her emotions back. She's glad Jean is safe and she's glad that she doesn't have to worry about becoming deputy. She can just focus on revenge.

"It's nice to be on the other side of this," Withorn says. "I haven't lost a teammate yet, and I'll be damned if Jean was the first one."

"We're lucky to have such a skilled medic," Scotty says.

"Pfft, I'm flattered," Withorn says. "Is there a punch line?"

Scotty laughs, the laughter turning into a sigh as the weight of responsibility lifts off her shoulders.

"What's the sigh for?" Withorn asks.

Scotty hesitates. "Well... when we were unsure about if Jean would make it, he said he wanted me to be Aster's deputy," Scotty says. "It's been weighing on me a lot."

Withorn laughs for a moment, his expression growing serious. "Oh, you're serious?"

Scotty frowns at him.

Withorn looks around awkwardly. "Er, I mean you'd definitely make a good choice, you—"

"No, I know I wouldn't," Scotty says. "But it made me realize how much Jean really values me. He's a good leader... and a good friend. I feel like I have a lot to live up to. Does he expect a lot out of me?"

"Scotty, you've worked hard for your place in the Raiders," Withorn says, his tone stern. "Jean doesn't expect a lot out of you, he knows that you're loyal and capable. People like you are hard to come by in the Sunbell City Guild. I mean there's an abundance of capable people, but loyalty is measured in gold there. It's what makes *most* of the Raiders different."

Scotty frowns, thinking about her nightmares, the ones that Jean said he shared about everyone else being untrustworthy. It feels lonely. Scotty looks to Withorn, she knows she can trust him at least. She should be able to trust the others, but there's a dark, haunting feeling deep inside her. Does Jean feel this too?

Withorn lets out a loud yawn, stretching his arms over his head as he stands up. "Well, I'm gonna hit the sack, I'm exhausted," he says. "See ya."

"Sleep well," she urges, shoving her sheets away.

She gets up, telling Katze to stay. She wants to check on Jean, maybe see if he's still even awake.

When she steps out of the barracks into the cooling summer air, she passes Jericho, the two exchanging tired nods. Jericho is walking comfortably with only a slight limp now. He disappears into the barracks, probably right behind Withorn to get some sleep.

Scotty finds her way to the infirmary, one of the newer construction buildings near the tower. It has that clean, sterile smell, the medics busy inside. Makeshift cots are set up, plenty of them filling the room. They must be preparing for the injured Cannonsburg rebels to return. No one pays Scotty any mind as she walks through the big building. She asks a lady if she knows where Jean is and after describing him, Scotty is pointed in the right direction into a small, cramped side room.

Scotty steps into the small room, a slight breeze twisting the curtains of the open window.

Jean and Aster are inside, both awake with heavy bags under their eyes. Jean sits in a chair and lights up when he sees Scotty. She smiles back, feeling a warmth in her heart.

"I'm glad you are okay," she says. "You guys look tired, though."

"No doubt," Aster remarks with a yawn, leaning cross-armed against the wall.

"Why don't you get some sleep then?" Scotty asks.

"You ever get so tired that it's hard to sleep?" Jean asks.

"I also sent a rebel to fetch Milos," Aster adds. "Might as well chat with him since we are back."

As if by command, someone raps on the moulding, Milos standing in the doorway. Jean tells him to come in and the rebellion's commander nods to Scotty in greeting.

"By Gadias, you definitely look like Cannonsburg put you through the ringer," Milos remarks. "Are you sure you want to discuss your team's next move now?"

Jean nods and carefully stands up from his chair. Aster looks concerned next to him, but holds back from offering help.

"Of course," Jean says. "I have a little ways to go with healing, but I'll be ready soon."

Milos dips his head and considers Jean's words before talking. "Do you think you will be ready by the autumnal equinox?"

"I'm certain of it," Jean says.

Scotty and Aster exchange hesitant glances and Milos responds.

"That's great," he says. "It's not a physically difficult mission, but it involves deception and I think it would be the perfect fit for the Acros Raiders."

Scotty frowns, thinking about Hartwood again. He sure was great at deception. Milos *is* right, the team is from the Sunbell City Guild, deception is a strong suit of theirs. Judging by the twisted look on Jean's face, he's having similar thoughts.

"What is the mission?" Jean asks.

"In Snowden, the Wingate Province's capital, a lot of the higher ups between Mohkan and Valko are gathering for the autumnal equinox. They're celebrating with a masquerade tea party at the Hearth Hotel. Unbeknownst to them, the Hearth Hotel is owned by one of our allies, a woman named Erin. She and much of her staff are Soharists, so when the event was booked at her venue, Erin reached out me because it is a great opportunity."

"A great opportunity for suicide?" Aster asserts. "The Valkoeans will have guards posted up everywhere, and so will the Mohkans, I'm sure of it."

"That's why I need a skilled team for this mission," Milos says. "I also need a team capable of more high-class manners."

Scotty almost laughs, thinking it's a joke, but Milos continues.

"I don't know much about the Sunbell City Guild, but I know the group had an affinity for lavish parties."

Jean frowns. "Yes, I've been to their pretentious parties, but I didn't quite enjoy them."

"We just need a team who can blend in," Milos says.

"We can certainly do that," Jean says.

Scotty thinks about Withorn or Ren acting with high-class manners. She can't even imagine it.

"What do we need to blend in for?" Scotty asks. She's used to working in the shadows, not in the open. Plus, she definitely doesn't have these manners Milos is talking about.

"Blending in will help you get intel at the party," Milos says. "The leaders of Mohkan and Valko will be meeting, so Prime Minister Amaranth, Mohkan's leader, will be there with part of her parliament," Milos explains.

"The leaders?" Aster asks, blinking. "High Priestess Tapscott will be there?"

"Yes, Tapscott will be there," Milos says.

Scotty's blood turns to ice, her skin pricking at the idea of seeing

Valko's leader. Will she be able to control herself if she sees the despicable High Priestess? Tapscott's death is how Scotty can get her revenge. She'll be so close. Revenge will be just in her grasp.

"No doubt General Halcomb will be there too," Aster says. His eyes grow wide.

"He's rumored to be the former leader of the Black Glove Scouts, so I'd imagine a man as high profile as he will be there," Milos says. "But I can't be certain."

Scotty cocks her head at the mention of the general. She had heard the name Halcomb around Hayward City, but she only heard of him ordering the guards of the Russet Province around. She wonders if Aster had a run-in with the general in his time in the rebellion before he joined the Raiders.

"That doesn't really matter, anyway," Milos says. "Your main target is a member of Prime Minister Amaranth's parliament, a womanizing engineer named Markos. He apparently has a hand in building the airships. A contact of mine in the city of Eve Hallow said that Markos now owns property there. There is a connection there that we can't make and we need some intel, something that only this man knows. There is close to no rebel presence in Eve Hallow, the city is protected vehemently by the Valkoeans, so we don't have the ability to investigate anything there further."

"So you want us to interrogate Markos at this tea party?" Jean asks.

Milos nods. "Like I said, Markos is a womanizer, and he's married with kids back in Mohkan. If threatening to leak his faithlessness doesn't get him to spill Mohkan plans, then I'm sure you'll have no issues... *intimidating* him."

"Don't you think it's in bad spirits to do this at an equinox party?" Aster asks. "It's not religiously holy, but it's culturally significant for everyone in attendance. It just seems like a low blow."

Scotty looks at Aster, confused by the softness for the enemy.

"The Valkoeans took Mike away from me at a spring equinox festival," Scotty says. "So I couldn't care less about tarnishing the day for them."

"Do you really want to stoop to that level?" Aster asks, concern flickering in his gaze.

Scotty can't help the disgusted expression spreading over her face. "Of course, I've done much worse, why would I care?"

Aster sighs. "I suppose I'm not much better. A bit of a hypocrite." He looks to Jean and laughs nervously.

Scotty eyes the deputy oddly. What could he mean by that?

"I understand that it is a significant day," Milos says. "We are running out of options, though. This man works between Mohkan and Valko and this is a time we will know where exactly he will be. We can get your team on the hotel staff or among the patrons of the party. While the parliament member Markos is your main target, there will be a lot of information discussed at this event among the Valkoean and Mohkan allies. Any information helps.

"Erin has a room booked for you at the Hearth Hotel. It is a suite that will be set up for your interrogation. Get creative with how you lure him in there. The main intel we need is weaknesses of the airships, why Mohkan is involved with the airships, and where these ships are mostly being housed. My scouts saw the airships leave Cannonsburg already, they went somewhere to the north. I'm not sure what the Valkoeans are up to, and I think this masquerade is our key to finding out."

"This sounds doable," Jean asks. "I think I need to get some sleep and think about this more. Get me a list of questions you need answers to and my team will get it for you."

Milos smiles. "I can do that. Thank you Jean. Let me know if there is anything you need."

Milos bids them farewell. The small infirmary room is quiet as Jean shuffles himself into the bed, Aster looking impatient beside him.

Scotty thinks about the mission, wondering where her place will be in it. She doesn't want to attend a tea party if she can help it, but she will do what she needs to if it means getting closer to ending this war and getting her revenge.

She looks at Jean as he struggles to get into bed, worry swelling inside her.

"Jean, do you really think it's a good idea for us to do the mission?" she asks.

"Of course," Jean says immediately. "It is perfect for our team."

"I think Milos is underestimating the stakes," Aster speaks up. "There will be high profile people there. Talented, horrible people."

"We are just as talented," Jean says.

"I don't think you understand what we will be dealing with," Aster says.

Jean's face twists at his deputy as he settles into the bed. "Can we discuss this later? We both will be more sound of mind after a good rest."

Aster's serious composure melts a bit and he sighs, stress obviously tugging at him. "Sure, Jean."

Aster and Scotty wish Jean a good sleep, leaving the infirmary together. As Scotty steps out, she catches a glimpse of a gothic building in the distance, the warden's description of the prison coming back to her. A longing pulls her towards it.

I need answers.

25
THE TREE'S STRENGTH

A flash of brown zips in front of Ren, bringing his sheathed bayonet up to block Jericho's own leather-lined blade. The small blade packs a punch, throwing Ren away from his opponent.

He yowls as he stumbles back.

"Good!" he shouts at the boy, panting hard. Jericho sought out Ren for training, Ren surprised by his ambition and prowess. Ren is still exhausted from the battle at Cannonsburg and the walk to Hightower, and he got much more sleep than Jericho did today.

"What's the matter, old man?" Jericho teases. "Am I getting too strong for you?"

Ren frowns and puffs air out his nose.

"Getting cocky's the last thing you need," he warns, stepping around the sturdy boy.

Jericho smirks as he pivots on his prosthetic, his gaze following Ren, ready to defend himself. The little dirt clearing in the city is lined with overgrown weeds, butting up to a line of crumbling wooden fences, some residential houses sitting on the other side.

Ren steps to the left before dashing to the right, Jericho already leaning his weight to counter a left blow. Ren lunges forward, rage fueling him. Jericho brings his blade sloppily to the side, Ren throwing all his weight into him.

Jericho howls as he staggers back, struggling to find the balance on his prosthetic. He tumbles into the dirt and Ren places the steel tip of his sheath on Jericho's neck. Rage bubbles in him as he presses a bit too hard, Jericho's blue eyes widening.

"I told you to not be cocky," Ren bites.

Jericho glowers at him.

"I keep getting you with that fake out," Ren says. "It's going to get you killed in a real battle!"

Jericho swats the blade away and scrambles to his feet.

"Well, I don't know what you want me to do about it!" Jericho says. "You tell me to get better, you tell me to do things right, but all you do is come at me with all your might and tell me to figure it out!"

"You *need* to be able to figure it out yourself," Ren says. "You need to be able to figure out what to do in battle. You want me to hold your hand through the next battle we are in?"

Jericho glares at him.

"Huh?" Ren says, leaning towards the boy. "Do you want that?"

Ren thinks he sees tears pooling in Jericho's eyes, but the boy lashes out.

"I don't know where to start, I need *some* answers, Ren!"

Ren blinks at him taken aback by his harshness, Jericho's words bringing him back to what Cosette had said.

"If you're really trying to help him, try being nicer to him when his form is off. Try being constructive when you help, try being nice — see how much quicker he makes progress."

Ren's nose scrunches at the thought.

The Acros Raiders need to be clever. They need to be about to come to their own conclusions in battle! Being nice doesn't win wars.

Ren lets out an impatient huff, rubbing his necklace locket between his fingers as he ponders how to approach this. They don't have much time left. Besides, Cosette doesn't need to know, she'd mock him for days about it if she knew he listened.

"Here," he says, planting his feet firmly on the ground. "Make sure you're always centered, always standing like a tree. If a tree is off balance, a strong wind will uproot it. Keep your roots, your feet, sturdy, and stay strong and centered."

Jericho is hesitant as he looks at Ren, almost unsure if his mentor is being serious, but he follows his motions.

"So my blade is like my branches?" Jericho asks, holding his blade close to his center like Ren.

"What?" Ren asks. "No, that's dumb."

Jericho frowns.

"Just be sturdy," Ren says. "Don't lean in to take a predicted blow. You'll want to lean into it *some*, but not as much as you are used to. That's what all that core training is for. "

"Oh!" Jericho exclaims. "That makes sense. I wasn't so sure why we were doing that."

Ren blinks. "Really?"

He turns away to hide his cheeks glowing red. Was Cosette right? Did he just need to explain himself better for Jericho to get it?

"I can feel those muscles you were having me strengthen in this position," Jericho says, twisting his torso. "I see why they need to be strong, so I can keep my roots strong."

"Uh, yeah," Ren says. He can't help the pride whelming in his chest. Maybe Jericho has a chance.

"I've accepted I'm not very mobile," Jericho says. "But maybe I can move faster on the battlefield by keeping my center low."

Ren nods. "Now you're getting it. We will need to get some more strength in your thighs, but we can add that to the routine if you're up for it."

"Of course!" Jericho exclaims.

"Let's go another round," Ren says, crouching down, blade positioned in front of him. "Put your new knowledge to the test."

Jericho nods and gets back in his sturdy position.

Ren lunges out at him, the two exchanging blows. Ren grows tired as the sun crawls through the sky, his blows growing weaker and weaker. Ren's necklace comes out from its tucked spot in his shirt, the metal locket flicking over his face as they battle. The sparring goes on, Jericho pushing Ren back with a powerful parry. Ren stumbles back pretty far, but remains strong, his boots firm in the dirt.

Ren hisses and notices Jericho's gaze on his hips. Ren steps to the right, then to the left, lunging at Jericho. The boy keeps the blade close to his chest, parrying the blow, sending Ren tumbling to the side.

"Gah!" Ren spits. The boy's parry in response to the fake out was stronger than Ren anticipated and he drops his sword, hands flailing out in front of him. His thumb snatches his necklace as he falls, the thing snapping as Ren tumbles into one of the ramshackle wooden fences, splinters of rot flinging out around him.

"Woah!" Jericho exclaims, his footfalls sounding behind Ren. "Are you alright."

Ren scrambles to his knees, embarrassed as he brushes the broken wood away. "Of course I'm alright," he says. His eyes search the ground, his heart leaping as he looks for his locket. *Where is it?*

He turns to see Jericho kneeling, his hands pressing into the dirt as he picks something up. Ren notices the locket in his fingers, the two oval halves split to reveal the pictures inside.

Ren gets up and steps over to Jericho.

"Dammit!" Ren hisses. "I broke it."

Jericho stands up next to him, still looking at the pictures inside.

"This is your family?" Jericho says.

Ren nods as Jericho hands it back to him carefully. He looks to the pictures, his beautiful wife, Curlew, and his infant daughter, Rosie.

"Yes," Ren says.

"Looks like you have a happy life," Jericho says. "I really want a family one day. I have a decently big family in Jareath, er, well I have a couple sisters and my mom. It feels big at times."

"I'd like for my daughter to have a couple siblings," Ren says.

"Well, she's young enough that there won't be much of an age difference," Jericho says. "I feel like I'd be closer to my siblings if the age gap was smaller. But we got along as well as siblings do, you know."

Ren frowns. He's an only child, so he doesn't know.

"Rosie is much older. I've been in this war for almost three years," Ren says. "This is what she looked like before I left. I... I wouldn't recognize her now."

"Oh, I'm sorry," Jericho says.

"Don't be," Ren says. "It's my choice. Mine and Curlew's. She won't bow to that false god Castus, it's my duty as man of the house to protect them."

Jericho gives him a hesitant glance. "I understand that desire to protect. I'm here to avenge my father, but I also want to protect my mother and sisters. If another draft happens, my oldest sister could get drafted, and she's probably a lot like your wife, she won't bow to Castus either. She's no apostle, but Soharism is important to her."

Ren smirks, thinking of Jericho interacting with someone as hard headed as Curlew. Maybe his sister made him so soft.

"Curlew is an apostle of Yuna," Ren says. "But she's got a certain edge to her. She's like Yuna's hard hand of justice more than the motherly love side. She's a wonderful mother still." His smile fades. "A much better mother than I am a father."

"I'm sure you're a fine father," Jericho says.

Ren thinks to his neighbor, Treacher, who's probably more of a father to his daughter than he is. Jealousy churns in his stomach.

"Maybe, if I was ever there."

Jericho hesitates. "This is how you're a good father. This war has already moved to Ghent. You're doing what you set out to, you're protecting your family."

Ren feels touched by his words but when he looks to Jericho he just sees a boy — a young, freckled face and naïve blue eyes. What would he know of the issues of a man?

"I admire that," Jericho continues. "It's good to protect the ones you love. My father didn't have a choice to get drafted, but he had to go to protect us."

"Oh, your father was a Valkoean solider?" Ren asks.

Jericho nods. "In the Navy."

"And you became a rebel?"

"Well, the rebels killed him, but he was an apostle of Gadias. *I'm* an apostle of Gadias. I need to do what's right, I need to do what my dad wanted to do. I hold no resentment for the rebellion because my dad wouldn't. Gadias is the god of war, strength, and protection. We need to be warriors with honor, we need to be strong in any way we can, and we need to protect those we love."

"That's an awfully mature take," Ren says.

Is he judging Jericho too harshly? Ren's parents are still alive and his limbs are all intact. He has seen horrors, mostly from his willing participation in the Sunbell City Guild's schemes and the war. Jericho has been unwillingly tossed into his shortcomings.

"You're an alright kid," Ren says. "You know that?"

"Well, I'm not a kid," Jericho says.

Ren laughs. "Maybe not. You're a kid to me."

"And you're an old man to me," Jericho quips back.

Ren looks to the broken chain of the locket and frowns.

"You know, Cosette can fix that," Jericho says, his eyes shining at the mention of the quartermaster. "If you ask her nicely."

Ren rolls his eyes. Jericho spends a lot of time with the quarter-master, and Ren wonders if it's really just about her repairing his leg. Jericho has that look in his eyes that many mocked Ren for when he first met Curlew.

At least the boy is right about Cosette being able to fix the neck-lace — Ren will have to find her after this. He flicks the locket shut and tucks it into his pants pocket. Stinging pulses on his arm and he lifts it up, a red scrape running down it from his scuffle with the old fence.

"Gah!" Jericho says. "That looks like it stings. We should see if Withorn will clean it out." He looks to the fence. "And maybe Milos will be able to get that family's fence fixed."

A woman stands in the window of the house the fence belongs to, arms crossed as she looks at the two soldiers. A young girl giggles next to her, excited about the fence getting busted. The woman shakes her head, but doesn't come out to nag them.

They start to make their way to the barracks to find the team's medic, Ren admiring the wound.

"Withorn's never gonna let me live this down, getting scuffed up in a sheathed sword spar with you!" he jokes.

The two laugh as they leave. Pride swells in his chest at the day's progress. He doubts Jericho can beat Aster, but maybe with this training, he will have a chance.

26

THE PRISON'S DEPTHS

The spires of the prison stretch into the sky above Scotty, the metal gate lined with barbed wire. Two armed sentries are posted on either side of the gate, watching Scotty approach. One is puffing at a cigarette, smoke snaking from his lips.

Her heart thumps hard as she thinks of what to say to them. Should she just turn around?

She needs answers from Hartwood. He probably won't even cooperate but if there's one thing she knows about the man is that he's an apostle of Ludon, that much he wasn't faking. Maybe that will mean something to him.

"Good afternoon," she greets with a nod. "I need to speak with one of the prisoners." She stares at them expectantly, the two exchanging glances.

The one takes a drag from his cigarette and lets out a puff of smoke before responding. "Which one?"

"His name is Hartwood," Scotty says. "He's an old member of my team. I just need some answers."

"We're always trying to get answers from these people," the guard says, sounding bored. "They don't say much."

DOWN IN FLAMES

Scotty feels her brows furrow. "Please, this is important." *To me.* She's careful to keep that part in her head.

The guard shrugs and flicks his cigarette to the ground, extinguishing it with a stomp from his boot. "Whatever," he says, turning to unlock the gate. "You got five minutes and I'm coming with you." He pushes the gate open with a sharp screech, Scotty wincing at the harsh noise.

Scotty wants to argue, she'd rather not have this guard listening in, but if one rebel guard thinks she's crazy, what's it matter?

"Thanks," Scotty says, stepping through the gate at the guard's beckon.

Two more sentries are posted at the large, dark doors of the gothic building, letting them in with little persuasion. More rebel guards are inside the prison, the inside as dark and ornate as the outside. Oil lanterns light up the darker areas, the tall, pointed windows doing the rest of the work letting the sunlight in. The stone interior feels cool, a draft making Scotty shiver.

The guard leads her to a cellar, the stairs carved into the ground, losing the building's charm as they descend into the dingy basement. The guard plucks a lantern from a hook on the wall and the basement opens up in front of them. High up, windows are cracked at the surface to let the basement breathe, but the air is still stale down here.

The guard greets his comrades as they step through one of the cell-lined walls. Iron bars pierce from the ground to the high ceiling, a brick wall thrown at intervals to divide the cells up. Reinforced sections hold the cell doors, thin entry points lined with locks. Few are empty, but most are holding men and women, some looking angry, but a majority are sad, heads hanging and not even turning to face the two as they pass. Scotty thinks she can see some of them wince in anticipation.

"Hartwell, right?" the rebel guard says, leaning towards Scotty.

"Hartwood," she corrects.

"Bah, thought I had it." He stops to ask another guard and they're pointed in the right direction.

193

The guard takes his bayonet and bangs the pommel against the metal bars of one cell, the noise echoing in the sad prison. A hunched figure in the cell cringes at the sharp noise, but doesn't turn around.

"Hartwood!" he exclaims. "You got a visitor!"

The rebel takes a step back and gestures for Scotty to step forward.

Scotty does so cautiously, peering into the dark cell. The figure is staring upwards at a high window, the sunlight pouring in. She notices something perched on his shoulder and the faint smell of smoking lavender hits her nostrils.

She wants to be angry looking at him, she wants to feel so many things as she stares down the traitor, but she just feels numb.

"Hartwood," Scotty greets.

He snaps around and the sound of her voice, stepping towards her into the lantern light. Shako is on his shoulder, the weaver looking depressed, his grey fur is matted, his white face brown with dirt. Hartwood stares at her with narrowed green eyes, his brown hair unkempt. His beard is much longer, looking like he puts no effort into keeping himself clean.

"You're the last person I expected to see come through here," Hartwood says, leaning his arm against the bars and pressing his head against it, lowering himself a bit to her level.

Scotty looks to the guard hesitantly, the man leaning back against a wall. "You got five minutes," he reminds her.

Scotty turns to Hartwood. "I... need answers about Ludon."

Hartwood frowns and relaxes a bit, confusion plastered over his face. He sighs. "Fine. You've got my attention, what is it?"

Scotty is surprised by how willing he is to cooperate. If she didn't see his treachery with her own eyes, she would find it hard to believe this is the traitor that haunted her for the first few months of her time on the team.

She tells him about her encounter in the Red Forest, the sharfawks, Ludon. She explains the omen, how she needed more from Ludon, how it led to Cannonsburg's fall.

Hartwood stares at her with a bored expression the whole time, a few moments of silence passing when she stops talking.

"The Red Forest tea is used to channel relationships with the gods," Hartwood tells her. "It's not specific to Ludon. I wouldn't trust what your brain comes up with in the holy ground of Cassius." His tone grows disgusted, his face scrunching up. "And I wouldn't think Ludon would chose someone like *you* to be His apostle."

Scotty's blood starts to boil, her fists clenching. "Like you have room to talk," she remarks, his comment draining the validity from the rest of his words.

"You're *not* an apostle of Ludon," Hartwood says, standing up to tower over her beyond the bars.

"Maybe I am!" Scotty bites back. "And maybe *you're* not! Maybe you're a Castist and that's why you betrayed us!"

Hartwood lets out a frustrated sigh and turns around, throwing his hands up to his head.

"By Ludon!" he hollers.

He snaps back around, Shako jerking on his shoulder and holding on tight, chattering at Hartwood's sudden change.

His hands lash out at the bars and he leans down to be on her level again, Shako leaping off his shoulder and retreating to a dark corner. Scotty jerks back slightly and for a moment Hartwood looks like a caged hound, barking and howling to be freed from his cell.

"Listen to me!" he demands. "I didn't do it, Scotty."

Scotty's brow furrows. "I *saw* you placing the bombs! Are you saying my eyes weren't working right?"

"Yes, I am!" he shouts. "Yes, exactly! I was *disarming* them! No one listens to me!"

"Bullshit!" Scotty spits.

"Aster didn't believe me either. We got separated and he lashed out at me when he saw me disarming one. He must have thought I was placing it too." Hartwood is shaking now, his eyes darting around as he recalls the day. He falls to his knees, his hands still gripping the bars and Scotty takes another step back as he starts to sob.

"If you were innocent, *why* did you run?" Scotty asks. "Do you think we're stupid?"

"I was scared!" Hartwood cries. "Guns were pointed at me! Guns of my comrades! I didn't know what was going on — I thought everyone was turning on *me!* Aster was so convinced, I thought he was going to kill me!"

"You broke Aster's arm!" Scotty exclaims.

"It just doesn't make sense!" he cries. "I feel like I'm going insane, no one will listen to me! Do you have any idea how much I've thought about it in this cell? Scotty, I'm going insane in here. Scotty, listen to me, I didn't do it! I didn't do what you think I did! I don't know why you and Aster are so convinced! I don't know why the team believed some forsaken Valkoeans! Maybe you guys are the traitors! You and Aster and that Jericho kid! All Valkoeans, all evil!" As he cries and shouts, spit flies from his lips. "Damn you all! Did you just come here to mock me? Is that what this is about? Do you enjoy this, Scotty? Whatever you got going on, I don't care! Get out of here, just leave me alone already!"

"Okay, we're done here," the guard says. He bangs his bayonet's pommel against the bars again and Hartwood winces and falls back. He curls up in a ball and continues sobbing, Scotty's stomach turning.

"Keep it down, will ya?" the guard says. He shakes his head and turns to Scotty, putting his arm on her to guide her away. "Why'd you have to get him all riled up like that? The others are gonna start going at it soon now!"

Scotty grimaces at him, the two walking away side by side now. "They're prisoners, they're not animals, stop talking about them like that."

"You don't work with these things," the guard says. "They're all like that Hartwell guy. They all put on shows like that, they all say they're innocent. Don't believe their deception."

Scotty shivers, her stomach still feeling uneasy at Hartwood's display. "He sounded so... convinced," she says.

The guard shrugs. "I think they go crazy and convince themselves of the lies they've been telling for so long. It happens, it's a thing. It's like Cassius gets ahold of their heads or something, I don't know."

Scotty thinks back to Hartwood's comment about the Red Forest being Cassius's holy ground. Unease swells through her and she regrets coming here. The guard leads her out of the prison and the sunlight washes over her as they step into the fresh air again.

More questions swirl through her head than when she entered, a darkness lingering inside her. She saw Hartwood placing the bombs, but he sounded so convinced. Why does he seem so certain Scotty isn't an apostle of Ludon? Ludon spoke directly to her, what else would that mean?

A buzzing sound rings in her ears and she scowls as a bee flies by, landing on her nose despite attempts to dodge it. She swats it away angrily and looks to the sky. *Ludon, what do I do?*

27
PASSION

That night, Scotty's dreams are haunted by Hartwood's crazed hollering. She twists and turns all night, waking up intermittently as his yowls echo in her head, doubts crawling their way into her mind.

The restless night bleeds into the morning, hazy sun cutting into the barrack windows. She gives up on sleep and gets ready, her arm wound stinging from her constant turning. She glances around the cots in the room. Most of the Raiders are still sleeping, but some of the cots are abandoned. Unease swirls through her as Hartwood's words of denial haunt her. Her doubts about the team were reinforced by his words. Her face scrunches up as she pulls her long socks up her calf.

Why would she trust him for even a moment?

She lets out a little sigh.

Katze realizes she's awake and steps over to her, placing her muzzle on Scotty's leg.

Scotty smiles and scratches behind her grey, pointed ears.

I can trust you, Katze.

She takes a deep breath to calm herself from the dream.

Katze pesters her as she finishes getting ready for the day, padding excitedly next to Scotty when she gets up. Scotty heads for the door, Katze elated for a morning walk.

The morning air is cool as fall approaches, the air around the island damp. A light fog hugs the land, Scotty heading towards the main road of the town.

She glances behind her and sees the tower the harbor is named after stretching high into the sky, much like an unlit lighthouse. The top is cut off by the fog, Scotty wondering what it looks like for Milos up there.

Some trees are changing colors to herald in fall. Most of the trees on the island are pines, but the golden leaves stand out against the dark green needles. The fall equinox approaches, Scotty growing nervous for the team's next mission.

Some people are out at this hour, a silhouette hobbling towards the barracks. Her heart leaps when she realizes it's Jean and rushes to him.

"Jean!" she exclaims, hugging him. "You're up!"

He smiles and hugs her back. "Good morning, Scotty."

She pulls away and glances behind him towards the infirmary. "Do the medics know you're out and about?"

"Actually, they dismissed me this morning," Jean says.

Scotty smiles. "That's amazing!"

"I know I'm still not walking the best, but they said the healing's nearly done and that I won't hurt myself or make it worse getting back to normal duty. I'm getting so sick of doing nothing and holding the team back."

"No one saw it as you holding us back," Scotty tells him.

"I appreciate that you didn't, but I'm not so sure you speak for the others," Jean says.

Scotty frowns, thinking back to what Hartwood said, her doubts about the team resurfacing.

"Do you wanna come for a walk with me and Katze?" Scotty asks.

"I'd love to," Jean says with a smile.

They head towards the downtown area, the gothic spires of the city's square faded from the foggy haze. Scotty breathes in the cool,

SARA TUNDER

damp air, tiredness from the restless night tugging at her. She looks over to Jean, bags under his eyes too.

She frowns. "Was it hard to sleep in the infirmary? You look tired."

"Hard to sleep is an understatement," Jean says. He lets out a sigh, stuffing his hands into his trench coat's pockets. "Anymore I'm having nightmares more often than not. It gets exhausting."

Scotty nods. *I know too much about that.*

"What were the nightmares about last night?" Scotty asks. She looks at Jean expectantly, wondering if they had the same dream again somehow.

"Fort Vail, again," Jean says, the darkness in his eyes deepening. "The team turning on me, again." He lets out a soft sigh and looks to the foggy sky.

Scotty considers telling him about her talk with Hartwood last night, but the hopeless look in his eyes makes her decide not to. Sowing more doubt in his mind won't help right now. Hartwood is a traitor and Jean's surely already heard it all from him.

Jean turns to face Scotty. "I'm glad I can trust you at least."

Scotty smiles back.

"Seeing good people like you gives me hope for the future, you know," he says. He laughs. "I'm only in my thirties but I sound like an old man."

"I'm glad you trust me and I'm glad I have someone on this team I can fully trust too," Scotty begins. "But I don't know what you see in me. I know *why* you trust me, because there were hints of a traitor before I joined, but I just don't get why you think I'd make a good deputy. I know the others won't understand either." She hesitates, thinking back to her dreams, back to Hardwood's seeds of doubt.

"I... still distrust the others," she admits. "I could never be a good leader. I'm too selfish, I'm a lot of things, and none of those things would make me a good leader or deputy."

"You have a deep passion in you," Jean says immediately. "For your fiancé. You are invested in this war and that passion will take you far, even if it takes you out of your comfort zone."

Scotty's heart swells at the praise, but sinks as she thinks about her late fiancé. She swallows hard. "Sometimes..." The words stick in her throat. "Sometimes I wonder if that's selfishness too. Fighting for Mike. I'm fighting for me. I... I know Mike wouldn't approve of me doing this."

"Trying to free your country?" Jean says.

Scotty pauses. "Trying to get revenge for him."

Jean cocks his head. "Is that really all this is about?" he asks. "Is that really what you risk your skin for?"

"It is," Scotty says. "It's all that drives me."

"You really fight for no other reason?" Jean challenges.

Scotty thinks hard, a few other reasons coming to mind.

"Well, after seeing the destruction in Ghent, I'd like to get revenge for that too," Scotty says. "Or right the wrong we did. We were why those bombs fell. Withorn's a good friend now." She hesitates as she thinks about his mother, High Priestess Tapscott, and the stories he told Scotty about her. Jean doesn't know this, though, and never will. "Jericho shares my passion for revenge, he's fighting for his dad, and I'd like him to see that through, I'd like to help him make a difference."

Jean smiles as Scotty goes on.

"It might be different now," Scotty admits. "But that doesn't change this burning hatred I feel when I fight. I don't know if I'd fight *just* for them. I don't know if I'd fight if those bastards didn't take Mike from me!"

She realizes her hands are clenched into fists and her voice was growing, but she lets out a breath to try to relax, looking to Jean ashamedly.

"Scotty, that hatred comes from a place of love," Jean tells her. "Trust me, I know. I hate the Valkoeans too." He laughs slightly. "The government and army I mean, I know you're technically Valkoean. Maybe we are the same in that regard, though. I fight to protect those I love back in New North Ash, I fight to do what's right, I fight for revenge, especially now since half of my team is gone... I fight to prove myself, I fight to try to make their sacrifices not be in vain." He frowns and looks to the ground. "None of us want to think our loved ones die for no reason, we always want to find meaning in it."

"I've been struggling to find meaning in Mike's death," Scotty says. "I just know that I'm sad and angry, even two seasons later."

Jean passes her a sympathetic smile. "That's alright, it takes time to heal, Scotty. I don't think your passion is selfish."

Scotty feels tears pooling in her eyes and turns away.

Why am I crying? I don't believe him!

She can't help but feel the validation deep down. If Jean believes in her so much, she'll work harder. She can become this person Jean thinks she is. Regardless of her doubts, she knows she can trust Jean, she does have friends in this war who want the same thing she does.

Once she regains her composure, she turns to face him. "I'll... I'll do my best, Jean," she says. "Thanks for believing in me."

"Thanks for trusting me as your leader," Jean says back with a polite dip of the head. He halts and Scotty stops a few steps later, turning back to him.

"Since I'm feeling better, I'm going to brief the team on the equinox masquerade," he tells her. "We'll be setting off on that mission soon." He hesitates. "I... would like your input. Do you really think we aren't ready for it?"

Scotty looks Jean over, impressed by his recovery and inspired by their shared passion. "We can do it," she says definitively. "We'll get the information we need to stop these damned airships."

28
THE FIRST TRIAL

Tiredness tugs at Ren at the briefing, a couple cups of tea with breakfast not enough caffeine to kickstart his day. The Raiders surround Jean, showering him with excited comments on his fast recovery. Cosette's shrill voice pierces Ren's ears as she nags at Jean, making sure he's fully recovered. Farsing is the only quiet one next to Ren, sipping at a metal flask, an annoying sloshing noise coming from the container. Ren drags his hands across his face, rubbing his eyes.

"Can we make this briefing *brief?*" he says.

Jean crosses his arms, turning to face him. "Did you have somewhere you needed to be, Reiner?" he asks.

Ren sniffs frustratedly at Jean's use of his full name. "Somewhere I can wake up a bit more."

Farsing thrusts the metal flask in front of Ren, the sloshing noise of the alcohol making Ren grimace.

"This'll sure wake you up, give it a try," Farsing says.

Ren swats his hairy arm away. "You know I don't drink," he says, not trying to hide the anger in his tone.

"We're all just excited that Jean is doing better," Jericho says to

Ren. Jean side eyes Jericho when he speaks, his gaze turning back to Ren. "Why can't you just be excited too?" Jericho finishes.

"I don't get excited about things," Ren says blandly. He can't even say he was excited when he married his wife or when his daughter was born. That was mostly fear, both times. Getting too excited in battle is how to lose focus and die. Getting excited this early in the morning? He just doesn't understand it.

Jean finally gets around to briefing the mission, talking about the team attending a masquerade tea party in Snowden, the capital of the Wingate Province. They need to lure a dewick engineer named Markos away from the party and interrogate him about Valko and Mohkan's alliance and the airships. Ren grimaces at the idea of attending an uppity tea party with some people he probably wants to kill. He lives in the middle of the woods for a reason.

"Milos thought our team was the best for this mission?" Ren blurts out at the end.

"Of course," Cosette says. "It makes sense, we've had similar parties in Sunbell City. Ever been to one of our clients parties in the cities?"

"I only went to the cities when a contract demanded it," Ren says.

Cosette rolls her eyes. "I'm excited to see what a Valkoean tea party is like!"

"You're excited?" Jericho asks from her side. "These aren't nice people we will be around. They want us dead!"

She waves a dismissive hand at him. "What do you think the parties were like in Ghent? Not much different. C'mon, it'll be fun!"

Jericho stands wide-eyed next to her. "Sometimes I forget this team's past. But Gadias knows it's not my past!"

Ren glances to Connie and Reagan, the two looking like they want to ask more about the team's past. Of course, they were told briefly about Ghent and the Sunbell City Guild. Reagan was still excited to join, Connie as hesitant as ever, but staying on Reagan's leash at the end of the day.

"We aren't going for fun," Jean asserts.

Cosette shrugs at him. "We can try to have fun."

Ren can hardly believe Cosette has been a guild member her whole life.

"High Priestess Tapscott will be attending," Jean says. "We need to take this seriously."

"Really?" Withorn blurts out. "We will be in the same room as the High Priestess." His hazel eyes are wide in fear.

"So what's stopping us from killing her there?" Ren asks.

Farsing and Reagan cheer in support, Jean hushing them.

"Because it'd be suicide," Jean says. "Guards will be everywhere, we need to lay low and gather intel. I will not entertain that idea further." His gaze sweeps over the team before he continues. "We'll be split into two teams. One will *not* show face in the party, the other will be on the floor gathering information and bringing Markos into our assigned hotel room. The team inside the room, or the interrogation team, will be me, Reagan, Connie, Farsing, and Ren."

Relief floods through Ren's veins. Jean isn't dumb enough to make him socialize.

Jean continues. "Out on the floor, the social team, will be Aster, Merryweather, Cosette, Withorn, Jericho, and Scotty."

Ren's face scrunches up and looks over to Jericho and Scotty. Odd choice. Jericho is already anxious about it and Scotty is a shut-in hitman. Judging by the look on her scarred face, she's just as confused as he is.

"You all need to gather what intel you can from the guests," Jean says.

"Jean," Aster speaks up. The whole team looks to him, anxiety plain as day on the deputy's face. "With all due respect, I'd like to be on the interrogation team."

Jean raises a brow at him.

Aster's eyes dart around. "And if General Halcomb, the former leader of the Black Glove Scouts is there, some other Scouts might be attending." He shuffles nervously. "I... because of my past in the war, I can't run into General Halcomb. Please."

Jean nods. "Of course. I'll be on the social team and you can be on the interrogation team."

Aster smiles weakly at him. Ren frowns, wondering what has Aster so stressed.

"Hey," Farsing speaks up, his raspy voice grating on Ren's ears. "If the Scouts might be there, don't you think they might, just *maybe* recognize us and try to kill us?"

"It's a masquerade, those in attendance will have masks," Jean says. "It's why this will be possible, we will all be hidden." Jean's gaze turns to Merryweather, smirking at his old friend. "Merryweather, you'll play a special part in this mission."

Merryweather's eyes light up. "Oh, me? What is it?"

"Markos is a known womanizer," Jean says. "You have some certain... social skills that I think could help lure him into the hotel room."

Merryweather lets out a laugh and places her hand on her chest. "Oh, you want *me* to flirt with the old man? Well, I might just be your woman of choice! All these boys think I'm flirting by just being myself, it's like they've never interacted with a woman before!"

"Get creative with it," Jean says. "Just make sure you bring him back to the right hotel room."

"Something tells me that'll be the hardest part," Merryweather says with a sly shrug.

Ren rolls his eyes. Merryweather is excited to have fun for the mission, but the thought of having to interact with a cheating man in any other way than interrogation irks him. She'll help make that happen, though.

Ren thinks to his own wife, alone at home, a nagging darkness inside him. Curlew knows cheating is wrong, but Ren's been such an awful husband abandoning them for so long.

He shakes the doubting thoughts away. He needs to focus on the mission and not dwell on some made up situation.

Ren meets Jean's eyes, his icy gaze lingering as he speaks. "If anyone has questions about the mission, let me know. If not, you're dismissed."

The Raiders disperse and Ren gets ready to leave towards downtown to get some more caffeine in his veins when Jean's voice catches him.

"Ren, Jericho, I'd like to speak with the two of you."

Ren winces and turns around to him, looking to Jericho first. The boy is frozen, his freckled face pointed at Ren questioningly.

"What is it?" Ren asks, meeting Jean in the middle of the room, Jericho following soon after.

Jean looks down to Jericho. "I'd like to test you," he says. "I know you two have only been working together for a little over a week, but we need quick improvement. Spar with me."

Jericho pauses before letting out a deep breath. "Of course, I'll show you all I've learned," he says, feigning confidence.

Ren grits his teeth and only nods at Jean when he looks to him expectantly. Ren would rather be waking up more right now, but he'd also like to get a few more lessons in for the boy before he spars with the commander. Last training session was promising, so hopefully the boy retained the knowledge and muscle memory and will impress Jean.

"Let's go out to the yard," Jean says. "There's a nice shady spot by the tower."

Before they head outside, Jericho passes a panicked look to Ren, not helping Ren's confidence.

Gadias, give him strength! Ren doubts that praying to the god of strength and war can even help him.

———

The Greater Asperetti Mountains in the west cast shadows on the island in the early morning hour, a thin layer of dew sparkling on the grass blades. The fresh smell of the lake is strong out in the cool late-summer air. The air reminds Ren of his home in the mountains at this time of year, air from a nearby lake in the valley lifting up to the mountainside.

He looks at the two men in front of him, bayonets drawn, covered with sheathes.

Jean and Jericho stand across from each other at the base of Milos's tower, a few sword-lengths between them. Jericho stands strong, taking some deep breaths as he holds his ground, pivoting on his prosthetic as Jean steps around him.

Jean's trench coat wavers as he lunges forward, his bayonet's tip aimed at Jericho. Jericho pivots, bringing his blade down to divert Jean to the side. Jean leans into the motion, swinging back around to bring his blade down on the boy. Jericho has already turned, rooted to the ground as he blocks the blow.

Pride whelms in Ren's chest as he watches Jericho deflect Jean's blows. The commander is still slightly recovering, so he's not fighting at one hundred percent, but he seems to be taken off guard by Jericho's built up strength. Jericho can't just keep playing defense, though.

As Jean zips around him quickly, Jericho adjusts, the boy's eyes snapping around and meeting Jean's blade.

Ren grits his teeth, unable to stop himself from blurting out, "Defense doesn't win battles!"

Jericho cocks his head towards Ren when he shouts out, Jean taking advantage of this and landing a blow on his arm.

"Gah!" Jericho shouts, leaping to the side. He winces as he stands unbalanced. The blades are sheathed, but Jean packs a powerful punch regardless.

Ren grimaces. A gash like that would likely take him out of battle. If it landed in the right place he'd be bleeding out.

Jericho recovers quickly, standing strong on the ground as Jean comes at him again. Ren thinks he can see the gears turning in the boy's head as he tries to figure out how to switch to offense.

Jericho locks in on Jean, bending his right leg to brace for his next blow, bringing his bayonet to his center. Jean lashes out and Jericho howls, deflecting the blow with timed precision towards his leg. Jean's blade hits the metal prosthetic with a solid thud, his arms shaking from the force. Jericho kicks his prosthetic forward and slices his sheathed blade, licking Jean's flank as he stumbles away.

Jean coughs at the blow, regaining his footing. He smiles admirably at the boy, stepping around him, bayonet aimed forward.

He takes no time to lash forward, Jericho pivoting around as they exchange blows. Jericho starts to get more comfortable, stepping around slowly to move with Jean's force, trying to keep his core strong.

Anxiety pricks through Ren as he sees him move more and more.

"Keep rooted!" Ren shouts. "You have no chance!"

Jericho grimaces, trying to keep his attention on Jean, growing more offensive as their blades meet. He manages a blow so strong that Jean goes on the defensive, Jericho stepping forward slowly as he lashes out. The two men are slicked with sweat and as Jericho slices forward, Ren notices how strong he's actually gotten.

Another blow from Jean sends Jericho stumbling back.

"No, no!" Ren shouts. "This is why you need to be rooted!"

Jericho looks like a fuse has been set off, flailing his arms up in the air. "Would you shut up?" he shouts.

"Keep your attention on Jean!" Ren demands.

Just then, Jean's blade meets Jericho chest and he yowls as he falls back, grunting when he lands hard on his back. Jean stands over him, holding the metal tip of his sheath against Jericho's neck.

Jericho swats the sword away with a balled fist and scrambles to his feet.

"What in the name of Forez was that?" Ren says, stomping over to them.

"What was that?" Jericho echoes in disbelief. "What were *you* doing shouting at *me*? I was doing fine!"

Ren hesitates, realizing the boy might be right. No, Ren was just trying to help. "You need to be able to fight well with a bunch of distractions around you," he says. "What if I was someone with a gun covering Jean? You'd be dead."

"Then I'd be dead and I wouldn't have to care. *I was doing fine.*" Jericho's freckled face is twisted in a scowl.

"You do need to be able to fight with distractions," Jean butts in. "Ren's right in that regard."

Jericho looks like he wants to shout at the commander, but his attention stays on Ren. "You couldn't just let me succeed on my own. I need to make my own decisions in battle."

"You don't understand, I'm responsible for you, boy," Ren says.

"I'm not a boy first of all," Jericho says. "And what makes you responsible for me? Huh? You're not my dad."

"If you fail, I fail," Ren says. "You are the way you are because I failed you at Salina Village."

"I'm the way I am because I decided to join a war," Jericho says. "I'm the way I am because of choices I made, it has nothing to do with you." Jericho hesitates, lingering on Ren's words for a moment. "So this has never been about me? You're only helping me because you think I'm *your* failure? Right? This is about you."

"Of course it's about you, you dumbass," Ren says. "But you are also my failure."

The emotion fades from Jericho's face as if he can't believe what he just heard.

"I'm *nothing* to you," Jericho says. "I've never been strong, I've always needed to work on my strength. Losing my leg *has* been a burden, it *has* made life harder for me, but I'm stronger now because of it. I'm more motivated. I've grown close to Cosette because of it. *My* decisions led to this and it's *my* decision to use it as motivation to get stronger. If I fail it's not because of you. If I succeed, it will *not* be because of you!" He straightens his back. "And I'm going to get stronger and beat Aster without your help."

He stomps away, Jean watching him with worried icy eyes. "Jericho, wait!" Jean shouts.

"I just need to go for a walk," Jericho says, his voice shaky now. "I just need to be alone, Jean."

Jean nods, turning to Ren when the boy is out of earshot.

Jean lets out a sigh. "I see promising improvement in Jericho," he says. "This mission we are going on isn't one where he will need to fight. I was testing his wit, and I'm confident he will be able to do what's needed at the masquerade. He used his prosthetic to his advantage, deflecting my blow to it. That's the wit of a Raider."

Ren opens his mouth to speak, but Jean cuts him off. "I'll let him know once he cools off. But, Ren let go of your guilt with him. I understand why you feel the way you do, but this is about Jericho, it's not about you. Get your emotions under control. If we all let guilt get to us like that, we'd be one dysfunctional team."

Ren grimaces at Jean's words. "You're one to talk," he says.

Jean stares at him, unmoved by his remark. "Why do you think I'm giving you this advice?"

Ren gets ready to defend his outburst, but bites his tongue, thinking to what Merryweather said to him after she collapsed.

Jean affixes his sheath back to his belt under his overcoat and steps away from Ren, leaving him as the morning sun peeks out from behind the distant mountains.

Embarrassment and anger swirl through Ren as Jean's words set in, as he thinks about Jericho's outburst.

What do they know?

The anger ebbs as their words echo in his head. He lets out a sigh. He thought he was doing what was best for Jericho, he thought he was being selfless.

Is he being selfish?

Maybe they're right...

29
THE HEARTH HOTEL

T he autumnal equinox approaches, now only days away. Jean's nearly fully recovered, the team on their way to Snowden, a Valkoean-controlled city south of Hightower Harbor.

Milos gave the Raiders a carriage drawn by two valen. The carriage is big enough to fit the team and the large valen are strong enough to tow them. Aster and Jean are at the front of the cart, Scotty hearing their quiet murmuring and intermittent laughing on the long journey. The back doors of the carriage are solid bullet proof metal and the sides are metal bars lined with a short metal wall.

They take a road alongside the lake southwards, the lakeside breeze wafting through the carriage windows, keeping the team cool. Between the cool breeze and the floor cushions, Scotty can't complain about this way of traveling.

Scotty feels closed in with the Raiders, Hartwood's words still haunting her.

Hartwood was lying, she reminds herself. *That's what people like him do.*

Withorn and Jericho are at Scotty's side, playing matekart. Withorn has a handle on it now, Connie's eyes poking out from under his round glasses as he watches them flip cards down and mutter about the game. The carriage bumps and jerks as they move along the road, the cards refusing to stay in place on the floor.

Jericho's leg is removed, Cosette taking a little screw driver to it. She had already helped the others field strip and clean their guns — Scotty thinks she just needed something else to do with her hands for the ride.

Grassy fields give way to a dryer ground with short pines, the land rising higher above the lake. Scotty peers out past Jean and Aster, the main part of the city still in the distance up the gently sloping ground. Cliffs dive down from the rounded spires of the skyline, far down towards a crescent shaped bay of Mayhew Lake.

The city rolls down the spiral sloped land, buildings sparse down here. Farms are dotted with cattle and the Snowden port is down here at the lower part of the city. The large port stretches all the way across the bay to the bottom of the cliff, a massive machine puffing out ethner steam breathing along the cliffside. Scotty can just barely make out a mechanical pulley system bringing goods up from the far side of the port to the top of the city, an impressive display of the good steam technology can do.

The road is busy with carriages, the money in this place evident from the lavish towers, large buildings, and pompous looking citizens. Their clothes are made with furs or brightly colored fabrics and their hair is pinned up and looks like they've never done a dirty day of work in their lives.

No gates or guards hinder entry into the city, the team strolling in quietly among the other carriages. Valko's blue, gold, and white flags hang proudly around the city.

The brick houses engulf them, the towering buildings casting shadows over the road. Aster and Jean maneuver the carriage through the roads, winding around the buildings. The city's bank is massive and large shops are in the market area. Scotty's brow furrows when they pass a Castist temple, a statue of the bearded man Castists call their god standing near the door.

Reagan sits next to Connie, hands against the carriage wall as she peers out the window, beaming. "The buildings here are beautiful!" she says.

Scotty glances to the buildings, some built with grey bricks, others painted soft colors. She wonders what's got Reagan so excited about them. It's just a city.

The carriage careens around a tall, blocky hotel with rounded spires, shadows fully dousing them as they pull into a stable smelling sweetly of hay.

When the Raiders step out, Scotty sees the top of the pulley system from the port on the other side of the yard. A warehouse sits at the edge of the cliff, the scale of the pulley platforms astonishing to Scotty. A full carriage could fit on the things. The ethner steam blows away across the water, unease tugging at Scotty's gut when she realizes how close they are to the cliff.

The employees at the warehouse watch the Raiders curiously, Scotty growing nervous under their watch. The Raiders are out of place, dressed more like the warehouse workers than what would be a normal guest at the hotel.

Scotty notices the rest of the team giving the workers hesitant glances as they step out.

A beautiful garden sprawls in front of them, a small frog pond in the center. Large rocks jut out among the bushes and flowers and a few winding paths lead to a door in the hotel's rear.

"Greetings!" a shrill voice calls out.

A young woman with pale skin and short, curled brown hair approaches them through the garden. She wears a casual, flowing dress, made of an expensive looking material.

"Miss Erin?" Jean asks, reaching a calloused hand out to her.

She nods and hesitates before shaking Jean's hand with a white glove. "And you must be Jean," she says. "It's nice to meet you all."

"Your hotel is beautiful, Miss Erin," Reagan says, her hands clasped together. Erin smiles at her.

Jean cranes his head around towards the warehouse workers without being obvious. "We got some onlookers back there," he tells

Erin. "I don't think I trust them. We can leave and come back later if it makes things less suspicious."

"Oh, nonsense!" she exclaims. "The warehouse workers are rebel-aligned. Most are Castists, but their treatment by the rich in town is... less than desirable. They're on our side."

Jean nods slowly, though Scotty knows he still doesn't trust them. She assumes he doesn't want to be rude and speak out again. Erin leads the team into the hotel, taking them in through the garden to the quiet back entrance.

They're led through a hall with intricately patterned carpet and noisy wallpaper, Scotty put off by the unnatural look. The hall spills into a large lobby adorned with beautiful furniture. Floral scents waft through the building, fresh bouquets displayed in crystal vases atop the tables. High ceilings lead to a wrap-around loft, iron spiral stair-cases leading upwards.

The lobby is void of guests, some staff members in soft grey suits setting up tables and silverware for their important event. Other staff members have clean white clothes on with aprons, and Scotty thinks they look similar to the cleaning staff at the Brunswick Manor. A massive wall in the lobby has a huge painting of Castus on it, his beady amber eyes watching over the team as they pace through the room. His arms are crossed as if ready to judge them, black gloves balled into fists as they rest on his arms. His hair and beard are a matching orange.

Erin takes them into a hall, halting at the first door. Erin lets them in, squeaking the door close behind them. "This is where you will be for your mission... Please do keep it clean, the cleaning staff has a lot of work as it is keeping these rooms nice and tidy."

Scotty looks around the place — it's gaudier than even the Brunswick Manor. The living space is massive, complete with a slumbering fireplace. Leather couches and chairs face the mantle, a tea table sitting on the carpet between them. A door to the bedroom is beside the fireplace, closed off right now. A small kitchen and dining area is on the far side of the room, open windows letting in a lovely breeze behind the dining table. In the middle of the large windows is a door with access to a back patio. Farsing looks around the room curiously, lifting up pillows and peeking in drawers while Connie and Reagan seem to be in awe of everything. The rest of the Raiders are unamused, save for Jericho, who takes everything in quietly.

Scotty smirks at the grandeur of it all. They're going to be interrogating a man in here. It's feels cozy and safe right now.

Erin steps over to the dining area, gesturing to the door.

"I picked this room not only because it's close to the venue, but it is one of the few rooms with a bottom floor patio. Er, an escape space, if you need it."

Jean smiles and nods. "Very thoughtful, I appreciate it."

Erin smiles at his praise. Scotty wonders why she is so eager to help. She's young but seems to be prim and proper.

Farsing thrusts a chef's knife in the air. "Found a cool blade for the interrogation!" he exclaims. "Aster, whaddaya think?"

"Oh, please put that down!" Erin exclaims, putting her gloved hand up. "Please refrain from... dirtying any of the property during the interrogation."

"Yeah, Farsing, just put that down," Aster says, unamused at the dewick.

Farsing grumbles and puts the knife back, but continues picking through the silverware drawer.

"This was just an idea Milos and I threw around when I visited him in Hightower Harbor," Erin says, facing Jean now. "If you think of any better ideas, let me know and we will accommodate you."

"No, I think it's a solid plan," Jean says.

"Are we going to all be sleeping in here before the party?" Farsing calls out, flopping down on the couch. "I call this spot!"

"Well, actually, I have rooms set aside for each of you," Erin says. "They aren't as big as this one, but you're honored guests and will be treated as such."

"Us? Honored?" Farsing echoes.

Scotty blinks in shock. She wasn't expecting the grand hospitality.

"I'll show you to your rooms after I show you the venue space," Erin says.

Erin takes them across the hall to a grand event space with wooden paneling, striped cream and orange wallpaper, and the same gaudy carpet as the lobby. Crystal oil chandeliers hang from the high ceilings and tall tables adorned with silk cloths stand intermittently across the floor. There isn't a lot of seating besides some couches against the walls and some chairs around a few lower tables. A massive stage with flowing scarlet curtains is on the far side of the room, showcasing a grand piano, and a couple doors on the side of the venue lead to a backroom and what Scotty can just barely make out as a kitchen.

Afterwards, Erin shows them to their rooms, each of them getting their own private room along the same side of the hall.

"I left masks on the beds in each room," Erin says. "They'll be your masks for the party, so make sure they fit and let me know if they don't. We'll get you set up with tailored clothes later so you look your best for the event."

"Tailored?" Jean asks. "Surely we'll be fine with whatever party attire you have. No need to empty your pocketbook for us."

"I insist," Erin says. "You must look your best for this. Fitting in seamlessly is necessary, and trust me, an ill-fitting suit will turn heads."

Scotty scrunches her nose at the thought. The Brunswicks were posh, but not that pretentious! Someone making the Brunswicks look less out of touch is not someone she wants to be around.

After the tour, Scotty settles into her room with Katze, lighting the oil lamp. Scotty takes in a deep breath — the room smells remarkably clean — and lets herself relax. The room is simple, it's as colorful as the rest of the place, having a soft bed with clean sheets, a few down pillows, a dresser where the oil lamp sits, a desk, and a plush chair. Scotty sits back into the chair, putting her feet up on a cushiony rest. Katze is excited to leap up with her and nestle her bony haunches into the small section of chair between Scotty's butt and the armrest.

Katze settles on her lap, Scotty letting out an "oof" as her gut gets squished by flailing paws. The two relax and enjoy the serene hotel room.

"Wouldn't this kinda be nice all the time?" Scotty muses, Katze's ears twisting to listen. Scotty rakes her hands through Katze's grey fur. "After the war, maybe we can have a place with a nice chair like this," Scotty tells her.

Warmth swells though her chest. She usually doesn't look to the future.

A pang of sadness hits. The future would be a lot nicer if Mike could be there.

"What I wouldn't give for Mike to be back," Scotty mutters. *I'd trade all the soft chairs in the world to have him again...*

A knock on the door makes Scotty yowl out, then again when Katze leaps off her gut, tail whizzing around at the door now.

Scotty hobbles over to the door, yanking it open.

"Jericho?" She can't help her greeting coming out more like a question. She wasn't expecting the blond young man to be on the other side of the door. Being one of the only people she feels she can trust on the team, it's a welcomed surprise.

"Hey, Scotty," he says, a bit distraught. "Can we talk?"

Scotty blinks. "Er, yeah, sure. Come on in."

He sits down on the end of the bed and Scotty takes a seat on the footrest, looking to him hesitantly.

"What did you want to talk about?" she urges. She tries to keep herself from looking back at the chair, she'd really like to be lounging back in it right now.

"It's just..." he begins, trailing off. "Jean said I'd be kicked off the team if I can't beat Aster in two months. Well, it's more like one month now."

"What?" Scotty blurts out, her blood starting to boil. "Why would Jean say something like that?"

"Well, it's because... I'm *not* very good at fighting," Jericho explains. He tells Scotty about the mission down by Fort Kip and how he got in the way. Scotty nods as he speaks. She hadn't realized how close he had come to dying then. Jericho feels guilty for almost getting Jean killed too. "It's not *just* because of my leg," he tells her. "I have a lot to learn. I've always had a lot to learn." His voice trembles a bit. "I'm a lighthouse keeper, a lighthouse keeper's *apprentice* for Gadias's sake!"

"You're not a lighthouse keeper anymore," Scotty tells him. "You're a member of the rebellion, a member of the Acros Raiders."

Jericho faintly smiles at her.

"That doesn't change the situation I'm in," he says. He explains how Ren of all people offered to help him get stronger, how Ren helped him adjust his fighting style to work with his new leg and limited mobility.

"But it turns out he was only doing it because he felt *guilty*," Jericho says. Scotty's face scrunches up.

She knows Ren has felt guilty since the day the three were paired together and Jericho lost his leg, but she hoped he'd be over it by now.

"He's the reason why we survived in Salina Village," Scotty says. "He shouldn't feel guilty. He led the Valkoeans away from us. What is he thinking?"

"Right?" Jericho says. He hesitates before continuing. "But he said... that I'm just his failure."

"Wow," Scotty says. Ren can be harsh, but it usually comes from a place of care. Scotty can't poke enough holes in that to make it sound like sympathy.

Jericho nods. "I thought I was doing well. I thought I was getting better, but now I feel like I failed myself. I didn't realize he thought so lowly of me. I know it shouldn't get to me, but it *does*."

"Ren can be an asshole," Scotty says. "Just... don't listen to him."

"Easier said than done," Jericho says.

Scotty nods, unsure of what to say.

"But I need some help training now," Jericho continues. "Would... you help me?"

Scotty is taken aback. "Me?" she says. "Why?" When Jericho frowns, she realizes that was the wrong reaction. "I'm not a very good teacher." She gestures to Katze, the fallion wriggling her back on the carpet, her skinny belly exposed. "I can't even train Katze."

Jericho laughs when Katze flips over, her pointed ears pricking towards Scotty.

"You're a good fighter and had to adjust to a new style too," Jericho says, Katze padding up to him. He runs a hand down her neck. "I think I just need someone who believes in me. And I know you do."

Scotty smiles, thinking about Jericho's desire to avenge his dad. They have similar motives to aiding the rebellion — the Valkoeans made it personal for them. When she met him, she knew he had a lot to learn, but his passion made Scotty vouch for him and his wits made Withorn endorse him joining. Because of their input, Jean let Jericho join the team.

"I can certainly give it a try," she says.

"Thanks, Scotty."

"Er, we'll start when we are out of Snowden," Scotty says. "I don't think training here will be beneficial. Besides, this is a mission where we finally don't need to fight."

"That sounds good," Jericho says. He lets out a sigh of relief, his spirits raised now. "I'll leave you be to relax. I really appreciate it."

Scotty bids him farewell, still shocked that she was the person Jericho decided to come to. She walks over to the bed to get ready for the night and notices something out the corner of her eye as she reaches down to pull the plush comforter back. Scotty picks a mask up from where it rests on her pillow.

The mask is the face of a sharfawks, the top half orange, the bottom half white. Sequins flutter around the cheeks and pointed ears spread out to the sides. Thin wooden antlers poke out the top and the hollow eyes seem to mock her.

An unsettling feeling rocks in Scotty's gut as she thinks of Ludon visiting her in the form of a sharfawks.

Is this supposed to be another omen from the god of beasts?

30
STRIKE A NERVE

The next day, the Raiders prepare for their mission, the fall equinox only two days away now. The guests for the masquerade arrive tomorrow, so Erin wanted the Raiders to get acquainted with rebel-aligned staff and to get comfortable in the venue. Erin and staff get everyone fitted in their party attire, Scotty already wearing a soft blue dress — a color Erin said would accent Scotty's brown hair and grey eyes well. The dress's bottom is puffier than Scotty is used to, and the waist tighter, but she's confident she can fight in this dress if needed.

She flips her mask around in her hands, wondering if it has any meaning.

Erin teaches Scotty about some manners, the posh woman getting impatient with Scotty as she is quizzed on the three-tiered trays served at tea parties. Erin grows frustrated when Scotty mixes up the scones and sweets.

"They're both sweet, it doesn't matter," Scotty says, an edge to her voice.

Erin huffs and leans down next to her. "Everything has to be perfect," she whispers.

Scotty can't help but to roll her eyes. "A small detail won't ruin the party."

"Won't ruin the party?" Erin echoes, her lips parted in disbelief. "Won't ruin the party! High Priestess Tapscott will be here! I'm not outright risking my life like you, but do you understand what's at stake for me here? This is my life. If something goes wrong, I can't run, I can't hide." The anger and disbelief fades, fear taking over. "If things don't go perfectly, blood could be on my hands. Not just my own. Your team's, my staff's... It's a heavy weight. Things *do* have to be perfect."

Scotty frowns, her face growing hot in embarrassment. She doesn't understand these high class manners like the elites or even her own comrades, she's just a lowly hitman! Her hands ball at her side as she grows frustrated, not at Erin, but at herself. *Mike would be better at this than me.* Loneliness pangs in Scotty's chest at the thought. Mike always attended parties like this with his family where she wasn't allowed. He hated acting like the other elites and preferred when he could be himself with Scotty. *If only he was here he could do a better job teaching me. If he was still here, I wouldn't be in this mess in the first place.*

The longing thoughts of her beloved can't pull her away from reality, Erin's terrified gaze burning into Scotty. "I'm sorry," Scotty says. "I just have a lot to learn." Her voice strengthens. "We'll make sure everything goes well. And I won't forget that the scones are in the middle tray." She faintly smiles at Erin, hoping she believes her. "Thank you for the help."

Erin smiles lightly, the fear in her eyes not ebbing. "Thank you. Don't hesitate to ask if you need a refresher on anything. I'm going to see if the others need anything."

Scotty bids her farewell, embarrassment still twisting inside her at her judgement of the posh woman. *She's risking a lot just having us in this place.*

Scotty lifts her hands up and ties the sharfawks mask behind her head. The mask fits perfectly, like it was made for her. Her lips and cheeks are exposed along with some of her scars.

Scotty looks at the others, frowning as Hartwood's words still buzz in her head. She's unsettled about going into another mission while the doubts about her team swirl around her head.

They're good people, she tells herself.

Doubts aside, it's odd seeing everyone else dressed so snazzy.

Merryweather, Cosette, and Jericho are all talking to each other around a table, Merryweather and Cosette both excited to be wearing lavish fabrics. Merryweather's dress is a deep indigo and her mask is blue and feathery, coming to sharp points on either side of her face. Cosette's mask is a simple metallic gold, bright against her blonde hair. Her dress is pale grey, the bottom poofy. Jericho has a nearly full-faced white mask, somehow making him look frightened even with his face covered. His suit is a light grey, a forest green bowtie on his neck.

I can trust Jericho... Merryweather seems trustworthy, but she is from the Sunbell City Guild. I want to trust Cosette. I don't think she could be deceptive. What if she's deceiving me into thinking that?

Scotty's heart races as her thoughts zoom around, paranoia buzzing in her head like a hive of bees.

"Scotty," a voice murmurs.

Scotty snaps around, noticing Withorn behind her. He's wearing a white suit, accented with a gold tie. Only his blond hair and striking yellow eyes are visible behind his full-faced novak mask.

She's yanked away from her thoughts, a smirk twisting over her lips at her friend dressed so handsomely.

"A white suit for you?" Scotty asks amusedly. "Be sure you don't spill tea on it."

Withorn hesitates after her comment, Scotty realizing this is not a time for joking.

"Is everything okay?" she asks.

He glances around before lifting his mask up to his hair. Scotty frowns at the disturbed look on his face.

"Scotty, my mother will be here tomorrow," he says quietly.

Scotty nods in understanding but can't stifle a shiver as fear resonates through her — High Priestess Tapscott, the woman behind this war, will be here, in the same room as Scotty. Besides Scotty's own reservations, the High Priestess was not a kind mother to her friend, which is why he ran away when he was still young, only to be adopted by Civran, the former medic of the Acros Raiders.

"I know," Scotty says softly. "Do you want to see if Jean can switch you to the interrogation team?"

Withorn shakes his head. "I don't know if I can handle myself knowing she's here. I-I'd rather be with you. You know the truth."

"Do you think she will recognize you like your aunt did?" Scotty whispers.

Withorn swallows hard, a new worry plastered on his face. "Luckily the mask covers my face, but I'm... I'm worried about my eyes."

"You think she will recognize your eyes?" Scotty asks.

"I know she will." Withorn sounds entirely convinced, so Scotty doesn't argue.

"We'll stay close, but we don't want to raise too much suspicious being together," Scotty says. "Just... don't look at her, okay? If you get uncomfortable and need to leave—" she hesitates, thinking how this mission needs to be a success, how they need to get intel in order to get the upper hand on the Valkoeans, and for Scotty to get her revenge. "—if you need to leave, I'll be right there beside you," she finally finishes. She winces internally at the words.

Worst case scenario, I can take Tapscott out myself. It'd be suicide but my mission will be complete...

A disturbing comfort sinks into her heart at that idea and she shivers as a darkness sneaks in.

But if I did that, what would happen to the team? To Withorn?

Withorn faintly smiles at her. "Thanks, Scotty," he says, bringing her out of her thoughts. "I don't like looking this weak. I don't like feeling this weak. But I'm scared."

"I don't get why this can't be a hit mission on Tapscott," Scotty says, her voice coming out almost like a growl. A large part of her needs revenge, but seeing the usually cranky medic murmuring at her like a lost child makes it feel somehow more personal — this is Tapscott's *son* for Gadias's sake.

"Jean said it'd be suicide with all the guards," Withorn says. "Besides, the Valkoeans need weakened before we can take her out. It would be hard for Milos to take power right now. Tapscott's influence is strong and will last when she dies."

Scotty thinks she can see tears forming in Withorn's bright hazel gaze, and he pulls his mask down to hide them. He stares behind Scotty and nods, bringing Scotty's attention behind her.

"You two are looking dapper," Jean's cheery voice forces Scotty to turn around. Scotty's heart skips a beat when she sees an identical sharfawks mask staring back at her, Jean's blue eyes peeking out behind it. A bowler hat sits atop his head and a long black suit, reminiscent of his long trench coat, is accentuated with a maroon-brown tie.

He moves with ease now, no trace of his ethner scar bothering him.

A smile spreads over Jean's lips as he looks at Scotty's mask. "Hey, we got matching masks, what are the odds? Must be a symbol of great minds."

Scotty just stares back at his mask. *What does it mean? Does it mean anything?*

"You guys ready or do you need to learn more about *manners* from the staff?" Jean asks.

Scotty's face scrunches up at the idea. Despite Erin's struggles to teach her, she's confident she can replicate it.

"I think we are ready," she says, praying Jean doesn't press Withorn to talk.

"Good, good," Jean says with a nod.

"It's weird seeing everyone looking so fancy," Scotty remarks, looking at the rest of the social team.

"I know," Jean says, turning to face the others. "You should see the others in the hotel room, you'd be shocked, Farsing actually can clean up."

Scotty laughs at the thought, darkness fading from her mind as she tries to imagine Farsing even cleaned up like a normal person. "That's something I'd have to see to believe."

Scotty turns around and notices that Withorn has disappeared. A pang of sadness hits her — this mission is really going to be a strain on her friend. She considers asking Jean to put Withorn on the interrogation team against his wishes, but she trusts Withorn's choice.

"Jean, there you are!" Aster's voice calls out.

He's dressed in a similar black suit, tailored wider for his body shape, a sleek blueish black acros mask over his face. An icy blue bowtie accents the suit.

Jean smiles at the deputy.

"The interrogation team is ready," Aster reports. "Farsing's as briefed on manners as he can be. We will... avoid him getting out and interacting with guests."

Jean laughs. "I figured. He will certainly be an asset during the interrogation at least."

Scotty thinks she can see Aster shiver. The deputy doesn't have a past as dark as the others, so maybe he isn't too keen on the interrogation. She's confused as to why he would chose that over a potential run in with General Halcomb.

Having the deputy and commander in front of her brings Scotty's thoughts back to what Hartwood said.

She points her eyes at Aster. Jean already brought him in on their secret.

She takes in a breath and holds it, contemplating what she should do. She hasn't been able to stop thinking about Hartwood since she visited him in the prison. She looks to Jean's mask, wondering what it could mean. Is it a sign there is still a traitor?

"Do you guys think everyone can be trusted?" she blurts out.

Aster and Jean blink at her awkwardly behind their masks.

"If there's still a traitor among us, this could be a disaster," Scotty says.

"Scotty, where is this coming from?" Jean asks.

"Hartwood was the traitor," Aster says firmly.

Scotty shuffles uncomfortably.

"I…" she hesitates. "When we were in Hightower, I went to the prison and spoke to Hartwood. At first, I wanted to ask him some things about Ludon." She prays they don't press further about that. "But it ended up with him shouting about how he didn't do anything wrong. He sounded so… convinced."

"Sometimes when people tell themselves a lie enough, they believe it," Aster tells her.

Jean nods, frowning at Scotty. "I've heard it all from Hartwood. We *aren't* going back to this. It's over."

Jean's entire demeanor has shifted, his eyes terrified behind the mask, his stance less authoritative and more unstable.

Scotty takes a step back. "I'm sorry," she says. "I just—"

"And don't go sneaking around behind my back to talk to him again," Jean says, anger growing in his voice.

"It wasn't that," Scotty says. "It's just that—"

"I don't care what it was, *don't* do it again!" Jean's last words come out as a shout. "Understand?"

Scotty dips her head ashamedly, taken aback by the commander's sudden change. *I didn't expect it to hurt Jean this much.*

"I'm sorry," she says. "I won't."

"Jean, it's okay," Aster says, placing his hand on his shoulder. Jean loses tension in his stance, but still looks unstable. "It's easy to get swayed by lies when someone is that convinced. I'm sure she didn't mean to stir the pot." Aster looks to Scotty, his brown eyes flashing behind the acros mask. "Thanks for bringing your concern up, but that situation is handled."

Scotty looks at him, unconvinced. "I understand," she mumbles.

Jean sits down on one of the couches.

"We'll get you some tea," Aster tells him. "It'll help you relax."

Jean just nods at Aster from his seat.

"C'mon," Aster whispers to Scotty, placing his hand on her back as he leads her towards the kitchen.

"I'm sorry," she says once they're out of Jean's earshot. "I just thought it was something he'd want to hear. I didn't realize how it would effect him."

"This is an important mission," Aster says. "Jean's just tense. There will be a lot of... big names here tomorrow."

Scotty shivers. "I know. I guess that might be why I'm so worried too."

They dip into the kitchen, counters lining the walls. An icebox sits between the counters across from a couple stoves. A few of Erin's staff members are prepping pots and pans for the event, laughing and talking loudly.

Aster walks up to the one stove and fills a saucepan with water, pulling a matchbox out of his pocket. "Do you *really* think there's still a traitor?" he asks, his voice hushed as he strikes the match.

Scotty watches as the flame dances on the stove, Aster swishing the match out in the air. She nods. "I'm worried there is. I don't have any proof, just paranoia."

Once the pot is on the stove, Aster turns to her. "You know Hartwood broke my arm, right? You *saw* him placing the bombs. Why are you paranoid?"

Scotty frowns. "I know, I just... I don't know why I'm paranoid!"

Aster sighs. "Sometimes, things effect us more than we think," he says, Scotty seeing a flicker of hurt in his brown eye behind his acros mask. "Same goes for Jean. Since he opened up to me about the mission he gave you when you first joined, we've talked more. I can tell the paranoia is getting to him too."

"What Hartwood said just sounded so... real. So emotional," she says.

"Hartwood's full of it!" Aster exclaims, reeling his tone back down. "Do you really believe that? Scotty, he tried to kill me. He broke my arm with those bombs! If it hit me and not the wall next to me, imagine what it would have done to me."

"Well, I mean, I did see him placing the bombs," Scotty says. "Hartwood said he was deactivating them, but with what you just said, it just doesn't make sense." Of course Hartwood did it. Scotty remembers seeing Aster's broken arm, a sickness stirring in her gut at the memory.

"I know Hartwood is a traitor, but maybe he had a partner in it." Aster looks to her expectantly. "Do you think that's possible?"

Scotty shrugs. "I really don't know. Wouldn't Hartwood have spilled about it in interrogation?"

"Interrogation isn't a surefire way to get everything out of someone," Aster says. "Maybe he's manic like he is as a defense mechanism, maybe they broke his mind. There's no way to know, but I don't think there's harm in investigating the others."

"Do you not trust them?" Scotty asks.

"Well, I'd like to," Aster says. "You saw the Sunbell City Guild. Those are the kind of people we work with."

"The Raiders are different," Scotty says.

"Hartwood isn't," Aster says. "Farsing has some screws loose, who knows what his logic is for anything. Jean has told me about the missions Ren took to feed his family while part of the guild. He doesn't care about anyone but himself and his family, probably because he sees his family as something his *owns*." Aster's voice grows disgusted, Scotty surprised at the deputy's disdain towards some of their comrades.

She thinks to what Ren said about Jericho. She couldn't argue with Aster on those points.

"Merryweather would do anything to fuel her gambling addiction," Aster continues. "Cosette is a Castist. She's a sweet girl, but if anyone would know how to deceive others, it's someone who grew up with the Sunbell City Guild's influence."

Aster sighs when he sees the unsure look on Scotty's face. "I like the team, I've known most of them for some time now," he says. "But I've always kept one eye open around them. All of them, but Jean."

"So you're fine with going behind Jean's back to do this?" Scotty asks.

Aster nods. "It will save Jean a lot of stress." His voice hushes even more. "I'll keep an eye on the interrogation team for this mission, and you make sure everyone on the social side is in line."

Scotty nods. "Is there anyone specific you'd suspect?"

Aster shakes his head. "I don't think there's another traitor, but if keeping an eye on them could help eventually ease Jean's stress, I'm here for it."

Scotty smiles. "I'm glad I'm not alone in this. Thanks for taking me seriously, Aster."

He smiles back. "Thanks for trusting me."

The water is now boiling, and Aster pours it into a mug lined with cheese cloth and curled tea leaves. "They got the fancy tea here. Hope they let us have some in the interrogation room," he muses. "Not sure if I'll have the stomach for anything then, though."

Scotty looks around the room, noticing only a few of Erin's staff on the far side.

"Aster, can I ask you something?" she asks.

Aster looks to her hesitantly. "Of course."

"You're more in tune with the rebellion than me. Is there any Valkoean I need to steer clear of?" She recalls his reaction to finding out about General Halcomb possibly being in attendance. "Is that General Halcomb guy dangerous? I've heard of him living in Hayward City, but never knew much about him."

Aster's gaze shoots to her at the mention of Halcomb.

"Very dangerous," he tells her sternly. "Stay away from him. There's no information you can get from him."

"What's he look like?" Scotty asks.

Aster hesitates. "He's usually glued to Tapscott's side at these social events. This is a masquerade, you won't see his face anyway, but Tapscott will be a dead giveaway. All you need to know is he used to be the commander of the Black Glove Scouts, he's one of Tapscott's most trusted men, and that he has killed a lot of people, and won't be scared to kill a young girl like yourself." His tone is low and dark, sending shivers over Scotty's skin. "He was a spy in the Ghent-Valko War. He's used to being a deceptive man."

Aster swallows hard, tossing the cheesecloth and tea away. Scotty didn't realize that he was shaking until droplets from the cloth miss the trash entirely.

"Thanks for the information," Scotty says with a nod. She reaches out to the distressed deputy. "I didn't mean to stress you out. I'll take that back to Jean."

Aster pulls it away quickly, some tea sloshing out and onto the floor.

"I'm fine, no need," he says quickly. "I'll take this to him. It's fine."

He steps out of the kitchen quickly, Scotty blinking confusedly as she watches the masked deputy disappear out the door.

Guilt swells through her chest, she's just upsetting everyone today. This is why she shouldn't be on the social team! She never says the right things.

She peeks out the door to watch Aster and Jean reunite, the two unusually quiet in each others presence now. Although she has already decided to not bring it up with the deputy again, the nagging question tugs at her.

What is it about General Halcomb that strikes a nerve with Aster?

31
THE EQUINOX MASQUERADE

Two tense days pass as the Raiders await the fall equinox. The sparse city trees begin to fade to orange and the coolness in the air extends through the full day. Grey clouds are blotched through the sky, the damp scent of fall strong.

Scotty stands against the wall and shivers as elegantly dressed people pour into the venue room, Erin's staff scurrying around to put a drink in each guest's hand. Windows are open, silk curtains flowing on the fall breeze.

Three tier trays are brought out by suited wait staff, temping Scotty as they pass by with finger sandwiches, scones and jam, and sweets. Teacups rest on the tables, awaiting their accompanying pots to be filled.

Scotty feels for Tex and her daggers hidden among the rolls of her soft blue dress, the rebel tailors having sewn the perfect pockets for her weaponry. The feel of her weapons calms her, but a bloodlust surges through her as she looks around for High Priestess Tapscott.

Atop the stage near the piano stands a woman with a snow white dress, pulling a bow across the strings of a teardrop shaped sumera. Scotty should find the soft, honey sweet melody relaxing, but she's struggling to hide her tenseness among enemies.

Scotty tries to not look suspicious as her eyes snap from guest to guest, wondering how each would react if they knew the Raiders were there. She thinks to the interrogation room, Katze keeping Aster's team company. Navigating this mission without Katze makes Scotty feel naked, like she's missing an important part of herself that makes her more vulnerable at a time she needs all the comfort she can get.

The masks ease some of Scotty's anxiety, feeling safely hidden by the sharfawks face covering her own. The Valkoeans and Mohkan diplomats mingle, the Mohkan people standing out beyond their masks with their curved horns.

Scotty makes a mental note of where the other Raiders are. Merryweather is doing a great job socializing, her voice carrying over the room. Scotty winces at her direct approach. Drawing attention isn't bad, especially for someone as social as her, but it still unnerves Scotty. Cosette and Jericho are chatting, Cosette probably trying to calm her friend. Jean blends with the crowd, chatting and laughing with some men his age.

Scotty's all too aware of Withorn shadowing her further down the wall, the medic not making an attempt to socialize — much like herself right now. She can't exactly blame him, but she has no excuse.

One more pass over the group and Scotty notices Markos. Jean staked out the hall by the room Erin said Markos would be in and reported back to the social team what the dewick man looks like. He stands out in a deep blue suit, a striped blue and white tie, and a blue devil mask. Beyond the horned mask, his S-curved horns poke out painted blue to match, his hair similar to Farsing's.

Scotty knows to keep clear of him, but Merryweather's loud voice already seems to have caught his attention. As more guests fill the room, her voice gets drowned out and the crowd of taller people stifles Scotty's view of the other Raiders.

Scotty glances around and realizes she needs to make herself useful. Reluctantly, she pushes off the wall and steps into the party, letting the chatter of people and hum of the sumera wash over her.

She feels uncomfortable as masked eyes look at her, though the guests are only cheery and welcoming. Among a break in the crowd, Scotty catches a glimpse of someone standing alone at a table, in a darker recess of the room, plucking at the sweets on top of the three-tiered tray with black-gloved hands. Scotty remembers Erin telling her it's bad manners to eat before the tea is out, on top of it being bad to eat the sweets first.

If there's anyone she would get along with here, it's probably that person.

As she approaches, she gets a better view of the taller man — donned in a cream suit with gold accents. Blond hair pokes out from behind an owl mask, the faint trail of scars poking out on his cheeks. The soft sounds of the sumera and chatter of people are quieter here, making this corner much more comfortable to Scotty.

"Happy equinox," she greets with a nod, startling the man.

He snaps around and swallows hard and Scotty can faintly smell alcohol as he speaks. "Hey there," he says, seemingly annoyed to be disturbed. "Happy equinox."

He looks bored and Erin's employees come out with pots of tea, whisking the cloth wrapped ceramic pots around to the tables. Scotty studies this man, an odd sense of familiarity taking over. There's no way she would know him from anywhere, so she pushes the thought away.

Scotty leans over and grabs a small chocolate muffin from the top of the tray, popping it into her mouth, letting the sweetness flow over her tongue. The man laughs, grabbing an identical muffin and popping it in his mouth.

"You're unlike the others," he says though a mouthful of muffin. "Most these folk care about manners."

"Yeah," Scotty says, swallowing. "I can't stand it, honestly." It probably isn't in her best interest to be so honest, but relating with this guy is a good way to get any information from him — if he even has any. She doubts it as she watches him pick at the tray, this time eying the finger sandwiches. He wipes his hand off on his pant leg and she snickers. She doesn't need Erin to tell her that's in bad taste.

"You're downright uncivilized," she teases.

234

"I take that as a compliment," he counters, mirroring her tone. "Eating's a good way to pass the time, try it. Castus knows there's nothing else to do." He hands her a cucumber sandwich, Scotty quick to take a bite.

A light herbed cream cheese is rich and savory, the cool cucumbers snapping against the soft bread. "That's actually really good," she says. She didn't realize something so simple could be so delicious.

"Eh?" the guy says. "It's just a cucumber sandwich."

One of Erin's staff members steps up, her suit immaculate as she grasps a tea pot with black-gloved hands. "Breakfast tea?" she offers, lifting the pot in question. Her eyes are narrowed as she watches the two munch, disgusted by their lack of manners.

"Of course," the man says, nodding to the flipped tea cups on the table. The woman flips the cups over into the saucers, pouring two cups before placing the pot on the tablecloth.

"Enjoy," she bids, whisking herself away into the kitchen.

The man produces a small flask from within his suit, splashing some alcohol into his mug.

"Want a dash?" he offers.

Scotty shakes her head. "Uh, I think I'm fine with plain tea."

"No sugar? No cream? *No alcohol?*" he asks. "Who's the uncivilized one now?" He takes a sip of the tea, hissing and pulling the cup away when the too-hot liquid hits his lips.

Scotty finishes the sandwich and blows a wisp of steam away from the top of her teacup. With the breath, she feels some anxiety fade from deep within. Watching the steam in such a relaxing setting is almost funny when she's so used to the steam of guns constantly trying to kill her.

Scotty eyes the man again, off put by the lingering familiarity. She studies the small scars poking out from the owl mask, but decides while this man has alcohol in his system, it's a good time to strike up a conversation. She doesn't have to worry about prying.

"What brings you here?" Scotty asks. "You don't seem to want to be here."

"What are you, a *spy*?" he says darkly.

Scotty freezes and almost chokes on the hot tea, which the man seemingly mistakes for a laugh. He laughs along and nudges her shoulder playfully.

"Kidding, kidding! You know how these things are," he says. Scotty nods although she doesn't, her heart still racing from his joke. "I'm just here representing my team. My uncle dragged me along." He grumbles at the mention of his uncle.

"Your team?" she asks.

"Bah, I don't want to talk about them," he says. "What about you? What brings you here? You also don't seem too enthused."

Scotty's mind races as she searches for an answer, taking a long sip to give herself time.

"I'm here with family too," she says, praying to Cassius that he takes the lie and doesn't press further.

"Oh, a noble woman?" he asks. "Never seen a noble woman with scars like my own."

Scotty brings a hand up to her cheek, feeling the rough outline of the scars. She forgot they were visible.

Her mind snaps back to the bombing of Vincent.

"Ethner is indiscriminate," she says darkly. "It doesn't care how much money you have when it tries to kill you... My family's business is ethner technology." That isn't exactly a lie.

The owl-masked man nods. "Sorry, I didn't mean— Er, I get a little dumb when I have alcohol in me. I... know that's not an excuse."

"It's okay," Scotty says. "Unlike the others who mention my scars, you actually understand it."

A silence falls over the two as they sip at their tea.

"Hey, you look a bit familiar, you know that?" the man says.

Scotty freezes, the familiarity of that same voice saying that same thing washing over her.

"You've seen a scarred sharfawks woman before?" she asks jokingly, trying to make out where she's met him. The Brunswick Manor? No. Hayward City? No, it can't be.

Aspen.

The newer rebel intelligence hub in the mountaintop town flashes in her mind. Is he a rebel too? No, a rebel wouldn't act like this. Besides, Erin would have to know.

"I'd surely have known if we met before," Scotty says. "What's your name?"

"Harland," he says.

Harland.

The memories come rushing back. This was the drunkard she met in a drinking competition in Aspen. She recalls the manor he stayed in, with the images of Castus on the walls. What stands out the most was his hospitality. His wife passed away years ago and having someone to relate to so soon after Mike's death was comforting to her. They shared each others pain and it felt like someone truly understood her. That's why it hurt so much when he ran after leading her back to the new rebellion intelligence hub.

Scotty frowns at the memories. So what is he doing here?

"So," Harland says through a mouthful of food. "What's your name?"

Scotty hesitates. He'd probably recognize her name too. She looks past him at a bouquet of roses on one of the tables, the floral scents filling the room. "Rose," she says.

Harland smiles. "That's a beautiful name. But it doesn't ring a bell."

"Ah," Scotty says, trying to not be angry with this man. "We must have never met before."

I still don't know what that was all about in Aspen. I need to be careful.

Harland grows tense, peering behind Scotty.

She feels someone looming over her and a deep, dark voice forces her to turn around.

"What are you doing?" the voice growls, Scotty tensing up, ready to snatch Tex out from her dress's folds.

She spins around to a tall mountainfolk man in a clean, tidy suit towering over her. Brown eyes glare from behind a feathery acros mask.

She opens her mouth, but words don't come out.

Does he somehow know who I am?

"I expect better of you," the man grumbles. "Your tray is almost gone, has my sister failed to teach you manners? Do you know your actions effect me?"

Scotty spins back around to see Harland frowning at the man.

This must be his uncle. Scotty's eyes snap between the two. She'd never guess Harland is part mountainfolk.

"I'm sorry, General Halcomb," Harland says with a dip of his head. "I'm just... You know I'm not cut out for stuff like this."

Scotty freezes. General Halcomb, the man Aster warned her about. The deputy's words swirl in her head.

He's one of Tapscott's most trusted men, he has killed a lot of people, and won't be scared to kill a young girl like yourself.

Is Tapscott nearby? Scotty's eyes snap around the crowds. First she searches for Withorn, noticing him nearby, then she searches for Tapscott, failing to see the country's leader.

"This is an important day, Harland," Halcomb chastises. "Our family must look good for High Priestess Tapscott."

"You're the High Priestess's most trusted general," Harland says matter-of-factly. "Don't worry about that."

"And Milos was the most trusted general to her and Enzo before the rebellion," Halcomb says. "Tapscott knows that things change which is why it's so important to show our loyalty. Don't be a failure like my son. He's already tarnished how she sees us. You're pushing our luck."

Harland scoffs. "Hawks is a fine man, he hasn't *tarnished* our reputation."

Scotty shivers at his tone with this man. If General Halcomb is as connected to Tapscott as they claim, speaking out is the last thing she'd do. Harland is either brave or stupid. She expects the general to lash out with the same ferocity Tapscott brings down on nonbelievers, but General Halcomb's voice comes out as a warning growl.

"Hawks's failures are on your hand. Of course you'd think that."

His voice lowers to an eerie warning. "Do you need to be reminded what happens if you and Hawks don't get your acts together?"

"Can we discuss this later?" Harland murmurs, eyes snapping to Scotty.

Halcomb nods and sighs. "It's just a tense day for me." Scotty still senses a strong divide between these two, an edge on Halcomb's voice.

"I understand," Harland says with a polite dip of the head. He looks to Scotty. "This is Rose, she's a noble from a family of ethner tycoons."

Panic surges through Scotty's chest as Halcomb extends a tan hand to her.

"Happy equinox, Rose," he says. "I'm General Halcomb, leader of the Citadel Vanguard in Hayward City."

"Happy equinox, general," Scotty says back, giving him a firm handshake. The general smiles respectfully at her, not picking up on her anxiety.

"Such a strong handshake for a noble girl," he observes. "What family are you part of?"

She freezes.

This may be a stupid option, but this man is well connected in the government and Hayward City. Lying about something she doesn't know about could be detrimental. But honesty might be just as detrimental.

"I'm married into the Brunswicks," she tells him.

"Hmm," Halcomb muses. "I'm a friend of the family."

She tries to not wince behind the mask. That, she didn't know.

"They have so many sons, I've never been able to keep track of their wives," Halcomb continues. "I'll have to keep an eye out for the others. It was nice to meet you, but I must be going."

"Nice to meet you too," she says with a nod.

There are so many people here, he may not realize they're not actually here.

She lets out a quiet sigh as she watches Halcomb step away, Harland not hearing it.

Scotty looks over the room and she spots Merryweather flirting with Markos, the two laughing haughtily. Merryweather keeps her hands on him and he seems to enjoy the attention. Scotty grimaces, she's not jealous of Merryweather's position in this mission, but the older woman seems to be having fun at least.

"Sorry about my uncle," Harland mumbles, Scotty's attention reeling back to him.

"Do you not get along with him?" Scotty asks. Halcomb seemed kind to her, unlike what Aster implied, but then again, Aster also said Halcomb is deceptive. Regardless, the tenseness between him and Harland, his nephew, was palpable.

Harland shakes his head. "We used to." He turns to the three-tiered tray, picking up a scone from the middle tier, shooting a spiteful glance where the general disappeared to. He breaks it in half and passes Scotty a piece.

"This one's vanilla," he tells her. "Give it a try!"

Scotty hesitates as she takes a bite from the scone — it is sweet and delicious. Despite her enjoyment of the scone, her eyes linger on Harland. He certainly has some information in him, and she needs to get that out.

She'd just like to know who he is to the rebellion over anything. He seems like a decent guy, but she wants to know more about what he and the general were talking about.

Harland's eyes trail to her hands and he swallows his scone. "So, you're married, but no hand tattoo?"

Scotty swallows her own scone hard, almost choking on the dry morsel. She hadn't realized her blunder. She can't help her wide-eyed gaze as she struggles to find an excuse.

"Hey!" a voice cheerily greets behind her. Scotty snaps around, thankful for someone pulling Harland's attention away from her error.

The man is wearing a grey suit and red tie, his simple mask an interesting metallic purple. The woman next to him is a dewick, holding a cup of tea in her hands. Horns stick out from behind a fiery looking mask. She's also donned in a light grey suit, a soft blue bowtie at her neck, standing out against her dark skin.

Harland nods to the man. "Arlo," he greets.

Scotty's eyes snap to Arlo. She takes a sip of tea nervously.

Arlo? Is this really Arlo from the Black Glove Scouts? If anyone would recognize me, it'd be him!

Harland nods to the woman. "Jessong. Good to see you."

Scotty stares at Arlo — this is absolutely the man that almost killed her commander. Behind his mask are brown hair and pale skin, she's seen him enough in battle to know.

Her heart races as she recalls what this man did to Connie and Reagan's team, what he did to Jean.

He doesn't have that steam weapon right now, calm down!

Her eyes snap around the room. Is Commander Halcy here too? Fear strikes her heart as she imagines running into him. But she doesn't even know what the armored leader of the Black Glove Scouts looks like!

Scotty hadn't realized Jessong's hand extended to her.

"Hey there, happy equinox!" Jessong greets, a slight accent in her voice. Scotty grabs her hand and gives it a shake. Is she also from the Black Glove Scouts? Scotty doesn't recognize her from the Scouts and the accent tells her she's from Mohkan.

"Happy equinox," Scotty says. She has to think for a moment, remembering her made up name. "My name's Rose."

"I'm Jessong, I'm a pyrotechnic in Mohkan, for Prime Minister Amaranth herself."

"Gives her quite the hot head," Arlo jokes.

Jessong laughs. "Maybe. I just got the position and I'm proud of it. It brings honor, and more importantly money, to my family."

"Money's always appreciated, right?" Harland says.

Jessong nods. "I've yet to get the posh manners, I'm still a military girl at heart."

"Yeah, I haven't evolved from that yet," Harland says, looking over the room disdainfully.

"Figured I'd bring her to someone she could relate to," Arlo says. "We're just a few fish out of water."

"I'm trying to stay low since I'm so new," Jessong says. "I don't want anyone's attention today, besides friends I've already met."

"That's smart," Harland says. "That's how people like us get far, especially with the state of the world right now."

"That's why we waited until we could steer clear of General Halcomb," Arlo says. "I respect him but he looked cross with you. I'd hate to set him off today."

"Yeah, I accidentally did that," Harland says, stuffing the last finger sandwich in his mouth. "My uncle's just tense."

Arlo lowers his voice. "Where's your respect? Refer to him by his title. You know that ticks him off. You better watch testing him like you do."

The darkness in Arlo's tone sends chills over Scotty's skin. He seems innocent enough in this situation, but the sinisterness in his voice reminds her what he would do if he recognized her.

"How about *you* show some respect? My uncle's not here and you're not gonna tell, *right?*" Harland challenges. His tone takes on the same darkness, almost threatening Arlo.

Arlo lets out a huff. "No, Commander Halcy."

Scotty stares at Harland, the owl-masked man pouring another cup of tea, adding a splash of alcohol. Her eyes widen behind her sharfawks mask, her heart racing. With each beat of her heart, it feels like the breath is sapped from her lungs as panic settles in.

Stay calm! They don't know who you are yet!

Disbelief overtaking her, she takes a step back and feels herself press into someone, the room hushing as the sumera player stops. She snaps around to see who she's pressed into. Fear settles as she wonders if she's already been found out, her ears ringing at the new silence.

She sees Withorn behind her, his yellow eyes wide behind his novak mask, pointed towards the stage.

No, no, no! Not now! What if Arlo recognizes both of us? What if Halcy suddenly recognizes us?

Everyone's attention is turned towards the stage, Arlo and Harland — *Halcy* — not paying any attention to the medic's arrival.

If only Withorn knew who these people are!

She follows Withorn's gaze to the stage, General Halcomb standing beside the grand piano, his watchful gaze washing over the crowd. Next to him is a woman who has a terrible presence, sending shivers down Scotty's spine. She has a burnt orange dress and sleek black hair. Scotty's heart leaps when she sees her mask — a sharfawks. Scotty immediately knows who it is, the image plastered in newspapers everywhere.

High Priestess Tapscott.

As Tapscott's view passes over the crowd, her eyes meet with Scotty's, staring deep into her identical mask. Scotty freezes, feeling a weird connection with the woman. A red aura laps around the High Priestess and Scotty almost thinks she can see it take the shape of a sharfawks, much like her mask.

Is she looking at me? What is this feeling?

Scotty shivers and glances at Withorn.

Has she somehow noticed her son?

Tapscott's gaze lingers too long to be coincidental, but soon passes. The weird connected feeling fades with the aura, Scotty quick to push that aside.

I'm just stressed and paranoid.

In Tapscott's black-gloved hand is a megaphone, and she lifts it to her mouth when the crowd stays hushed.

"Thank you for joining me this morning to celebrate the fall equinox," she announces. "Today, we also get to celebrate the alliance between two Castist countries. Thank you to the men and women who traveled from their posts around Valko or their homes in Mohkan to be here with us today."

She pauses and raises her free hand, soft claps rising from the crowd.

"Know that all this hard work will bring us peace one day. I deeply appreciate Mohkan's dedication to Castism and Prime Minister's Amaranth's shared vision for the future." She gestures beside her, Scotty taking a step to the side to see beyond the crowd at a beautiful, older dewick woman at Tapscott's side — that must be the Prime Minister of Mohkan. Amaranth waves a black-gloved hand at the crowd, a smile sitting below her sleek black mask.

"I know most of your faith is blind, both in Castus and in me," Tapscott continues, "and I'm honored to have such a loyal team at my side. My faith in Castus is not blind, I've been blessed to have *seen* the truth."

Scotty frowns. Soharists have seen their gods too. Soharists have seen the truth, the real truth. What is she on about?

"On Saint Maxson's Day of Silence, years ago, in my day-long vow of silence, I was chosen by Castus to hear His voice," Tapscott says. "That day, my destiny was made clear to me. When Castus spoke to me, He said in order for Him to be able to bring peace to the land, the world had to be united under *one* religion, under the *true* religion, Castism. After all, what is more chaotic, what causes more conflict than opposing religions?"

Scotty's blood boils. Sure, wars have been historically fought over religions before, but more death is just adding to that conflict and chaos. Scotty wants to shout out against the crowd. Her gaze sweeps around and she sees everyone smiling or nodding. Do they really agree with Tapscott? Their most recent war was fought over borders with Ghent, not religion. Surely, the High Priestess hasn't forgotten about that. Scotty passes a glance to Withorn and while he doesn't look to her, she feels his hand tighten around hers, giving it a tight squeeze. She squeezes his hand back softly, trying to urge her friend to stay calm as his mother speaks. She recalls how Withorn reacted to seeing his aunt in Salina Village, and how she had to pry the gun from his hand to keep him from killing her. Will he be able to hold himself back now?

"I knew what I had to do after that day," Tapscott says. "However, Chancellor Enzo, my predecessor, did not agree with my mission — Castus bless his soul." She dips her head and closes her eyes for a respectful moment of silence. "He was an avid Castist, as most of this country (and Mohkan) has always been, but he could not see my vision, he did not hear His voice. It's a lofty goal to convert a whole country to Castism, but with our passion, with our righteous goal to achieve peace, I know we will be able to convert the world!"

She raises her gloved hand and the crowd claps, happy murmurs spreading through the masked people.

"It's not an easy task," Tapscott says. "Many still don't understand, many have not heard His voice like I have. When we are all connected under His love, we will have peace. We will be able to get along. My heart sincerely goes out to all who make the biggest sacrifice to achieve this goal — when they reach Niveah, then they will know the truth, then they will understand our goal. After we succeed, future generations will look back and wonder why so many resisted when the path to peace was so obvious. The rebellion is nearly eradicated. Once the last nonbeliever is converted or removed, we can spread our vision for a peaceful future to the rest of Harkive!"

Scotty's nose scrunches up. Why does Tapscott care about the future? She couldn't even properly care for the future of her bloodline. This woman is delusional! She squeezes Withorn's hand tighter. The rebellion is *not* nearly eradicated! Hightower Harbor stands strong! Scotty thinks to Cannonsburg, guilt for the lost fort heavy in her heart. Her mind fades to the airships, wondering why the massive sky-beasts haven't been sent to bomb Hightower Harbor yet.

Would that end the rebellion instantly?

The rebellion is still strong, isn't it?

Scotty's gaze snaps around, trying to see Merryweather or Markos. She can't make them out in the crowd of taller people, but pride whelms in her chest knowing they are taking the next step to potentially stopping the airships — and right under High Priestess Tapscott's clueless nose too.

"Again, thank you for gathering for this equinox masquerade!" Tapscott calls out. "Let us eat, drink, and look forward to a prosperous future!"

Everyone claps and cheers and the crowd disperses towards the tables. Scotty finally catches a glimpse of Merryweather and Markos, his hand in hers as she leads him across the room.

She did it!

She watches them disappear out of the venue's door, Merry-weather flirty the entire way out, the two hidden by the natural flow of the crowd.

Gods, please let the interrogation go well!

Scotty turns to see Withorn, still frozen in fear, Harland — *Commander Halcy* — and Arlo behind him. The hope for their mission is replaced with fear as she realizes she's still among their worst enemy.

32
INTERROGATION

R en taps his foot irritably as he waits for Merryweather. His shiny black dress shoe clicks against the floor, Ren hiding behind the door of the hotel room's bedroom.

Ren adjusts his mask, Erin having left a stupid looking weaver mask on his bed. As if he wanted to be reminded of that dumb rodent after Hartwood's betrayal.

Connie and Reagan hide in the closet, the two wearing matching suits. Reagan's mask is a pure white and Connie's is floral. Katze waits patiently with Connie, the annoying fallion actually keeping quiet. Aster and Farsing are behind a chair caddy corner to Ren. Farsing is rather dapper, wearing a well-fitted suit and a metallic red mask. A bowler hat sits atop his mess of hair to hide his horn stubs.

Ren glances at the clock in the bedroom, growing irritated.

Come on, Merryweather! Has something gone wrong?

The bed sits in the middle of the room — that's where Merryweather should be bringing Markos soon. Ren itches to start the interrogation, the questions buzzing in his head. Aster tasked Farsing and Ren with being the main interrogators, Connie and Reagan in charge of recording the information. Aster said he's going to make sure nothing goes wrong. Ren scrunches his nose as he thinks of the deputy. It's as if he doesn't trust them!

A click at the main room's door pulls his attention back, his foot stopping on the floor. The sweet sounds of a sumera pour in, a chattering crowd in the distance. Merryweather's voice pierces above it all, the soft murmuring of an accented man following her.

That must be Markos.

Ren shuffles, excited to get to the purpose of this mission.

A tense air falls over the room as the bedroom door squeaks and presses slightly against him, Merryweather and Markos's murmuring growing louder. Ren frowns when he sees the two walk in, Merryweather keeping Markos's attention talking to him, but also guiding him along with her hands, something he seems to enjoy judging by the smile below his blue devil mask.

Merryweather does well controlling him, bringing him to the bed. Ren grimaces at the man, thinking about his wife back in Mohkan.

Disgusting.

Unease pricks through Ren as he thinks of his own wife back in Ghent.

She wouldn't be unfaithful like this man, he tries to convince himself.

In a quick flash, Merryweather whips her twin cutlasses out from the bed's sheets, pressing them against Markos's throat.

"Woah, woah!" he bellows, throwing his hands up against the pillows. "I am not into this sort of stuff!"

He whimpers as Merryweather presses the blades into his soft throat above his deep blue suit's collar. "Not a word!" she hisses. "A peep and you're dead!"

"Wh-wha—"

Markos's words cut into another whimper as Merryweather applies more pressure. He tries to scamper back, but hits S-curved horns press into the bed's headrest. Beyond the devil mask, his eyes are wide in fear and realization floods into his gaze. He swallows hard, wincing as his throat flexes into Merryweather's sharp blades.

"C'mon out, boys," Merryweather says, not keeping her eyes off Markos.

Ren, Aster, and Farsing slink out of their hiding spots, converging on the bed. Aster stands back as Ren and Farsing grab Markos's arms, yanking him up.

"Hey!" he grumbles.

"Not a word!" Merryweather demands.

Markos grits his teeth as he's yanked towards the chair, pulling back on Ren and Farsing's strong grasp. With a strong lurch, he pulls his arm free of Farsing, and Ren gasps as a fist swings around towards him. Ren ducks to the side, twisting Markos's arm in the process. His punch weakens and he hisses as he's brought to his knees, but he adjusts his arm and flows with Ren's twist, grunting as he thrusts his horns towards Ren. His blue devil mask snaps and splats to the floor, his face scrunched up in hatred as his brown gaze tears into Ren.

"Gah!" Ren spits, bringing his free arm up to block the horns.

The cock of a gun makes Markos freeze, giving enough time for Farsing to yank his arms behind his back. Markos and Ren turn to see Merryweather aiming her gunpowder revolver towards their prisoner.

"Behave," she demands. "Understand?"

Markos grimaces, shooting daggers at Merryweather and nods.

"Damned succubus," Markos hisses.

"I've been called worse," Merryweather teases.

Farsing grabs Markos by the blue horns and thrusts him into the chair he and Aster hid behind, the deputy ready with ropes to bind his hands behind the chair.

"What do you what?" Markos asks. The anger has been replaced with terror, his eyes snapping around, his chest heaving with shallow breath as he panics.

This is just an engineer, Ren thinks. *A man who studied at a university and has never seen battle like we have. He should be easy to break.*

Aster steps away from tying the binds, looking up to Ren and Farsing, giving them a hesitant nod. Aster seems uncomfortable — despite having been a rebel before joining, he's still soft. But not as soft as Markos.

Ren has seen Aster do some awful things with his longsword and duck foot pistol, painting his Panzer Suit red with blood of his victims. Maybe this is too personal for him.

"Markos, right?" Ren asks, leaning down. Markos trembles and whimpers, Ren energized by his weakness. "Right?" he presses.

"Uh huh," Markos says, coming out naturally with his trembling.

"A Mohkan engineer, responsible for building the airships. The airships that bombed our capital." Ren doesn't feel any kind of patriotism for his home country, but his mind flashes back to the things he saw among the rubble of Vincent — things this man would never be able to stomach.

"I helped," Markos admits. "It wasn't my doing! I didn't drop the bombs!"

Ren nods.

"Keep your voice down," Merryweather hisses.

"We just have some questions," Ren tells him. "If you cooperate, this will be a lot easier."

"Don't hurt me!" Markos pleads. "Please, I-I can't tell you anything! The Valkoeans will kill me!"

"Oh, they don't have to know," Ren says. "Besides, if you don't cooperate, you'll also be dead. You don't have a lot of options."

Markos swallows hard and winces. Ren thinks he can see Markos's heart beating under his tailored blue suit.

"This will be our secret," Ren says. "The only way they know this is how we got the information is if you tell them." Ren pauses, trying to recall the list Jean had him remember.

"Why is Mohkan involved with building these airships?" Ren asks.

"I-I don't know," Markos says.

Ren frowns at him and looks to Merryweather.

"Merryweather," Ren says, pointing to Markos with his eyes.

Merryweather unsheathes her blades, bringing the cutlasses down to her side and she starts to stride over to the chair.

"No, no!" Markos says. "Get away!"

His eyes dart around.

"It's because—" he gasps as Merryweather stops in Ren's shadow.

"It's because we get to keep the airships when the war is won. We get to keep what we helped make and we get to spread Castus's peace."

Ren scoffs at the idea of Castus being peaceful.

"You really believe that?" Ren asks.

This sours Markos's expression, the fear being overshadowed by contempt. "Your days are numbered, nonbelievers," Markos says. "You are not just, you are not right, you're on the wrong side of history."

Ren rolls his eyes. "Merryweather?" he says again.

The man winces as Merryweather steps towards him, shutting his eyes hard and Ren laughs.

Pathetic.

"Where are these airships being housed?" Ren asks.

"In camps," Markos says right away, a light gleaming in his eyes. "Around the Greater Asperetti Mountains!"

Ren recalls Milos saying his scouts disproved that. The rebels knew they were kept there once, but they need to know where they went.

Ren sighs and shakes his head, grabbing Markos's blue horn. Markos gasps as Ren pulls his head forward.

"Listen, it's really easy for us to get along," Ren says. "Don't feed me bullshit. Tell me where they went."

Ren catches Aster shooting him a disproving glance.

I'm hardly touching him, he wants to shout. *Get over it!*

Markos lets out unintelligible hushed stammering, like a frightened, babbling baby.

"What's that?" Ren asks, yanking him forward again, leaning his ear towards him.

"E-Eve Hallow," he says. "We have a hangar... in Eve Hallow."

"Where in Eve Hallow?" Ren yanks Markos's horns harder, bending his neck at an odd angle. Markos gasps in pain.

"A hangar!" Markos says.

"You said that!" Ren hisses.

"It's-it's—" He gasps. "You're really hurting me."

"It's going to hurt even more if you don't spit it out!" Ren warns.

251

"On the northern side of the harbor," Markos hisses out. "Thirty-eight Industrial Drive! In that hangar!"

Ren thrusts his arms forward, throwing Markos's head back onto the cushy chair. "Thirty-eight?" Ren asks.

Markos nods.

"Industrial Drive?"

Markos nods again and whimpers, "Uh huh."

Ren pauses, allowing time for Connie and Reagan to jot it down, the two former rebels still stifled behind the slotted closet doors.

He knows the address by heart, what else does he have in that horned head of his?

"Tell me, Markos," Ren says. "What are some weaknesses of the airships?"

Markos's eyes dart around and he swallows hard and shakes his head. "N-none," he tells him. "There are none."

Ren frowns. Surely he isn't serious.

Ren lashes out and grabs Markos's one horn again, Markos flinching as Ren tugs them.

"I'll ask again. What are the weaknesses?"

"Stop, stop!" Markos blurts out. "They-they can't fly in storms! But that's all I know! That's all I know!"

Ren releasing his grip and turns to Farsing, nodding at the other dewick. "Wanna take over?"

Farsing cracks his knuckles and snickers. "My pleasure."

Ren notices Aster frowning at Farsing.

Let us have some fun, this isn't a good man.

Farsing produces a bone saw from Withorn's cabinet, scowling as he looks over Markos. Markos shivers as Farsing removes his hat, showing off his horn stubs.

"I used to have a nice set of horns like yours," Farsing tells him, tapping at his skull. "You have any idea how much it hurts having those removed?"

Markos shakes his head, brown eyes locked on Farsing's stubs.

"The pain never fully goes away," Farsing says. "You can never think straight with a constant headache. They're not supposed to be removed, you know."

He puts the hat back on.

"I would like my horns back," Farsing tells him. "I know that will never happen, mine were ground off, turned to dust. I'll be much kinder to you than the people who took my horns were. I think yours would make a *nice* replacement for mine."

"Still don't know any more weaknesses?" Ren asks.

"I don't! I swear, it's all I know!"

Ren grabs a cloth from Withorn's cabinet and stomps over to Markos. He grabs his sleeve where the soft part of his bicep is and twists, Markos opening his mouth to shout. Ren stuffs the cloth in his mouth before a noise can come out.

"Don't spit it out," Ren warns. "Unless you want to lose some teeth too."

Markos only blinks in response, as if to ask if they're really going to go that far.

Farsing takes Ren's place, towering over Markos again, bone saw in hand. Without a word, he leans in, firmly grasping Markos's right horn. Markos jerks, to no avail, as Farsing leans in with the saw.

Farsing hesitates, waiting for Markos to give in.

He shrugs and starts sawing, the grating sound and muffled shouting rough on Ren's ears. Markos twitches and spits out the cloth.

"Stop!" His beg is a whisper. "Stop, stop!"

Farsing keeps sawing.

"The weaknesses!" Markos hisses. "The weaknesses are—"

Farsing stops sawing, but keeps in the position.

"Yes, I'm listening," Farsing says.

"The sails on the sides of the airships," Markos says. "They're a canvas material. If you pierce even one when it is in the air, the airship can't stay up. And the engines, they're positioned towards the back of the stern. There are four of them. The exhaust pipes pump air into the sails to keep them up. Without the exhaust, it also can't keep up or steer." He gulps. "And the balloon is filled with excess steam, but that's nearly impossible to pierce."

There's a silence and Farsing leans in with the bone saw again.

"Wait!" Markos hisses. "And-and the engines' fuel tanks are exposed on the sides, makes it easier to fuel. They're a soft metal, like ethner cartridges for guns, so they're easy to break too! Water in the front and ethner in the back. Or is it the other way around. I-I don't know!"

"Which is where?" Farsing growls. "Your horns depend on it!"

"I don't know!" Markos heaves. "E-ethner in the front!"

"You're lying!" Farsing hisses.

"I don't know, I can't remember!"

"I have another question," Ren says, stepping in. "What are the future plans with these airships? Who has these plans?"

Markos nods at Ren, refusing to make eye contact. He glances at the bone saw again and curses under his breath.

"The Valkoeans will soon be done with the bombs," he whispers. "And once they're done, the rebellion's capital will be destroyed. But that's all I know. That's all I know!"

"Where are the bombs being made?" Ren asks.

"I don't know! I swear to Castus, I don't know!"

Ren grimaces.

"You do know!" Farsing says, grabbing at his horns again.

"I swear on Castus, I don't know!" Markos says. "Please don't do it, I don't know!"

Farsing yanks him forward, adjusting the saw in his hand and Markos peeps again.

"I-I'd assume somewhere in Eve Hallow too. I just design airships! I just design engines! I don't know anything about bombs! Really!"

Ren puts a hand on Farsing, reeling his hostility back a bit.

"Markos, how soon will the Valkoeans be done with the bombs?" Ren asks. Ren feels a disturbance stir in his stomach. If it's soon, it's going to be a race against the clock to win this war, and the odds won't be in the rebellion's favor.

"I told you, I know nothing about the bombs!" Markos says. "I just know it's soon. The airships all needed to be done before the bombs would be finished. The fleet is almost done, but I don't know a thing about the bombs!"

"I won't stop at your horns," Farsing warns. "We'll start sawing fingers, then limbs, and if you survive, well it won't be for long. Rethink what you said. *How soon?*"

"I really don't know!"

Farsing grabs his horn and starts sawing into the notch he made again.

"No, no! I don't know! I don't know!" Markos jerks around, hyperventilating.

"Farsing, that's enough," Aster demands, pulling him away.

"He's about to spill!" Farsing hisses. Ren frowns at Aster, he agrees with Farsing. He doesn't want to show a divide in front of Markos, though.

"He's about to have a heart attack," Aster says. "Let's take a break and let him think. Maybe taking some pressure off will allow him to gather his thoughts. He's cooperating well enough."

Farsing grumbles and tosses the saw to the ground, producing a cigarette from a pack in his pocket. He steps behind the chair, facing the curtains leading to the patio, puffing at the cigarette, filling the room with a dry smoke.

Merryweather relaxes, sitting on the bed and Ren looks to the closet, wondering what the scribes are doing in there.

"Aster, can I talk to you in the main room?" Ren says.

"Of course," Aster says, following Ren out.

They leave the bedroom door ajar, stepping out into the main room, the smell of Farsing's smoke still slightly wafting from the cracked door.

"This is the breaking point," Ren tells Aster, an edge to his tone. "That's exactly how we get more info. He's spilling in there, he just needs more pressure and he'll be *gushing* with information."

"Do you think Jean would approve of what you guys were doing?" Aster counters.

"It's an interrogation! Yes!" Ren says definitively. "Jean has done stuff like this before."

Hurt spreads over Aster's face. "Really?"

"You think you're better than us because you're not from the guild," Ren says. "Well, this is how the people who get stuff done operate. We're getting valuable information, throw your morals out the window for one minute. This is not a good man." Ren recalls how Aster treated Hartwood upon their old friend's betrayal. "Like Hartwood," he adds.

Aster still looks hurt, but a pained shout from Farsing forces their attention to the bedroom. A thump sounds out and Merryweather curses, the bedroom door slamming open between Aster and Ren.

What—

Before Ren can even think, Markos bursts out the door, throwing his weight into Aster and Ren. The two men shout as they tumble to the floor, caught off guard. Merryweather bursts out the door behind him, tripping over the tangled Aster and Ren with a shocked shout.

"He broke lose!" Merryweather hisses.

"No shit!" Ren says, scrambling back to his feet. "How?"

Markos is already to the front door, shouting out as he yanks the door open.

"Help!" he bellows. "Help! There are rebels! Help me!"

"We need to get out of here!" Ren shouts. "Let's go! We'll take the carriage to the rendezvous point. Pray the others make it there safely!"

As well dressed Valkoeans pour into the room, Ren notices some suited guards on alert, ethner revolvers primed in hand.

"Guns!" Merryweather says.

Aster, Merryweather, and Ren burst back into the bedroom, ethner hissing as bullets pierce the wallpaper around them. The door slams shut and Ren locks it tight, a couple bullets having pierced through the wood.

Too close!

Farsing holds his groin, his cigarette extinguished on the floor.

"Bastard kicked me in the balls and knocked Merryweather over," Farsing says with a hiss of pain.

"It doesn't matter what happened now, we just need to get out!" Ren says. Connie and Reagan are already at the bedroom's glass patio door, unlocking and sliding it open.

"Come on!" Reagan shouts, gesturing a splotched hand at the others as Connie leaps out the door.

Rapid pounding thunks behind Ren as the Valkoeans struggle to break the door down, Ren dashing to follow Connie. Aster slings Withorn's pack over his back, and everyone slips out to the patio, the valen-drawn carriage waiting outside. Reagan and Farsing hop into the coach box and Ren follows Connie and Merryweather up into the carriage, Katze on their heels. Aster tosses Withorn's cabinet into Ren's arms, Ren helping lug the deputy into the back of the carriage.

"Go, go, go!" Ren shouts, waving his arms forward.

"What about Jean and the others?" Aster blurts out in panic.

Beyond the glass patio door the suited Valkoean guards have broken through, shouting as they raise ethner revolvers pointed at the carriage.

The carriage jolts when Reagan urges the valen forward and Ren shouts as he and Farsing slam the armored carriage doors shut. Bullets clunk off the metal doors not a moment later.

"That was too close!" Farsing exclaims.

"We about the others?" Aster repeats.

"We will meet them at the rendezvous spot," Ren assures the deputy, not shaking the fear in his eyes. "We need to trust their skills, they will be safe."

"So long as they aren't recognized, they'll be fine," Merryweather says.

"That shouldn't be possible," Ren says.

Aster still looks unsure, as if Ren and Merryweather's words only deepened his worry.

Ren has to admit, he shares the deputy's fears, but he won't say that out loud.

33
THE SNOWDEN ESCAPE

Cries of help force Scotty's attention to the hall where Merryweather and Markos disappeared a while back, fear flooding through her.

"Help!" an accented man's voice cries. "Help! There are rebels! Help me!"

They botched it!

Another intrusive thought presses into the back of her mind, the buzzing sound echoing in her ears.

Was it because there's a traitor?

Anger swells inside her and she meets Withorn's hazel gaze beyond his novak mask. As ethner hisses in the event space, she wants to shout the obvious out to the medic. *We gotta go!*

Just as she goes to step towards Withorn, she feels a strong hand clasp around her arm. She looks back and sees Halcy towering over her, and she can't help but to look into his calm, caring eyes in fear.

"Rose," he says. "I'll protect you from the rebels, get behind me."

"No!" Scotty shouts, trying to shake her arm loose. "Let go of me!"

Her eyes snap back and fort between Halcy and Arlo.

Don't recognize me, please Cassius let the mask work!

Halcy blinks in surprise and lets go of her. "Sorry, I—"

Just then, a flash of black catches her eye and she sees a pale fist lash across Halcy's jaw, his head jerking to the side as his owl mask flies off.

Scotty stares at Jean in shock, her commander now standing between her and the Scout commander.

"Let go of the woman!" Jean spits, not realizing Halcy was already releasing her.

Scotty wants to shout at Jean. This is Commander Halcy and Arlo!

As Jean reels back from the punch, his sharfawks mask snaps off, dropping to the floor. Halcy recovers from the blow and Arlo grabs onto him.

"What in the name of Castus do you think you're doing?" Arlo shouts. "Do you have any idea—" Halcy holds Arlo back, cutting off his words.

Halcy turns to face Jean. His scarred face is all too familiar. Scotty can hardly believe the drunkard she spent the night with in Aspen was Commander Halcy.

Sudden realization flashes in Halcy's gaze.

"You," he growls. "Commander Jean."

"I have no idea who you are, but we must be going," Jean says. "Scotty, Withorn, let's go!"

"Scotty?" Halcy blinks at her. Scotty wonders if he recognizes her name from Aspen. Judging by the look in his eyes, he finally gets it.

Without thinking about it a moment more, Scotty disappears into the crowd, pressed closely by Jean and Withorn.

"Stop!" Halcy demands, his voice getting drowned out by the feared voices of party-goers. Luckily, the wall of people washes over them, making for a good meat shield between them and the Scouts.

The three burst out the front door among a group of others, passing a quick glance to some of the suited guards. Anxiety pricks over Scotty, letting out a breath when they scurry down the hall with the other fleeing guests, the guards unsuspecting of them being involved.

The three race through the lobby and sneak out the way Erin let them in, dashing down the gaudy hall and plowing out the back door into the garden. Scotty's eyes snap around, seeing the warehouse workers loading a massive platform to be taken down to Snowden's port. The hotel stretches towards the cliffside, the acrid odor from the ethner pulley machine strong on the air. They race through the garden, past the little frog pond, and around the large rocks.

Hissing gunshots ring out, debris from the rocks scattering around. The three duck behind the tall rocks, Jean and Scotty together while Withorn hides behind another. Scotty pulls Tex from the hidden compartment on her dress, Withorn and Jean producing their own gunpowder weapons from their suits.

Scotty's heart races.

If they wanted us dead, they could have done it there! They want to capture us! But why?

"Stop!" Halcy's demanding plea calls out again.

Jean and Scotty poke out from their cover, Scotty's gun hissing as she fires, gunpowder booming out next to her.

Halcy, Arlo, and Jessong had followed them out, the three dashing to their own cover of the garden's stones. The back door of the hotel gets peppered with bullets, glass shattering as the window explodes.

Scotty hisses as ethner steam settles in her eyes and lungs, wincing when she realizes she doesn't have her protective gear.

Gadias, give me strength!

She pokes out to fire again, bullets sloppily piercing the stones around her. They exchange a few rounds of gunshots, chipping away at the stones and outer walls of the hotel. As Scotty dips back behind the rock, she notices the warehouse workers on the cliffside, looking on in terror. Some flee, but others can't look away.

Scotty recalls what Erin said about them: they're rebel aligned.

"The warehouse workers," Scotty whispered to Jean. "They can get us out of here! Down that big pulley thing!"

"You trust them?" Jean asks.

"Erin said she does, and I think it's our best shot," Scotty says. "And we'll be close to the rendezvous point."

Jean looks to her, unconvinced. "How do we shake these three?" Jean presses.

Scotty hesitates for a second, recalling the frog pond in the center of the garden.

"Cover me," she tells Jean. "I have an idea!" She grabs a couple spare ethner cartridges from the hidden compartment of her dress, meeting Jean's icy gaze. Jean just nods and pokes out from behind the stone, firing cover shots to keep their assailants hidden.

Scotty peeks out and focuses on the little frog pond. She bites the frail metal tips off the ethner cartridge and heaves it across the garden, the vials splashing into the pond. Steam erupts from the garden's center, a thick, toxic, wall of fog veiling them.

"Let's go!" Scotty hollers.

Bullets fly through the steam wall, peppering the garden aimlessly. Withorn shouts out and Scotty feels a bullet graze her leg through her poofy dress. She lets out a gasp and takes in a mouthful of acrid air, her lungs screaming out.

Go, go, go! she urges herself.

She cranes her head around as they flee, the early afternoon sun casting shadows of their opponents into the wall of steam. Halcy is in the center, fists balled at his side. Jessong, the horned silhouette, is to his right, and Arlo looks like he's reloading his gun to the left.

Scotty shivers and thanks the gods that Halcy doesn't have his armor. He'd burst through it no problem. The veil won't last forever, though.

Jean, Withorn, and Scotty run to the warehouse workers, one standing in awe at what just happened.

"We are rebels," Jean blurts out. "Erin thinks you can help us?"

He nods hesitantly. "W-what do you need?"

"Take us down to the docks!" Jean says. "Can you do that?"

The warehouse worker looks to the wall of steam and nods. "C'mon, c'mon," he urges, waving his hand towards the fenced platform. "There's a gap between these crates, room enough to hide. Soon as you're settled, I'll lower you."

"Thank you," Jean says, the three slinking between some wooden crates, another worker pointing to the best spots to hide. It's no problem for Scotty to hide, but Jean and Withorn look uncomfortable, fear plain on their faces as they stay scrunched up, waiting for the pulley system to start.

A few heartbeats pass, nerves pricking at Scotty as the pain from the bullet grazing her sears in her leg. *Lower it! Let's go!*

Was it a mistake to trust the warehouse worker? Did they just let him lure them into a trap for the Scouts?

Fear overtakes her when she peeks out a small crack to see the steam dissipated, Halcy, Arlo, and Jessong racing towards them.

"You!" Halcy shouts, pointing an arm at the warehouse worker. Scotty can't see the warehouse worker from her vantage point and when the platform stays in place, she grows more and more worried that she doomed her comrades.

"Yes?" the guy asks shakily.

"Three people just went through here. Where'd they go?"

"There," he says. Scotty imagines his arm pointed at the crates and it feels like her heart gets caught in her chest.

"Thank you," Halcy bids. Scotty winces, but their footsteps grow louder and pass them, growing silent soon.

Just then, the noise of a machine huffing and puffing sounds out and the platform jolts. A cacophony of pistons and grating chains is accompanied by sour ethner smell. As the platform lowers, fresher fall lake air replaces the ethner and Scotty can breathe a real sigh of relief.

She looks out at the other side of the crates, the rock cliff passing behind her. In front of her, a breathtaking view towering above Snowden's port shows her criss-crossing docks spreading out across the harbor. They lead to the grassy farmlands they travelled through to get here and beyond that to the left Scotty catches a glimpse of the massive Greater Asperetti Mountains.

Scotty sighs and relaxes as much as she can with the pain in her leg, but she prays the others make it to the rendezvous point safely. As the platform descends, she wonders what made the interrogation team fail. Aster will hopefully have answers. Her mind trails back to Tapscott's speech, imagining the airships raining bombs on Hightower Harbor.

Doubts surface in her mind, one strong thought breaking through all the rest: The rebellion is still strong, isn't it?

34
THE LAST MISSION

The Raiders meet up at the rendezvous point, Jericho and Cosette the last to arrive. Ren's anxieties fade when the boy steps up to the carriage. His limp is still there, but he walks strongly now. Ren wonders if that has anything to do with their core and balance training.

Pride starts to swirl in Ren's chest, but it's replaced with shame as he remembered how Jericho reacted to Ren's slip up. Jericho avoids Ren's gaze as he lunges himself up into the carriage. Ren's face scrunches up.

He'll never forgive me...

No one asks any questions about what went wrong, but they are all loaded up in the comfy carriage, Jean and Aster at the lead again as the clunky ride back to Hightower Harbor starts.

Ren's mind sorts through what could have went wrong, but he's quick to shake it off. What matters is that they got valuable information. He doubts Markos knew when the bombs will be done. He didn't have that same bullshit tone the other times he lied.

Once the city is behind them, silent relief falls over the group. Withorn treats a graze on Scotty's leg and Connie patches up a bullet wound on Withorn's thigh. Withorn doesn't seem too enthused to have the former rebel medic working on him, bossing Connie around. Connie seems too tired to snap back.

The sun crawls through the afternoon sky, diving into Mayhew Lake as the carriage is carried over the eastbound bridges and through the gate into Hightower Harbor.

Most of the Raiders are asleep by the time they stop, Ren wishing he could doze off. Jericho passed out next to Cosette, Ren thankful he didn't have to withstand an awkward silence with the boy.

Cosette gives Ren a hard stare, more judgmental than usual.

Those two sure are close anymore. No doubt Jericho's already told her what an ass I am.

Ren looks away from her. It irks him that she was right about how to train the boy. He'll die before he admits that to her, he'd never hear the end of it.

The sleeping Raiders are jostled awake, and they start to unload. The dapperly dressed gang gets some odd glances from the rebels in the moonlight, but it's quickly shrugged off. As Ren slides off the back of the carriage, he's all to aware of Jean and Aster staring him down. Aster looks tired, the interrogation reports Connie and Reagan wrote up in his hands, but Jean is still wide awake.

"Ren, come with us," Jean demands.

What now? Ren bites back the remark. "What do you need?" he asks, trying to keep his tone polite.

"We're reporting to Milos now," Jean tells him. "I'd like you to be there so we have a more accurate report along with Connie and Reagan's notes." Jean shoots an unamused glance at Farsing as he walks by, sipping at a flask. "And the other interrogator is already *on break.*"

Tiredness tugs at Ren as he thinks about walking up all those steps to Milos's office in the tower, but who would he be to say no? This is urgent. "Of course. Let's go."

As they walk away, Jean looks back to make sure the other Raiders are far out of earshot.

"So, you two, tell me," Jean says. "What happened? What went wrong?"

Aster and Ren exchange hesitant glances. Neither of them know for sure.

"Aster got soft seeing Farsing hassling the guy and paused the interrogation," Ren says. "We don't know what happened, we were arguing outside the door when the bastard burst out."

"We were *discussing* the mission," Aster says.

"He would never have gotten out if you didn't pause the mission during an important breaking point," Ren says. "We could have gotten more information, but *you* wouldn't let us."

"It was a team mission, Ren," Jean argues, an edge to his tone as he defends his deputy. "Don't put the blame on one person."

"No," Aster speaks up. "He's right. It was just difficult for me. I... just don't like seeing someone get hurt like that."

Jean blinks at Aster, taken aback by his admission of guilt. After he realizes Aster is serious, he speaks up again.

"You've killed plenty of people," Jean says, a twinge of amusement in his tone. "What, was this too personal?"

"I don't kill for fun, I kill to protect people I care about." Ren frowns at Aster's desperate tone, as if he's pleading for his friend to forgive him. "I-I'm really sorry Jean." If Ren didn't know any better, he'd think Aster actually believes Jean would kick him out for that.

"You're a caring man, Aster," Jean says. "It's why you make such a good deputy."

Aster lights up at the compliment.

"I know these past few missions have been really tough for you," Jean continues, "and you couldn't have known Markos would break out. In the future, if there's anything you're uncomfortable about like that again, let me know. I won't force my men to do something they don't want to do. You're my best friend, Aster, the last thing I want is to put you in a bad situation."

Aster slightly smiles, but it's quick to fade. "I appreciate it, Jean." He pauses before adding, "Farsing was the last person closest to Markos during the mission, maybe you should ask him for a full report later. After pausing it, I don't think I'd be the right one to ask. I know the rest of the team thinks it's my fault, and I don't blame them."

"I'll do that," Jean says. "But really, if you think you're why he got out, don't worry about it. No one got terribly hurt. I've certainly made my mistakes, you know that."

Their conversation ends when they get to the foot of the tower, a rebel sentry letting them inside. They scale the stairs to the top, rapping at the door to be let in by Milos. He welcomes them in, Aster and Jean taking a seat in front of his desk, Ren standing back, cross-armed. The room is simple, the walls mostly windows. The corners of the room are filled bookshelves. Maps with markings on them and papers are strewn about his desk, Milos apologizing for the mess.

"It's been a busy week," Milos says, not trying to hide his tired tone from the Raiders.

"Hopefully it doesn't get busier," Jean says.

Milos sighs. "We'll see. Tell me about your mission. You're back much earlier than I expected."

Jean goes into detail briefing the rebellion's leader on the mission, Milos listening on, horrified upon hearing the Valkoeans plan to bomb Hightower Harbor.

"Dear Gadias," Milos murmurs.

An eerie silence falls over the room, Milos standing up and pacing. Ren thinks he can see the gears of the rebellion's commander spinning in his head.

"This needs addressed as soon as possible," Milos says. "Commander Jean, I'd like the Raiders to look into this as well. Take your team to Eve Hallow in the next few days to investigate."

"I think we should head out tomorrow," Aster says. "The sooner the better. Those bombs could be finished tomorrow, we have no way to know besides this investigation."

Ren frowns at the idea of traveling again the following day, but he actually agrees with the deputy.

"I doubt Markos will tell the Valkoeans that he spilled," Milos says. "Tapscott would surely have his head, but I have to agree with you, the sooner we act on this, the better." Milos turns to Jean. "Do you think your team can leave tomorrow."

"Of course," Jean says.

"I need you to investigate where the bombs are being made and to destroy the airships," Milos says.

Jean blinks at Milos in surprise when he mentions destroying the ships. "How?" Jean asks.

Milos smiles. "I have some ideas."

Jean turns to Ren. "Ren, go tell the others to get prepared for another day of walking tomorrow," he says. "And get some sleep. Milos, Aster, and I will get details together."

Ren wants to argue, he'd love to help with the planning process. Even he knows not to argue now, preparing the team is an important step. Jean looks unusually stressed too. It wouldn't help to add to Jean's problems.

Ren just nods and turns away, descending the tower steps.

Excitement buzzes through him as he leaves — this is going to be a great mission for the Raiders' skills. Concern overtakes the excitement, Ren wondering just how they're going to destroy the airships without being seen.

35
NEW EVIDENCE

S cotty is swept into her haunting dream again. Her comrades hunt her in the dark forest and she goes through the motions. Harland appears from the darkness, in all his armor but the helmet. His scarred face shouts out at her, like a snarling hound's jaw going for her neck.

Scotty runs from him and falls, face-to-face with the amber gaze of the sharfawks. She shouts and scurries back, unsettled by his stare.

"Ludon!" she exclaims. "Why didn't you tell me about the other camps? Cannonsburg fell!"

"Why didn't you ask me for more?" The voice pounds into her head. "My knowledge isn't free. I need your commitment."

Scotty recalls seeing the sharfawks aura in Tapscott at the masquerade, and something holds her back.

"What do you gain?" she asks.

The sharfawks's tail flickers in annoyance, the voice booming in Scotty's head, making her wince. "I'm a god! What right do you have to question me? Mortals couldn't understand the motives of gods! We do what's best and I think you know what's best for the rebellion."

Scotty hesitates still.

"Fine." His tail flicks. "I'll find another." He disappears into the darkness.

"Wait!" Scotty exclaims, hungry for more answers.

She wakes up in a panic, a persistent buzzing humming in her ears. She wants answers, but something held her back from accepting Ludon's help. The image of Tapscott with the aura of the sharfawks is etched into her head.

Were the sharfawks masks just a coincidence too?

The Raiders prepare to get on the road again, Scotty's nightmares and thoughts of the god of beasts and nature being pushed to the back of her mind. Her leg throbs as her bullet graze wound heals, her eyelids heavy from the haunted sleep.

She looks over to her comrades, anxiety surging through her veins. *Another mission and I don't know if I can trust anyone!* They got valuable information at the equinox masquerade, but Aster's team was such a disaster, it feels like the gods were reinforcing her doubts with bright signs.

Farsing is helping some rebels load dynamis onto a carriage, the explosives expert uncharacteristically careful as he handles the chemicals. They're at a weapons warehouse near Hightower's front gate, getting ready to leave for their long walk.

Scotty shudders as she looks at the wooden boxes of the unstable explosive. It's too volatile — an early detonation is all too common with the material. Scotty and her brother, Grover, used it for a mission in the town of Layton. The dynamis detonated early when exposed to the heat of a coke oven and caught the attention of the guards which led to her brother's death.

The dynamis would be easy to rig. Grover and I were being so careful, he was a chemist for gods' sake. This could be a disaster even worse than Vail! This could be the death of us all!

Her eyes fall on Aster, the deputy busy bossing rebels around. He has a twinge of paranoia in his eyes, demanding they get going as soon as possible. Scotty wants to talk to him about the tea party masquerade and what happened with his team, but he's too busy now. She wonders what's lit a fire under his ass.

She lets out a breath. *We can sort everything out before the mission officially starts, I'm sure of it.*

Soon, the team heads out on the road. Withorn rides on the carriage loaded with dynamis, the medic nervous to be so close to the unstable explosive. He said he'd rather chance it than make himself sore walking with the bullet hole in his leg, especially since it's at a spot difficult for him to see, so Connie is the one tending to it.

The Raiders venture over the bridges taking them away from the crescent island. They take the path north towards Eve Hallow, Scotty craning her head back one last time to see the island. The mismatched steamship navy bobs on glassy blue water, the walled island hugging the harbor protectively. Pine trees stretch into the sky on the island, dwarfed by the gothic spires of the town square. Milos's tower soars high above it all.

The weight of their mission is heavy on Scotty's shoulders. If they fail and the airships and bombs don't get destroyed, Hightower Harbor could fall. If that happened, it would surely be the end of the rebellion.

As they march alongside the carriage, Scotty falls back, stepping slower until she's brushing by Aster's shoulder at the back of the group, Katze heeled at her side. Jean usually has Aster in the back to protect their rear as the team's tank. While Aster's Panzer Suit is tucked away in the carriage, he still guards the team's back, duck foot pistol in hand.

The two slow to fall out of earshot of the others. Aster must know why she's here.

"How's your leg?" Aster asks.

"It hurts, but it's just a graze," Scotty says. "I've marched with worse."

"A long march with a small wound can be tough on you," Aster says. "I'm sure Withorn wouldn't mind company on that death trap of a carriage." He laughs.

Scotty's nose scrunches up and she feels a shiver crawl up her spine. "No thank you!" she says.

"Yeah I wouldn't want to ride with Withorn either," Aster says jokingly.

Scotty laughs, the laugher fading as she thinks of how to open the question up to Aster. She lowers her voice, hoping they're well out of range of the others, her eyes burning into the backs of Farsing and Ren's heads ahead of them.

"I've been meaning to ask you," she murmurs. "What happened at the masquerade?"

Aster sighs, glancing off to the side. "I'm not entirely sure, honestly," he says, his voice quiet. "Markos got free when I wasn't in the room."

Scotty frowns. "Do you think it could have been the work of a traitor?"

Aster hesitates. "I don't know," he says. "It's hard to say anything with certainty. But what I do know is Farsing was behind the chair last I saw him. He'd have easy access to untie Markos without being seen by the others."

"Farsing?" Scotty echoes. She grows all too aware of Farsing ahead of them, marching along among the other Raiders.

"It's a good lead," Aster says. "Farsing's been on edge with me since that mission, I've been wondering if it's because he knows I'm suspicious of there being a traitor."

"Who knows what Farsing is ever thinking," Scotty comments. "I'll investigate him, though. We want to keep his sights off you if he does suspect you're looking out for a traitor."

"That might be dangerous to investigate alone," Aster warns, a darkness in his tone. "He's a loose cannon. If he gets suspicious of you, who knows what will happen."

"I've done it before," Scotty says. "I'll be fine."

Aster smiles at her confidence. "Thank you, Scotty," he says. "If we have to do any split missions, I'll have Jean put you with Farsing. I won't have to tell him why. Let me know if you find anything suspicious, we'll keep Jean out of this until we are certain of something."

Scotty shivers, paranoia creeping its way back in as she looks at Farsing. She glances over to Aster and some of the weight lifts off her shoulders.

"I'm glad I have someone to share this mission with this time," Scotty says. "It's hard when you feel like you can't trust someone around you."

Aster nods. "It's hard when you feel like you can't trust *anyone* around you," he says. "It's nice to have at least one person to trust."

Scotty smiles at the deputy. "It really is."

The two grow silent, pacing faster to blend into the group better. Scotty steps just behind Farsing, a tense air falling over the hornless dewick. Questions swirl through Scotty's head. Was Farsing working with Hartwood the whole time? Or did Farsing frame Hartwood?

Anxiety pricks through her as she thinks to Aster's warning, a stronger question overtaking her — could Farsing really be so dangerous?

36
THE BEACHES
OF EVE HALLOW

The team makes one stop between Hightower Harbor and Eve Hallow, Scotty and Jericho training before bed. Scotty's injured leg aches during the sparring, the graze wound still healing. It stings even more from the long march as they make their way into Eve Hallow the following day.

Groves of dead dwarf blooddew trees line the road before the causeway leading into the Valkoean city that juts out into Mayhew lake. The Raiders sneak their way in among a caravan of traders, the guards on the land bridge paying no mind to the rebel carriage packed with explosives sneaking in under their noses. While the guards are aloof, their numbers are many, anxiety pricking over Scotty's skin at the sight. Valko's colors fly proudly at the end of the causeway, the light blue, golden V, and bright white flags fluttering nearly straight on the backdrop of the grey fall skies.

Scotty's tension ebbs once they're out of sight of the causeway guards. The city of Eve Hallow is old and built up with stone buildings, massive orange trees shading the place. It has a natural beauty, like the ones who built it were mindful of Ludon's art of nature. Towering steamstacks are in the distance beyond the patchy fall trees. Plumes of ethner discharge puff into the air, the steam clouds blowing away in the wind. The acrid odor of ethner is light on the air, the natural city not being spared from industrialism.

Up in the branches of the autumn trees, Scotty catches a glimpse of a messenger swift — a soft yellow and grey bird with a single black feather in its mohawk. It almost seems to be watching the Raiders, cocking its head at them to focus. A leather X is on its chest, a capped message tube on its back. Scotty wonders what the thing is doing up there. Usually they only stop when they reach one of their swift stones.

Her eyes trail down and a pang of sadness hits Scotty when she sees a wooden "Welcome to Eve Hallow" sign tucked among the large sprawling oaks greeting people. Eve Hallow is a name she heard her brother say many times. Grover went to the University of Eve Hallow to study ethner technology, and he was a great tinkerer, having built Tex. He was about to become a full time engineer at Hayward City Steel. His last mission before he was to retire from being a hitman ended up being the mission that took his life. He sacrificed himself to save Scotty.

Scotty sighs, a knot of guilt settling in her chest. She's not smart like Grover. She should have never let him go. It would have been much better for both Grover and Mike if she died that day instead.

Why am I who is left? Why have the gods spared me?

As she thinks of her brother's involvement at the school, the grief and guilt is replaced with a spark.

Ethner technology! The university! We are looking for where bombs are being built! Could the school be what we are looking for?

When they stop, she will mention the idea to Jean. Maybe they can investigate the school's grounds somehow.

They slip off the main road and find their way down some roads that lead to the shore, Jean referencing a vague map of the city Milos had managed to get for him. Jean splits from the team to drop the carriage off at a boarding stable, the Raiders watching from the distance as the carriage is parked and the valen are left to roam in the facility's corral. Leaving the carriage alone there is a risk since there are no known rebel allies in the city. For the same reason, the Raiders have no housing and must camp out in a secluded area just outside of town and pray no guards find them and pry.

They put the stable behind them, Jean meeting up with the team again. The corral butts up to a patch of woodlands, the team following the gently sloping hill down through the forest. Trees envelop them and the fresh scent of fishy lake water wafts over Scotty. They stop at a rocky beach on the north shore of the city's land, Jean declaring that they will make camp there. Cosette passes rations out with Jericho's help, Katze scarfing down part of Scotty's dried meat.

Scotty walks to the rocky shore, Katze padding at her side with her tongue lolling out of her mouth. The cold wind whistles, the sun already dipping beyond the horizon. As the sky darkens, Scotty focuses on the beach, the rocky shore reminding her of where she and Mike used to spend time together in Hayward City. Just outside the metal city's walls, along the shoreline where the water sparkled purple with ethner. Scotty closes her eyes and breathes in, taking in the mingling smells of the lake and ethner from the city. The cool air brushes over her skin and the sounds of the waves bring her back to Hayward City, the only part she missed about it.

Mike.

She imagines for just a moment, him sitting next to her in the spot he first confessed his love, where they spent many nights, where he suggested they run away to Ouellette and get married.

She almost thinks she can smell Mike's sweet scent, feel his warm touch again.

She opens her eyes to reality, a quiet loneliness settling in. After a few heartbeats, she notices a dark silhouette on the beach, the bottom of Jean's trench coat flowing in the wind behind his knees. For just a brief second she could be brought to nostalgic solace, but the weight of the rebellion comes crushing down on her.

I do this all for you, Mike.

She sighs and looks to Katze, her companion staring out at the water, eyes wincing in the wind.

Things sure have changed a lot.

Scotty steps forward to Jean's side, the commander staring at the array of colors in the sun-set sky.

"Quite beautiful, is it not?" Jean asks, his gaze turned back to the massive lake.

Scotty shrugs. "It's water. I've seen plenty of views like this growing up in Hayward City."

"We never got views like this on Kip Lake," Jean tells her. "I don't think I could get used to it like you."

Scotty frowns. The only view of Hayward City she wants to see anymore is of it being destroyed by the rebellion. A fire burns inside her at the thought, her mind turning back to their mission at hand.

She glances over to the camp, the Raiders settling for the night.

"I have an idea on where the bombs could be built," Scotty says.

Jean raises a brow at her. "Oh? Why don't we take a walk and you can tell me about it?"

"Of course," Scotty says. As they step away from the Raiders' makeshift camp, Scotty can't help but to wonder why Jean wants to talk about it away from them. Is it because he can't trust the others?

Scotty recalls how he acted last time she mentioned her trust in the others, how the paranoia crawled in and turned him into someone else. She opens her mouth to speak, but Jean cuts her off.

"Before you tell me," he begins. "I just wanted to say sorry for how I acted at the tea party."

Scotty blinks at him, shutting her mouth after a moment.

"I appreciate you coming to me with any concerns. I don't want you to think you shouldn't because of how I overreacted. Hartwood's betrayal is still a heavy weight on my shoulders. You struck a nerve, which I know is no excuse for me to lash out. Hartwood is silver tongued, blessed in the art of lies by Cassius."

Scotty realizes he wanted to talk to her away from the others for the apology.

"Uh." Scotty hesitates as she thinks of what to say. "Thank you. I wasn't all that offended by how you acted, but more... worried about you."

Scotty considers telling Jean about her and Aster's mission to investigate Farsing. She bites her lip and lets out a small breath, deciding against it. She wants to believe that Jean wouldn't lash out again, but he shares her paranoid dreams and as she looks into his blue eyes, she feels something dark deep within. She will bear the burden herself and investigate the explosives expert soon. If anything is found, then she and Aster will report to Jean.

"I appreciate the concern," Jean says. "But I'm fine." His words come out a bit broken and he clears his throat. "Tell me what you're thinking about the bombs. Where are they being built?"

Scotty hesitates on her answer, wondering if she should address his broken tone. The crunch of rocks under their feet is loud against the wind and waves as silence falls over the two.

It's Jean. He's fine.

"I think they're being built at the University of Eve Hallow," she tells him. "It's where the Brunswicks got their best engineers from for Hayward City Steel. They train a lot of skilled chemists there too."

"I'm glad we have you on the team," Jean says. "It'd have taken us a while to get that information. Very good, Scotty. We'll have two teams for our missions here, smaller teams will be best in a city crawling with enemies like this anyway. I'd like you to help investigate the school since it's your lead."

Scotty smiles at him, pride whelming in her chest at his accolade. She casts a glance at the water once more, hope for her country swelling in her chest. "Hopefully because of what we do here, the war will be over soon," she says.

Jean halts, Scotty pausing and turning next to him. There's a difficult look in his gaze.

He lets out a small laugh. "Truthfully," he says, looking out at the water. "Sometimes I don't want this to end."

Scotty blinks at him. "What do you mean by that?"

"I don't have much to go back to," Jean says. "My family in New North Ash wasn't happy with my running off to join the Sunbell City Guild. The guild sure isn't taking me back. I know it's selfish not wanting this war to ever end — I'm happy with this team, as broken as we feel sometimes. Maybe I'm just drawn to the chaos." He lets out a broken laugh and casts a sidelong glance towards the camp. "And once this is over... I don't want to leave Aster behind. I worry that when the war is done, he will stay in Valko and I'll have to return to Ghent. I don't want to lose him. I've never been so close with anyone before."

Scotty frowns at the sadness in his voice.

"If Ghent isn't welcoming, why don't you just stay here?" Scotty says. "We'd love to have you in Valko. I know the team will still be broken up, but you'd have a home here."

Jean sighs, staring longingly out at the water. "Maybe. But maybe I just don't like change. Don't worry, though. Despite how I feel, I'll be trying my hardest to help end the war. Starting with this mission."

Scotty frowns, wishing she could say something that would help Jean feel more like he has a place to go when this is all over. Instead, she finds her mind racing, struggling to imagine herself once the war is over.

"Honestly," she says. "I don't know what I'll do when this is over either. I might be just as lost. My life might get a bit... meaningless if I reach my goal. If I avenge Mike."

"That's exactly how I feel," Jean says, sadness laced in his tone. "We're really messed up, huh?"

They let out pitiful laughs.

Scotty points her face towards the darkening sky, the stars peeking through the moonless night.

"You're a good person," she tells him. "Your life would never be meaningless, Jean."

"I'm a member of the Sunbell City Guild," Jean says. "I'm not exactly the cream of the crop."

"That's not who you are anymore. You're a hero in Valko," Scotty says. "If no one else in the country agrees, take it from me. I can't speak for my whole country, but you're a hero to me." Scotty feels embarrassment grow on her cheeks at the honesty. "You believed in me and allowed me the chance to avenge Mike." The words get harder as she thinks of her late fiancé. "You have no idea what that means to me."

Jean passes her a sympathetic glance, the sadness in his eyes softened. "Thanks, Scotty," he says.

Scotty faintly smiles at him, a comfortable silence falling over the two.

"Let's get back to the others," he eventually tells her. "We have a mission to tackle in the morning."

37
THE UNIVERSITY

The Raiders stir awake before the crack of dawn. The echoes of a nightmare sit in the back of Scotty's head, but she's just thankful her graze wound has stopped hurting after some rest.

The team gathers around Jean and Aster, hard tack and tea passed out for breakfast. Scotty holds her cup close, letting the warm steam wash over her face. The mornings have become cooler and cooler as the trees grow bare.

Scotty glances over her comrades, everyone in good spirits to get this mission started. Withorn is the grumpiest of them all, sitting awkwardly from the bullet wound in his leg.

Scotty's gaze hovers on Farsing, as if staring hard enough would allow her to read his mind.

How do I go about investigating him?

Jean's voice brings her to the center of the group.

"Today is an intel gathering day," Jean tells them. "Thanks to a lead from Scotty, we have decided to split the team up again for this mission. One team will be in charge of investigating the airships in the hangar, and the other will try to figure out where the bombs are being built — starting with the Univestity of Eve Hallow. We'll set up the teams today, discuss strategies, and do the first rounds of scouting this afternoon. On the airship team will be Aster, Ren, Connie, Jericho, and Cosette. That leaves the University team as me, Scotty, Farsing, Withorn, Reagan, and Merryweather."

Farsing frowns. "Why don't I get to be on the team demolishing the hangars? Blowing things up is my speciality!"

"Because identifying explosives is a bit more important for the University team," Jean tells him. "Wherever we find the bombs are being made will need destroyed too, along with possible defusing of larger explosives. So we will need your expertise, Farsing."

Farsing nods, satisfied with Jean's answer. Scotty considers his reaction. Did he want to sabotage the hangars' destruction?

They split off into their teams, Aster and Jean murmuring to each other before dividing away from the spot Jean spoke at. Jean gathers up the University team near the pebbly shore, everyone looking to him expectantly.

"We don't know anything about the University," Jean says, "besides the fact they study ethner technology there. Eve Hallow today is not well known by the rebellion, so we have no leads to go off of. We don't have good maps, we don't have the location, so we are starting this out very bare bones. Does anyone have strategies in mind?"

"Stealth, duh," Farsing says. "Get in unseen and sap all the information we can out of it."

"We'd have to wait until night time for that," Scotty argues. "And if they have night guards, we'd have to figure out their schedules. It's a long time investment for something that might not even be the place we are looking for."

"Do you have any better plans?" Farsing challenges. "Wasn't it your bright idea that led to us investigating the school in the first place?"

"That doesn't mean I'm entirely certain," Scotty says, her hands balling in fists at Farsing's antagonizing tone. "It's just a lead, our only lead so far."

"Does anyone have any better plans to investigate?" Jean asks.

"Um," Reagan speaks up. "There was a university in Nettlecrest, where I'm from, and they offered free tours to potential students. Maybe we can see if this school does it too?"

"That's a great idea," Jean says.

Reagan smiles, looking pleased with herself.

"Yeah, not a bad idea," Farsing remarks.

Merryweather shrugs. "We're an awfully suspicious looking group to be inquiring about getting an education," she says. "Maybe only a few of us should go, or we should go in teams."

"Younger people usually go to these schools," Withorn says. "Farsing and Jean might raise some suspicions."

"Hey, dewick live like twice as long as you all, I'm still young," Farsing says.

"It's a fair point," Jean says. "Same with Merryweather's point. Merryweather, Farsing, and I will stay back. Scotty, Withorn, and Reagan can take a tour."

"Me?" Merryweather exclaims, slapping Jean's shoulder. "Are you saying I look old?"

"Merryweather, you have children who could be students there," Jean says.

"I adopted them as teens, I'm not *that* old!"

"What's the matter, you don't want to spend time on a mission with me?" Jean teases. "Like the good ole days?"

Merryweather laughs. "Well, if you miss me *that* much, I guess I don't have a choice."

They divide up into their groups and head out into the city to find the location of the school, promising to meet back up at the camp at lunch time. Scotty cranes her head back to watch the other three depart from them, her eyes lingering on Farsing.

Great! How am I supposed to figure anything out while split from my target?

Aster at least convinced Jean to put Scotty and Farsing on the same team, but he didn't anticipate another divide, especially not one based on age.

As they walk away, the three fall silent, Katze padding at Scotty's side. Withorn still has a slight limp from his bullet wound, a frustrated look on his face. Reagan is distracted, looking around at Eve Hallow's unique stone buildings.

Scotty drops her frustration about being split from Farsing. She's not entirely certain if there's another traitor, but one thing is certain: they must succeed for the rebellion to survive.

Scotty looks to Reagan, thinking of something to say to get her mind off of this lingering paranoia.

"It was a good idea to get a tour at the school," Scotty tells her.

Reagan smiles. "I just hope they are the same as the school in Nettlecrest. I don't see why they wouldn't. I've toured a few in Valko, they seem to be the same."

"A few?" Scotty asks. "Did you end up going to a university?"

Reagan sighs. "I was... *accepted* at Nettlecrest's university."

"Accepted? Why didn't you go, what happened?" Scotty asks.

"Tapscott happened," Reagan says, an edge to her tone. Scotty notices Withorn's gaze turn to the clansman woman, guilt in his eyes.

"When the war started, I knew as an apostle of Yuna, I needed to help bring Tapscott to justice," Reagan says.

"That's noble," Withorn chimes in. "But it shouldn't be your burden to bear. You should have been bettering yourself. The rest of the Raiders, we didn't exactly have bright futures ahead of us."

"I didn't feel like I had a choice," Reagan says. "I'm a proud Soharist, I evaded Tapscott's men as much as I could. My uncle was lost to the first round of genocide, most of my family converted to Castism... And our church..." Scotty hears her words get strained. "It's gone, along with most of the community."

"Oh," Withorn says, looking away awkwardly.

"I'm sorry to hear that," Scotty says, her heart aching. She's felt enough grief losing Grover and Mike. She can't imagine losing any more than that, it would have broken her.

"It is what it is," Reagan says dully. "You know. But thanks."

"What were you going to university for?" Scotty asks.

"To study architecture," Reagan says. "I want to be a designer."

"Wow, how do you even go about designing a building?" Scotty asks. Reagan must be smart and creative to even consider that career. That's how Grover was too.

Reagan laughs. "I'm honestly not sure yet. I've always sketched up designs in a notebook, I wonder if it's similar to that."

Their conversation fades as they get deep into the tree-filled city, wary of the eyes and ears of the guards around them. A slip up even talking about Soharism would be detrimental to the mission.

They wander through the city, scoping out the eastern side while Jean, Farsing, and Merryweather scout the west. The smell of the lake grows strong, mixing with an acrid ethner odor as they near the industrial part of the city.

Following the smells to a sloping road, they are brought to the city's port, the trio walking along the seawall with docks pouring into the lightly white-capping bay. The city wraps around the bay, making a perfect crescent shape against the water. The fall foliage reaching up the hills into the city stand out brightly against the churning water reflecting the grey skies. A plethora of factories line the water, steam stacks blowing ethner into the air.

They head south along the seawall, finding signs directing away from the port into the city. A sign pointing south shows them the way to the University of Eve Hallow.

As they make their way towards the school, they pass a large Castist church, the building pointed and sinister looking. It's made of the same dark stone as most of the city, the slate roof jagged and streaked with orange leaves from the towering trees. The church holds a dark, pulling energy to it and Scotty shivers, unsure if it's from the church or the cool wind picking up from the water.

The feeling is similar to what she felt when she saw Tapscott at the masquerade.

It's probably just anxiety.

As the building falls behind them, Scotty can't help but to feel its presence too strongly. The foreboding feeling passes when Reagan speaks up.

"The university, this way," she says excitedly.

Scotty turns with the other two, Katze padding ahead. Scotty is taken aback by what's in front of her. A massive iron sign with intricate floral details serves as an entryway into a red brick walled courtyard. Atop the sign reads the building's name: The University of Eve Hallow.

They walk into the courtyard, a beautiful garden sprawling in front of them. Around the edges of the brick wall are evergreen shrubs of varying sizes, looking dull in the shady fall skies. Old trees around the outside of the wall cast shadows into the garden.

A brick pathway cuts through a manicured lawn, dividing at the middle where a massive, orange, sprawling oak serves as the garden's centerpiece.

"Grover never told me about this," Scotty says as they walk along.

"Makes you wonder how much it costs to attend," Withorn adds dryly.

As they step around the sprawling oak, Scotty hears a breath of awe from Reagan.

"Wow!"

The school towers over them, like an old, sturdy castle. The massive building is made of grey stone and sits on the edge of the city, the lake visible just over the garden's brick wall.

From here, Scotty can see the center is the shortest part of the university, the sides reaching up high to wrap-around balconies overlooking the garden. The entryway, though the shortest part of the building, has twisting pillars and a triangular overhang, a group of students chatting under its protection. Scotty doesn't have to share Reagan's passion for architecture to appreciate the beauty of the building.

Reagan keeps walking, staring upwards in amazement.

"Hold up," Scotty says.

Reagan freezes and turns around, passing Scotty a questioning glance.

"Our mission is just to find the school, and we did that," Scotty says. "We can go in later. Now, we need to report to Jean."

38
INDUSTRIAL DRIVE

R en's team heads out before Jean's team finishes their scheming. Their mission today is simple: find the hangar.

They have the address, thirty-eight Industrial Drive. Ren sighs. A lot of boring scouting will need to happen before they can crack into the fun parts — destroying the airships.

Aster leads them along the shore, saying he's heard rumors of where the industrial district is in Eve Hallow. Ren has to admit, having Valkoean natives on the team does come in handy sometimes.

Aster brings them out of the more natural part of the land, the city wrapping around them. Ren can't help his gaze shifting around to the city's guards, growing uncomfortable being in a bigger group in the city. They're not a convincing family, so he worries they will catch the wrong attention. He recalls being interrogated by the Valkoeans in Salina Village just because they looked out of place. That was a small town, though, with an easy to track population. Maybe the Raiders will be more inconspicuous in a big city like this.

They're heading to what Aster explains as the industrial district, apparently something the city is well known for. He hushes up after he reveals that knowledge about the place, and leads the team down the dusty city roads.

They walk past some houses with lawns strewn with fall leaves. Some of the city folk on their porches wave to the group walking by, welcoming and trusting of the rebels. Ren just nods back to them, wondering what they're being so friendly for.

Dying flowers line the gardens and plants are getting ready for winter's slumber. Ren thinks back to his homestead and clutches his fixed locket in his hand. How are Curlew and Rosie getting along? Winter can be a challenge on a homestead, but it's their third winter alone, so they'll probably manage just fine.

He sighs. *Just fine without me.*

As they make their way deeper into the city, the buildings grow taller. Among the tall buildings, the dusty road widens into a circle, wrapping around a tall statue that Ren immediately recognizes. He's a Soharist, but he's seen enough Castist imagery in Valko to know Castus when he sees him. A tall, normal-looking, bearded man stands triumphantly, black gloves painted on the deep grey stone. At the bottom of the statue is a small house with a metal gate, tiered trays full of sand holding lit candles.

Ren looks at the statue and huffs. He's just a man. The Soharist gods are hardly defined, most people and cultures seeing them differently. What's so special about a guy?

Cosette pauses at the foot of the statue, shutting her eyes as she says a prayer to her god. Ren's first reaction is to mock her, but when she opens her eyes, they hold an unshakable passion.

"So, what is this? A shrine?" he asks, walking up to her.

Cosette glances over at him, seemingly shocked Ren's comment wasn't a negative one.

"Yes, it is," she finally says. She turns back to look at it. "The candles are to communicate with the dead. Some see it as a way to pass a message along, others to honor those who passed."

"Huh," Ren says, surprised by his genuine interest. "That's just like what we do for Soharist funerals."

"Yes," she says with a nod. "Funny how similar our traditions can be considering the war."

Ren sighs. "Right?"

"Come on you two," Aster says. "Stop holding us up, we have work to do."

Cosette flashes an angry glare at Aster, clearly he doesn't respect her praying to her god at a shrine. Ren catches Aster staring up at the statue, his eyes lingering on the grey stone for a moment after Ren and Cosette catch up.

The residential buildings thin out and they follow a dusty road up a hill, grassy land reaching out on the left side, leading further up the hill into some woods, the right still holding a few homes. Once they reach the crest of the road, it slopes downwards toward the harbor. Steamstacks and industrial buildings line the small bay, looking especially dismal under the fall skies. A strong breeze from the bay brings the acrid odor of ethner up the hill, the grasses rustling with the wind.

"I'd take it this is Industrial Drive?" Ren asks.

Aster nods, his eyes locked on the warehouses.

Ren narrows his eyes as he tries to make out the workers at the warehouse. The largest building by far is a rectangular hangar, towering terrifyingly high over the other buildings. Ren isn't sure if he's ever seen anything that big before.

A metal gate surrounds the massive hangar, barbed wire twisting around the top. Armed guards donned in ethner gear look like bugs from atop the hill.

"I think I know which one is the hangar," Ren remarks, still in awe at the massive building on the harbor. He can't see in the building's huge windows, but he knows that's the only place the airship fleet could be.

"We need to gather intel, go closer in," Aster says.

"Closer in?" Jericho asks with wide eyes. "With all due respect, it's broad daylight! I'm nervous here on this hill! Look at the size of the place, and all the guards!"

"It's not illegal to stand on this hill," Aster says. "Going closer would certainly be trespassing, but we need intel."

Jericho shuffles through his small field bag and produces a small scope from his bag. He casts a glance over the hill, points to the woods, and says, "We all have spotting scopes in our field bags. Why don't we go in the woods and gather intel from there?"

"That sounds much safer," Connie interjects. "We're sitting ducks even up on this hill. It would be nice to avoid *another* disaster."

Aster turns around, frustration plain as day on his face.

"The woods are obviously the safer option," Ren says. He nods to Jericho. "Good idea, Jericho."

Jericho doesn't look at Ren, ignoring his praise as he stares down Aster. Guilt pricks at Ren. *Worrying about what Jericho thinks of me now isn't a good idea. Focus on the mission.*

"We don't need safe," Aster says. "We need results."

"This city is crawling with Castist extremists and we don't know if Markos or the Valkoeans have upped the guards to be on alert," Cosette says. "Jericho has a solid plan with little risk. Why not go for it?"

Frustration flickers in Aster's brown eyes, darting back and forth over Cosette's face as the gears seem to turn in his head. He sighs.

"The majority rules," Aster says, defeated. "We'll scout from the woods."

"Scouting closer is not an awful idea all together," Ren says. "But later tonight while we have the veil of shadows to hide us."

"It's how we handled missions like this in the Sunbell City Guild," Cosette says.

Aster's lips twitch. "I forget this team's past sometimes," he says.

Ren wants to point out that Jericho's idea was the smartest one and that he's not from the guild, so it should have been obvious to Aster too. The deputy seems to have a darkness to him, like something is bothering him deep down. Ren decides not to press it further. What matters is that they are starting with the safest and smartest plan.

"Let's swing back around on the road into the woods," Aster says, beckoning the four back with him. "We've probably caught the eye of the guards already."

Ren proudly smiles at Jericho, but the boy doesn't even glance in his direction. Ren's smile fades as Jericho falls into line next to Cosette, Connie at Ren's side.

Even if I apologized, there's no way he will forgive me. He hates me, and I don't blame him. I deserve it.

They backtrack up the road away from Industrial Drive. Aster leads them across the stream of grass into the woods, out of view of the warehouse guards.

The team disperses throughout the woods, tucking away into the still green bushes on the forest's floor. Ren nestles down into a spot to keep comfortable, his belly pressed on the ground. The sweet smell of fall leaves is strong and he pushes himself into a bush, getting his scope and notepad out. He sighs, regretting leaving his field rations at camp.

It's going to be a long day. Gadias give me strength!

He presses the cold end of the scope up to his eye, focusing on the hangar below. It's just a formality at this point, but Ren double checks the address of the hangar, pointing his scope at the mailbox at the gate's entrance.

Thirty-eight.

Ren watches the guards closely, scratching notes about their schedules and rotations in his journal. They aren't incredibly predictable, meandering around somewhat aimlessly, but they follow a path around the hangar. Pines are around the yard, nearly reaching the top of the building. The hangar is against the water, but Ren can't see the water side.

Ren tries to peer into the hangar with his scope, the large, high windows not revealing any secrets as they reflect the image of the woods back at him. Ren can make out skylights at the top of the hangar, noticing some of them left ajar, presumable to air out the chemicals in the place. He jots a quick note down on that.

It's an entry point, but how on Harkive would we even get to the top of the beast of a building? And then we'd have no way to make it to the floor safely.

The fall clouds start to break, becoming patches of grey against blue. Ren tries to not focus on the sun intermittently peeking out as it crawls through the sky, all too aware of the time passing slowly. Ren's eyelids grow heavy and his stomach growls.

Investigating closer would have been more exciting, he decides. But they'd certainly have been caught.

As the sun shifts and the clouds grow patchy, sunlight cuts down over the land, Ren growing warm in the light. Sunlight pierces into the skylights of the hangar, the glare of the side windows fading as the interior becomes visible. Ren brings his scope over to focus on the interior, getting a glimpse into the building.

Ren sees the tops and backs of two airships — one's body mostly yellow, the other red. The wing-sails are folded up at their sides, like a perched bird. The tails of the beasts are shaped almost like a shark's back fin. On the pointed part, he notices bold lettering, the sunlight highlighting them: Dodecanese M003 on the red one, Explorer V004 on the yellow.

Ren ponders for a moment. He recalls seeing Mohkan's snake symbol, much like the country's flag, on the sides of the red airships they have seen. The M must be for the Mohkan ships, the V for Valkoean ones. He jots down the names and what he saw quickly with a question in the notes: How many of these things are there?

He notices scaffolding against the windows of the hangars, the sunlight showing workers pointed towards the massive ships. Ren feels like a rock settles in his stomach as he realizes the scope of the airships. The workers are tiny compared to the big ships, their hands waving towards the airships as they discuss something, the one referring to a clipboard.

The airships are massive! Markos told them how to destroy them, but how will they even do that? It's like taking down a beast of legend!

Ren has seen the airships in the skies, but their size against the clouds does not compare to the scale of them on the ground. The Raiders have a carriage packed full of explosives, but would that even put a dent in these things? Could they even destroy just one?

As Ren peers in, hope flutters inside him. The scaffolding goes all the way to the bottom of the window and presumably the ground. The skylights had to be opened somehow, so maybe the rows of metal walkways could bring the Raiders from the skylight entryway to the ground.

But how do we get on the roof of the hangar in the first place?

He grows frustrated as the answer remains unclear and a cloud casts a shadow over the hangar, being cut off from his inside view.

He prays to Ludon to bring the sun back so he can get a better view of the interior. The grey fall sky returns, Ren's prayers going unanswered. His stomach twists into knots as hunger overtakes him, and new information grows sparse.

Aster calls the mission over, telling everyone to get back to camp to discuss their findings and get a meal in their bellies. Ren is thankful to roll off the ground, clutching his book of notes tightly. He wishes he had gotten more information, but it is a good start.

With any luck, they'll be back later tonight to scout the hangar. Ren shivers as he thinks of the size of the beasts and trying to take them down. The five stay silent as their feet crunch over the fall leaves, Ren casting one last glance to the hangar before the forest hides it from view entirely. Is this mission even possible?

39
THE TOUR

S cotty, Withorn, and Reagan find themselves back at the university's courtyard, Katze left behind at the camp. Jean, Merryweather, and Farsing are scouting the outside of the university, hiding out and gathering notes on points of entry or where bombs may be built.

Scotty is bothered to be away from Farsing again, but she prays that Jean will be on alert. He is as paranoid as Scotty, so he should be on top of things.

They step under the overhang at the school's front doors, students passing the trio odd glances. Most of them seem to be eyeing Scotty, worry starting to surge through her. She wonders if she has a gun or dagger out, glancing down at her shirt, then her pants. She is wearing baggy jeans, Tex concealed, the imprint not even noticeable.

Scotty realizes their gazes are on her face, on her scars.

The rebels are much more used to seeing people like me.

The front doors open up, tall ceilings greeting them. A wall divides the entryway into two halls.

"Where do we go?" Withorn asks, looking to Reagan.

"There is usually an office where you can get an employee to give you a tour," Reagan says. She glances around and leads Scotty and

Withorn across the front room to a door, the word "office" carved into a wood plaque. Scotty peers into a window giving a view into the office. Desks, cabinets, and bookshelves line the walls, parchments sticking out from folders packed into the shelves. A wrinkled woman with curled grey hair writes with a quill, peering at the paper through small glasses on the bridge of her nose. Scotty notices a few other younger people at other desks, wondering what they could possibly be doing.

Reagan smiles as she looks in and turns to the two. "I'll go in and request a tour," she tells them. She knocks on the door and with a beckoning call she is allowed in.

Reagan greet the woman behind the desk, nodding in respect at her before shaking her hand and saying something. They talk for a bit and the old woman laughs. Reagan gestures to the window and the woman's gaze move from Withorn to Scotty, the woman looking pitifully at Scotty.

The old woman says something and gestures to another employee. A middle-aged woman steps gracefully over to her, nodding politely. The old woman points to the door and Reagan and the middle-aged woman leave, Reagan smiling at Withorn and Scotty.

"We got the tour!" she says excitedly. Scotty thinks for a moment that Reagan is genuinely excited to see the school and consider it for education.

"Hello," the woman says with a polite nod. "My name is Lisa, I'll be your guide today. Reagan told me she's here to check out our architecture program, but she said you two are here for general studies."

Scotty nods, shaking the woman's hand when it is extended to her. "My name is Scotty." *What even is general studies?*

Lisa turns to Withorn and shakes his hand. "I'm Withorn," he says.

"Withorn, Reagan said you might be interested in our medicine program," Lisa says.

Scotty sees Withorn's face scrunch up. "Did she now?" Withorn shoots daggers at Reagan and Reagan's face goes red, her pale blotches glowing brighter.

"Er, I said you *might* be," Reagan tells him.

Withorn just swallows his pride and nods. Scotty stifles a laugh bubbling in her chest. Withorn has a bone to pick with Valkoean medicine, so she can't imagine he's happy at the thought of being a prospective student of it.

"Follow me," Lisa says.

Reagan steps alongside Lisa, the guide taking them down the left hall. Lisa explains some of the rooms to them, nothing that really strikes Scotty as useful. The hallway is built beautifully with wooden pillars and wood paneling. Oil sconces line the walls, leading to high, sloped ceilings. Reagan and the guide talk about the building and the beauty, and while Scotty agrees it is nice, it gets old quick.

Scotty glances out the window and wonders where the other half of their team is. The school feels high up, the land sloping far down into the harbor. There is a nice view of the lake and a small overgrown yard.

The guide points out math and science classes, but nothing chemistry related, Scotty wondering where the classes her brother took might take place.

They weave through the halls, Scotty legs aching from walking around the students. She starts to doubt there's any useful information to be gotten on this tour.

"And this is the library," Lisa says, opening one of the doors on the left to let them see more.

They step into the library, this being one of the large spires of the building. Scotty looks up in awe at the height of the tower. Books line the walls to the top spanning multiple lofts, massive windows between the shelves letting in natural, clouded daylight. Potted plants are strewn about the floors, still lush and green despite the dismal fall outside. The lofts are lined with wooden guardrails and connected with spiral staircases, long, old ivy vines wrapping around the ironwork.

Students study on the ground floor, their tables set atop a maroon and white rug. The dewick librarian yawns at the checkout desk, reading a book of his own. Next to the checkout desk is a dark grandfather clock, a bronze pendulum ticking behind its long glass door.

"Feel free to look around," Lisa says, smiling at the room. "Our library is one of our proudest features."

Reagan looks around in awe. "This is amazing! You have much to be proud of."

Scotty shuffles as irritation washes over her. They're wasting a lot of time on this tour and not getting any good information. Was her lead a bust?

Lisa goes over to chat with the librarian, the dewick beaming at her as she approaches.

Reagan looks to Withorn and Scotty. "Well, we can see if there is any useful information in here."

"A library?" Withorn says, unconvinced.

"It's a start. Let's look around," Reagan says.

Reagan is quick to split off from them, starting at the ground level.

"I think she's more interested in the school and the books than the mission," Withorn grumbles once she's out of earshot.

"We're being given free rein, so she's right, it's a start," Scotty says. "Let's check the top loft first."

"My leg's killing me, do we have to go all the way up there?" Withorn asks.

"We can start at the second loft," Scotty suggests.

"Fine," Withorn says, pointing his blocky nose upward. "There are less people on the second loft anyway."

They step up the steep stairs, the loft floor soon echoing underfoot as they browse the shelves.

"This is all useless," Withorn says, thumbing through the higher books. "We aren't going to find information on the location we are looking for here."

"We at least look interested," Scotty says, pulling a book from the shelf. It's a leather bound hardback, the title reading "Ashlar Abyss". She reads the blurb printed inside and it looks to be a story about an underground kingdom, each lower layer of the city doused in more secrets. She flips through a few pages. The technology is weird, engines using something called diesel rather than ethner to run.

Sounds cool.

She tucks the book back in its place.

Withorn groans and sits down on a soft stool next to a window with thick curtains tucked to the side. He casts a sidelong glance outside and Scotty sighs.

"What's your problem now?" she asks, glancing over another book. She turns to look at him and he's rubbing his leg, wincing.

"That stupid rebel medic," he mumbles. "I'd have this wound healed by now."

"Connie is trying his best," Scotty tells him, shelving the book. "It hasn't even been a week. *You* can't even heal a wound in that amount of time. You're just usually not wounded, so you're not used to it."

Withorn huffs. "I... I know. You're right."

Scotty gives him a sideways glance. "You being agreeable? What else is wrong?" She smirks at the tease, but when his expression stays sad, she frowns.

"*Is* something wrong?" she repeats more carefully.

"I haven't felt the same since... since I saw *her*," he murmurs.

His mother, High Priestess Tapscott. Scotty nods in understanding. She recalls the day of the masquerade, the odd dark aura over High Priestess Tapscott. Scotty shivers as she remembers the knowing look from Tapscott. *I still don't know what that was.*

A look of fear overtakes Withorn's hazel gaze and Scotty feels like she's looking down at a scared boy.

"I wanted to lash out," Withorn continues in a hushed tone. "But my body wouldn't move."

Scotty sits down on the ground next to Withorn's stool, picking at chipping paint on a bookcase.

"Good thing you didn't lash out," Scotty says. "You'd be dead, you know."

"I know that," Withorn says, frustration laced in his tone. "Maybe you grounded me. It was nice just knowing that someone else there knew my secret. Knew *Tapscott's* secret. But I still feel haunted by her presence."

Scotty hesitates as she considers what to say, her heart aching at Withorn's pain. "Maybe it is just something that takes time to heal," she says. "Like your leg wound."

Withorn sighs, the fear in his eyes ebbing as his body relaxes. "I hope so. If this was a physical wound, I'd know just what to do. I don't know what to do about... whatever feels broken in my head."

"Nothing is broken up there," Scotty tells him.

Scotty hesitates a silence falls over them, shivering as she thinks about the dark aura she saw around Tapscott.

"Tapscott sure had a weird energy about her," Scotty says.

Withorn gives her an odd glance.

"What do you mean?" he asks.

"Did you not sense it?" Scotty asks. She frowns, wondering if she's crazy. "Er. I don't know. It felt like a weird connection. It was like the aura of a... of a sharfawks overtook her."

"She did wear a sharfawks mask," Withorn says. "And you did too... Didn't Ludon come to you in the form of a sharfawks?"

Scotty nods. "In the Red Forest. Do... do you think those things are connected?"

"When I met another apostle of Nikos, I saw the aura of the dark god in them or felt a pull to them," Withorn says. "It happened when I saw Doctor Hewett in Ghent and Aunt Margarette in Salina Village."

"Well, I keep having dreams of Ludon," Scotty says. "I... I don't exactly know if I'm his apostle." She thinks about how Hartwood said they don't share a god. If what Withorn said was true about apostles being able to sense each other, wouldn't she have sensed it in Hartwood too? Or has Hartwood been lying about being an apostle after all? It seemed to be the one thing that made sense of the man.

"If I am an apostle of Ludon," Scotty continues, her voice hushed, "then does that mean High Priestess Tapscott is too?"

Withorn laughs, the guttural noise catching the eyes of a few students for a moment. Withorn lowers his voice, waiting for the attention to pass before continuing. "Have you forgotten *everything* about this war? She's a Castist through and through," he says.

"Er, yeah," Scotty says. "That was a stupid thing to think."

Withorn frowns as he considers what all Scotty has said. "It's definitely weird, though. Maybe we can check out the Good Book sometimes. See if we can find anything about a sharfawks. It... it really doesn't make sense that you'd feel that connection with Tapscott unless you shared a god."

Scotty shivers at the thought of having something in common with Tapscott. "She said she has spoken to her god, though," Scotty says. "Is she just crazy?"

"Well, I think she is," Withorn says. "There's plenty of evidence supporting it."

"Scotty, Withorn!" The two jolt at the call of Lisa's voice.

Scotty goes to the guard rail, Lisa waving up to them. "Ready to continue?" Lisa asks.

Scotty cranes her head back to Withorn, the medic standing up. He hisses and falls back into the stool.

"Are you okay up there?" Lisa calls.

"Uh," Withorn calls back. "My leg is cramped up. Er, from the walking."

Scotty turns back to look down at Lisa. "Can you two continue without us?" she asks. "We will catch up later, he just needs to rest."

Reagan looks at Lisa and nods as if to urge her to say yes.

"Certainly," Lisa says, turning back to Scotty. "Take as much time as you need. If you have any questions, feel free to ask when you catch up."

Reagan and Lisa bid them farewell, leaving the library.

Withorn gets to his feet slowly. "So, you said your brother went here?" he asks, glancing around.

"Yes, this is where he worked on Tex."

"Why did the Brunswicks spend all that money on a hitman?" Withorn asks. "Er, no offense. I've just dealt with tycoons in my time in the guild and I've never heard of them promoting indentured servants."

"My *parents* were indentured servants," Scotty tells him. "They chose that life. Grover and I didn't. We were slaves to the Brunswicks." Scotty leans on the rail, keeping her voice low. "It wasn't a promotion, it was a way to stay tied to them. We were just tools for Hayward City Steel. When Grover showed prowess in his tinkering, they just saw him as a thing to invest in. Like spending money to clean and put shoes on a valen. It was not out of kindness."

"Oh," Withorn says, leaning next to her. "I didn't think it was out of kindness, it just seemed odd. Your brother must have been something special then. This place is really something."

Through the pain and frustration, a smile spreads over her lips as she thinks of her brother. "He really was special. The Brunswicks send all their best chemists here. I think some of Mike's brothers even were interested in coming here. Grover was smarter than all of them though."

"Sorry if I set off some bad memories," Withorn says.

"This is where my brother felt the happiest," Scotty says. "Where he actually felt free. It's nice to think that's possible for people like us."

Withorn faintly smiles at her.

"This is actually a good opportunity for us to scout," Scotty says. "Let's not waste it."

They descend the stairs to the ground floor. They try to make themselves look busy for a little longer, trying to not catch the suspicion of the librarian. He doesn't seem to mind their presence, his nose already stuffed into a book again. Still, Scotty and Withorn give enough time for Reagan and Lisa to get further on the tour so they don't have to go back if Lisa catches them.

Bong! Bong! Bong!

Scotty snaps around with a racing heart, expecting an ambush in the library. Embarrassment burns hot on her skin when she notices the chiming grandfather clock next to the librarian's desk. She looks to Withorn, the medic clearly shaken too.

The students around the library leave, probably moving on to their next class. After the group leaves, more students getting off of classes fill the library, some stepping up into the lofts, others settling around at the tables.

Scotty and Withorn exchange knowing glances, silently agreeing to get out of the library. They make their way towards the door, pressing against the flood of students coming in. Scotty glances up at the people as she walks, Withorn towering over most of them.

She catches the gazes of a few students, but feels herself lock up when she notices familiar brown eyes. The stare of a brown haired man gawks back, studying her scars. Scotty quickly averts her gaze, her heart thumping hard.

That familiar face.

A close mirror image to her late fiancé. For a moment her heart aches, wishing it was Mike, but panic swells over the pain at the realization.

Ezekiel Brunswick.

One of Mike's younger brothers.

She prays he didn't recognize her, but a strong hand grabs her shoulder and she yowls as she is pulled back.

Withorn snaps around at her scream. "Scotty!"

Scotty is jerked around, Ezekiel's hands now tight around her shoulders.

"You!" he hisses. "Scotty! You whore!"

"Whore?" Scotty says back in shock. He could call her many true things, but that? Scotty jerks around, trying to free herself, Ezekiel only tightening his grip as she struggles.

"You're why Mike is gone!" he says. "You're why I'll never see my brother again!" He shoves her and she falls to the ground, gasps sounding out. Scotty hadn't realized the crowd they have gathered.

Withorn kneels at her side, helping her get up.

"Your *parents* killed Mike," Scotty tells him slowly, trying to hide the fury in her voice. "Your *parents* put the hit out on him." Scotty holds back the fact that Mike talking about Soharism was why the guards turned on him in the first place. *It's all their faults!*

Ezekiel steps back with wide eyes. "No!" he says. "You're wrong!" Scotty almost feels bad as she sees panic start to overtake his pose.

"Guards!" Ezekiel howls. "Someone call the guards! There is a fugitive in the school!"

This sets off a panic, gasps waving around the crowd.

"A criminal?"

"She's just a girl!"

"Stop standing around and someone get the guards!" Ezekiel howls.

Ezekiel lashes out to grab her again, but Scotty parries to the side, Ezekiel stumbling as she throws her body weight into him at his side. He lurches and curses as he spins around, this time throwing a balled fist towards her.

Scotty dodges it again, her brow furrowing. He's sloppy, no one's ever trained him to fight. She's all too aware of Tex tucked in her pants, but she feels her fists clench.

He's a Brunswick, he's as guilty as his parents for Mike's death.

He needs to pay.

Tex would be too easy.

With all her might, she lands a blow into his gut, Ezekiel lurching back, coughing.

"Fighting a girl? I know your mother has taught you better than that," Scotty teases with a smirk. She knows he was raised by nannies. He doesn't know his mother very well besides what her money provided to him.

Ezekiel's face turns red, his teeth grit.

"Bitch!" he yells, lunging forward again.

Scotty buzzes as she gets ready to lay into him, feeling like a screaming tea pot, ready to scald him.

"Okay now," Withorn says, wrapping his arms around Ezekiel. "We're done here."

"Hey!" Ezekiel shouts, wriggling in Withorn's grasp. Withorn leans back, Ezekiel's feet lifting off the floor. His polished shoes kick into Withorn's shins, but nothing fazes the medic.

"Put him down!" Scotty demands. Her rage boils over, like a feral hound possesses her. "Let me kick his ass!" she snarls. "I can take him! Let me kill him!"

"As if!" Ezekiel bites.

The seriousness in Withorn's gaze grounds Scotty and she remembers why they are here. The crowd murmurs around her and a voice shouts from the hall, "Guards, this way! There's a fight!"

Scotty is a wanted woman still, and Ezekiel knows this. It wouldn't take much for the guards to confirm it and ship her off to Hayward City to her death.

Temptation tugs at her to end Ezekiel right here and risk it all, but she forces the dark thoughts away. What would happen to Withorn if she did that?

"Shit," Scotty hisses. "Withorn, let's go!"

Withorn heaves forward, throwing Ezekiel a good distance. The crowd shouts and parts as Ezekiel tumbles, a panic erupting. Withorn turns and pushes out the crowd into the hall, more people having gathered among the ruckus. Other students are running, some in panic from the chaos, others in fear of Withorn and Scotty.

Withorn and Scotty disappear into the mass of students, Scotty's shoulder brushing against the ribs of a guard as he runs to the library to investigate.

The students fleeing the fight mix in with students walking to class, unaware of what happened in the library. The people calm and Withorn and Scotty slow, but Scotty is all too aware they went further into the school along the path of least resistance.

"We need to hide," Scotty whispers to Withorn.

"I know," he hisses back, his eyes darting around the hall.

"There!" he says.

They move out of the flow of walking students to be against the wall by a door reading "Authorized Personnel Only".

Scotty wants to argue with the choice, but Withorn yanks the door open and they slip inside, a couple of students looking at them curiously. A few heartbeats pass as they sit on the other side of the door, as if waiting for a guard to come bellowing through the door.

Did we really make it in unseen?

Scotty turns around, fear overtaking her as she realizes they're trespassing now.

Thankfully, no one is behind them, but a long, wooden staircase leads into darkness. Scotty and Withorn exchange hesitant glances in the shadows, nodding at each other in agreement to go down.

They carefully step down towards a soft light. The stairs creak and they find themselves in a walkout basement. The slope from the land lets the university's basement overlook the lake, close to the water level. The windows down here are small and secretive, metal bars on the outside making it look like they're inside a jail cell.

The windows illuminate the place with soft blue light. First, Scotty notices there are no people in the room. Weird metal instruments hang on the wall, Scotty wondering if they're for science or for torture. Or both?

A couple bookcases sit on the walls, some desks near the windows and what look like tool chests are also in the place. In the middle of the room are long tables with weird metal projects on them, nothing familiar to Scotty. A few tall wooden cabinets sit ajar, seemingly empty inside towards the front.

"It's some kind of workshop," Withorn says.

"But is it for making bombs?" Scotty whispers, stepping around the tables. She picks up a weird metal contraption, some gears in the center.

"I'm no expert, but it doesn't look like it," Withorn says. "Farsing would probably know."

Scotty shakes her head. "It looks like stations to make prototypes, like the research rooms at Hayward City Steel. I've seen plenty like it from their competitors too, when the Brunswicks had me rob them. Either way, it's not a full blown factory in any way."

"Why do you think this place is only for authorized personnel?" Withorn asks, his voice hushed. "It doesn't look like anything special."

"Maybe this technology is a secret for whatever reason." Scotty dangles the gear contraption in front of her, wondering if it'll suddenly make sense at a different angle. "The Brunswicks and their competitors guarded their new tech like their lives depended on it."

Their pondering stops as a click sounds from the top of the stairs. Panic surges through Scotty as the door creaks open. *Is it the guards?*

"Hide!" she hisses to Withorn.

Her eyes snap around the room, eventually landing on the large ajar cabinets. She dashes across the room, Withorn on her heels. She hears thunking as people lumber down the stairs. The two duck into the same cabinet, pushing a mop and bucket aside as they stuff into the place. Scotty would fit fine, but Withorn has to bend at an awkward angle. They struggle to shut the door, but settle on keeping it cracked when they hear the voices of two men grow loud.

Scotty prays the darkness of the room keeps them hidden, but fear overtakes her. They can't stay in here forever and they can't be seen or else they could risk the whole mission.

Withorn stands next to her, fidgeting slightly. Scotty stands up fine, but irritation swells inside her at being pressed up against Withorn — it's not her ideal situation.

The men make small talk, one placing a mug on one of the tables in the center of the room. He pulls a coat off, putting it on the desk too.

"That was a good lunch," he says, patting his round belly.

"I think you need to cut back on the sides," the other man remarks.

The first man lets out a bellowing laugh and the other sighs.

"We have a lot of paperwork to get through for the student internships," the skinnier, more serious man says. He disappears from Scotty's view and comes back to plop a large binder in front of the big-bellied man.

The big man lets out a sigh. "Yeah, the internship."

"It's what they pay us to do, Damian."

Damian opens up the binder, looking to the skinny man. "An internship with the government is the last thing I wanted for our students. They're bright minds, Adam. There's more to their futures than this."

Scotty was about to drown out their talk and focus on ways to get out of this situation, but the mention of the government piques her attention.

Is this actually where they are building the bombs?

Adam sighs. "It's an internship, it's a start. It's good experience to lead to a good future. It's certainly not forever. You saw that through the first batch of interns, it led to great careers for them. The second batch is already getting job offers while in the program."

"It's... used to destroy," Damian says. "If... *when* the government uses it, don't you think it will weigh heavily on them? We're talking about bombs, Adam. You heard what they did to Ghent, the people they killed."

"They're adults," Adam says. "They can make their own choices."

"Don't you think as professors, we should be guiding them down the right path?" Damian says.

"We *are* guiding them to a better future." Adam sighs. "Listen, stop this talk now." His voice grows hushed. "You know the other professors would report *both* of us for it, and we'd soon disappear. You don't know who could be listening."

Damian nods.

Scotty sees a hint of regret in Adam's boney face. "Working with the explosives will give them opportunities to work with airships," he says. "And that's... that's a good thing. If more of our students learn about airships, think of the good that will do." His voice grows optimistic, like he truly believes it. "They can be used for transportation from Hayward City all the way to Snowden in record time. They could transport sick and injured from rural communities to hospitals in big cities for better care. And imagine how logistics would be changed! Damian, most innovation starts at war. That's just how things have always been."

Scotty frowns. So they *are* using student interns to work on the bombs. She thinks to the accidents she has seen at Hayward City Steel working with engines and guns, certainly a much smaller scale than bombs! And those have killed many, what would an accident building bombs entail? Do the students know the risk? Do these professors know?

"Yeah, you're right," Damian says, his tone more upbeat. "It's just a tough hurdle to get past."

"Speaking of which," Adam says, looking to his watch. "It's about time for us to get to the old blooddew shipping facility. We can get through this paperwork when we get back."

Damian picks up his coat again, slinging it over his arms. "I almost forgot! If this internship program does one good thing immediately, it's making the old warehouse useful again. It's weird to think we went from a school of agriculture and innovation to... doing *this*."

Scotty wishes she could look to Withorn to see his reaction, but judging by his slight fidgeting, he's probably not paying great attention. She makes a mental note about the blooddew shipping facility. It sounds like a likely candidate for where the bombs are being made.

Adam ignores Damian's comment about the internship. "We don't have to be too punctual," Adam says, stuffing his hands into his coat's pocket. "You know how these captains are with time."

"We should still be there on time," Damian says. "I'm... anxious to get the chemical shipments in."

"I think we have an aluminum shipment today too," Adam says. Their footfalls echo across the room, the two moving out of Scotty's line of vision. "We'll meet the interns here later."

A door creaks open and it feels like a long time of the two chattering at the open door before it shuts again. A few moments pass as Scotty and Withorn wait to assure they're far away and like breaking the surface of the water, they spill out of the cabinet, Withorn gasping for breath.

He stretches and rubs his neck. "That was miserable!" he complains.

"We have a lead!" Scotty tells him.

"A old blooddew shipping facility," Withorn says with a nod. "It shouldn't be hard to figure out where that's at."

Scotty and Withorn sneak out of the university's basement, meeting up with Reagan before returning to camp. Reagan said despite going in with them, the staff didn't suspect her of anything and she managed to slip away without them noticing.

Jean, Farsing, Merryweather, and Katze return to the camp a little later. Scotty reluctantly meets with Jean, reporting what happened with Mike's brother. She expects him to lash out, wincing in anticipation.

"What are the chances of that happening?" Jean asks. "Encounters like that are in the hands of the gods."

Scotty relaxes at the commander's words.

"But the guards are probably on the lookout for you now, Scotty," Jean continues, Scotty's heart sinking. "If your fiancé's brother filed a report about someone with a bounty around the city, they'll be searching. I doubt they suspect you're connected to the rebellion, but I don't want you out in the city during daylight again."

"But I want to keep helping!" Scotty blurts out. "I don't want to be useless!"

"You've done plenty to help," Jean tells her. "Besides, I don't know how much more daylight scouting we will be doing. We will go inspect this blooddew shipping facility now, but since we may be on a time crunch, I'd like to get back out there tonight. Daylight scouting is risky and we need to be quick but careful for this mission."

"So I get to help tonight?" she asks.

Jean nods. "Of course. I want you, Withorn, and Farsing to stay behind and relax so you can handle the bulk of tonight's mission. Merryweather, Reagan, and I will find and scout the shipping facility where we suspect bombs are being made. If we confirm that, I'd like the three of you to get inside when it's dark out. You guys will be able to investigate better if you've gotten a bit of rest."

Scotty nods, pleased to hear she's not the only one being set aside for now. "That makes sense." She glances across the camp to Farsing, already lazing around. It'll be a good opportunity to investigate him too.

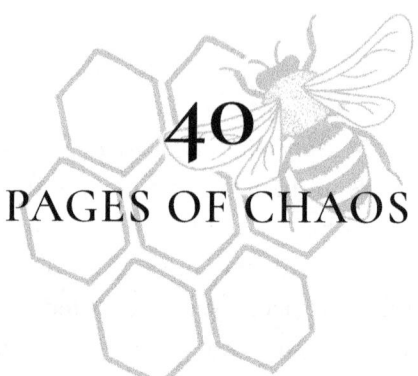

40
PAGES OF CHAOS

Jean, Merryweather, and Reagan head out, leaving Scotty, Withorn, and Farsing alone at the camp. Scotty watches Farsing from a distance, the dewick settling by his bed roll, using his bag as a pillow. He passes out, his snores echoing out on the beach.

She wonders if she could sneak behind him and search through his bag for anything incriminating, mapping out how to come around from behind and get the bag open. His head rests on the main flap, his scruffy hair draped over the bag.

Unless he's a deep sleeper, it doesn't seem possible.

"By Nikos, his snoring is unbearable," Withorn grumbles from behind Scotty, startling her. She snaps around to face him, trying to hide her surprise.

"Er, yeah," she says. "It's pretty awful."

"Since Connie's not here to be useless, can you help dress my wound?" Withorn asks. "It needs cleaned especially after all the walking today."

Scotty and Katze follow Withorn to where his tent is set up, his cabinet protected inside. He pulls out some supplies and rolls his pant leg up, sitting on top of his cabinet so Scotty can reach the gash. He unwraps the bandage and tosses it aside, handing Scotty a sterile-smelling rag. She kneels on the gravel and wipes the wound down, wincing at the bright red color and deep bullet hole. Katze sniffs the wound and Scotty shoos her away from it.

"It's bright red, is that normal?" Scotty asks.

"It's very irritated, so yes," Withorn says. He hesitates before adding. "I'll have Connie check it over later to be sure. Even he should be able to tell if it's the start of an infection."

Scotty winces as she works on the wound. She's not sure how Withorn can stomach this sometimes.

"I was just thinking about what you said in the library," Withorn says, keeping his voice lower as if the sleeping Farsing could overhear.

"About Tapscott?" Scotty says.

Withorn nods. "I wanted to look through the Good Book with you again, in Ludon's section, to see if there's anything you can find that reminds you of what you felt when you saw Tapscott. I know I pretty much said the idea of her being an apostle of Ludon is insanity, but I can't stop thinking about it. We have a book that might have the answers."

Scotty considers Withorn's words as she finishes wrapping the wound, pinning the bandage in place carefully.

"There wasn't anything helpful in there before, but another read through might give us some more insight. I'm down to try to make sense of it." Scotty laughs. "It'd be nice to read something that makes me think I'm not crazy!"

"I can't promise we'll find that," Withorn teases. He rolls his pant leg back down and seems excited as he retreats into his tent to retrieve the book his old mentor, Civran, gave him.

He opens it to Ludon's chapter, sitting next to Scotty on the gravel beach. His wounded leg is splayed out to the side, but his eyes are locked intently on the book.

They flip through the sections, the words the same as before. Just as useless, nothing reminding her of the feeling she felt when she saw Tapscott.

"Nothing sounds like any of the experiences I've had," Scotty says sadly. "It just doesn't make sense."

"Are you sure it's Ludon?" Withorn asks.

As Withorn flips the last page of Ludon's section, Scotty notices the Teachings and Commandments page for Cassius, god of chaos and lies. The flame symbol almost dances off the page for her, Scotty drawn to the logo. She hears a buzzing and a bee lands on the page, hopping on the flame for a moment before Withorn shoos it away.

"Give me that," she urges, Withorn releasing his grasp on the book curiously as Scotty snatches it away from him.

"What is it?" Withorn asks.

Scotty can't answer, she doesn't know what's drawing her to this section. Intuition? What kind of answer is that? She flips through Cassius's pages, frowning at the texts. They're all abstract poems.

"It's all gibberish in that section," Withorn tells her.

Scotty reads through the poems, trying to make sense of the teachings and commandments of the god of chaos. One poem fills two pages, repeating the phrase "The more you obey, the deeper the grasp." More speak about the realm of chaos, but give no hints what that means.

Scotty pauses on a page, one poem leaping out at her.

> Hands and feet of black
> Hair of orange
> From the flames of Chaos
> He is born
> As the drone bees
> Leave the hive
> His grasp of the mind
> You cannot hide

Dread spikes through her, the words sinking in.

"Hands and feet of black," Scotty murmurs. "Hair of orange."

"Yes?" Withorn says. "Does... does it make sense to you?"

"Well... as a whole it doesn't make sense, but this line: Hands and feet of black, hair of orange." She thinks to the sharfawks speaking to her in the Red Forest, the one that haunts her dreams. The one she believed to be Ludon. "Does that not sound like a sharfawks to you?"

"A sharfawks?" Withorn hesitates. "I mean, I suppose it does." Realization spreads over his face. "A sharfawks! You think *Cassius* has been speaking to you?"

"He did come to me in the Red Forest," Scotty says. "Maybe it truly is the holy ground of Cassius." She shivers at the thought. "Is he drawn to Tapscott too?"

"The god of chaos being attracted to my mother makes sense," Withorn murmurs. "But you? Why?"

"I... I don't know," Scotty says. "In Tapscott's speech, she was so certain her god had spoken to her. Was it actually Cassius then?"

"Considering I've seen the god of plague, I have to say that's the only way for it to make sense," Withorn says. "Castus *can't* exist." He sighs. "I never thought I'd say this, but I wish Storn was here right now. He was an apostle of Cassius, he'd probably have answers... If we could even trust a word he says."

Scotty frowns and realizes Hartwood wasn't lying to her. They don't share a god. "Does this mean I'm an apostle of Cassius?" Scotty asks, her stomach churning.

"I don't know, Scotty," Withorn says. "I don't think so. You haven't accepted him, have you?"

Scotty shakes her head. "Something has been holding me back."

"You're far from being like Storn," Withorn says. "He was alright, but he was a lot like Farsing, you know, a bit... off." He glances over to the dewick.

"Do you think Farsing follows Cassius?" Scotty murmurs.

"He's never hinted at it," Withorn says. "All I know is he's from a Soharist family."

Scotty casts a glance at Farsing, feeling like the puzzle pieces are coming together. *A traitor would bring chaos.* "Is Farsing here to sabotage us then?" Scotty asks, freezing up when she realizes Withorn isn't in on her and Aster's mission.

"What?" Withorn asks.

Scotty hesitates, looking up to the confused medic.

"Er..." She lets out a sigh. "I haven't been entirely honest with you," she begins.

Withorn blinks at her. "Well, are you about to start?" he asks, a bit frustrated.

Scotty tells him about her mission when she first joined and how Jean was certain there was a traitor. She explains to him about her and Jean's lingering paranoia about the situation and how Jean confided in Aster about it. She then tells Withorn about her and Aster's current mission and how Aster suspects Farsing of sabotaging the interrogation.

"Wow," Withorn breathes. Hurt swells in his yellow gaze. "Did... did you ever suspect me?" he asks.

"After you told me about your mother, about Tapscott, I was worried for a moment," Scotty says. "But you've been too good a friend to me. It wasn't something I considered for long."

Withorn pauses, as if trying to figure out how he feels about it. He eventually nods. "I see. This is a lot of information to wrap my mind around."

"I know," Scotty murmurs, looking to the Good Book. "All of this is. The last words of Cassius's poem echo in her head. "But the last line of the poem," she mentions. "His grasp of the mind you cannot hide. How... how do people keep out of his influence?" She shivers and lowers her voice. "Can I get him out of my head?" A knot tightens in her chest. Does the dark god make her a liability to her team?

"You need to remember, those are the ramblings of an apostle," Withorn says. "The ramblings of a madman."

Scotty's stomach churns as the weight of the situation settles in. The god of chaos is drawn to her. "Am I going to become a madman?" she breathes.

"No, Scotty," Withorn says defiantly. Scotty wonders if he's certain of that or if he's in denial.

He doesn't have to live with it, of course he'd be quick to come to the best conclusion!

"You're a good person, Scotty," Withorn tells her. "You've got a good head on your shoulders."

"No I don't!" she exclaims. "I'm here for selfish reasons, I'm here to get revenge for Mike! I'm not here to make the world a better place. I'm just a gods forsaken hitman and I've caught the attention of the worst god. It's all because of who I am, because I'm a terrible person!"

"Scotty," Withorn says, sounding hurt again. "You're not any of those things. You're not selfish, you're not a hitman anymore, and you're *not* a terrible person."

"You haven't even known me for a year," Scotty says. "You don't know the things I've done, the people I've killed." Her mind flickers to Grover, then Mike. "The people I've *gotten* killed." Her feet pace under her, her nails digging into her palms. Her head buzzes strongly, a headache pulsating at her ears.

She shuts her eyes and the buzzing grows around her and she winces. The bees are back! These gods forsaken bees! The bees! She swats them away around her head and yells out in frustration when the noise doesn't stop.

Withorn's strong hands clasp onto her shoulders and she feels herself halt. Her eyes snap open and among all the buzzing, she sees no bees. The buzzing mocks her, the words of the madman's poem mock her.

> As the drone bees
> Leave the hive
> His grasp of the mind
> You cannot hide

Her body vibrates and she feels like she wants to cry. Instead, she fall to her knees. *I can't hide. I can't hide. I can't hide.*

"You kept insisting we should recruit Jericho because you cared about his cause," Withorn says. "You saved Katze from her handler and have given her a new chance at freedom — she's always stayed because of her love for you. And you've always been caring to me, even when I've gotten out of hand. You're not a terrible person, and I'd have a hard time believing you're anything but a good person."

Scotty stays silent, letting her friend's words sink in. Katze presses her body into Scotty's chest, the warmth soothing her as Scotty wraps her arms around her grey fur. Scotty sobs into her fur and the buzzing ebbs, but doesn't go away.

Is that Cassius trying to get a grasp on my mind?

"I'm going to make some tea," Withorn says. "To calm your nerves. Stay here."

Scotty hardly feels like she blinks before Withorn returns, thrusting a cup of lavender tea into her hands. Katze steps out of his way, pressing her flank against Scotty as she sits.

"Drink," he demands, sitting cross-legged next to her.

Scotty scrunches her nose at the floral scent but obeys, letting the hot, bitter liquid wash over her tongue.

"You'll only become a madman if you keep up like this," Withorn says. "Like I said, *we have free will.* It was *my* choice to let Nikos in. It's *your* choice to let Cassius in."

Scotty lets out a sigh, relaxing even more. "This is just a lot of information," Scotty murmurs. The buzzing fades as she drinks.

"I know," Withorn says. "But I'm here for you through this."

Scotty's heart swells at her friend's support, combined with the warmth of Katze next to her. "Maybe this is a good thing," she says. "Hartwood said it was clear to him that we didn't share a god." She swallows a sip of tea. "But it just reignites my paranoia."

As she says this, Aster's team returns to camp. She frowns. "Great, now there's too many eyes around to investigate Farsing."

"We'll have plenty of time tonight," Withorn assures her. The weight lifts off Scotty's shoulders at her friend's words. "We need to help take Tapscott down, and we'll do *anything* to get there."

41
THE CLIMB

Ren's team returns to the camp, Faring fast asleep on his bedroll. Scotty and Withorn are murmuring next to the medic's tent, Katze sitting in the gravel next to Scotty.

Aster gathers the hangar team around the coals of the camp's fire, asking for everyone's notes. "I'll compile them together and come up with a plan," he says.

"We should all discuss it now," Cosette mentions. "I think Ren and my experience from the guild can help us come up with a good plan."

Aster frowns at Cosette and looks to Ren. Ren nods at him. "She's right."

Cosette smiles at Ren's support and Aster glances to Jericho and Connie.

"Good idea," Aster says. "Well, what did you all find?"

They sit down on the gravel beach, some heat still radiating from the grey coals in the fire pit.

Cosette reads off what she found about the guards' patterns, Connie and Ren backing her up. Jericho mentions some details on the hangar where downspouts and supports are, things Ren didn't even notice. Ren nods as the boy reads his notes, impressed.

Connie talks about the interior. From his vantage point, he was able to track some of the inside guards. Connie and Aster got the names of the other airships, completing the fleet with Ren's information: Avalon V001, Magnolia V002, Liberty V003, Explorer V004, Maragos M001, Arfaras M002, Dodecanese M003.

There are seven total, Connie also reporting the shell of an eighth being built.

Ren reports his information about the skylights, Aster nodding along silently.

"Going in from the top is impossible," Aster says. "The building is massive, there's no way to the top. A low window or breaking in a door would be best."

"If the guards patrol the same during the night as the day, that will be nearly impossible too," Cosette says. "It takes too long to break in so we'd surely be seen and it's far too loud."

"If we can get in through the top, we could just unlock a window from the inside," Ren says. "No glass breaking, no noise to worry about."

"The downspouts looked strong," Jericho says. "And the building supports I saw could be a way to climb up."

"Climb up?" Aster echoes. "Are you insane? How am I supposed to do that in my armor? And how is Jericho going to get all the way up there?"

"A couple of us could go in to get information," Ren says. "We don't need five people to gather information on the inside. Whoever doesn't go in can stay outside and get more intel."

Cosette nods. "I think it would work."

"I think it is too risky to go inside now," Aster says. "You guys were hesitant to go closer earlier, and I think that's the best way to handle this."

"We do need information on the inside," Connie says. "We aren't getting a better view than I had from the woods, especially at night."

"If we get caught breaking in or raise suspicion in any way, that's it," Aster says. "The mission would be a bust. Guards would be increased and it would be impossible to get in to destroy the ships later."

"We don't have time to be careful like that," Ren tells Aster. "Going closer earlier would have compromised our position, but we *do* need to get in closer. If we try to get inside tonight, we will have the shadows on our side. Aurthuras and Nikos will be thin again tonight."

"You're trying to compromise this mission, aren't you, Ren?" Aster accuses.

"What?" Ren spits.

"Woah!" Cosette exclaims. "Aster, calm down. Ren's not compromising the mission. He's making good points. You're the only one not agreeing with the rest of us."

Aster and Ren's eyes stay locked on each other, Ren's brow furrowing. He wants to lay into Aster for accusing him of that when Ren has so much on the line in this war, but he knows now isn't the time to argue. Ren, for once, has everyone else on his side.

"Aster," Cosette repeats. "Do you have anything to say about that?"

"We can try to get in through the roof," Aster remarks, turning to look at the woman. "Cosette, Ren, since you two are the biggest supporters of it, *you* can go in. Connie, Jericho, and I will gather intel from the outside and work out another, safer way in. We will *not* be able to help if you fail."

"Works for me," Cosette says, an edge to her tone as she glares at the deputy.

"Me too," Ren says.

"You think you'll be alright?" Jericho asks, concern in his gaze. Ren frowns when he realizes Jericho is looking at Cosette.

"Of course," Cosette says, the frustration not leaving her voice.

"We have to go in to help if something happens," Jericho says, turning to Aster.

"We'll be fine," Cosette assures him. "Worry about yourself, will you?"

Jericho looks like he regrets his words, but stays quiet, seemingly searching for words. Ren knows that Jericho shouldn't worry about

Cosette — like she said he should worry about himself more — but despite the regret in his eyes, they still sparkle with longing as he looks at the quartermaster.

"I'm... I'm sorry, Cosette," he finally says.

Cosette's frown softens, but Aster speaks up.

"Everyone get a good meal in," Aster says. "When the sun starts to set, we'll head back to Industrial Drive."

———

The sun dives into the eastern horizon, and the team heads out again. Ren and Cosette leave Aster, Jericho, and Connie on the hill. The three lay down in the tall grasses, camouflaged by the shadows, ready to gather more intel during the dark night.

Ren and Cosette head into the woods, flanking the hangar to enter from the quieter side. Ren looks to the sky. The glow of the sunset has faded to a dark blue, Aurthuras and Nikos together in the sky as slivers. Their silver light is duller than usual, and patchy fall clouds that look almost black in the night intermittently hide them.

They near Industrial Drive, keeping low in the grasses at they approach. Ren looks over the metal fence, searching for a good entry point. Guards step around, Ren counting to confirm they follow the lose patterns from earlier in the day. The guards carry oil lanterns, the soft glow giving their positions away.

As Ren's gaze passes over the grounds, he sees where the hangar butts up to the water, docks stretching out from it, lit with oil lamps.

"The fence ends at the water," he whispers to Cosette. "Let's get in closer."

Cosette nods and they cross the dirt road into the grass across from them. The grass is shorter here, so they crawl behind a small hump in the land, another less important warehouse behind them. The dry grass scratches Ren's stomach through his shirt, his elbows stinging as they dig through the grass into the stoney dirt.

The guards are unaware of the two Raiders crawling yards away from the fence, Ren thankful for the grass and small hill covering them. A copse of pine trees is near the water, Ren and Cosette standing up when they're stifled in their shadows. Waves lap up against the cracked seawall, the soft noise enough to hide their whispers and footsteps from the guards.

The clouds momentarily split from the moons, dull silver light showing Ren and Cosette the side of the hangar they hadn't seen earlier in the day.

Four bay doors face the docks, eight steamboats tied up in front of them. Large, sturdy posts stretch high into the sky where the docks meet the land.

Ren and Cosette sneak along the fence in the cover of shadows, and halt at where the land meets the waters. Waves lap at the seawall, the splashing sending droplets over the cracked wall. The fence extends a little ways into the dark water, Ren glancing back at Cosette hesitantly. They need to get around the fence, and the water is the best route.

They nod at each other, and Ren hands his revolver and munitions over to Cosette. He winces as he slides off the seawall, holding his breath, expecting the water to wash over his head. He lets out a quiet gasp as water engulfs his waist, but is thankful when his head doesn't go under. Cosette snickers quietly at his reaction, handing him his weapons back and holding her own above the water as she takes the plunge.

They wade farther out, casting glances back to the guards patrolling on land. Thankfully, the darkness and sounds of the waves are enough to hide them.

Ren's boots drag along the mushy bay floor, trying to not gasp when the cold waves rise over his belly as he moves towards the end of the fence. As the water deepens, he grabs onto the fence with his free hand, his boots lifting from the floor. Cosette struggles behind him, huffing in the chilly water as she keeps her own weapons high. She half swims, half climbs towards the end.

The two round the fence and move closer to the shore, Ren chilled to the bone in the cold water. They crawl up onto an area where the hangar's seawall has fully deteriorated, a concrete spot free of water pressed up against the shore — a perfect place to scout their next move.

Ren winces at his wet clothes, he and Cosette taking a moment to ring out their wet pants, not looking at each other as they do. It'll be bad enough having to climb with wet clothes, but it would be impossible to tackle soaked. Ren shivers even after putting his clothes back on. Part of him wants to turn back now, frustrated at the deep coldness. They've come too far to not give it a try, though.

They peek over the broken seawall, Ren's gaze sweeping over the side of the hangar, in awe at how massive this building is.

Cosette nudges Ren, pointing his attention towards the right side of the hangar. A pair of guards, visible thanks to their bobbing lantern, step around the corner closest to Cosette and Ren. Tall pines grow against this side of the hangar, stifling the corner from their view. The trees nearly go to the top of the hangar, Ren still shocked by the scale of this operation

"The other corners had the gutters and support Jericho reported," Cosette whispers. "If it's the same for the back side, the one closest to us will be mostly covered by the trees."

"Good catch," Ren whispers, genuinely impressed. "Let's see if it's even possible to climb them."

"I think we got this," Cosette says.

Ren and Cosette wait for the next group of guards to pass with their bobbing lantern. Once the guards have well passed the corner and Ren sees the next lantern getting closer, they dart across the ground to the trees against the hangar, their wet boots squishing with every step. The swashing of the waves covers the noise, the moonlight spilling over the land when they're under the cover of the pines.

They're dangerously close to the guard path now, but Ren feels comfortable in the shadows. Still, he looks to the moons peeking through the pines and he sends out a silent prayer, *Aurthuras, Nikos, please help hide us!*

Ren and Cosette press up against the side of the hangar, the metal wall cool against Ren's palms. Another pair of guards pass, this time with a tracking fallion in tow. Among the strong smells of ethner, Ren doubts it'll be able to spot them, but when it points its muzzle towards the pines, its eyes flashing in the moonlight, Ren holds his breath.

The guard tugs the fallion's chain and its muzzle turns back to the path, its feet scraping over the ground. Ren lets out the breath, thankful for the unsuspecting guards.

He turns to Cosette, her eyes wide. She shakes the emotion away and they both face the wall, the bottom branches of the pines just inches away from the building. A window is covered by the trees, Ren and Cosette careful to keep away from it's view.

Cosette gestures him over with a swinging arm, her hand on a wide, rectangle downspout. Ren nods at her, this is where they go up at. Ren glances up, his stomach churning at the gently sloping wall towering over him.

It's taller than the trees. By Gadias, was Aster right? Is this impossible?

Ren inspects the downspout, its clasps firmly screwed into the building. The downspout is close to another round metal support on the very edge of the building. Between the clasps and the support, it *should* be possible to get to the top. A sweaty palm or slipped foot could be the death of them. Ren's waist is still soaked, his boots slippery, but his hands are dry.

Ren is about to open his mouth to voice his concerns to Cosette, but she's already hauling herself upwards, the clasps and downspout proving themselves to be sturdy. Ren grits his teeth, embarrassed that the younger Raider has more confidence than he does. Once she has cleared twice his height, he follows.

The metal downspout is cold, Ren grasping it tightly as he pushes off the ground. His left hand desperately latches to the wide downspout, his right getting a good handle on the space between the clasp and the wall. As he ascends, the bottom of his left boot presses into the wall clasp, his right slipping against the corner support to the right, putting him at an awkward angle.

Gadias, give me strength!

For a while, the scent of pine overtakes him, the trees brushing against his back as he hauls himself upwards. When the small guard patrols pass, Ren and Cosette pause, Ren holding his breath as he waits for the increasingly distant lantern light to disappear around the corner beyond the trees.

Ren's anxiety grows when the branches stop brushing his back, his arms starting to burn. His breath grows labored, but the top gets closer. Cosette has slowed considerably too, the two still pausing when guards pass below. Their lights look tiny and Ren doubts the guards could see them if they were looking, but neither he nor Cosette are willing to risk it.

The stops get more numerous, not just when the guards pass, Ren breathing harder now. He looks back to check for guards, the ground hardly visible in the darkness. The dull moonlight shines off the harbor's waters, Ren swallowing hard to fight off encroaching nausea. He's not afraid of heights, but he is afraid of falling!

His arms scream at him to stop and his hands grow clammy as his body heats up from the movement. The ground is far away, the roof closer now. There's only one option, so he can't wimp out. The wind strengthens, chilling Ren to the bone as it pierces through his wet clothes.

Determined, he lugs himself up a few more feet. His hand tightens around the downspout, his grasp firm. He heaves upwards, but the clamminess makes his hand slip and he lets out a yowl as his feet slip from under him. His right hand tightens on the clasp, his heart racing. Blood rushes in his head, the wind echoing in his ears as he dangles from one hand.

"Ren!" Cosette yells out in fear. She cranes her head around to look at him, panic plain on her face.

The clasp starts to pull away from the building under Ren's full weight.

Shit! No, no!

With a grunt, Ren's feet flail out in a desperate attempt to find something to grab onto again, his left hand slipping against the cold downspout. His right arm shakes, his heart racing. His feet finally find solid footing back on a clasp and the corner support.

Cosette still looks on in panic, watching as Ren finally struggles upwards, getting away from the breaking clasp. He glowers at Cosette, as if to urge her on.

She stays still for a moment, watching the guards below. Ren doesn't dare to look behind him, not wanting to know how far he would have just fallen to his death. He grows frustrated in himself, remembering his shout when he thought he was falling. They're high up, and the waves are loud, but that and Cosette's shout could have put the guards on alert.

Ren just says a prayer to the gods to keep them hidden, he and Cosette continuing after a moment's pause. Cosette moves faster again, Ren's adrenaline fueling him forward.

Just keep going! Don't look down!

Relief floods over him when Cosette hauls herself over the edge of the roof, fear still in her gaze as she extends her arm to Ren. Ren is quick to take it, Cosette helping lug him over the study gutter onto the rooftop.

Cosette falls over onto her back, breathing heavily. Ren does the same, the wind and cold roof cooling off his sweaty body. They remain silent as they gasp for breath for a few moments, Ren the first to sit upright.

Cosette follows. "No way we are going back that way," she whispers, Ren hardly hearing her over the wind.

Ren just nods, thinking if he opens his mouth, his racing heart will leap out his throat. He calms down a bit, swallowing hard before speaking again.

"Agreed," he says.

"Let's—" Cosette takes another swallow of air. "Let's take a breather before going in."

Ren nods in agreement, the two sitting in silence next to each other.

Flickering lights from boats are strewn over the harbor, the silhouette of a beautiful spired building across the round bay. The moons peek out from the clouds again, the city lit with silver rays, looking small from here.

"I hope the guards aren't on alert," Ren says, his voice hushed. "It was stupid of me to yell when I slipped."

"Hey, I yelled too," Cosette says. "The patrol I was watching didn't seem to notice the noise."

"Thank the gods," Ren murmurs. "I'm glad the downspouts worked. It was a good idea, Jericho's a bright kid for noticing them."

Cosette purses her lips at him. "He doesn't like being called a kid," she tells him.

Ren rolls his eyes. "He's not here, I can say whatever I want. He won't know."

"I know and it pisses me off too," Cosette says. "I know what it's like to be that person always looked down on for being young."

Ren frowns at Cosette. "I've known you since you were a kid, it's hard to see you as anything else." Guilt twinges in his belly.

Cosette huffs. "I'm the team's quartermaster for Castus's sake! It feels like I'm constantly disrespected, and Jericho feels the same way."

"I... I didn't mean it to come across as disrespect," Ren says. "You're a great quartermaster, if that means anything to you coming from me."

Cosette softly smiles at him, seemingly unsure of how to respond. "It does. Thanks Ren." She hesitates before speaking up again. "You know, Jericho really looked up to you."

Ren feels his teeth grind, his fists balling against the rooftop. "Really? You want to talk about this here?"

"He told me what you said to him," Cosette presses.

"Of course he did," Ren hisses, making sure to keep his voice low. "You two are *awfully* close anymore."

"I build and maintain his leg," Cosette says in defense, Ren noticing a red blush in her cheeks among the moonlight.

"Right," Ren says, rolling his eyes.

"Don't change the subject," Cosette says. "You *really* hurt him."

"I know," Ren mumbles, placing his chin on his knees. "I've been an ass to him." The guilt grips at his chest and Cosette's gaze softens on him. "I can't take back what I said, as much as I'd like to."

"You can *try* to take it back," Cosette says carefully. "Jericho doesn't have to accept it, but you for once seem to genuinely regret how you acted."

Ren lifts his head and furrows his brow at her.

"You don't think I regret stuff every day?" he hisses.

"Uh," Cosette says. "You sure don't act like it."

"I miss my wife, I miss my daughter," Ren whispers. "I miss Eliska, I miss the rest of the team that died at Fort Vail. I regret not doing more to keep them alive, I regret leaving my family behind. And now I regret pushing Jericho away."

Cosette stares at him, wide-eyed. Her gaze softens as Ren sits on the roof fuming, his regrets eating him like acros on carrion.

"Lets just get into this hangar," he huffs. He stands up, not giving Cosette time to respond. She follows him.

Ren's anger ebbs, Cosette's words sticking with him. Ren would talk to Jericho if the boy didn't keep avoiding him! He hasn't tried to approach Jericho out of respect. Is Cosette saying Jericho might not push him away?

He shakes his head, ridding himself of the thoughts. That's to worry about later. He and Cosette need to focus on this mission and not gossip all night on this forsaken roof.

They step over to one of the skylights, the hatches cracked even at night. An acrid ethner odor lifts up from the hangar's interior, Ren wincing. Through the glass hatches, Ren can't spot lights from any guards, but he sees the metal scaffolding below. The moonlight casts squares of light over the airships, Ren shivering as they face the beasts from above.

Ren cracks the skylight open more, making enough space for them to shimmy through.

"Alright," he whispers. "Let's get in there."

42

THE BLOODDEW
SHIPPING FACILITY

Jean's team returns to the camp with directions for Scotty's team. They found the blooddew shipping facility and scouted the guards and compiled a short document with other useful information. Scotty, Withorn, and Farsing look it over before heading out, Scotty all too aware of Farsing's presence as they walk towards the shipping facility. As anxiety prickles through her veins, she lets out a breath in an attempt to relax. Withorn is on her side and he knows her mission. Katze trots next to her, looking up when Scotty lets out the small sigh.

Darkness has settled over the land, Scotty more comfortable having her face is hidden by shadows. They make their way through the city, passing by a handful of unaware guards.

Scotty keeps an eye on Farsing, noticing Withorn watchful of him as well.

Jean wants them to scout the inside of the facility, the mission document having a rough sketch of where windows are located on the building. Their mission is just to confirm the bombs are being built there, but any extra information, if it can be gathered safely, is welcomed.

Where they would head up a narrow road to get to the university, a fork forms and they step down the sloped path. The road is wide enough for a single carriage and surrounded by woods. Moonlight casts dappled shadows on the road, the small team walking in a low spot bore in the ground by many carriage trips down this road.

"The road is worn," Scotty murmurs. "It looks like this spot gets a lot of carriage traffic."

"Probably traffic towing bombs out of the facility," Farsing comments darkly. Scotty frowns, wondering if he says this from hidden knowledge. Even if he did have hidden knowledge, he probably wouldn't comment on it. He's just making an observation.

Scotty can just barely make out the road turning ahead, but she notices unnatural yellow lantern light through the woods beyond the turn.

"Into the trees," she whispers, pointing ahead to the lights.

Withorn and Farsing don't question her and step into the cover of the patch of woods, Katze following suit.

They sneak through the trees towards the distant lights. At first, Scotty thought it was a carriage leaving the facility. As they near, she realizes it's the front gate, recalling Jean's notes on the warehouse.

"The front gate," Farsing whispers. "This is the western side of the facility, then."

"Well, we can't go that way," Withorn comments.

"Jean's notes said there's a clearcut section around the western and southern sides of the fence," Farsing brings up. "The northern side is the water and the eastern side is apparently overgrown. I think the overgrown side is the best place to enter."

Scotty wants to argue because of her suspicions, Withorn speaking out on those feelings.

"There has to be a better way," Withorn remarks.

Scotty glances at the facility, her mind racing through what she remembers of Jean's notes. Farsing is correct about what the commander's team had mapped. From here, she can see the metal fence and the guards posted at the entrance. Jean's notes said the guards are stationary and don't patrol and Scotty can make out some of the posts on the corners of the yard, highlighted by oil lamps. The old shipping facility sits in the center of the dusty, fenced yard, the windows of the building higher up, close to the roof. It's a huge, dilapidated warehouse butting up to the water. She can't see the far side of the fence, where the supposed overgrown section is, but it's clear they can't enter anywhere nearby. "No, he's right," Scotty finally says. "It's the safest place to enter."

Withorn passes Scotty a hesitant glance and Farsing huffs. "Of course I'm right," Farsing says. "I've been doing missions like this long before you two were even born!"

Farsing takes the lead, beckoning the two along to the far side of the fence. Scotty winces as Farsing stomps through the thicket. They take a wider than necessary path through the woods, the brush getting thicker. Scotty and Withorn step carefully through the sticks, Katze struggling behind them.

"Farsing, be quieter," she hisses to him. "Do you want the guards to hear?"

"There's no path, what do you want me to do? I'm sure plenty of valen or weavers stomp through here," Farsing says. "The guards won't notice."

"It's an unnecessary risk," Withorn whispers.

"Whispering like we are is an unnecessary risk," Farsing retorts. "Now shut up unless you can cut a path better!"

Withorn pushes forward, Farsing huffing when the medic presses his hand into the dewick's chest. "I'll gladly do it better," Withorn whispers.

Scotty steps past Farsing, the dewick fuming at the medic. Farsing stays quiet as he follows them, Withorn careful as he presses through the brush. Scotty grits her teeth, her anxiety rising. She's happy Withorn knows about her mission, but the medic is being standoffish because of it.

They find themselves pressed up against the metal fence, careful to stay silent as they push through the branches. Thick, weaving vines grow over the fence, the browning leaves falling off as Scotty presses into them.

Scotty can see into the yard from her vantage point, thankful for

DOWN IN FLAMES

the darkness to keep her hidden. The lights from the corner guard posts are visible. The overgrown woods cast long shadows in the moonlight all the way to the facility, the side of the building a stone's throw away.

Old shrubbery grows against the building, looking more like overgrown undergrowth from the woods rather than purposeful landscaping. Where shrubs don't engulf the side of the facility, wooden barrels and boxes are stored under the overhang.

That would be great cover, but how do we get in?

Katze rustling at Scotty's side, Scotty getting ready to chastise her for making any noise. She realizes Katze is pawing at the bottom of the fence, revealing a worn out space where weavers or a stray fallion dug under.

Scotty look to Withorn and Farsing, the two nodding in understanding, looking pleased with Katze's find.

Scotty kneels down to assess the hole under the fence.

It's enough for me to get through.

She looks over to Farsing, the older dewick a bit wide in the stomach. Withorn's broad shoulders would have a hard time fitting.

Scotty cups her hands at the dirt, the ground crumbling easily where the critter path is. She digs the hole deeper and wider, Katze even helping, pawing forward and tossing dirt into the brush.

Scotty leans in towards Withorn and Farsing. "I'll go in first," she whispers. "There's plenty of cover alongside the building."

"Good idea," Farsing whispers. He looks down to the grey fallion. "And good find, Katze."

Katze looks up at him happily, tongue lolling out of her dirt-dusted muzzle.

Scotty's gaze shifts back and forth between the guard posts. She can't see the guards, but can hear the deep notes in their voices as they talk and laugh over the wind and waves. With a prayer to the gods, she pulls herself through the hole, her shirt dragging through the loose dirt. Once she's on the other side, she dashes to the warehouse, aware of Katze's feet scrambling behind her. Her heart beats in her ears as adrenaline pulses through her veins, still feeling the rush

331

when she ducks into the shrubbery, pressing her back against the frail warehouse wall.

Her breathing steadies as she assesses her surroundings, satisfied that she hasn't caught the attention of any guards. Her nose scrunches up at the smell of rotted wood, the building dank and old. After a few heartbeats studying the guards, she gestures for the next Raider to come over.

Withorn shimmies under the fence, Scotty having a hard time spotting him as he pushes his way to the warehouse side, the medic keeping low as he strides across the yard.

They wait a few more moments before gesturing Farsing over. Withorn keeps watch of the guards, Scotty holding her breath as the explosives expert struggles under the fence. When he yanks through, the fence catches on his pants and jingles, the sharp sound piercing over the waves.

"What's he doing?" Withorn hisses, his tone accusatory.

Scotty shushes him, her chest tightening. She might have not dug the hole deep enough. Or did Farsing do it on purpose?

Farsing sneaks across the yard, huffing when he's beside Scotty and Withorn, keeping his breaths low.

"What was that?" Withorn hisses to him.

Scotty shoots daggers at Withorn. "Shut up," she whispers, nudging him.

Farsing opens his mouth to defend himself, but stops when one of the guard post lanterns bobs towards them. Scotty shivers when she hears a voice over the sound of the wind and waves. "What was that?"

The Raiders freeze, crouched in the shadows and brush. Katze lays low, her beady eyes locked on the light as it gets closer.

A pair of guards investigate the noise, shadows morphing as the one swings his lantern around to get a good view of the land. He thankfully keeps the light close to the source of the sound.

The other guard speaks up. "Do you think a branch fell on the fence?" she asks. "It's a windy night."

"Maybe," the first guard says, but his tone sounds doubtful.

The shadows warp over the hole where the Raiders entered as the guard's lantern passes over it.

"Here," he says.

"The fallion hole?" the woman asks, leaning up against the fence, uninterested.

"It's dug deeper," he says, kneeling down.

"Oh?' the woman says, crouching next to him.

Scotty's eyes snap around the yard, looking for escape routes. The fence is tall and lined with barbed wire, and the guards are many and armed. Her gaze falls to the water — if it comes to it, that's their only route out, if they don't get shot full of bullets first.

Her muscles tense up, ready to run if needed.

"You dunce!" the woman finally says. "Look, more fallion prints where the hole's been dug out. They must be getting fatter with all the scraps they're eating from our trash."

The man huffs. "Yeah. We'll just shoo 'em away if we see them again. Damned hounds."

"I'll shoo 'em away with my gun," the woman remarks frustratedly, lifting her ethner rifle. "Let's get back to our post. It's too cold in this wind."

The guards turn away, becoming a distant bobbing light again and Scotty lets out a breath she didn't realize she was holding.

Scotty has to stifle a yowl of shock when her shoulder gets prodded. She turns to see Farsing standing there, the dewick pointing further into the brush and up a little. Scotty realizes he's pointing at a window, higher up, but still hidden behind the bushes. Withorn is able to stand under it, looking upwards.

"All the windows are too high to scout properly," Withorn whispers. "Doesn't matter that this one is covered."

Farsing gives him a blank stare. "Scotty weighs less than that cabinet you carry around all day," he whispers. "Lift her up there!"

Scotty's face scrunches up at the idea of Withorn lifting her up, but it seems to be their only option. Definitely a helpful idea on Farsing's part, but it could just be a trick to hide suspicion from trying to tip off the guards.

Withorn sighs and kneels down.

"Get on my shoulders," he says, unamused.

Scotty presses her palms on his shoulders, shuffling her legs up around his neck. She hears Withorn swallow a breath as he lifts upwards, stifling a grunt. He topples uneasily, Scotty pressing her hands on the splintery siding to help stabilize them. The wood flexes a bit under her weight and for a moment, she fears she will fall right through the wall.

"You're supposed to be light!" Withorn bites out through gritted teeth.

"And you're supposed to be strong," Scotty remarks.

"Focus, you two!" Farsing whispers.

Withorn finally finds his balance, hands wrapped around Scotty's calves as he lifts her upwards. She glances behind her, making sure she's well within the cover of the tall brush. The soft lantern lights at the guard posts flicker through the bushes, almost hidden from view.

Satisfied, she turns back around, being faced with her reflection in the dusty window. She cups her hands around her face and leans in, the smell of the wood dry up here.

Her eyes adjust to the new darkness beyond the glass, and she makes out faint silhouettes in the massive building. Nearby, she sees workshops tables and massive industrial looking machines, the silhouettes blocking a majority of the room. It's hard to make out anything in the darkness, but the lack of light means one thing: no guards patrol inside.

Scotty jabs her heel into Withorn's ribcage, and the medic lets her down, the rotten wood smell growing stronger.

"What's it look like?" Farsing whispers, excitement glimmering in his dark eyes.

"There are a lot of machines in there," Scotty whispers. "But I can't see much in the darkness. There are no guards, so if we find a way inside, we shouldn't have any troubles."

"We're far from any door," Farsing says.

"And the windows are too high to get in," Withorn says. "Even if we could get one open and I get you in there, you wouldn't be able to come out."

Scotty frowns, another wave of the pungent odor of rotten wood hitting her nose. Her face scrunches up, but realization strikes her. She falls to her knees, the ground damp, and she brushes her hand along the siding towards the bottom. She feels a weak spot and presses in slightly, the wood flexing under the pressure.

"What is it?" Farsing asks.

"Don't you smell it?" Scotty asks. "Rotten wood!"

"My sense of smell has been destroyed since I started working with ethner," Farsing comments.

Farsing kneels down next to her, Withorn crouching on the other side. They poke at the wood and find the weakest spot, Withorn's finger pushing through it.

"This building's old," Farsing whispers. "Looks like it's been flooded a few times and never repaired."

"The *perfect* place to produce ethner technology," Withorn comments sarcastically.

"Do you think we can pick our way inside?" Scotty asks.

Farsing ponders for a moment and nods. "If a rodent can do it, we can do it, I'm sure. But a hole will be suspicious. Scotty, I think if you go inside, we can keep the hole smaller and hide it from the guards more easily."

Scotty frowns at the idea of going inside alone. Farsing does have a point, though. "I can do that," Scotty finally says. It's a helpful point, doubts of Farsing being a traitor growing stronger.

Without another word, the three pick at the rotten wood, making a hole just wide enough for Scotty to shimmy through to the side of a stud. A layer of soft paper is on the other side, Scotty dragging her daggers through it. Balsam wool is packed into the paper, the stench of mold spilling out with the dusty wood. Scotty pushes her way through the hole, piercing through another layer of rotted wood on the other side.

Scotty pulls herself to her feet in the warehouse, the musty scent of the room strong even over the ethner odor. She steps through the old room, the sounds of the wind and waves muffled from here.

She gets her notepad out and jots observations down about the room: the strange machines, the smell, the roller doors towards where the building butts up to the small port.

It has the same technology as Hayward City Steel's factories, Scotty almost imagining herself walking among one of their faculties in the country's capital.

The warehouse is deep and creaks in the wind, Scotty half expecting it to fall down on top of her. Her eyes fall on the notes scratched on the paper, tiredness already tugging at her. The building has three distinct stations, one with the presses, one with newer welding gear, and one with large hoists. Odd looking shells sit on the welding station's tables, abandoned to be worked on again in the morning.

Scotty finds some parchments near the shells squinting to see them in the darkness. Her heart sinks into darkness when she realizes it is instructions — instructions to build a familiar shape, one she saw falling from the airships to fall onto Ghent's capital. A pointed oval with a tail, much like a small, wingless airship.

She was already certain this is where the bombs were being built, but seeing the proof in her hands, and the realization of the volatile technology around her makes her shiver. When she notices other similar instruction pamphlets around, she folds up the one in her hands and tucks it deep into her pocket for safe keeping. The rebellion might find it useful. She continues stepping through the warehouse, her heart thumping hard.

Well, our suspicions are confirmed. We can work towards taking this place down.

Scotty glances around, noticing a suspicious lack of finished explosives. The last station is where she assumes the final assembly would happen, if it is anything like Hayward City Steel's factories. Large, metal hoists indicate that big, heavy items are processed here. No big items are to be seen, Scotty only being faced with the closed roller doors going towards the port.

Have bombs already been shipped out, or have they not been built yet?

Massive metal boxes sit by the roller doors, the boxes used to ship ethner a familiar sight to Scotty. More than a dozen crates of the acrid liquid are here, enough to destroy this whole facility in an accident. Scotty makes a note where they're located.

The faint moonlight cuts through the high windows as the autumn clouds part. Dust pirouettes in the rays, the light bringing Scotty's attention away from the ethner boxes to a desk at the far side of the room.

The desk is relatively tidy, but Scotty's eyes fall on a tray on its corner with a handwritten label reading "Unfinished Work Orders."

She pulls the parchment out, noticing the date: Baymoth 5th, Alignment 26, Year 271. That's today. She reads over the details, anger boiling inside her. It is a request for the students to build thirty ethner bombs for the Valkoeans. She has to force herself to relax when her hands start to crumple the paper.

Hope replaces the anger when she notes the date it must be completed by: Baymoth 14th, Alignment 26, Year 271. It stresses that they need shipped early in the morning on the fourteenth, but provides no further detail.

Is that date when the Valkoeans plan on bombing Hightower Harbor?

Excitedly, she copies every word of the work order into her notepad. She puts the order back in its place and makes her way back to the hole she entered from. She scoots an old crate labeled "Eve Hallow Orchard" over her entry point, meeting Farsing and Withorn on the other side.

She tells them what she found they head out. Withorn races to the fence first, then Farsing, the dewick getting through the fence quietly from this angle. Once they've cleared the other side, Scotty and Katze dash over next, stifled by the shadows. Scotty ducks down to dive into the hole, she has to hold back a yowl when she's faced with twitching white whiskers. She pulls back in fear when she catches the amber gaze of a sharfawks. She falls back on her butt, her heart racing. She stares forward confusedly when she realizes the sharfawks is gone, Katze already slipping in after Withorn and Farsing.

"What are you doing?" Farsing hisses. "Hurry!"

Scotty blinks. They didn't see the sharfawks there? She shakes her head to try to clear her mind and pulls herself through the gap, Withorn reaching an arm out to help her up. As they flee through the woods, the gaze of the sharfawks stays burned in her mind, the darkness from its presence lingering.

Was that Cassius again? What does he want from me?

She tries to stay optimistic, but she can't help but feel it was a dark omen.

43
INTO THE HANGAR

Ren slips into the skylight, his feet landing on the scaffolding with a thud. Ren winces at the noise, but turns his attention up, catching Cosette to make her landing softer.

Moonlight washes over the airships below them, the massive beasts nearly reaching the hangar's ceiling. Ren wonders how many people — and how many bombs — can fit in them.

He makes a mental note of where the guards are below, toting small lanterns like the exterior guards. All of the guards are scattered throughout the hangar's floor, the scaffolding dark and empty. Chemical smells puff up from the ground, bringing a warm, stale air.

"Should we go down now?" Cosette whispers hesitantly.

Ren nods. "Our priority is finding a way to get the others inside, but we'll see what information we can get on these beasts. I take it not a lot of rebels have been this close to them and lived."

They make their way across the top layer of scaffolding, Ren's hands clasping tightly on the metal railing. They're careful to keep their footfalls quiet, but the scaffolding sways from side to side, Ren's heart tightening in his chest. It feels like a sudden movement would take the whole platform down.

The platform moans as they descend the stairs, keeping to the spots void of moonlight to avoid the attention of the guards. Luckily, the rushing wind outside makes the building creak louder than the platform.

As they get to the lower platforms, Ren stares at the airships in awe. They descend near a red Valkoean airship, brandishing its name, Explorer V004 on the back. Its huge wings are folded at its side like a sleeping bird. Its body is a bit deflated, its massive skeleton sticking through like the ribs of a hungry fallion.

They dodge the lights of the guards and reach the hangar's floor, Ren thankful to be on solid ground again. He takes another glance at the airship, his neck aching as he struggles to see the top. Even the platform they entered on looks small from here.

He looks to the slumbering wings, remembering Markos's words on how to cripple the airships — puncture the wings. Ren wonders how that would even be possible, the sails are so massive and so high up! Surely a bullet wouldn't be enough to destroy it.

Below the wings are what look like valves. Ren thinks back to his interrogation and decides that steam must come out of those to help fill the sails and lift the ships.

The bottom of the airship has some kind of large housing facility made of metal with windows wrapping around it. Steam engines are on the sides towards the back, two of them on this side.

Ren brings his attention away from the airship to try to focus on their mission — finding an entry point. He cranes his head around, looking for any place they might be able to let their comrades in at. The windows are all out in the open, too difficult of a space to enter at with the guards in the building. Ren also tries to keep his eyes on the lights bobbing around the hangar in the distance, wary of the guards' presences.

Ren nearly runs into Cosette, the woman suddenly stopped. He wants to hiss at her to move it, but she points forward, eyes wide.

Ren glowers and follows her finger, seeing the rear of the airship, a back hatch wide open making a ramp into its belly. Deep within are oval objects secured on wooden stands, the shape all too familiar.

"Bombs," Ren whispers to Cosette.

"A lot of them," Cosette whispers back. "This is awful."

Ren looks around to the other ships. Are they all just as full? His heart sinks, Cosette speaking his concerns out loud.

"Are we too late?" she breathes.

Ren is about ready to get out, but a sudden wave of optimism rushes over him.

"No," he whispers. "We have the perfect opportunity to destroy them! They're full of explosives. We just need to set them off and the whole building will fall."

Cosette smiles at him. "You're right. But how do we do it? We can't be too close, we don't know what the range of the explosion will be."

Ren frowns. "We will consult Farsing. He should know. This is great information." He looks around. "Now let's shut up and move along."

Cosette nods and they continue sneaking around in the shadows, still hugging the side of the building closest to where they entered the skylights. They confirm that some of the other airships are loaded up as well, careful as they investigate the massive beasts. They near the corner of the facility, changing their pace as the guards meander around, sometimes backtracking before finally moving forward.

They come across an office door, Cosette frantically gesturing at Ren to go inside. He quickens his pace and slides in, Cosette carefully closing the door behind them. Frosted glass on the door glimmers in the peeking moonlight, the room illuminated slightly by dirty windows on the far side.

"Was there a guard?" he asks, his voice low.

She cocks her head at him and then shakes her head. "There might be useful information in here."

Ren frowns. "Right now we need to focus on ways to get the others inside, not raid the office," he whispers. "There are guards out there."

"This is just as important," Cosette assures him.

"We can't be wasting time," Ren says.

Cosette hushes him, making Ren's blood boil.

"Calm down," she hisses. "Start looking for information."

"No!" he whispers. "We need—"

A thump sounds as a strong gust of wind makes the building creak, Cosette and Ren freezing. Once the wind calms down, footsteps echo outside the door. The frosted glass glows yellow as a lantern nears.

"Hide!" Ren whispers.

They duck further into the office, Cosette nestling between the wall and a bookshelf. Ren dives under a desk, pressing up against the front cover, his heart racing. He grabs at his revolver, ready to use it if needed.

After a few moments pass, he peeks around the desk to check the door, the yellow light growing dimmer as the guard passes the door.

Cosette starts rustling again, pulling binders from the shelves, placing them on the desk. Ren pulls himself from his cover, tucking his revolver away as he turns to Cosette.

"Really, what on Harkive are you doing now?" he whispers.

"Ren!" she whispers excitedly, looking up to reveal wonderment shining in her blue eyes. "I've found schematics for the airships! There's a whole wealth of information in here!"

Ren scrunches his nose at her naïvety. "What's it matter if we're going to destroy the things? We have a solid plan, don't mess up this mission by letting curiosity get the best of you."

"You think the Valkoeans won't try to build more?" Cosette asks, ripping pages out and tucking them into her field bag. "And what if the rebellion wants to build their own?"

"Build their own?" Ren echoes. "They hardly can fund their arms."

"Things change," Cosette says, replacing the defiled binders.

"Don't you think the Valkoeans will notice their notes ripped up?" Ren asks.

"What's it matter if we're going to destroy the building?" Cosette asks in a mocking tone.

Ren frowns, his blood boiling at the young woman.

"You've found some information, now let's go do what we're actually here to accomplish," Ren says.

Cosette smirks at him, seemingly happy to know she struck a nerve with Ren.

Ren heads towards the front door, growing irritated when Cosette stays behind in the office. He decides to keep quiet as he peers through the frosted glass, only seeing faint lights in the distance.

He turns and gestures to Cosette, now is their time to get out.

"Cosette," he hisses when he sees her at the back of the room.

"Ren, look," she says, paying no mind to his harsh tone.

Ren realizes she's peering out the window's back office — a possible exit point. He steps across the office to be at Cosette's side.

"Get back from the window," he whispers. "Guards might see!"

Cosette points out the window and Ren realizes there's no chance of the guards seeing inside. Soft moonlight cuts through a copse of pine trees outside. This is the window by the place they climbed up at, covered well by the trees.

"This is the place we can get in at," Cosette says. "The guards won't be able to see from the outside, and they seem more preoccupied with patrolling the hangar compared to the office."

Ren frowns. He misjudged Cosette. Coming in here was the best thing they could do for this mission.

Cosette huffs. "But it's not like we can leave the window unlocked." She pulls the lever style lock to the open position, cracking the window. "It's a bit obvious."

Ren looks at the locks, Cosette stepping aside for him to investigate it. He pulls a knife from his field bag, cutting the part of the wooden lever that holds the window in the locked position. He does that on the window's second lever, pushing them back into what looks like the locked position. He then pulls the window open, still appearing locked.

"Clever," Cosette whispers, putting a hand on her hip. "Let's pray to Castus the wind doesn't open it or whoever uses this office doesn't like to work with an open window."

"With any luck, we will only need this space for one more night," Ren says. "It's hardly noticeable and quieter than breaking the glass. It's less of a risk any way you look at it."

Cosette purses her lip. "I suppose you're right." She looks out the window, a pleased smile spreading over her face. "How about we get back to the others to let Aster know he was wrong about our plan?" Her tone is sly and for once, not aimed towards Ren, much to his relief.

Ren can't help but to let out a quiet laugh. "With what we found today, we might not need a way to sneak the others in."

44
CONFRONTATION

The sun sets and the flames from the camp's fire send dancing shadows across the pebble beach. Scotty sits beside Withorn, cards in their hands as Withorn attempts to teach her how to play matekart.

The Raiders' spirits are high, Cosette and Jericho passing dinner around to everyone. Some are laughing and telling stories as dinner is served, others quiet in content happiness.

Scotty finds herself growing happy among her comrades, but the feeling hits a brick wall when her sweeping gaze falls on Farsing, drinking something and chatting with Connie and Reagan. This mission is a small misstep away from being a disaster, and Farsing could be the link to the destruction. He's been helpful, so doubts prick at Scotty.

Scotty and Withorn place their cards on the ground when Cosette and Jericho hand them bowls of bean stew. Scotty breathes in the warm, savory smell, recognizing it as Jericho's recipe. He had served the same meal to Withorn and Scotty the night they met him.

"Cosette, I think Jericho is vying for your job!" Withorn calls out over a mouthful of food.

Scotty laughs when Cosette shoots daggers at Withorn, Jericho looking flustered at her side.

"I'm better off as an assistant!" Jericho blurts out. "Besides, I don't know how to clean a gun, I could never do her job!"

Cosette's frustration at Withorn turns to amusement at Jericho's panicked answer.

"I appreciate the assistance," Cosette says with a laugh. "But everyone's fed, so relax and eat."

With that, she walks away, Jericho sitting next to Scotty and Withorn. He looks at their card game, quietly eating a spoonful of soup.

"Not eating with your girlfriend tonight?" Withorn asks.

"She's not my girlfriend!" Jericho whispers. "W-why do you think that? Did she say something to you?"

Scotty laughs. "You two spend *a lot* of time together."

"So do you and Withorn," Jericho shoots back.

Withorn makes a gagging motion and Scotty's face scrunches up, Jericho laughing at their expense.

"I think you two get a long a lot better than me and Scotty," Withorn remarks.

"I... I like Cosette," Jericho says. "She's a good friend, she's helped me a lot with my leg."

"Ask her out already!" Withorn says, gesturing wildly with his arms, soup bowl sloshing around. "By Nikos! You two obviously like each other!"

"Is it really obvious?" Jericho whispers.

"Even to me," Scotty says.

Jericho turns to look at Cosette, his blue eyes shining as he watches her. The happiness fades and he sighs.

"I wouldn't do that to her," Jericho says. "Especially since I might have to leave soon."

"What?" Withorn asks, swallowing and swiping his arm across his mouth. "Leave the Raiders?"

Scotty frowns. She has hardly had time to train Jericho, and even then Scotty's not a great teacher. They tell Withorn about Jean's impossible task, the medic growing angry as they speak.

Withorn stands up. "I'll talk to Jean!" he exclaims. "Jean couldn't even beat Aster!"

"No!" Jericho says, shooting up to grab Withorn's arm. His movement on his prosthetic has improved greatly, wobbling only slightly at the fast motion. "No, sit back down! I've decided I'll give it my best, even if my best isn't enough." Jericho's voice crackles as if he's damming back tears.

Withorn looks like he still wants to go chew Jean's ear off, but he nods and sits back down. "You're really certain about that?" he asks.

Jericho nods. "Sometimes life isn't fair. I learned that when I had my dad ripped away from me. Being a failure here... it isn't the worst thing that could happen to me."

"You're *not* a failure," Scotty tells him. Her hands tighten around her soup bowl. Jericho needs to avenge his father. There has to be a way he can still be in the Raiders.

Jericho lets out a pitiful laugh. "Not yet."

Everyone quiets down as Jean stands up, moving to the front of the fire to address the team. Scotty stops eating and puts her bowl down to focus on the commander. He should be going over their intel from the day and coming up with a plan to take out the shipping facility and hangar before it's too late.

The smoke twists over Jean's face, the fire gently crackling as it casts orange highlights over his trench coat. The bags under his eyes look deeper in the fire's shadows, making the commander seem more stressed than usual. Scotty almost thinks she sees a reddish aura around him, but when she blinks, it fades.

It was probably just a trick of the light from the fire.

When he talks, the stressed look melts away and his voice booms with confidence. "We got some vital information today," he begins. "Information without which the rebellion would surely fall. The shipping facility team found that there is a set date for the Valkoeans to make their move on Hightower — nine days out from today. The hangar team found an easy way in and learned that the airships have already started to be loaded with explosives."

Goosebumps crawl over Scotty's skin, imagining the bombs dropping on Vincent again. The goosebumps turn to dread when her gaze falls on Farsing.

Jean's voice pulls her away from it all as her doubts start to take over.

"We have plenty of time, but Aster and I have decided that we will act on this tomorrow night," Jean says.

Agreeable murmurs spread through the Raiders.

"Farsing," Jean says, nodding at the dewick. "I wanted your input on the mission as the team's demolitionist."

Scotty glances at Aster, the deputy shooting her a worried look. She wants to urge Aster to speak out against Jean's request for Farsing's help, but the deputy stays silent.

Aster! Do something!

Farsing nods. "My advice is to blow them up!" He laughs.

Jean sighs and shakes his head.

"Well, if the airships are already stuffed with explosives, it'd take one well placed shot to take the whole hangar down," Farsing says. "It'd take some calculating to figure out the scope of the explosion. As for the shipping facility, one ethner grenade to the ethner shipments by the bay doors would ruin their entire supply and possible fall that whole piece of shit building. It wouldn't be an explosion, but it'd sure be destructive. But that all just seems like common sense to me."

Scotty muses over Farsing's words. There are no holes to pick in his plan, it's pretty cut and dry.

"If we want it done at the same time, we'd only need two men on the mission," Farsing says.

"We'll bring the whole team into it," Jean says. "As soon as the buildings fall, we need to be on the road to Hightower Harbor again. We won't need our valen or carriage full of explosives, so they can just remain at the stable here. It'll be a better life for the valen anyhow." Jean looks to the rest of the team, his blue gaze stopping on Aster. "Does anyone have any concerns about that?"

Silence falls over the group, Scotty hoping Aster can think of a way to speak out against Farsing. Doubt pricks at her. Is Aster's lead just wrong? As she looks at Aster, she wonders if he thinks this too.

Aster stands up, pacing over to Jean's side.

"We're going to solidify the plan tomorrow morning," Aster says. His head is turned towards Jean, half of his face covered in shadows from the flickering fire. "When we have the veil of shadows to cover us at night, we'll be able to safely take this on."

"Why don't we just do it now?" Farsing asks through a mouthful of food, leaning back on a large rock.

Murmurs of agreement roll across the Raiders.

"I'm exhausted, but if it's as easy as Farsing says, I'm down," Merryweather remarks excitedly.

"It makes sense," Ren comments.

"Right now?" Jericho asks in a panic.

Jean opens his mouth to speak, but the deputy's voice booms out.

"We will *not* do it right now," Aster says firmly. "We need to rest up and Jean and I need to plan this out. We have over a week to get this together. We are rushing it as it is, no need to rush it more."

Jean nods at the deputy's words. "We mostly need to plan a route out of the city. If word on the destruction gets around faster than we can move, the causeway could get shut down, and that could be disastrous for us. We need to be quick, but most importantly, we need to be careful."

Farsing shrugs. "I suppose I could use some sleep."

Scotty's anxiety lifts. Aster is buying her time to investigate Farsing. She *must* find something tomorrow, or risk the rebellion falling.

———

The night passes, Scotty awoken by nightmares throughout her sleep. Cassius is there in the form of the sharfawks, his gaze burning into her from afar. Scotty runs through the void, but the distance between them stays the same. Despite her body running, it's like her mind is pulling back towards him. The Raiders are there with menacing faces of darkness, the blackness suffocating like a weight on her chest.

She wakes up, heart racing, Cassius's gaze burnt into her mind.

She trembles as she pushes her bedroll open, shaking the nightmare away.

It's just a nightmare. Don't let Cassius get to you.

The gaze of the dark god refuses to leave her mind and she shivers, unsure if its from the cool fall morning or from the eerie feeling that won't leave.

She sighs, the tent walls feeling like they're closing in on her. Grey fur stirs beside her, Katze raising her head. She looks uneasy, as if Scotty's dark dreams had also reached her companion.

Scotty's hands rake through Katze's fur, and she relaxes with Katze's warmth. Katze also calms down, eventually getting up and giving herself a good shake in the tight confines of the tent.

"Katze!" Scotty whispers, laughing when her long, fluffy tail smacks over her face.

Katze slips out of the tent's flap, knocking over Scotty's bag in the process. A few things spill out and Scotty starts pushing the stuff back in. Her hand stops on Hartwood's lighter, the honeycomb symbol catching her eye. She picks it up and looks it over, thinking of the pull she felt towards Cassius in her dream before stuffing it into her pocket.

Scotty gets ready for the day and follows Katze. The morning is wet, a layer of dew formed over her tent. The clouds are puffy and grey, moving slowly as the fall breeze blows on the surface.

Katze's muzzle points upwards, her haunches placed in the gravel. Scotty follows her gaze, Katze looking up into the branches of the forest behind the camp.

A faint flash of yellow stands out among the orange leaves — a messenger swift perched in the branches. The soft yellow and grey feathers are familiar, a single black streak on its crest. It stares down at them, moving its head around as it assesses the camp. It has a leather strap around its chest.

Scotty frowns. She thinks its the same messenger swift she saw when they first entered the city. Is it following them? Is it lost?

Before she can think too much about it, Jericho's voice brings her attention away.

"Hey, Scotty."

She turns around to face Jericho, casting one last glance to the trees, noticing the bird has already flown away.

"Er, what are you looking at?" he asks.

"It was just a messenger swift," Scotty says. "He might have been lost." Paranoia prickles through her. *Or taking a message of espionage away.*

"Poor guy," Jericho says, genuine concern in his tone. "I hope he finds his way home."

"Did you need something?" Scotty asks.

Jericho nods, looking a bit distracted. "Let's spar. We have some time this morning, and I have strength to build up."

"Sure thing," Scotty says.

The rest of the camp is nearly awake, Withorn one of the few still snoozing in his tent. Aster and Jean talk among the coals of last night's fire, Merryweather there to advise her old friend.

Scotty gets her twin daggers and she and Jericho head to the water where the waves gently lap at their feet over the pebbles of the beach. Katze steps over with them, laying down in a dirt patch where the pebbles end.

Scotty faces Jericho, daggers held up defensively. She finds her vision trailing behind him, Farsing stirring awake out of his tent. She grits her teeth as she thinks about how to investigate him. He lingers by his tent, but he should leave it unguarded at some point and Withorn can help her when the medic finally wakes up.

"Ready?" Jericho asks, pulling Scotty's attention back.

"I'm ready," she says.

Scotty lunges first, Jericho's new style more stationary. He blocks her first blow, swinging his blade back around to lash at her. She jumps back, his blade crashing into the gravel. Her feet scramble as she rushes him again, pulling around the back. Jericho pivots and blocks her blows skillfully, stepping towards her, retaining his strong stance.

Jericho grunts and yowls as they slash at each other, moving with more ease as they go. He's become stronger than she ever expected.

Maybe losing his leg has motivated him more than when he first joined.

The first few fights, Scotty is able to use her speed to knock Jericho off his feet and overpower him. As they go, Jericho grows more determined, Scotty losing a few fights. Pride whelms in her chest at his growth, but it's a long stretch away from beating Aster.

Scotty's stomach growls, her arms aching as they spar. Jericho keeps insisting they spar longer and Scotty go harder on him. Her attention keeps snapping back to the camp, searching for her chance to investigate Farsing.

Withorn finally stirs awake, the medic poking his blond head out of his tent flap.

Jericho knocks Scotty to the ground with a sheathed sword hit to the chest, knocking the wind from her lungs. She heaves on the ground, Jericho extending an arm to her.

"Er, sorry," he says. "I think I went a bit too far."

Scotty takes a moment to regain her breath, wincing at the pain. "Going too far in a spar means your opponent is dead," she says. "You're fine."

"You good?" he asks, concern flickering in his blue gaze.

"Yeah," she says. "I'm fine..." Her gaze trails back to Farsing. "Er, can we take a break? I, uh, I have to—"

"Of course," Jericho says, though Scotty doesn't think he means it by his tone. "You don't need a reason. We need to keep our strength up for tonight after all."

"Are you sure?" Scotty asks, unconvinced by his tone.

"Yeah. Thanks for the help, Scotty," he says.

Scotty grits her teeth, but tries to hide it. She wants to stay back and help him more, but she can't explain to him what she needs to do. There's no point sowing more doubt among her comrades. Jericho has other things to worry about right now.

"I'll be back soon," Scotty tells him, turning around to head back into the small camp. She tells Katze to stay with Jericho, the fallion cocking her head at the command, but decides to listen.

Scotty finds her way to Withorn's side, the medic blinking tiredly at her, a cup of tea in hand.

"What do you want?" he grumbles.

"I need your help," she says. "Can you distract Farsing? I want to investigate his tent to see if I can find anything incriminating."

Withorn downs the rest of the tea, placing the cup in the gravel. "Yeah, I think I can do that. Now?"

"Yes, now," Scotty says.

"I can't wake up a bit more?"

"Withorn," Scotty bites out.

Withorn lets out a small laugh and waves a dismissive hand at her. "I'm joking. Kinda. I'll help." He's starting to look more awake. "Er, how should I do it?"

"I don't know, just talk to the guy," Scotty says.

"I'll think of something," Withorn says. He turns around to find Farsing in the little camp. "Good luck," he bids quietly.

Scotty watches as Withorn gets to Farsing's side, chatting with the dewick. Luckily, Jean and Aster join them, which will certainly buy her more time. Scotty assumes the commander and deputy want to bring the explosives expert into the discussion for safety reasons. Probably an idea from Jean, but she's thankful Aster is there too, so he can make sure their plans will definitely keep the team safe.

When Withorn makes sure Farsing is facing away from his tent, Scotty sneaks inside on her knees. Her face scrunches at the smell of sweat, booze, and smoke and she has to hold back a cough.

She pulls his pack forward, keeping quiet as she goes through it. She is careful as she digs around, all too wary of the grenades belt strapped to the side.

She places some of the stuff on the stinking bedroll: a couple flasks of alcohol, packs of cigarettes, far too few changes of clothes, a barely used bar of soap.

Her hand brushes against a notebook and excitement flutters through her chest. She flips through the pages, praying to find something incriminating. She frowns when she realizes there are very few notes. They are straightforward notes from their previous missions, nothing that strikes her as possibly being coded. His handwriting is horrendous and everything is written in shorthand, but it's legible in the very least. Doodles of stars and explosions are scattered throughout the notebook, doubt swirling through Scotty.

This isn't an act. Farsing is just like this.

Withorn's voice gets louder outside the tent. It sounds like he's trying to convince Farsing to turn away.

"Oh, so you're going to your tent?" Withorn shouts.

Scotty cringes, regretting pulling Withorn into the mission as she frantically stuffs Farsing's gear back into his bag.

The tent flap snaps open, Scotty freezing with the contents of the bag still in front of her.

"What?" Farsing exclaims. "Scotty, what are you doing?" Anger is strong in his tone.

"Uh," Scotty says, turning around. She looks to the bag. "Oh, is this your tent?"

"Who else's tent smells like smoke and booze?" Farsing spits. "Of course it's my tent! Get out of there!"

"I, uh, thought this was Jericho's tent," Scotty says. She wants to pray to Cassius for Farsing to take the lie, but she stops herself from praying to the dark god.

"Bullshit!" Farsing spits. His hairy hand grabs into Scotty's shoulder and tugs her out of the tent, Scotty letting out a grunt as she falls into the gravel.

"Hey!" she hisses. She can't say she didn't deserve it, but she can't help but to be pissed. "What, are you hiding something?"

"Hiding something?" Farsing echoes in disbelief. "Hiding something? Woman, what are you on about? Don't go through my shit!"

His voice booms over camp, drawing the attention of some of the others nearby, but no one comes over to investigate.

Withorn stands wide-eyed above Scotty, helping her to her feet.

"What are *you two* hiding?" Farsing challenges. "Huh? Is that why Withorn was being so weird?"

"Weird?" Withorn asks.

Scotty hears a buzzing in her ears, growing stronger as the two men fall into an argument. Farsing's voice booms in her left ear, Withorn's in the right. The buzzing grows and grows and Scotty hears another voice shout out, "Shut up!"

Farsing and Withorn freeze and Scotty realizes it was her own voice, the buzzing ever present now, frustration and paranoia bubbling inside her.

I'm sick of this game! We don't have time for this! Being straightforward is the only way!

"We're investigating a traitor," Scotty says, her voice low.

"A traitor?" Farsing echoes. "A traitor?" He starts to laugh, Scotty and Withorn taking a step back as the laughter becomes deranged. He steps closer and closer to Scotty as he speaks, his breath hot on her skin.

"You think *I'm* a traitor?" he growls.

She pushes him aside.

"You untied Markos at the masquerade!" Scotty accuses.

"What?" Farsing booms.

"You're the only one it can be!" Scotty exclaims.

"The only one?" Farsing says.

His brown gaze stays locked with Scotty's, the two scowling at each other. Scotty grits her teeth, more doubts poking through Aster's theory.

"And you'll find proof of this in my tent?" he challenges.

Farsing doesn't let Scotty respond and dips into his tent to pull his bag out. He opens the flap and spills the bag out on the gravel in front of them. "Show me what's incriminating! Show me why I'm a traitor! I think I'm not a traitor because if I was we'd all be fucking dead!"

Scotty looks at the stuff on the ground. It's all just typical gear, nothing indicating he could be traitor. She grows frustrated as she pokes through the stuff on her knees.

"I've lived your life twice," Farsing says. "I've lost more than you could ever imagine, seen more destruction than you could ever fathom, killed more people than you ever could in an entire lifetime! This is all I have left." He gestures around the camp. "These are the only people I can trust, the only place I belong. You think I'd just throw that away? I'm a lot of terrible things, but I'm loyal. At the end of the day, that's the only thing I have, and I'm not letting go of it even when I'm dead in the ground or my brain's splattered against a wall. *I'm. Loyal.*" He looks down to Scotty. "Now, tell me, *what's incriminating?*"

"Well, someone's a traitor!" Scotty exclaims. "Someone has to be a traitor!"

"You're *paranoid*, Scotty," Farsing growls. "Hartwood was the only traitor! None of us would betray the Raiders!"

"You-you don't know that!" Scotty exclaims, shooting up.

"Scotty," Withorn says calmly, placing his hands on her shoulders.

Scotty shakes him away. "Get off me!" she hisses. The buzzing grows louder and her head starts to pound. "Someone is a traitor here, and I need to figure it out!"

"You're so sure about that?" Farsing asks. "If you're *so certain* someone's a traitor, here, I'll help you out!"

45
CONFESSION

Ren's feet crunch over the gravel as he makes his way across the camp, the morning fall air cool on his face. His eyes fall on Jericho, the boy sparring with Scotty. Ren frowns. He's glad Jericho can lean on someone else for training. If the raid in Salina Village taught him anything, Scotty is a good choice as a mentor. She can be very thoughtful and sympathizes with Jericho because of their shared desire for revenge.

Something makes Ren want to approach the boy. He hates to admit it, but Cosette is right. Ren should try to take back what he said. He cringes as he recalls his outburst.

I'm just an idiot.

Ren's attention turns to Aster, Jean, and Merryweather, the three chatting over the remains of the campfire. He thinks about Farsing's idea of having someone shoot the explosives in the hangar that Ren and Cosette found. Jericho is a good shot, maybe putting in a good word for him will help Jean realize he's an asset to the team and drop the impossible task of beating Aster.

Ren inserts himself into their talk.

"Ren," Jean says with a dip of his head. "Is everything okay?"

"Or are you just here to argue about something?" Merryweather asks, crossing her arms at him.

Ren rolls his eyes, but ignores her remark.

"I have a suggestion," Ren says. Merryweather stares at him and he wonders if he's being pushy. "If you're open to it, that is."

"Of course," Jean says. "What is it?"

"You need someone who is a good aim to take out the hangar, someone who is capable of getting it done in one clean shot," Ren says. "I wanted to nominate Jericho for that. The boy's a skilled marksman."

"I hadn't thought of him," Jean says. "You really think he's that good of a shot?"

"He saved my ass with his aim," Ren says. "Absolutely."

Jean considers his words, but Merryweather speaks up first.

"Jericho is young and sure has better eyesight than me," Merryweather says to Jean. "We're talking *long* long distance. I'm a good aim, but my eyesight isn't as sharp as it used to be. I think it's a great choice."

Ren assumes they were talking about having her be the sniper for the mission initially. Her aim was one of the best of the Sunbell City Guild, her quickdraw a force to be reckoned with. Ren didn't know her personally back then, but he knew of her. A small smile twists over his lips at her endorsement.

Jean ponders for a moment and finally speaks. "I'll think about it."

"He's the best one for the mission," Ren continues.

"Yes, yes," Jean says. "I said I'll think about it, Reiner."

Ren wants to argue more, making a bigger case for Jericho and asking if it would solidify Jericho's place on the team, but he decides to not pester the commander further.

"Let us know if you have any other ideas," Aster says, seemingly trying to push Ren out of the conversation.

"I will," Ren says, stepping away from the three.

He glances over to Jericho on the beach, Scotty stepping away from the boy. Jericho looks disheartened, and Ren watches Scotty walking away, wondering what she's doing. Ren sighs, thinking about what Cosette said on the roof of the hangar.

Jericho really looked up to me. Can I make things right again?

A lump grows in his throat as he thinks of the words to say. He swallows his pride and heads towards the boy. Jericho sits in the gravel, petting Katze. She gets up and shakes her pelt before trotting up to Ren, tongue lolling as she greets him. Jericho just frowns at him.

"Jericho," Ren says with a nod. He puts a hand on Katze's head, giving her a short scratch before she settles by Jericho again.

"What do you want?" Jericho asks, his voice unamused.

Ren frowns, the boy's tone stinging him. He freezes, sorting through his thoughts to figure out what to say.

"Well?" Jericho presses.

"I'm sorry," Ren finally blurts out.

The anger melts from Jericho's gaze and turns into shock. After a moment, the anger returns.

"For what?" he asks.

Ren's cheeks grow hot, half in embarrassment, half in anger at Jericho for making him say it out loud.

"For calling you my failure," Ren says.

When Jericho stays silent, Ren speaks up again. "It was a stupid thing for me to say. It was a stupid thing for me to feel. I just felt responsible for what happened to you. I could have prevented it, and it ate me up." He sits down a few feet away from Jericho in the gravel. "I know there's no excuse for what I said. I'm just a shitty person." His heart tightens up as he thinks of Rosie and Curlew back home. He grabs the locket around his neck and thinks of how he's neglected them over the past couple of years. "I always have been. But I'm trying to change that."

Jericho frowns at him, the anger in his eyes fading to sympathy. He lets out a sigh. "You're not a shitty person, Ren. I know what you said comes from a place of care."

"No," Ren says, his fist tightening around the locket. "I was selfish. Thinking you were my failure was just me thinking about myself.

After seeing how it effected you, I just... I realized I'm a shitty person."

"You feel bad because you care," Jericho says. "What you said was shitty, but I don't think that makes you a shitty person."

Ren's throat tightens up and his eyes grow wet. He swallows hard to control himself. He wants to call Jericho naïve, he doesn't know the things Ren has done in his past with the Sunbell City Guild. Ren looks down at the gravel. But that was in the past. Ren joined the Raiders to protect his family. Becoming a father and joining the rebellion has made him soft. He sniffles, growing embarrassed that he's on the verge of tears after being complimented.

Maybe I'm different now. Maybe it's not a bad thing.

"You're a good kid, Jericho," Ren says after he composes himself. "If my daughter ends up being half as good as you are, I'd say I succeeded as a father."

"That's great and all, but I'm not a kid," Jericho tells him.

Ren smirks. "You're a fine young man," he corrects himself.

Jericho looks like he wants to stay serious, but a smile spreads over his lips. "Thanks, Ren. I forgive you."

A wave of relief overtakes Ren. "Do you want to train together again? I have plenty of ideas that I think would—"

"I don't think that'll be necessary," Jericho says, sadness in his tone.

Ren frowns. He's probably content with training with Scotty. He can't blame him, though. Ren is just happy Jericho forgave him.

"I'm planning on sparring with Aster today," Jericho says.

"What?" Ren blurts out.

"If I'm not ready now, I won't be ready in a couple of weeks," Jericho says. "I'll help with this mission, but we'll be passing Jareath on the way back to Hightower Harbor. I'll leave when we're passing my hometown again. I... I know I can't beat Aster. I'll give it my best shot, but I know it's impossible. I've known it from the start."

Ren just nods at Jericho. Ren isn't entirely sure *he* could beat Aster. Anger flares inside him at Jean's impossible task, growing even angrier when he remembers Jean not immediately receptive to the idea of having Jericho as the sniper for this mission.

"Jean's a dumbass," Ren sneers. "If he can't see that you're a fine fit for the team, then I don't think he's as good of a leader as he thinks."

"Do you want to come when I spar with Aster?" Jericho asks. "I... I don't want to go alone. And Scotty seems like she's got a lot on her mind."

"Of course," Ren says. He wants to feel happy that Jericho accepted his apology, but sadness overtakes him. He knows there's nothing he can say to make it better. "If Jean still wants to kick you out after all the progress you've made, I'll rip him a new one!"

"No," Jericho says. "I accepted the terms knowing what it meant."

"Don't just roll over for Jean," Ren says. "It wasn't fair, and you shouldn't stand for it."

Jericho sighs. "We'll see how the fight goes. I appreciate your support though." The hurt in his gaze softens. "And thanks for apologizing."

Ren smiles at him and opens his mouth to speak, but a voice booms over the beachside camp.

"There's a traitor among us!" Farsing hollers. "We're gonna settle this! Everyone, get over here!"

46
BEE & HONEYCOMB

"Farsing!" Scotty booms as the dewick stomps to the center of the camp, bellowing out her mission. "Farsing, stop it!"

"Everyone, get over here!" Farsing calls.

The Raiders gather around Farsing, Jean and Aster pushing towards the front.

"What's this about?" Jean says, his brow furrowed.

Scotty's panicked gaze falls on the commander, his icy eyes turning to her.

"Scotty says there's another traitor!" Farsing exclaims. "I caught her rummaging through my stuff and she started making wild accusations that I untied Markos at the masquerade."

"Hartwood was the traitor," Ren says certainly.

"Was someone working with him?" Cosette asks.

"It's nonsense," Jean says.

Scotty turns to Aster, trying to plead to him with her gaze. She doesn't want to call the deputy out, but she feels herself rearing up to shout at him, the murmurs of the Raiders growing louder.

"Stop!" Aster hollers. "It's my fault she was investigating you, okay?"

"What?" Farsing booms, stomping over to Aster. "You're just a gods forsaken Valkoean, what do you think you know about *anyone* on this team?"

Farsing's words make Aster's gaze grow dark, Scotty shivering at the look.

"Farsing, that's enough!" Jean shouts. "Aster is the deputy, you'd better show him some respect."

"How can I respect him if he thinks I'm against the team?" Farsing asks. "Do you understand what he's saying about me? About my loyalty? Even *you* shouldn't stand up for that, Jean!"

Jean grits his teeth and turns to Aster. Aster's dark gaze grows fearful, like he becomes a young boy chastised by his father.

"Jean, wait!" Aster blurts out before Jean can get a word in. "I-I just—" He looks to Scotty. "We were just worried about you." He lowers his voice. "It didn't make sense that Markos got loose, so we figured we'd make sure no one was working with Hartwood. You seemed stressed about it, so we—"

"That's no excuse to accuse my men of mutiny behind my back!" Jean hollers.

Scotty looks at Jean in shock. She never expected him to raise his voice at Aster like that. Aster looks equally as shocked, dwarfed by the yelling commander.

"I said to drop it, and you just wouldn't listen!" Jean says. He turns to Scotty and when their eyes meet, Scotty sees the red aura around him. He's fuming, the outline of a sharfawks around him, the ears and antlers visible, like the aura Tapscott had.

Cassius?

Scotty is too shocked by the clear aura to say anything.

"I say we take everyone's bags and dump them out in the clearing!" Farsing exclaims, pulling Jean's attention away from her. "Starting with Scotty's! If there's a traitor, we'll surely have proof of who it is then!"

Scotty opens her mouth to speak in favor of his plan, but a voice booms over hers.

"That's insanity!" Aster exclaims. "We aren't doing that." The deputy turns to Jean. "Jean, I'm sorry. We really just thought we were doing what was best for you."

"You should be doing what's best for the *team*," Farsing sneers.

Scotty's gaze snaps around to her teammates glaring at Aster, shocked murmuring still going around the group. As she looks at them, she feels like she can see their prowling faces from her dream, the buzzing noise pulsating in her head. The presence of Cassius is heavy on her soul, the darkness creeping through the camp.

Arguing erupts in the camp, Aster and Jean the loudest of them all. Hartwood's words echo in Scotty's head, his broken movements etched into her mind as he begged in front of her.

I didn't do it! I didn't do what you think I did! I don't know why you are so convinced!

The buzzing grows louder and louder, Scotty's head throbbing at the noise around her. Her paranoia bubbles up inside her, exploding in a loud accusation.

"Someone's a traitor," she shouts. "Someone has to be a traitor!"

The camp falls silent, the team all looking at Scotty now.

"Scotty," Aster says. "Drop it. I think it's clear. Farsing was the only lead, and it was a shoddy one at that. No one is the traitor. Let it go."

"Aster!" Scotty pleads. Did his mind really change so fast?

"What makes you so certain of this, Scotty?" Jean asks.

"Hartwood was so convinced! Hartwood said he didn't do it!" Scotty says.

"Of course he'd say that!" Ren shouts.

"It *was* shocking to me that Hartwood would betray us," Cosette says skeptically.

"Hartwood *is* the only traitor," Jean says firmly.

"How can you be so sure?" Scotty shouts. "Why have things gone wrong? Why was Markos untied? *Someone* is against us!"

Her eyes snap around to her comrades and she trembles. They're all getting closer and closer, just like her nightmares. They all wear looks of concern rather than malice.

"Scotty, are you okay?" Reagan asks.

"Just relax," Cosette says. "We'll get to the bottom of this."

Despite the concerned looks, she still feels like she is being suffocated, her heart racing as her breath shortens.

One of them is a traitor!

She can't handle their gazes on her, the buzzing and pain in her head making her thoughts swirl.

"Get away from me!" she hollers, taking a few steps back.

Withorn pushes through to the front. "Scotty, calm down," he says.

Scotty meets Jean's gaze again, but quickly averts her eyes out of fear of seeing the aura of the dark god again.

"I-I just need to be alone!" she blurts out.

"Scotty!" Aster calls.

Scotty feels her feet moving and she's racing down the beach away from the camp. Voices of concern shout out to her, but she doesn't listen.

I just need to be alone!

She finds a spot along the gravel beach where a couple fuzzy pines grow on the shore, the dirt around their roots eroded away. She sits between them, her heart thumping hard in her chest.

A cold breeze cuts in from the water and Scotty shivers, stuffing her hands into her pockets for warmth. Her right hand brushes over something cold and metallic and she frowns, pulling it out.

Her head throbs harder at the sight of the lighter in her palm — the lighter of the traitor — the honeycomb symbol etched into it. The buzzing in her heads grows louder and a single bee lands on the symbol, as if the gods are mocking her.

The poem from Cassius's chapter of the Good Book echoes in her throbbing head as the bee taunts her.

> As the drone bees
> Leave the hive
> His grasp of the mind
> You cannot hide

Scotty stands up and yowls, chucking the lighter into the waves.

There is no traitor, there is no traitor.

She tries to tell herself that, tries to believe it, but certain doubt pierces her.

"Why do I feel this way?" she shouts.

The grey clouds blotch the sky and she grimaces. The question was aimed at the gods, but she knows they won't respond. She shivers. If they do respond, it'd be from the dark god, Cassius.

"Scotty," a voice says calmly.

Scotty snaps around, Withorn standing on the beach. Katze is at his side, looking at Scotty hesitantly.

"I said I want to be alone!" Scotty snaps, sitting down again.

"You can't be alone right now," Withorn says, walking closer.

His cape bounces on his shoulders as he steps to her, taking a seat next to her on the crook of the pine.

"Maybe there isn't a traitor," he tells her.

"I just feel like there is," Scotty murmurs.

Withorn sighs. "I think you're paranoid, Scotty. It was wrong for Jean to put the mission on you when you started with us. I don't blame you for still feeling afraid."

"I just can't shake the feeling," she says.

"Have you considered what you're feeling is just from Cassius's influence? You seem to have let him in if you realize it or not."

Scotty hesitates as she thinks of what to say to the medic. Cassius certainly has his grasp on her, she has no doubt about that.

"Jean... I think Jean has it too," she says. "He had an aura, an aura of a sharfawks. Of Cassius. Like Tapscott."

Withorn frowns at her. "Are you sure?"

Scotty nods. "Unless it's a trick from Cassius. He's the god of lies, what else can I say?"

Withorn sighs. "He's much more difficult to figure out than Nikos, that's for sure."

"Do you have any medicine that will make these thoughts stop?" Scotty asks.

Withorn shakes his head. "No, all I have is calming tea, but I think you need a bit more than that right now."

Silence falls over the two, the grey waves lapping up at the bottom of the trees.

"I think you need to consider that this is all a trick of Cassius," Withorn says. "He gets into your head and... and he messes with things up there. Storn, Cassius's apostle that died in the hanging, he wasn't okay. Mentally, I mean. I don't want you to go down that route. And I pray Jean isn't already on it."

Scotty shivers at the thought of Jean being under Cassius's influence too. "How do I fight it, though?" Scotty asks.

"I can't say for certain," Withorn says. "But if you work through this paranoia, I'm sure that'll be a good start. Cassius doesn't have control of you. Influence of a god or not, you'll always have free will. I'll help you though it, if it means anything."

Scotty's eyes water and she looks up at the medic. She nods and leans into him, his arms wrapping around her. Katze nuzzles up next to her on the other side, and as she cries, the pain in her head weakens and the buzzing stops altogether.

"When nothing goes wrong on this mission, that'll be a pretty clear indicator that there isn't a traitor," Withorn says. "If this fails, Hightower could fall and that would be the end of the rebellion. If there'd be any time for a traitor to act, it'd be now."

"That's true," Scotty says, his words actually making her feel better. The headache persists, but the logic is clear.

"Once we destroy these airships, I imagine Milos will have Hayward City and Tapscott in his sights next," Withorn says. "Then the streets will burn and we can get our revenge."

Scotty feels the fire burning in her chest once more. "You really think we are that close?"

"It might be wishful thinking," Withorn admits. "But the airships give the Valkoeans a huge advantage, and they've clearly been pumping money and resources into it the past six months. With those out of the question, who knows what that would do to Valko and Mohkan's alliance. If that alliance is weakened, the rebellion and Ghent would have a chance, don't you think?"

"I hadn't thought of that," Scotty says. She imagines storming the streets of Hayward City and seeing the Brunswick Manor and Hayward City Steel fall. Seeing the stupid face of Ezekiel, Mike's brothers, and his parents as everything is ripped from them. The citadel will fall, and Scotty will do everything in her power to make that happen, to get her revenge.

"The mission will go fine tonight," Scotty tells Withorn. "I think I'll feel a lot better when that happens."

Withorn smiles at her. "Good."

The paranoia seeps away from her, strength returning at her renewed thoughts of her goal.

I'll see that Hayward City falls, no matter what! Even if that means defying a god.

47
JERICHO VS ASTER

After Scotty leaves the campsite, Withorn follows her. The rest of the Raiders stand around, murmuring among themselves about the possibility of a traitor. Ren's nose scrunches at the talk.

"Enough!" he shouts. "We have an important mission tonight. Having doubts like this isn't helpful. *Hartwood was the traitor.* Simple as that."

"I should never have entertained the idea of Hartwood having help," Aster says, shaking his head. "I thought I was being helpful."

"Yeah, helpful," Ren scoffs. "Look at what you've done!"

Ren glances in the direction Scotty disappeared at. Her outburst was strange. It's something he wouldn't even expect from Farsing. He wonders what's going on with her, but he trusts Withorn will be able to help.

His mind trails to Hartwood. Every fiber of his being wants his old friend to be innocent, but he needs to trust the team's decision.

But I still don't know why Hartwood would betray us.

The reveal shocked him, and maybe it shocked Scotty too. She doesn't know the team as well as Ren does, so maybe Hartwood's betrayal so soon after she joined made her distrust the rest.

Ren's gaze falls on Aster. But what was Aster's motivation to distrust them?

"Ren." Jericho's voice pulls him out of his thoughts.

"Er, what is it?" Ren asks, still a bit distracted.

"I think now's a good time to duel with Aster," Jericho says.

It feels like a rock sinks in Ren's gut. He swallows and nods. "If that's what you think is best."

"Can you come with me when I ask?" Jericho asks.

Ren wants to be happy that Jericho trusts him again, but only feels sorrow at what's about to happen. "Of course," he says. "Let's go."

Jericho walks with confidence despite his slight limp, Ren trailing slightly behind him.

Aster still looks a bit shaken by everything. He and Jean turn to Ren and Jericho as they approach.

"Jean, sir," Jericho greets with a nod. He takes in a breath and calms himself. "I'm ready to duel with Aster."

"Right now?" Aster asks.

"It hasn't been a full two months yet," Jean says. "Are you sure?"

"I'm certain," Jericho says, failing to hide the shakiness in his voice.

Jean nods. "If you're certain, then sure." He turns to Aster. "What do you think? Are you ready? We have a bit of time before tonight's mission."

Aster nods. "Ready as I'll ever be."

The camp falls silent as the rest of the Raiders disperse, Jericho and Aster standing across from each other on the gravel beach. Aster faces Jericho with his sheathed longsword. The deputy looks bare brandishing the sword without his armor.

Jean and Merryweather stand behind Aster, the commander examining the two closely, and Ren stands at Cosette's side, just behind Jericho.

Aster stands still, watching for the young man's first move. Ren frowns. For Jericho to fight the best, he needs to be the stationary one, but Aster refuses to move.

Jericho bounds at him, letting out a mighty yowl as he leads with his prosthetic. Aster brings his sword down to block Jericho's bayonet, moving with ease out of his armor.

Jericho grunts and stumbles from the force. Aster swings his sword wide, Jericho bouncing backwards, the tip barely missing his gut. Jericho stumbles more, but he takes a firm stance again in time for Aster to barrel down on him.

Aster's longsword swings down and Jericho pulls his sword up in a block, his arms bending from the force. Ren winces at the hit, but Jericho recovers, pushing forward, and Aster leaps back to aim his blow again.

Jericho steps around as Aster swings at him, Ren watching his prosthetic closely. The young man is moving with more ease, still with a limp, but the movement looks natural. He takes a blow here and there, blocking well with his sword, his arm muscles rippling as sheathes meet.

Jericho grows tired, sweat slicked over his freckled face, mouth agape as he calculates Aster's movement.

Aster comes on strong, the deputy's face twisted into a scowl, hollering as he slices his sword around, Jericho retaliating with powerful lashes. Aster reels back and lands a strong blow, Jericho wincing through a well timed block, only taking a single step back.

"You sure can take a strong hit," Aster grumbles.

Jericho looks too exhausted to respond, taking advantage of Aster's slight distraction. He howls as Aster reels back, Jericho swinging low with his blade, nicking Aster in the shin. Aster hisses in pain, stumbling back, but stays on his feet.

Ren can't help but to cheer out, and Jericho smirks, Aster's face twisting in anger. Aster's eyes snap around his opponent and he lunges forward with terrifying speed. Jericho pulls up his bayonet to block, but Aster keeps going, using his longsword as a buffer to ram into him. Aster's boot stomps on the metal foot of Jericho's prosthetic and thrusts him to the ground.

"Gah!" Jericho hisses, falling on his back with a thud.

In a flash, Aster brings his longsword down on Jericho's chest, pressing the metal tip of the leather sheath into his heart.

They both freeze, chests heaving as they pant.

Ren's heart sinks. Jericho gave it his all, but Jean is going to cast him aside. Despite the looming sorrow, Ren can't help but to feel pride — Jericho would never have been able to make it that far when he first joined, prosthetic or not.

Without a word, Aster pulls his sword away and takes a step over to Jean, the two murmuring to each other.

"Jericho!" Cosette bellows. Ren follows her over to Jericho's side, the young man accepting the quartermaster's help to his feet.

"I don't know what I was expecting," Jericho mutters.

"You fought really well," Cosette says.

"You did," Ren adds. "It was impressive. You gave Aster a run for his money."

"Thanks," Jericho says, not meeting the gaze of either of them. "But I'd still be dead. I still lost. I'm... I'm not a Raider anymore."

Ren knows there's nothing he could say to help, but he tries anyway. "Your father would be proud of you regardless."

Jericho looks away, but Ren thinks he sees tears forming in his eyes as he moves.

"Thanks, Ren," he mumbles.

"Jericho," Jean says, the three turning to face the commander and deputy.

Ren can't help but to scowl at them. He wants to shout out, to scream, he wants to beg, his blood boiling as the two look at Jericho.

"It was an impossible task!"

Ren is surprised the voice wasn't his own and turns to Jericho, the young man glowering at the two.

"I fought well, I fought with the strength of Gadias!" Jericho shouts. "You can't turn me away, not after everything I've been through, not after how I've improved!" Jericho thrusts his bayonet into Jean's arms, the commander confused as he takes it. "You show me how easy it is, Jean! You fight Aster! Do it, beat him!"

"Jericho," Jean says, blinking in disbelief.

"Yeah!" Ren cheers. "I want to see *you* beat Aster!"

Jean just stares at them.

"The goal wasn't to *beat* Aster," Jean says. "It was to *fight* him, to test Jericho's strength, so I could see his progress." He turns his icy gaze to Jericho. "And I think you've improved well, you're a fine Raider." He looks to the side. "Er, perhaps I should have made it more clear at the start."

"You think?" Ren spits out.

Jericho's angered expression fades and a few tears roll down his cheeks, now glowing red in embarrassment.

"I-I'm sorry, sir!" Jericho blurts out. "That was rude of me to say! I just— I thought—"

"You thought the goal was to beat me and you accepted it?" Aster asks.

"Yes," Jericho says.

"You're cut from a different cloth," Aster says. "I don't know many sane people who would take up that challenge." He laughs. "Farsing even knows better!"

"I'd do whatever it would take to prove myself," Jericho says firmly.

"And you did just that," Jean says, handing Jericho his bayonet back. "I'm sorry I didn't make myself clearer when I gave you the task. I imagine it caused you a lot of stress."

"I'd say that's an understatement," Jericho remarks.

"I have another task for you, if you're up to it," Jean says.

"Another task?" Jericho blinks. "What is it?"

"Would you like to be the sniper for our mission tonight?" Jean asks. "Ren nominated you for it and I can't think of anyone better to take the shot into the hangar."

Jericho looks to Ren, half in disbelief, then back to Jean.

"Yes, of course!" he blurts out.

Jean smiles at him. "Aster and I will brief you on the plan, come with me, I have a map drawn up in my tent."

"Actually, I'll catch up with you in a second, if that's okay," Jericho says.

"Of course," Jean says. "Don't be too long."

The commander and deputy leave for Jean's tent, Jericho turning to Ren and Cosette.

Ren opens his mouth to speak, but Jericho latches around him, hugging him tight, throwing him off guard. Ren's initial reaction is to shout about being touched, but he wraps his arms around Jericho.

"Thank you for everything, Ren," Jericho whispers.

"Sure thing," Ren says. "Jean's right, you're a fine Raider."

Jericho pulls away. "I really do owe it to you for your help," Jericho says.

Ren shakes his head. "You owe it to yourself for having the willpower. It was all you, buddy."

Jericho just smiles at him and after hugging Cosette, heads away to Jean's tent. Ren feels a smile spread over his face.

Cosette smirks at him. "Well, Reiner, you're more compassionate than I thought. I was wrong all along."

48
THE AIRSHIPS

S cotty and Withorn return to the camp, Scotty embarrassed to face everyone again after her outburst. When she looks around at her comrades, they pay her no mind, and she has to take a deep breath to calm herself more.

There's no traitor, they're your friends, your comrades. This mission will go well, it has to.

Aster is lazing away outside of Jean's tent, exhaustion tugging at the deputy's face.

Jericho rushes up to Scotty and Withorn, excitedly telling the two that he fought Aster and that Jean is letting him stay. Scotty's excitement grows for the fall of Hayward City. Jericho will be here to get revenge for his father's death.

Dinner time nears and Jean calls everyone around the fire where Cosette and Jericho are cooking. Beef steaks from the city's butcher sear over the open fire, sweet potatoes baking under them as bread with butter are passed around. Scotty's mouth waters as the food is served, the savory smells making her stomach grumble. It's not every day they get a meal like this. Jean must be feeling confident about this mission to spend their budget on this.

And I should be confident too, Scotty tells herself, letting herself get comfortable around her comrades.

The Raiders dig in to their feast, the steaks cooked to a perfect medium rare besides Farsing's, who asks for well done. Scotty first serves Katze a quarter of her steak, cut up into small pieces, giving her a small chunk of sweet potato to round out her meal. Katze inhales it all the same, immediately going around to the others to beg for more.

Jean briefs the team on the mission. They will be divided into the same two teams and head to their respective buildings to destroy them. Jericho will be the sniper of the hangar and Farsing will be the grenade-thrower at the shipping facility. The fall clouds blanket the sky in grey, so they won't have the clearest night for the mission, but it will at least be good cover.

After Jean briefs them, they fall into telling stories around the fire, laughing and joking to quell the anxieties of the upcoming mission. Their camp is already cleaned up, minus the fire, everyone's packs ready for a long hike through the night.

It should be an easy and relatively safe mission. Little to no fighting, only a couple of actions need to happen, and the hardest part will be fleeing the city after the destruction. Now, they just have to wait for the shadows of the night so they can do the mission and have a safe escape.

Aster looks a bit down next to Jean, having hardly touched his steak.

"Eat up, Aster," Scotty says. "You need your strength for the walk tonight."

Aster blinks at her as if he didn't hear her. "Er, oh, yeah," he says. "I'm just exhausted after sparring with Jericho. I think I'm a bit out of it."

"C'mon, I'm the one that lost," Jericho jokes, perkier than the deputy.

A small smile forms over Aster's lips. "Well, you'll understand when you're my age, kid."

"Pfft," Cosette says. "You can call us young all you want, but you're not *that* old!"

"You're making *me* feel old," Connie remarks dolefully. Scotty doesn't know how old the former rebel medic is, but he looks to be the same age as Aster and Jean.

"I'll tell you all about old!" Farsing exclaims, mimicking an old man's voice before laughing.

Aster just smiles at them and the attention is pulled away from the deputy. He goes back to picking at the food as Cosette and Farsing joke. Scotty watches him for a moment, unconvinced by his reasoning for being tired. She's seen him fight a battle in armor and march the same night without a complaint. Surely it's not his age getting to him.

Her attention lifts from the deputy as something flickers in the sky in the distance. At first she thinks it's a trick of her mind, but a faint noise hisses out over the voices of the Raiders and the washing of the waves.

The thing turns and lifts higher into the sky and she sees a flash of red, the yellow sun logo of the Valkoean airship bright on the side.

"Airship!" she yells out, almost choking on her dinner.

At her voice, the Raiders all stop and turn, some standing up and gasping.

"An airship!" Cosette exclaims.

"Is it coming for us?" Connie asks.

"We need to get over there," Jean says.

Jean rushes away from the beach, the rest of the Raiders close on his heels.

"Jean!" Aster calls out. The deputy's cry falls on deaf ears as the Raiders bound out, Aster and Scotty lingering behind.

"Did a traitor tip them off?" Scotty asks Aster.

Aster frowns. "I don't know, but it can't be safe to go over there. Those idiots! Let's go!"

Scotty dons her ethner gear and follows the deputy, Katze on her heels.

A traitor! A traitor had *to have done this!*

They follow Jean and the others to the woods atop the hill, dry grasses rustling in front of them. Scotty looks on in horror at the hangar, Valkoean and Mohkan soldiers working as the massive red airship hovers overhead, a second yellow Mohkan one already joining it. A third and fourth airship have already been pulled out of the hangar, huge, huffing steamboats still tied to them with a tow rope. The airships cough from their exhaust, the steam filling their wings and lifting them into the air as the tow rope is cut.

"By Gadias!" Jean exclaims.

As soon as they're clear, another pair of steamboats move forward, the yellow and red bodies pulling from the hangar once more.

"What do we do?" Jericho asks.

Jean scowls. "Raiders!" he calls. "Aim for their engines, their wings, the cargo latch, anything! Shoot, shoot!"

When the airships are in view and begin to rise, the Raiders open fire. Scotty hears the muffled yowls of the soldiers below.

"To cover, to cover!" Jean yells.

The Raiders snap behind the trees as bullets pepper the woods. Scotty hears some of her comrades yell out as she pops more bullets in Tex's chamber.

"I've been hit!" Reagan hollers.

Withorn turns his attention towards her and Jean's gaze snaps around. His eyes meets Scotty's for a moment and she thinks she can briefly see the red sharfawks aura in his fearful gaze, but that's the least of her concerns right now.

Someone here is a traitor! That's why this is happening!

"Shoot again!" Jean hollers. "We can't let them get up!"

Scotty peeks out and gunpowder booms around her. She aims Tex at the airship and fires six hissing shots. She grimaces.

"The ships are too far away!" Scotty shouts. "This is pointless!"

"No, they're not!" Jericho declares.

Valkoean and Mohkan soldiers shoot from the front of the hangar, moving closer and closer to the Raiders as they climb through the cover of parked carriages. Scotty snaps behind a tree as the bark splinters beside her, tasting the acrid steam twisting off the bullets.

She moves back out to fire and hears a hissing boom, the sound thumping in Scotty's chest. A red airship explodes into a cloud of steam, shouts of fear erupting as it crashes to the ground. The massive corrosive cloud is twice the size of the hangar, growing still as it bellows into the air. Scotty's stomach churns at the destruction.

There were people on that airship.

The twin yellow airship jerks in the sky at the explosion's impact but keeps rising.

"Go, go, go!" a command radiates from below and soldiers pour from the hangar, running up the hill. Scotty looks on, knowing even if these were new, untrained soldiers, their numbers are enough to take them out.

Jean grunts in frustration. "Raiders, retreat!" he calls. "Farsing, cover us!"

Scotty retreats with the others deeper into the woods and Farsing's peppered grenades hiss and blow behind her, her stomach turning at the news.

A traitor did this.

Hightower is going to fall.

Who is to blame?

Who do I kill to get revenge?

The Raiders are able to sneak out of the woods and through the city, hiding among the caravans as they cross the causeway to the mainland. Some are injured, though not gravely.

The cloudy sky darkens as dusk settles, the Raiders heading south towards Hightower Harbor. Jean sends Copper back to Milos with a warning message, but Scotty fears it won't give them enough warning.

The airships mockingly chug down the coast, too high for bullets to hit. Scotty can only watch helplessly as they disappear into darkness towards Hightower.

"Dammit!" Jean hollers. "Dammit, dammit, dammit!"

"We should relax for the night," Aster suggests, placing an armored hand on Jean's shoulder.

Jean grunts and pushes the deputy's arm away. "How did this happen?" he breathes.

Scotty feels the presence of the others around her, all too aware someone isn't as they seem. Her conversation with Withorn comes crashing back. If things went well, it meant there was no traitor, but now... "It's because there's a traitor!" she hisses out.

She instinctively turns to Farsing.

"You did this, didn't you?" she accuses.

"Not this shit again!" Farsing says.

"Someone tipped them off!" Scotty says, her gaze sweeping around the shocked faces of her comrades before landing on Farsing again. "And *you're* the only one it can be!" He had to have untied Markos, nothing else makes sense!

"Me?" Farsing grumbles. "What proof do you have? What proof do you want? I got us out of this shitstorm with my bombs! What did *you* do in all this?" Farsing stands tall and looks to the other. "I'm starting to think *Scotty* is a traitor!"

Murmurs swell through the others and panic swells through Scotty.

"I need to see Hayward City burn, to get revenge for Mike's death," Scotty shouts. "I'll do anything to stop *anyone* who stands in my way!"

"Likely story," Farsing mocks. "I'm starting to think there was no *Mike*."

Scotty's blood boils and suddenly she's leaping at Farsing, yowling like an animal as she latches on him.

"How dare you?" she spits.

Farsing digs his hairy hands into the back of her shirt and he flips her over, the breath sapping from her lungs at the impact with the ground. She coughs and chokes as she struggles to suck in air.

"You bitch!" Farsing hisses, reeling up to lash out at her.

Hands grab at him, Jean and Ren pulling him back. Withorn picks Scotty up, holding her arms tightly behind her back.

"Let go of me!" she shouts.

"Calm down and I will," Withorn hisses into her ear. "You're not making a great case for yourself. I know, it was a low blow, but you're accusing him of a lot too."

Scotty's breathing calms again and embarrassment burns hot on her skin.

"Maybe it's not Farsing!" she calls out. "Then it's someone else! It's someone! I saw a messenger swift in the trees of Eve Hallow! It must have taken a message away, a message from a traitor."

"Scotty," Aster says. "Calm down."

"I can't when there's a traitor here! There's no other reason the airship are going up! Aster, I know deep down you *know* this!"

Aster frowns and looks to the side.

"Enough, Scotty!" Jean shouts. He steps up to her and Withorn releases her.

Scotty looks up at Jean, the crazed look in his eyes making him look like an entirely different person. The red aura is plain as day, as if Cassius is staring her down himself. She averts her eyes.

"There is no traitor!" he says. "Our information was just old."

"The information was dated for *yesterday*," Scotty tells him.

"Things change all the time," Jean says.

Scotty's heart sinks. Did her information lead them astray?

"She obviously made the note up," Farsing accuses.

"Farsing, not another word from you!" Jean says.

"Jean," Scotty begs. "What does your intuition say about this? Do you think there's a possibility there could be a traitor?"

Jean's hesitance tells Scotty everything she needs to know. He glowers at her and Scotty sees the aura flare in him once more.

"Are... you okay, Jean?" Scotty murmurs when he takes too long to respond.

"Scotty, you need to get your shit together," he says. "Drop this traitor stuff. I don't want to hear another word of it! If I do, I'm not afraid to kick you off the team!"

"Jean," Aster says. "She's just concerned."

Scotty wants to shout out at him that it's Jean's fault she's on it in the first place, but she knows to hold her tongue. Maybe Aster can talk some sense into him later.

Relax. Calm down. Don't let Cassius get ahold of you.

She takes in a breath.

"I-I'm sorry, Jean," she says.

Jean turns away from her without another word, satisfied.

Scotty watches him hesitantly. She needs to ask him about his connection to Cassius. It's either a trick from the god of chaos, or Cassius's claws are getting deeper and deeper into the commander. She's not exactly on his good side right now. Her eyes point south. Regardless, now isn't the time.

"We need to head south now," Jean says. "Hightower is going to need our support."

49
THE SWORD & THE SHIELD

"Jean, no."

Aster's voice makes Ren turn around in disbelief. "What now?" he says.

"We sent Copper down to warn Milos," Aster says. "There's nothing we can do to stop the airships. They'll drop bombs on Hightower Harbor and the rebellion is *done*. We should... *You* should really think about heading back to Ghent. Ghent will be the next front of the war."

"Aster?" Jean asks, hurt. "You... you wouldn't come with us?"

Aster looks to Jean hesitantly. "Valko is my country. My home. I can't leave it behind, but... it's pointless for the Raiders to stay here. This isn't your battle. More of you can't die for this."

"I don't know if you've noticed, but almost half of us are Valkoean now," Jericho mentions. "Aster, we can't give up."

"I'm staying in my home," Reagan says.

"I can't leave," Connie speaks up.

"It's our fight now too," Cosette says. "We need to avenge the others."

"I ain't going back," Farsing says with a shrug.

"We can't go to Hightower!" Aster exclaims. "With all the men in Cannonsburg, we'll just die."

"Maybe we can help somehow," Merryweather speaks up.

"We can help better if we survive!" Aster argues.

Anger flares in Ren's chest at the deputy's words. If he went back to Ghent he'd be a sitting duck waiting for the Valkoeans to take over the mountains and kill his family. Valko needs stopped now! Somehow. He won't give up.

"Where do your loyalties lie, Aster?" Ren challenges. "You've never been such a coward!"

Aster turns to Ren, the armored man glaring at him. The darkness in Aster's gaze surprises Ren, but he's sure to not show it to the deputy.

"I don't want to see the ones I love die pointlessly," Aster says, hurt in his eyes. "I'm trying to keep you all as safe as I can. I've seen it too much already. The rebellion is done."

Ren frowns and looks to the others.

"What does everyone else think?" Ren calls out. "Do we just let Hightower fall, or do we try to do something about it?"

"If things are too dire when we get there, we can leave," Jean says. "We *have* to give it a chance. Just in case there's *something* we can do."

Aster sighs as Jean's look pleads with him.

The rest of the Raiders cheer out in unanimous support.

"Come on, Aster," Jean says. "I'll be your sword, but I need my shield. We need to do this. For Valko." He smiles at him, though there's sadness in his eyes.

Aster nods at Jean, though the darkness hasn't left him. "For Valko," he says.

50

AMONG THE REMNANTS

The Raiders march through the night towards Hightower Harbor, an air of dread growing as each dark minute passes. Without the carriage to slow them down, they're on the familiar shore near Hightower as the sun rises.

Tiredness tugs at Scotty, her stomach screaming for food after the long march. Her legs ache and her eyelids droop, but the guilt of their failure hurts the worst, cutting deep into her chest.

The grey clouds set a dreary aura over the grassy fields in front of Hightower. The six red and yellow airships hover above the island in the distance, Scotty hardly recognizing it.

Her heart sinks when she sees the ethner steam fogged over the island. What she doesn't see is the unmistakable silhouette of the island's namesake tower or the small skyline of the square.

Her stomach churns.

Is Milos dead? Did Copper get the message to him in time?

Purple shimmers over the water, much like the chemical-ridden water Scotty saw growing up in Hayward City. Some of the ships are up in flames or fizzling in steam. Other ships are moving between the island and shore and cannons boom as the rest fire onto shore, defending the front gate. Scotty hears distant screams and gunshots.

She shivers.

Has the rebellion fallen?

"Commander Jean! The Acros Raiders!" a hissing voice calls from the grass.

The Raiders race over to the source of the sound and Scotty has to watch her step, rebels laying in the grasses, hiding.

Survivors!

The source of the voice is Bramblewood, the woman bloodied and burnt from chemicals, but still alive. She crouches in the grass.

"Get down, get down!" she says, gesturing downwards with her hands. "Valkoeans are around!"

The Raiders crouch in the grass around her, Scotty noticing some of Bramblewood's comrades in rough condition. Some are already bandaged up, but they're all still holding on to life, holding on to the rebellion.

"What's going on?" Jean asks.

"The airships have been slowly bombing the island all night," Bramblewood says. "The damned ships are just out of our weapons' range. We-we can't take them down. It's impossible."

Scotty frowns.

They should have been quicker.

The Raiders are why the rebellion is going to fall.

Milos trusted them.

"The airships have been dropping leaflets, calling for a surrender," Bramblewood continues. "We won't surrender! We won't back down! They've been coming over and bombing survivor camps and boats they realize have rebels on them. They're relentless. We need to stay hidden in the grass, if they do a passover, they'll shoot us down or drop more of those bombs, those gods forsaken bombs!"

Jean considers her words, his face twisting.

"Is Milos... Do you know what happened to Milos?" Jean asks.

One of the rebels speaks up. "We don't know. We only know about the people around us and the people we've seen die. We... we haven't seen him, which could be a good thing."

"Milos did get your message, though," Bramblewood says. "He

began evacuating citizens just before the bombs started to fall. That was the last time I saw him."

Scotty recalls the missing skyline of the island, her mind turning to the prison.

Hartwood! Is he still alive?

If he's innocent, then...

Scotty feels herself growing sick.

"We've had some ships going back and forth, getting citizens off the island," Bramblewood says. "We're here trying to protect this line so we can take survivors northwest into the mountains towards Aspen."

"How can we help?" Jean asks. "Do they need reinforcements at the bridge? I hear gunshots."

Bramblewood shakes her head. "Those men know it's a suicide mission protecting the bridge. May Forez guide their souls. They're buying time to get everyone off the island, which is where you can help. Valkoean soldiers have been intercepting the ships at shore, trying to kill the Soharist citizens on board. They're... sickening. We have a few ships that could use guards."

Jean nods. "Take us to them."

"Look out!" a rebel calls. "Valkoeans!"

"Get down!" Bramblewood hollers.

Scotty falls to the ground, gunshots ring out around them. Bullets whiz overhead and her heart thumps hard.

"Cover us, cover us!" Bramblewood calls. "Raiders, lets go, to the shore!"

Gunpowder booms around them and they race among the veil of smoke. Scotty cranes her head around and the rebels start to fall in the flattened grasses.

Bramblewood instructs them to slow and lower in the grass, the clansman's face twisted into a tired scowl. Another rebel is at her side, the two leading the Raiders through the tall grasses. They stay low until they get to the shoreline, sliding down the bank held together by grass roots. Scotty's boots land in wet sand.

Boats are beached on the shore, some in ruins, some shot up by bullets, some covered in corpses. One intact steamboat has a pair of naval rebels on it, waving to Bramblewood.

"Ey! Over here!" the one rebel says.

"Leave your travel packs here," Bramblewood tells the Raiders. "The ships need as little weight as possible."

They leave their packs behind, minus Withorn, the medic keeping his medical supplies.

As they walk up to the ship, Scotty notices the name "Lady Iceberg" stenciled on the side of the boat. It's a beautiful, large steamboat, twice the size of the one she and Mike had been living on.

"Captain Sewall!" Bramblewood greets. "The Acros Raiders are here to help. What do you need?"

Scotty studies the rebels atop the boat, realization surging through her at the burly fisherman at the front, and the scarred, dark-skinned mountainfolk next to him, Tac. They offered her and Mike a job on their vessel in Edgewood Port just before Mike was captured. It seems fate dragged them into the rebellion too.

"Eh, I only need 'bout half that team," Sewall says, scratching his white beard. "Can get the most citizens on board that way, but I sure need the guns. Lady Iceberg's a fishin' vessel after all."

Jean nods, gesturing to the Raiders closest to him, minus Aster. "Scotty, Withorn, Jericho, Reagan," he says. "Come with me to protect the ship. Aster, stay behind with the others."

"Jean!" Aster shouts. "The airships, if they drop bombs on the boat, you're not making it out! It'll kill you!"

"We have to try," Scotty says. "There are citizens over there, Aster. More innocent people, like the ones we lost in Ghent. The ones *we* were responsible for." She wants to say they're responsible for this too, but she knows they all feel the guilt deep down.

"Jean, I don't want to lose you!" Aster cries.

"It's not about me," Jean says. "It's not about you, its not about what we want. There are lives to be saved. We're going!"

"Come on, come on!" Sewall says. "Stop yer bickering and get up here!"

Tac throws a rope ladder over the bow, the five chosen Raiders scrambling up over the gunnel into the deck. Katze stays behind with Cosette at Scotty's command.

Sewall pats Scotty on the back as she gets on board. "C'mon, miss, go go!"

Scotty scowls at the man, she's pretty sure he doesn't recognize her. When she makes eye contact with Tac, his scarred face mirrored in her own, he nods in greeting.

"You made it here eventually," Tac remarks, his voice deep. "Welcome aboard."

A large metal cabin is towards the stern of the boat, two steamstacks jutting up on either side of it. They puff out steam as the engine turns on. The engine rumbles, shaking the boat, and the sternwheeler splashes and scrapes the sand as it reverses into the purple-streaked waters.

Scotty watches as the rest of her comrades are pulled out of view, the bow swinging around as Sewall turns towards Hightower Harbor.

Steam fogs around the boat as they move towards the island, and Scotty's throat stings. She pulls her gaiter over her nose and her goggles to her eyes, dousing the island in a yellow haze.

She looks up to the airships, her heart thumping in her ears as she studies them. They hover around at different points of the island, Scotty praying they don't spot the steamboat puffing in the harbor.

A couple of them start to move and Scotty thinks her heart stops for a moment. A red Valkoean one and yellow Mohkan ship move forward and rotate, Scotty watching their bellies for bombs. The exhaust puffs into their wings and they head toward the south side of the island, away from the Lady Iceberg.

Scotty's anxiety fades, but it returns when she sees them stop over the sentry towers and bridges leading into the rebel city. Cannons boom from the towers as Valkoean soldiers march over the hillside from Cannonsburg towards Hightower's main defenses. The airships only hover for a moment before their bottom carriages open, a few ethner bombs dropping from their stomachs. A hissing explosion rings out with distant screams, and steam overtakes the sentry posts.

"The guard towers!" Jericho exclaims.

"Things are looking grim for the rebellion," Tac remarks.

"We just gotta focus on the civilians for now," Sewall calls from the helm. "Boats are their only ticket out, we can't be gettin' caught up on what's already lost."

"With the posts down, it's only a matter of time before the Valkoeans flood the island," Jean says.

"At least the bombing on the island will stop then," Tac says. "I don't know what's the worse way to go: blown to bits or at the hands of the soldiers."

The boat cuts through the steam and drags through sand until its bow is set into Hightower's shore.

"Get on out there!" Sewall calls out, shutting the engine off and running to the front deck.

Tac rolls the rope ladder out and goes down first, the Raiders stepping down with him.

Scotty's feet land in the sand and she looks up, her stomach lurching when she sees the island's wall in front of them, a massive hole blown in it. The rebel flag with its twisted logo hangs sadly to the right of the hole, half of the flag corroded away.

Down the coast, some of the flags are intact, but the wall is mostly destroyed, red bricks strewn over the beach. There is a distinct lack of trees beyond the wall, some chemical-burnt trees remaining on the other side.

Tac silently leads them forward, stepping over the rubble into the remains of the rebel city. Scotty is the last to enter, the land around her unrecognizable.

Splintered trunks of the once-tall pines dot the land around them, the grass seared from being washed with ethner. Dirt is turned up, craters blown into the ground, still hissing with steam. This seems to be a spot that was targeted harshly. Scotty can't imagine the whole island being reduced to *this*.

"Get down," Tac says calmly, bringing the Raiders into the confines of a fallen pine. The needles still crackle as they steam, but the Raiders push into the branches.

The humming of a patrolling Mohkan airship purrs in the sky. It doesn't notice them and turns further to the east, eventually halting to hover in the distance.

"When they see groups of survivors, they drop bombs," Tac tells them. "They're like cats toying with their prey."

"Best to stay out of their sights," Jean says.

Bombs fall from the belly of the beast, the ground below Scotty's feet shaking as steam erupts in the distance. She tightens her gloved hands around the branches, keeping her feet firm on the ground and trying to not panic.

The airship's hatch closes and it continues moving, leaving a steaming wall of destruction behind it.

"That's a good place to start looking for survivors," Jean says.

"More like a good place to find remains," Withorn says.

"Let's go," Tac says, his eyes pointed to the skies.

As they step out into the cratered land, they pass the crown of Milos's tower pierced into the ground, its roof cracked. Despite that, its rebel flag remains strong on the top. Debris from the rest of the tower and surrounding buildings are strewn around, cracked concrete showing where buildings once were.

"They spared no expense bombing the tower," Reagan says.

"It was the first place hit," Tac says.

Scotty remembers Bramblewood telling them Milos was helping evacuate citizens when the bombs initially fell, so she knows Milos at least didn't die then.

"The rest of Hightower Harbor doesn't look much better," Tac admits.

They walk through the broken streets and scattered buildings, Scotty realizing Tac wasn't over exaggerating. The less familiar areas of the city are even more unrecognizable, though some of the buildings still remain. Trees in the center of the island still stand tall but the bottoms are scorched by steam.

If only we could have stopped them...

Scotty's guilt is overtaken by rage.

A traitor is to blame! Not the Raiders!

Even through the gaiter, the sour smell of ethner hits Scotty. Her comrades cough and wheeze as they near the bombing site.

Tac keeps them under the canopies of trees and close to the taller buildings when he can, checking the sky for airships every once in a while.

Scotty's stomach stirs when they walk near a main road, bodies in the streets. Citizens, rebels, and Ghentians alike, indiscriminately killed by the ethner bombs. Some have lost limbs and look like they died from blood loss, others are covered in boils, clothes partially eroded. The stink of death is unmistakable, fresh flesh and blood in the air.

The steam flickers over the ground as they reach the site, this place unfamiliar to Scotty. Her mind is brought to Hartwood again, the former Raider tracker left at the island's prison. She glances around, trying to see if she can spot the spires of the prison, but she's so turned around, she has no idea where they're at.

"Tac, do you know what happened to the prison?" Scotty asks.

He shakes his head. "I doubt it was a target. Valkoean soldiers are kept there. But I can't say for certain. Sewall and I haven't spent much time in the rebel capital."

Scotty grows hopeful at his answer. If Hartwood is innocent, there's still a chance he's alive.

Crumbling buildings surround them, smaller craters lining the road, blood and flesh mixed in the debris. Scotty expects herself to get sick at the sight, but she can hardly process it as someone's remains.

A realization hits her — this is the city's square. It's unrecognizable in this state. Scotty becomes all too aware of where the prison is relative to where they're at.

They walk by the remains of a building, a sign brandishing the words "The Hungry Novak" split on the ground. Scotty tries to imagine the interior of the Ghentian restaurant, thinking to the morning she spend there with Cosette and Merryweather. Everything is rubble besides a few standing walls.

Maybe Milos was able to get the owner out in time. Hasn't this war taken enough from him?

"Spread out," Jean tells them. "They weren't wasting bombs, there are probably people around."

The Raiders and Tac move around to the buildings, the coughs of Scotty's comrades loud over the eerie silence. It's not long before a young voice calls out.

"Rebels! Rebels, over here!"

The Raiders surround the remains of a building, nervous eyes poking out from a blown out window.

"You-you're rebels, right?"

A teenage clansman boy stands in the rubble, watching the rescue team.

"We are," Jean says. "No Valkoeans are on the island yet."

The boy comes out a bit further, revealing blood on his arms.

"Come over here, a ceiling is still up," the boy says, his eyes pointing to the sky. "Those things... those things in the sky, they dropped the bombs on a rebel team in the streets. The house... it fell apart. Come inside and help, please!"

"Help?" Withorn asks.

The boy leads them into the remains of his home and Scotty hears moans of pain, her heart lurching.

"Over here!" the boy says.

Two clansmen, a man and a woman, who Scotty suspects are the boys parents, kneel down around something. Four other citizens are with them, most injured in some way, shouting out things. A rebel is there too, armed to the teeth, covered in blood and boils.

"The wall fell on him!" the rebel says when he sees the team.

The revel removes to reveal another rebel on the floor, wailing occasionally as the people try to move the bricks from his crushed legs.

The Raiders manage to get the bricks free, revealing a broken leg under the rubble. It is bloody and bruised, bent at an odd angle. Withorn splints the leg, taking his time to check vitals, and gets the man upright, but the rebel protests as he moans in pain.

"Just on one leg," Withorn says. "Use me to stay upright, easy now."

"Is he going to make it?" the other rebel murmurs. "Please, the rest of the team is dead! We were inside when the bombs fell. The others are... they're..."

"We saw," Withorn says, pointing his blocky nose towards the front of the house. "It's hard to say what will happen with a break, but it should be fine so long as we keep it clean."

They leave the house, moving slowly as they make their way back to the boat. Tac urges them to keep in the few areas where they're hidden from the sky. Two airships patrol in the distance, hunting for survivors like them. Scotty turns to face her team, moving as fast as the injured rebel can.

Gadias, protect us!

She looks to the sky and wonders if the good gods have abandoned them. They're supposed to be up above them, protecting them, but the only all powerful gods she sees now are the airships who could send them to the afterlife on a whim.

Scotty catches a glimpse of gothic spires beyond the seared branches of a browning pine, her heart lurching as she feels a pull towards it.

The prison! Tac was right, it wasn't a target.

Scotty glances over at the team, moving at a snail's pace back to the boat. Her eyes land on Jean, leading them alongside Tac through the ruined streets.

Jean would never allow me to see if Hartwood is there and safe if I asked.

Guilt pricks at her as she remembers Hartwood's pleading. She sees the man on his knees, his broken look. He was convinced.

Scotty realizes she's convinced of his innocence too.

What will the Valkoeans do when they realize he's not one of them? She has to do more than just see if he's safe.

"I'll be back!" she blurts out, racing out over the broken land.

She hears a couple of them yell out at her, but she keeps going.

I have to do this!

"Scotty!" Jean's voice booms out.

Scotty cranes her head around as she runs to make sure no one gives chance, but she sees Withorn convincing them to move along. Jean looks furious, shouting at the medic before giving in.

He's really not going to like what I'm about to do.

Her feet carry her to the prison, the pines keeping ample cover from the sky here. The grass is still green, the plants still alive. Through her gaiter, she can still smell the stink of ethner blanketing the island.

The gothic building stretches far above her and she yanks the front door open, the guards all evacuated. When the door cracks open, howls erupt from the prisoners below.

She snatches a key ring from the wall, running past upturned seats. The rebels were in a hurry to flee and she can't blame them. She rushes down the steps into the dank prison, running past cells of terrified men and woman.

Terrified Valkoeans, terrified enemies.

They yell out fearfully.

"Are we going to die?"

"What's happening out there?"

She grits her teeth and pushes through. They're Valkoeans, they'll be fine. She has no time to explain that.

Why do I feel bad? If I met them in battle, there'd be no guilt. I'd kill them without a second thought.

She runs through the prison until descending upon a familiar cell, a back donned in rags turned to her, facing the thin window at the ceiling.

"Hartwood!" Scotty exclaims.

Hartwood snaps around, Shako clutching tightly on his shoulder. She expects him to react with anger, but his eyes are full of fear and he trembles as he steps towards the bars.

"What's going on out there?" he bellows.

"Hightower Harbor has fallen," Scotty tells him.

The horrified look in his gaze makes Scotty even more certain of his innocence. She remembers Hartwood telling her about how he was in love with Eliska, one of the Raiders who died in the hanging at

Edgewood Port, the same hanging that took Mike. The rebellion is personal to him too, and she can see that plainly now.

As she unlocks the cage, Hartwood looks on in confusion, but she continues speaking. "Those airships that bombed Ghent, there are six of them now. The Acros Raiders were supposed to stop them, but..."

"How could it even be possible to stop them?" Hartwood says.

That doesn't help Scotty's guilt.

"A traitor ruined our plans," Scotty spits out scornfully as she opens the door. "The same person who framed you."

Hartwood blinks at her as if his bars weren't removed. At first, she expects him to lash out in fury, and she wouldn't blame him. She's the reason he's here. She fell for it.

He looks like he's full of questions, but among the yowls of the other prisoners, Scotty shouts out. "Let's get out of here!"

51
DOWNWARD SPIRAL

S cotty and Hartwood race over the cratered island, Hartwood's green eyes snapping around at the destruction.

"It's worse than Vincent," he breathes.

Scotty casts a glance to the sky, praying the airships are far away. Would they really waste a bomb on two people? She doesn't want to risk it to find out.

They move as quick as possible, pressing into the dying trees and against buildings of rubble for cover. They reach the crumbled wall that once protected Hightower Harbor, moving along it towards Captain Sewall's beached boat.

"What convinced you to save me?" Hartwood asks.

Scotty hesitates. She doesn't want to tell him about the dreams making her paranoid. "You just seemed so convinced when I spoke to you. And things have still been going wrong. I... I couldn't live with myself knowing you were in that prison... because of me."

"Aster was the first one to accuse me," Hartwood says.

Scotty frowns. It was so long ago, the details are fuzzy to her.

"Aster... he did say you threw the bomb at him," Scotty murmurs.

"I wasn't even in the room when the bomb went off," Hartwood says. "He might have been seeing things, unless..." His voice trails off as if he doesn't want to finish the sentence.

"Unless what?" Scotty asks. "Are you... are you suggesting Aster framed you?"

"Who else could have?" Hartwood asks. "We were paired up on that mission."

Scotty blinks. The deputy's been nothing but helpful on her mission to find the traitor. He's loyal to Jean, and that's apparent. He cares for the commander deeply. The two at times seem closer than she and Mike were, and she knew her fiancé for her entire life.

"Aster wouldn't do that!" Scotty blurts out. "There had to have been someone else in the guardhouse, someone who made Aster think you attacked him."

Aster was convinced someone was helping Hartwood, but Scotty's entirely doubtful of that. She decides to not tell Hartwood about Aster's involvement in finding the actual traitor. If Aster was a traitor, surely he would have dismissed the idea immediately.

"If there's any way I can help find out who did it, I'm in," Hartwood says. "I... I'm not the smartest, but tracking is my forte. Mine and Shako's." He reaches up to the little weaver on his shoulder and gives him a scratch behind his long ear.

Scotty nods at him, paranoia pricking at her as her ears start to buzz.

Aster wouldn't do that, she quietly affirms.

"Thanks," she says.

"You said a lot has gone wrong," Hartwood says, concern flickering in his green gaze. "Has anyone been hurt?"

Scotty shakes her head. "Things haven't gone *that* wrong."

"Good," Hartwood says. "I'm shocked that a traitor hasn't been able to take the team out after all this time. It's been some months, though I lost track of time in there."

Scotty frowns. He's right, it has been a couple seasons since the traitor starting making things go awry.

Why hasn't *the team been taken out?*
It doesn't make sense.

Nothing makes sense!

Scotty hushes Hartwood, trying to feign that there could be danger if they speak. She just doesn't want him instilling more doubts.

Scotty peeks around the cratered part of the wall they initially entered at, Jean's team and the survivors returning to the boat just now. A few new survivors are in tow and Jean still looks furious.

"I don't know how they're going to react," Scotty warns Hartwood, her voice low.

"Even if they kill me, it'll be better than that cell," Hartwood sneers.

She overhears Jean shouting at Withorn, pointing back into the island as Jericho and Reagan follow Tac up onto the boat. The survivors are already on board, being greeted by Captain Sewall.

"Go find her! She's compromising this whole mission!"

Scotty steps forward, gesturing for Hartwood to stay behind the wall.

"Jean!" she calls out. "I—"

"Where have you been?" Jean booms, stomping up to her. "Do you realize you could have compromised everything? You could have gotten us all killed running off like that! What in the name of Forez were you out there doing? Do you have Cassius's claws in your head?"

Scotty winces at his words.

Yes, apparently I do.

She narrows her eyes at him, the red sharfawks aura flickering as she meets his gaze.

And I suspect you do too. Do you see it too?

"Well?" Jean booms. "Explain yourself!"

"Hartwood is innocent!" Scotty exclaims. "I had to—"

"What is *he* doing here?" Jean asks. "Scotty, what have you done?"

Its as if he didn't even hear her. Scotty turns around to see Hartwood approaching earlier than she intended.

"Jean!" Scotty calls as the commander races up to Hartwood.

Hartwood holds his arms up, his green eyes wide as he watches

Jean approach. Even Shako winces, retreating behind Hartwood's neck.

"Jean, I'm innocent!" he bellows.

"Bullshit!" Jean hisses.

"Jean!" Withorn calls out, unsurprised by Hartwood's appearance.

Jericho seems shocked, but Reagan doesn't know Hartwood and just looks on awkwardly, much like Tac and Sewall.

"Jean, we can't be wasting time," Withorn says firmly.

"I was framed!" Hartwood exclaims. "Let me prove myself!"

Jean narrows his eyes at Hartwood.

"He stays on the island," Jean declares.

"Then I'll stay too!" Scotty says.

"Fine," Jean sneers back.

Scotty's heart sinks. Surely she means more to Jean than that?

"I'm not getting on that boat without *either* of them," Withorn says. "You feel like losing a medic today, Jean?"

Jean glares at Withorn and Scotty is suddenly thankful for bringing Withorn in on the mission of finding the traitor. At least someone trusts her judgement.

"Get on," Jean demands, eyes pointing between Hartwood and Scotty. "But know on the other side of this, if the rebellion survives, you'll both be rotting in a cell for the rest of your lives!" Cassius's aura flares up in him. "Traitors!"

"Jean," Scotty breathes. "You-you can't do—"

"I'm the commander, I can do what I want!" he says "Maybe Farsing was right, maybe *you've* been against us this whole time! My intuition has only led the team astray."

"Stop arguing or we'll leave you all behind!" Captain Sewall calls. "Get yer asses up here!"

"If Hartwood comes, he's coming as a prisoner," Jean says. He ties up the tracker, leaving Shako alone on his shoulder. Hartwood lets him tie the binds, saying nothing to his former commander.

The rest of the Raiders load up on the boat, Scotty's mind swirling at Jean's reaction.

Jean stays on the far side of the boat away from Scotty. Jericho,

Withorn, and Hartwood stay by her side. Reagan goes over to comfort the commander, the two murmuring to each other quietly.

Tac keeps the rebels and survivors together in the center of the boat, trying to keep morale high as the Raiders melt down around them.

The motor starts up, the steamstacks puffing, and the engine grumbles as the stern wheel drags the boat off the sand into the steam-coated water.

"I couldn't just leave him behind," Scotty says as if to defend herself from Withorn and Jericho.

"I'm innocent," Hartwood tells them. "I didn't do anything to Aster. I swear to Ludon on it!"

"I trust Scotty's judgement," Withorn says.

"I... I don't know what to think," Jericho says.

"I don't care what people think now," Scotty says. "We'll prove his innocence!"

"I don't know how well I can defend you from Jean's threat," Withorn warns her. "I don't want to see you locked up. I... I don't even know if the rebellion will persist after this, so maybe you don't have anything to worry about. Maybe there will be nothing to prove."

"The rebellion *has* to survive," Scotty says desperately.

If it doesn't, it means her failures led to the rebellion's downfall.

I couldn't live with that!

Withorn opens his mouth to speak, but Reagan's voice booms out instead.

"Airship!"

Shouts of fear erupt from the survivors as they huddle on the deck floor. The injured rebel looks up, terrified, his comrade standing protectively in front of him.

Scotty follows their gaze to the massive red ship heading towards them.

She snaps back to look towards their destination.

But we are so close to shore!

"Captain Sewall, can it go any faster?" Jean calls out.

"I'm topped out at five knots with all yer weight!" Sewall calls back from the helm.

"Yuna save us!" Reagan hollers out.

Scotty watches helplessly as the massive winged beast hovers closer from the destroyed island.

Soon, it's overhead.

"Hold tight!" Sewall calls out.

Scotty is thrown against the gunnel as the ship is thrown into reverse, the front swinging around. The boat jolts again as it goes forward, the rear swinging to follow the front as Sewall tries to evade the airship.

Scotty watches in terror as a trio of small bombs fall from the airship as it floats above the maneuvering steamboat. She grabs onto the gunnel tightly and the bombs splash around them.

"They missed!" a survivor calls out.

"Hold on!" Tac calls. "We're not in the clear yet."

Muffled explosions ring out as pillars of water shoot from the bay and the boat jolts harder. Scotty hollers among the yells of the others as she's thrown to the deck.

"We're hit!" Sewall calls.

"But how? They missed!" a survivor says.

Tac disappears and reappears at the door of the large cabin.

"We're taking on water!" he shouts.

The survivors shout in terror and Scotty's heart lurches.

"I'll get 'er in!" Sewall calls. "Don't worry!"

Panic surges through Scotty as she realizes Tex is tucked in a holster around her belt. The ethner gun will explode if exposed to water.

She gets on her feet again and the airship makes a wide turn back around towards the boat, humming and hissing as it maneuvers.

"She's coming back around," Tac warns.

"Not much I can do about it!" Sewall says angrily, focused on the shore.

The bow gets lower and lower, the boat slowing as it sinks. They approach the shore but water pools around the low deck.

Scotty tries to step away, but her feet only find more of the bay water.

"If the engine goes under, it'll blow," Tac says to Sewall. "Do we abandon ship?"

"We don't abandon her!" Sewall growls.

"It's going to explode?" the survivor clansman woman shouts out, grabbing onto her teenage son protectively.

"She's not going to explode!" Sewall snaps.

"The airship's closing in!" Jean calls out.

Scotty feels Jericho grab onto her arm, the young man trembling as he looks to the skies.

"Gadias," he mumbles. "Gods, anyone. Save us!"

Scotty winces as the boat sinks further, cold water filling her boots, and she expects the engine to turn the boat into a bomb at any moment.

The boat lurches and everyone shouts, but Scotty's eyes snap open when she realizes the bottom is dragging on sand. They're still a little ways out from shore, but the boat has sunk enough to lower the draft.

The engine grumbles as Sewall tries to move the boat forward and Scotty winces when the paddle grinds agains the rocks in the sandy bay. The boat slows and stops.

"We're aground," Sewall says, cutting the engine and stomping out to the deck. "We need to wade in. Go on, get out!"

When the others jump in, Scotty realizes the water is only about three feet deep. She keeps her ethner gear raised high as she takes the plunge off the bow. Withorn and Tac carry the injured rebel, keeping his broken leg out of the mucky bay.

The rescue team makes it to the sandy shore between the remains of rebel ships, Bramblewood and the rest of the Raiders greeting them and offering help.

Yowls of shock erupt from the other Raiders when Hartwood follows Scotty.

"Hartwood?" Ren blurts out.

"What's this about?" Aster booms out, stepping up to Jean. "Why is Hartwood here? Do you remember what he did to me? He tried to kill me!"

"We'll worry about it later," Jean says.

Scotty lets out a breath of relief when he doesn't immediately pin the blame on Scotty. The last thing she would want is for the deputy to be cross with her too.

Aster looks like he wants to say more, but the voice of a survivor calls out.

"The airship! It's here! Look out!"

52

BATTLE FOR THE HARBOR

S cotty's heart sinks as she turns around, the big red beast
approaching in the sky.

*The explosions were stifled in the water. What will happen if
they fall on land?*

The rear rudder of the ship shifts and the wings move, the airship
making a wide turn. Its spiral sun symbol flashes at them, and it
moves back towards the island.

"It's leaving?" Jean says.

"Looks like it," Ren remarks.

Scotty is about to ask why, but the answer comes as gunshots hiss
out. Everyone presses against the bay's bank as bullets pierce the dirt.
Bramblewood's rebels return fire, gunpowder smoke settling on the
thin beach.

Scotty glances down the bank when Jean's voice calls out.

"Bramblewood! Get the citizens and injured to safety. We'll
provide as much cover as possible."

"On it!" Bramblewood says.

She calls a few of her men and moves to the citizens, taking them
north with the bank's cover. Scotty doesn't watch for long before
peeking up over the grasses, firing where fresh steam clouds waft.

She spends six bullets and falls behind the bank again as retaliation fire hisses back. Gunpowder booms around her, reverberating in her chest.

She peeks back up when the hissing bullets slow and sees the heads of Valkoeans hiding back into the grasses, the grass rustling as they move forward. Scotty empties her chamber again and ducks down just as bullets whiz by, blood rushing in her ears. She plinks bullets in her chamber.

"They're coming!" Jericho calls out.

"Grenades!" Connie shouts.

Grenades clunk around Scotty, her heart racing as she scrambles up onto shore with Katze on her heels. Scotty rolls into the grass as the hissing explosions boom behind her.

She gets up and spins around, trying to get her bearings straight as her ears ring. She doesn't know which way is which, booms and hisses echoing around her as the battle erupts. The steam and smoke thicken and metal clashes against metal as bullets expend and swords lash out.

Scotty steps through the grass and hissing bullets whiz by. She yowls and falls to the ground, gasping for air as adrenaline rushes through her veins. At the sound, a person leaps towards her, the silhouette wielding a sword. Scotty shouts and rolls to narrowly miss the blade, spinning around and firing at the person until her gun clicks empty.

A yowl is cut short as the person goes limp, Scotty breathing heavily. She catches a flash of a pin on the corpse's chest, brandishing a familiar owl's wingspan symbol.

The Black Glove Scouts? Here? Now?

She scowls. She's sick of these bastards! Why are they always crossing paths?

She has no time to dwell on it before the grass rustles and a pair of snarling beasts leap out. The jaws of a black armored fallion clasp around her arm and she yells as she bangs the handle of her empty gun against his metal forehead. He yelps and lets go, another one rearing up to bite as Katze barrels into it, the two tussling together in a snarling fit.

Scotty falls to the ground, hissing at the new pain as she grabs her bleeding arm. She exchanges Tex for her twin daggers, just in time for a silhouette to show face where the fallion have flattened the grass.

A whistle calls the armored fallion back and Scotty finds herself facing the barrel of a gun.

"Found you! This is for Shisha, you bitch!"

Scotty recognizes Qailah, the Scout's fallion trainer on the other side of the gun. Scotty winces and holds her daggers up in a useless block.

Snarling hits her ears and Qailah yells out, hissing bullets firing out as Scotty cringes. Scotty's eyes snap open to Katze latched onto Qailah's gun arm, the woman emptying her chamber as she yells. The larger armored fallion barrels into Katze, ripping her from Qailah. Scotty takes this opportunity to lunge out at Qailah with her daggers.

Qailah yowls out and side steps as Scotty's one dagger licks over her cheek. Qailah pulls her bayonet out of its sheath and whistles, her two fallion returning behind her.

They face each other, pacing around the bloodied, flattened grass. Their fallion crouch as they stalk protectively in front of their masters, teeth bared in a snarl. Both Scotty and Qailah's arms bleed, the blood whelming as they breathe heavily.

We need medics. This fight has to be quick.

Qailah sneers and whistles.

"Gwen, Reese," she calls. "Out!"

The two fallion break away from Qailah and she turns to run back into the grasses.

She's fleeing?

Scotty turns around, expecting the fallion to flank her and attack.

She's probably buying time to reload her gun!

Scotty makes chase through the grass, Katze leaping ahead to follow the enemy fallion trainer. Scotty's feet skid onto the gravel road that lines the shore, low steam and smoke reducing her vision as swords slash around her. Silhouettes of Scouts and Raiders fight along with rebels, Ghentians, Valkoeans, and Mohkan soldiers. Cannons boom in the distance and explosions from airships holler out, shaking the land.

Scotty's arm screams in pain, the blood still flowing.

Scotty snaps around.

Where'd Qailah go?

Scotty yells out when two armored beasts bowl into Katze, Katze yelping in pain. Scotty runs over to help, daggers lashing out, but Qailah intercepts with her bayonet.

"You get to watch like I did!" Qailah hisses.

Scotty scowls and lashes hard with her daggers and sends her foot into Qailah's shin. Qailah howls out and Scotty throws her weight into her, taking the small woman down.

"Katze!" Scotty howls.

She runs over, Katze's grey pelt staining red under the Scout hounds' jaws. Katze is on her side, taken down by the weight of the armored fallen.

"Gwen! Reese!" Qailah calls. "Drop it!" She whistles and the armored fallion split away from Katze, Scotty sending her foot towards the one as it rushes past, Katze's blood on its maw.

"Katze!" Scotty hollers again, falling to her knees at her companion's side.

"See how it feels," Qailah hisses. "The worst I can do to you is let you live!"

Scotty doesn't check to see if Qailah leaves, her eyes sticking to Katze. Her mind snaps around to what Withorn would do in this situation.

"Katze," she breathes. "You're going to be okay, you're going to be okay." Her eyes stain with tears, but she needs to focus. For Katze.

She shouldn't have taken her rage out on Katze, it should have been me! Is another of my loved ones going to die because of me?

Scotty rips her gaiter off and tears the fabric, tying it around the deepest wound on Katze's shoulder. Katze breathes heavily, staying on her side. She whines a bit when Scotty works on her shoulder, but doesn't muster up any strength for anything else.

"I-I gotta find Withorn," she says. "I gotta find Withorn, he'll know what to do. It was a trap, I fell into her damned trap!"

Scotty stands up, snapping around the smoke and steam.

Where do I even begin to find Withorn?

The team has gotten so turned around and explosions and hisses ring out around her.

Her heart thumps hard.

I'm not going to lose Katze!

"Scotty!"

Relief floods through her when she turns around and sees Aster in his full Panzer Suit racing up the road towards her through the steam.

"Aster!" she calls. "I-I need help! Where's Withorn? Katze is—"

"We need to get out of here," Aster says, his voice echoing. "I'll carry Katze, don't worry, no one is going to die! I won't let anyone die!"

He steps over to the injured fallion, but a voice calls out over the clashing of battle around them.

"Blasphemer!"

Scotty looks up to a silhouette pacing towards them through the haze, the familiar blocky weapon clasped in his hands.

Arlo.

He's wearing a pointed gas mask, looking like another species as he steps towards them. He holds up his weapon, aiming at Scotty. Her heart thumps hard in her chest, holding her daggers up desperately.

"Stop!" Aster bellows at him, stepping in front of Scotty. "Take your men and leave! There are citizens being evacuated on this shore!"

"Why do you think we are here?" Arlo says, cocking his head as he lowers his weapon slightly. Scotty wonders why he's even entertaining Aster's words. "Citizens," he sneers. "They're blasphemers! Blasphemers who need redeemed, redeemed by Castus in death!"

"Valkoeans are supposed to be better than this!" Aster pleads.

Arlo seems to consider his words.

"My mercy extends to Castists," he says, "not nonbelievers and their *allies*." He lifts his weapon. "Which are you?"

Aster looks down to Scotty hesitantly. Arlo's words sound personal, like the two have history.

After a moment of silence, Arlo speaks again. "May Castus judge your souls."

Aster leans down and wraps his arms around Scotty and she hears a terrible, hissing noise.

Pain. Searing pain.

Scotty yowls as steam engulfs her body, Aster holding her tightly. Her hands sting as she grabs onto his cold, metal armor and she can't help but to scream out more.

Am I dying?

The pain worsens.

Please, just let me die!

Aster's hollers echo out and his helmet flies off from the pressure of the steam. Scotty feels herself go numb, her eyes still tightly shut and she feels herself thud to the gravel.

Aster's screams are loud on her ears and she opens her eyes, only now realizing Arlo is long gone. It feels like the steam lingers, the agonizing pain gripping her. She tries to move, but her body won't listen. Her eyes move around and she first sees her hands sprawled out in front of her. Her arms are licked with ethner boils, but her hands are bloody messes.

Her left hand trembles and she's able to flex it slightly but she fails to move her right hand, a sickening feeling making bile rise in her chest.

Where... where are my fingers?

White bone remains where the ethner boiled away the rest of her hand.

Her eyes move further up and she sees Aster in front of her, yowling out as he grabs at his face, his helmet on the ground next to him.

Aster.

She tries to speak, but she's too weak.

Aster!

He pulls his hands away from his face to reveal half of his face boiled away, his maroon hair singed.

"I can't see!" he hollers. "I can't see! That bastard!"

Scotty tries to reach out to help, but she only manages a slight flinch of her left fingers. Her heart thumps hard and she sees Katze on her side further away, her chest still heaving.

Struggling.

Dying.

As Scotty's vision starts to fade, she thinks of her comrades, the citizens of Valko, the citizens of Ghent. Tapscott will try to spread Castism over the whole world.

The traitor needs brought to justice.

Withorn needs justice.

Jericho needs justice.

Connie and Reagan.

Hartwood.

Katze.

Aster.

So much more still needs done.

The destruction won't end at the rebellion.

We can't let the rebellion die.

I don't want to die.

Another thought soothes her as her vision fully fades over.

Mike...

53
EVERYTHING WILL BE OKAY

Ren's bayonet lurches into the neck of a Mohkan soldier, slicing forward as they thud to the ground. His chest heaves, sucking in ethner and smoke, and he spins around to find his next opponent.

Valkoean and Mohkan soldiers descend upon the small rebel group defending the citizens fleeing at the shore. Ren notices a couple other rebel boats meet at the shore, but the rescues have been less frequent. Bramblewood's division has returned, but her men are falling.

The tall grasses have been flattened by battle, corpses piling up nearby. Jean heaves next to him, Jericho staying close to the two.

"Let's move forward," Jean says. "We need to regroup with the others."

"We need to retreat," Ren says, choking out the words.

Jean grits his teeth. "We can't give up! Citizens are still being brought in!"

"We can either give up or die!" Ren exclaims.

"We're tired," Jericho says. The young man is covered with sword licks and blood. He needs Withorn or Connie to look over him. "I-I don't think the rebellion is going to last after this, Jean."

Cannon fire is sparse and no gunshots remain, but swords clashing and yowls of death are loud. Ren assumes everyone's expended their bullets, even the Valkoeans with their seemingly infinite resources.

"Look out!" Jean exclaims.

Five Valkoeans descend on them from the haze, their swords lashing out.

Merryweather appears from behind Ren, making a wide swing with her dual cutlasses. She parries a swing from the Valkoean on the left and uses her second blade to slice into his shoulder, taking him down.

Ren doesn't see her lock into battle again, a Valkoean lunging at him with a rapier. Ren yells and leaps out of the way, the lethal tip barely missing him.

The Valkoean roars as she pokes at him with the thin blade. Ren steps around in a deadly dance, lashing the rapier's blade out of the way with his thicker bayonet. Her movements are quick and he is hardly able to parry her.

He just needs to get one slice in, she can't block, but she's too damn fast.

He swings too wide and realizes his mistake too late. The rapier pierces in and out of his flank, like a venomous snake's bite. He hollers and grabs the wound with his free hand, adrenaline surging through his veins as he lashes out at her harder and faster.

I can't die here! I need to see my daughter one more time before I go!

The Valkoean shouts and moves back as Ren's blade slices in front of her. His movements are fast, but sloppy.

I need to finish this!

She dodges his blade and pierces his other flank, Ren letting out a deep shout at the new pain. The pain is overshadowed by a new surge of adrenaline and he grabs his bayonet in both bloodied hands, piercing forward into the Valkoean soldier's chest.

She lets out a gurgle and falls back and Ren notices the other four Valkoeans have been felled too.

"Ren!" Jericho cries, running to Ren's side.

"Damn rapiers," Ren hisses. "She was fast, but at least she wasn't accurate." His body screams at him to sit down, but he knows that could be fatal. *Keep moving.*

"We need to find Withorn," Jericho says.

Everyone is licked with wounds, new ones piled on from this skirmish.

"I know where the others are," Merryweather says, one eye shut as a lash on her forehead bleeds into it. "Come on."

The four Raiders sneak around the hazy battlefield, Merry- weather leading them to where a handful of the others have been fighting near the bank, the medics cleaning everyone up. A few rebels are among them, some in rough shape.

Withorn and Connie tend to the new group's wounds imme- diately.

"By Aurthuras, this is awful," Connie says with wide eyes. "I thought I've seen a lot of death, I thought I've seen the worst of it. I was wrong."

"Stop your whining and work," Withorn grumbles. "We don't know when the Valkoeans will find us again."

"We need to retreat," Jean says, standing up once his wounds are cleaned and bleeding is stopped. "We will—" His eyes widen as he looks over the group. "Where's Aster?" he asks. "And Scotty?"

"No one has seen them," Withorn says, worry tainting his tone as he works.

"We need to get back out there and find them," Jean says.

"It could be a suicide mission," Ren says. His heart aches as he thinks of his comrades, but the place is ripe with enemies. He hardly feels safe against the bank here.

"I'd die before I left without Aster!" Jean blurts out.

Ren's gaze falls to Hartwood, the bound man pressed up against the bank with Shako. His old friend's hair is overgrown, making Hart- wood look like he's got the claws of Cassius in his head, his wide-eyed stare not helping.

"We have a tracker, you know," Ren tells Jean.

Jean follows his gaze to Hartwood.

"You think *he* should help?" Jean asks.

Ren shrugs. "I think he's the only one who can. Ask him." His last words almost come out as a challenge. Ren just doesn't want his old friend to truly be a traitor.

Jean glowers as he slides down the bank to Hartwood's side, Ren following closely. The former Raider just stares forward, paying the two no mind at their arrival. Scotty saved him, so even if he's a traitor, maybe he'll be compelled to help for her sake.

"We need help," Jean says.

Ren eagerly watches Hartwood, praying he helps. If he does, maybe it means he's still loyal. Maybe it means he was innocent this whole time.

"With what?" Hartwood asks, not hiding the curiosity in his tone.

"Scotty and Aster are somewhere out there," Jean says. "We need to track them down so we can retreat."

"I'd love to," Hartwood says, lifting his bound hands. "But I'm a bit tied up right now."

"You don't need hands to send Shako out there," Jean says.

"I'll sure need them to defend myself if we get into some shit," Hartwood says. "But I'm a bit out of practice because *I've been rotting in a cell because of you!*" He breathes heavily as if holding back an explosion of words. "I'll find Scotty, but I'll be *damned* if I find Aster!"

"You find *both* of them or I'll take you out right here," Jean sneers, brandishing his blade.

Hartwood sniffs as he looks at the blade blankly.

"Whatever," he scoffs. "Free me and give me a weapon and *then* I'll find Aster. I'm not too afraid of death anymore, Jean. Not that I ever was. I'd rather die than be in that cell again."

Jean huffs. "Merryweather!" he calls. "Spare a cutlass?"

Merryweather steps over to the two, her forehead bandaged now.

"For what?" she asks.

"I'm arming Hartwood," Jean says darkly. "He'll help us find Scotty and Aster. He's the only one who can."

Merryweather nods and hesitantly hands a blade to Jean. Jean lets out a yowl and slices Hartwood's bonds, the tracker wincing as the blade lashes by. He opens his green eyes and stares at the broken binds in shock, as if he wasn't expecting to be freed.

Jean holds the cutlass in front of him and Hartwood reaches out hesitantly to grab it. He holds the grip in his hand, giving it a few squeezes as he looks the blade over.

"Didn't think I'd get to hold one of these again," he mumbles.

Ren watches him closely, half expecting him to lash out at Jean with the blade.

Hartwood looks up to the commander. "Take me to their bags," he says.

Shako gets a good sniff of Aster and Scotty's gear, Jean, Merryweather, Ren and the tracker heading out into the depths of the battlefield again, the team keeping low. Most of the grass has been trampled and bloodied and they step over bodies in their search, Ren praying Shako doesn't stop at any of them. The smoke and steam proves to be an obstacle for Shako, Hartwood refreshing the scent often with clothes from the missing Raiders' bags.

Acros flock overhead, the scavengers landing in the nearby woods as the haze fades, waiting to take advantage of the battlegrounds for their meal. The battles have moved closer to the entrance of Hightower Harbor, swords and yowls echoing, but still too close for comfort.

Ren's flanks sting as his bandages glow red, but he clutches his bayonet tightly, anticipating lingering enemies. The lack of enemies worries him, only dead bodies remaining around.

What does this mean for Aster and Scotty? Did they move further towards the bridges to help the battles there?

"By Ludon," Hartwood murmurs.

The fear in his voice propels Ren forward and he sees Shako nuzzling into a limp body.

Ren looks on in horror.

Are they dead?

Scotty lays on her belly, her arms singed by ethner. Her hands are entirely boiled, Ren growing sick as he looks at the bones of her right arm. Katze is pressed up into her, a trail of blood leading from where the fallion dragged herself to Scotty's side.

Aster lays on his back, his helmet thrown on the ground. Half of his face is reduced to boils, Ren's stomach churn at the gore. Aster moans weakly and Ren realizes Scotty and Katze's chests are still heaving.

Ren is half relieved and half sickened.

"They're... alive," he says, unable to hide the shocked disgust.

Jean falls to Aster's side and tears stream down his face.

"Aster," he chokes out. "I should have listened! I should have listened to you, dammit! We should have never came out here!"

Jean wails out and Aster moans again as if to try to say something to the commander.

"Aster, stay with us," Jean begs. "We'll get you help!"

Ren swallows bile that was rising in his throat. "Jean, let's not waste time. Let's pick them up and bring them to Withorn. If... if anything can be done, it needs to be done as soon as possible."

Hartwood picks up Katze, and Merryweather and Jean lift Aster, the commander's composure breaking more.

Ren grabs Scotty in his arms, careful with her hands as he lifts her.

"R-Ren," Scotty chokes out.

Ren swallows hard. Usually he doesn't lie to make someone feel better, but he makes an exception for this.

"We'll get you to Withorn," Ren says. "Everything will be okay."

54
THE SON

The void returns, Scotty laying on the ground, sprawled out on her belly.

I can't move.

She recognizes the void as a dream, somehow more terrifying to her than reality. She can't see her hands in front of her, both replaced with wads of bandages.

She wants to scream out for help, but her lips won't move. No one is nearby, except a dark presence.

Footfalls sound from behind her and fur brushes over her cheek as the black-gloved feet of a sharfawks pace in front of her face. The thing sits on its haunches just in front of her paralyzed gaze, looking at her with sinister, amber eyes.

Fear prickles through Scotty and she wants to run.

I don't want to be an apostle of Cassius! Get away!

It cocks its head at her, its antlers glowing faintly.

Its mouth doesn't move, but its voice pangs in Scotty's head.

"Someone will give in to me eventually. Will it be you?"

Scotty shoots awake, covered in an all too familiar cold sweat.

She's in Jean's large tent, repurposed as Withorn's medic tent. It's been a few days since Hightower was lost, or maybe a week. She's been sleeping most of the time as she heals and the team has been moving ever so slowly towards the Flight Stronghold.

Scotty moves the blanket off her legs and pain surges through her hands.

She winces.

I keep forgetting.

She lifts her arms in front of her, her right hand reduced to a stub. Withorn was able to save her left hand, three of her fingers in splints, though the whole thing is covered in bandages. He had to amputate what was left of the right.

Katze moves at Scotty's side, looking tiredly up at her master. She's covered in bandages too, but Connie was able to patch her up well. She's weak, but so long as the bite wounds don't get infected, she'll make a full recovery.

No one came out of the battle without wounds, but Scotty and Aster got the worst of it. The deputy rustles awake beside her, half his face wrapped in bandages. Withorn said Aster's left eye would never fully recover vision, but truthfully, everyone's just shocked he's alive.

"Good morning," Scotty says with a nod.

Aster doesn't say anything back. She's not sure if it's hard for him to speak because of the wound reaching his lips or if he's shaken by the near death experience. His yowls of pain still echo in her head.

"Do you want breakfast?" Scotty asks. "I'm sure Cosette will have something for us."

Aster shakes his head. "No." His voice is slightly muffled, but Scotty is glad to get some kind of answer.

"I'll get up and get it myself when I'm ready," Aster says. "I'm restless."

His good eye points to her hands and she's not sure if it's pain or guilt she sees in his gaze. He's as hard to read as when he has his helmet on.

He grabs his helmet from beside him and digs through his bag for a small container of black paint. His hands brush over the Acros

419

Raiders' skull symbol on the forehead, the paint singed away from the steam.

"The paint never sticks," Aster grumbles, dipping a brush in the paint. "Never does..." He mumbles incoherently as he fixes the symbol, struggling with his lessened vision. Scotty almost wants to ask him if he's okay, but clearly he's not. After what happened, who would be?

Scotty steps out of the tent with Katze on her heels, the bird skull logo on Jean's tent flapping as she lets it fall shut. The grassy camp is small, set up against the shore of Mayhew Lake at the foot of the mountain that Aspen, the rebel intelligence hub city, is built on. Fiery looking fall trees grow bare at the foot of the mountain.

Despite the small size of the camp, it's packed with many rebels and Ghentians. They're a smaller group of survivors heading to the Flight Stronghold to establish it as the new headquarters. There is still no word of Milos's survival, but everyone is hopeful.

Bramblewood has taken control of the camp, and Scotty doesn't think Jean minds taking orders from her now. Ren seems to be opinionated, but Scotty suspects Jean feels guilty since Aster got hurt. Aster was the loudest voice to oppose helping Hightower and he's the one who got hurt the worst.

Scotty notices Withorn and Connie by where the larger medic tents are, the two carrying the body of a rebel towards the camp's gravesite. Another rebel carries a shovel behind them, trying to hold back sobs and stay strong for his comrade.

Scotty shivers, realizing she's not out of the water yet. Her fallion bite is healing well, but if she's not careful, infection could take her other hand away, or maybe even her life. She glances to Katze, her companion limping beside her. Or infection could take even more from her.

Scotty gets some food from Cosette, the quartermaster measuring her new stub to get fitted for a prosthetic before giving up a meal. Cosette spares some extra rations for Katze, the fallion gobbling up the food as if she wasn't injured. Jericho tells Scotty about what to expect missing part of her body, but she's too focused on Hartwood in the camp to listen. Scotty wants to get some extra food for Hartwood, but she realizes it's hard enough to carry food with two intact fingers. It's only a small serving of dried meat and bread, and Scotty knows Cosette is giving larger rations to the injured.

Still, she makes her way over to the prisoner, a Ghentian soldier guarding him. Scotty nods in greeting to the tired woman, her furs looking warm on this cool fall day.

"Hartwood," Scotty greets.

Hartwood nods at her, Shako curled up beside him. "How are you healing up?" he asks.

"I'm alive, so I'd say pretty good." Scotty places her wooden plate on the ground and tries to hand a piece of dried meat to Hartwood with two fingers.

He shakes his head. "You need it more. I don't deserve it."

"You can't just not eat," Scotty says.

"Cosette's been bringing me food," Hartwood says guiltily. "I think she feels bad for me. My stomach's still growling, but there are too many injured for me to take more."

"At least give it to Shako," Scotty says. "I'm sure he's hungry too."

Hartwood considers her words and grabs the meat from her in his bound hands before passing it to the weaver next to him. Shako eats the morsels up ravenously, looking to Hartwood for more.

Hartwood sighs. "Scotty, I'm sorry for what I said when you came down and visited me in the prison. About your loyalty. I... I was—"

"You don't have to say anything," Scotty says. "I understand."

Hartwood continues anyway. "I... I didn't want to see any of you then. Even though I'm in binds, I'm really happy to be back. I don't know if it's being in nature and the weather again, in Ludon's art, or if it's because the team is where I feel at home."

"I'm not sure how far out of the water either of us are right now," Scotty says. "I'm on Jean's bad side now, and I can't say I blame him."

Hartwood frowns at her.

"I know Aster's pretty beat up right now," Hartwood says, keeping his voice low. "But Scotty, I don't think he's what he seems. Please keep him away from me. I don't feel safe around him."

"Aster almost died to save me," Scotty assures him.

Hardwood sighs. "I know. It... it doesn't make sense."

Scotty frowns, craning her head around to the Acros Raiders medic tent, the deputy stepping out into the sun. He's wearing the poncho part of his armor, fresh acros skulls painted on the shoulders. It looks like he made an attempt to clean up the armor, but the ethner stains seem permanent.

"Nothing does anymore," Scotty murmurs. "But I'll make sure he doesn't come over. He doesn't seem happy that you're back, but I don't think you have to worry."

Scotty notices the deputy glaring at the two, or she thinks he's glaring with his one eye.

He turns away quickly, moving to Cosette and Jericho where rations are being served.

The guard urges Scotty along and she leaves after bidding farewell to Hartwood. Scotty steps across the camp to the water, sitting on the bank between two trees, wincing when she forgets her right hand is a healing stub.

She sighs and looks at her stub. She flexes her fingers on her right hand, or at least her brain tells her that's what she's doing.

It's like I can't comprehend that it's gone. Maybe I should have listened to Jericho more earlier.

A breeze wafts from the lake and Scotty winces, wishing she had her jacket from the tent. Red leaves fall from the trees above as the wind dies down and Scotty looks up into the blood-red trees. She shivers, thinking of the Red Forest, the holy ground of Cassius. The dream from last night comes back to her and she wonders what it could mean.

Someone will give in to me eventually. Will it be you?

"Scotty."

Jean's voice startles her, the commander sitting down on the bank next to her. His icy eyes study her, his black trench coat sprawling out on the dead leaves of the ground.

"Er, hi, Jean," Scotty says. Part of her wants to apologize for freeing Hartwood, but she wouldn't mean it.

Silence falls over them for a moment.

"Scotty, I'm sorry for threatening to kick you off the team," Jean says. "I know I'm the one who made you doubt the team in the first place. It wasn't fair to you."

Scotty blinks at him, not expecting the apology.

"Thanks, Jean," she says. "I—"

"Even if Hartwood is a traitor," Jean continues, "I... I don't think he should die. It's why I didn't have Milos execute him. I find myself feeling comforted knowing he's here and safe."

"I couldn't leave him there to die," Scotty says.

Jean's face twists at Scotty. "And I hate to admit it, but you were right about my intuition." Jean keeps his voice low. "It's been saying we might have been wrong. We might have been tricked somehow. I just kept lying to myself. I want to trust the others, but the dreams..."

"You've still been having dreams of the others too?" Scotty asks. "Worrying that someone else is a traitor?"

Jean nods. "I feel like an awful leader, suspecting any of my men."

"It's good to be cautious," Scotty says.

Silence falls over them.

"So who could it be?" Jean murmurs.

Scotty thinks to what Hartwood said about the deputy. But Aster almost died to save her. It's not possible.

"Jean," Scotty begins hesitantly. "Do you know anything about Cassius?"

Jean blinks at her. "What?"

Scotty tells him about her experience with Cassius, the sharfawks haunting her dreams, how she suspects the dark god has had his sights on Jean.

Jean lets out a pitiful laugh. "Oh, by the gods," he murmurs. "Is that what's going on in my head? Oh, when I've been telling Aster I feel like I have the claws of Cassius in my head, I've been right! Ha! I've been right."

Concern pulses through Scotty as Jean's laugh gets louder, worrying he's coming unhinged.

"Maybe the god of chaos is giving us the runaround," Jean says, his voice lowering again. "Aren't we just the playthings of the gods?"

"No we're not!" Scotty says. Part of her wants to think she can shake the influence of Cassius, but another part feels like she's in denial.

"Are you so sure?" Jean challenges. "They're gods after all."

"We have free will," Scotty says. "Everyone has free will. The gods can only influence us. Never can they control us." She feels doubtful at her words, but her own persistence breaks through. It *has* to be true.

"They can't control us, but maybe they can make us doubtful. Maybe they can make us wary of our comrades," Jean says. "I don't know why Cassius would meddle like that, but I'd rather not try to ponder the logic of the god of chaos."

Scotty sighs and Jean stands up.

"I'm going to go see if Bramblewood needs help," Jean says. "Let me know if you need anything."

Scotty frowns. She wants to talk about Cassius more, but there's not anything more to say. It's probably just Cassius making them paranoid.

She shivers as Cassius's voice echoes in her ears again.

Someone will give in to me eventually.

She turns, but Jean is already gone.

Will it be you?

Her mind swirls and she shivers as another breeze wafts over the camp.

I just need to lay down.

She gets up and returns to the medic's tent, Katze following her. She sits on her bedroll and winces as pain shoots through her arms and hands. She says a quick prayer to Aurthuras to heal soon and her head throbs a bit as she murmurs.

Katze lays her head on Scotty's thigh and Scotty gently places her bandaged hand on her grey fur. Scotty's eyes shift to the left and she notices Aster's bag sitting next to his helmet, the fresh paint having dripped a bit. Her good fingers twitch, thinking about what Hartwood said about the deputy.

It wouldn't be right to search Aster's bag. He saved my life. It'd be a mockery to his honor. It doesn't matter what Hartwood said.

She leans over anyway, prodding her broken fingers into the bag, moving his stuff around. Scotty freezes when she catches sight of something in the slightly opened bag.

A familiar honeycomb symbol.

Scotty blinks and throws her hand into the bag like a starving hound into fresh meat. She pulls out the rolled parchment in her good fingers, the plain honeycomb symbol stamped on it.

The same as the lighter.

The lighter of the traitor.

Her heart thumps hard in her chest and the pain in her hand goes numb. *It's something placed here. It's not Aster's.* Gently, she unrolls the parchment, praying it's just a trick of the gods.

Hawks Halcomb,

Your team wasn't supposed to intervene!

Arlo said he was forced to attack you to kill one of the Raiders. The whole team thinks you've gone soft. I can't keep vouching for you. You know what your father thinks. Don't forget both of us are on the line if you fail.

Meet us at the rendezvous spot and turn the Acros Raiders over. I want you to know it's not my call. It comes straight from your father. It will be nice having you by my side again, cousin.

It's been far too long.

-Commander Halcy

Scotty feels as if her heart gets caught in her throat as she reads.

She flips the paper back and forth in her hand, wondering if it's real.

It doesn't make sense!

She recalls hearing General Halcomb mention the name Hawks

at the masquerade. The mountainfolk general's son. A member of the Scouts, someone close to Commander Halcy.

Aster.

No, Hawks.

The son of Tapscott's most trusted general.

Kin to the leader of the Scouts.

The traitor.

It can't be true.

As she reads the note over, rage bubbles in her chest.

She rummages through the bag, trying to catch more incriminating evidence, but the note from Halcy is all she can find along with a swift stone — the stone he must use to communicate with the Scouts. He must have recently got the message.

Too many questions swirl in Scotty's head, pain pounding through her brain.

Why would Aster do it?

Who really is Aster?

Why did he save her?

Why did he ever act like he cared?

Is this even real?

The tent flap rustles behind Scotty and she snaps around, Aster stepping inside.

"You!" Scotty hisses.

Aster blinks at her, concern in his tone. "Scotty, what—"

Scotty lunges at him, pain searing through her wounds as she tightens her arms around his neck. Aster stumbles back out of the tent, stomping as Scotty's weight throws him around.

"Scotty!" Aster hollers.

"You bastard!" she cries. "You gods forsaken *bastard!*"

Voices murmur around them, Aster coming to a halt. He yowls and tosses her to the ground, Scotty coughing as air is sapped from her lungs.

"What's this about?" Jean booms. "Scotty!"

Raiders and rebels surround them, people yapping out words of concern.

Scotty scrambles to her feet and throws the crumpled note at Jean, the paper floating to the ground in front of the scowling commander.

"Look what I found in Aster's bag!" she says.

"You were going through my bag?" Aster growls.

Jean leans down and picks the paper up, his expression melting as he reads. Fear strike's Aster's face when he sees the note, Aster taking a few steps away from the commander, his gaze sweeping around the growing crowd.

Jean's icy gaze looks up to Aster, the two staring at each other with equal amounts of pain.

"Aster," Jean breathes. "Is this... is this some kind of joke?"

"Jean!" Aster pleads. His gaze snaps around as more rebels and Raiders congregate around them, panic overtaking the deputy.

"What's going on?" someone shouts.

"Aster is the traitor!" Scotty hisses.

"Not this shit again!" Farsing calls out.

"Aster would never betray us!" Cosette cries.

Jean looks like he doesn't know what to say. "Aster," he pleads, holding the note out. "Defend yourself. What is this?"

Scotty expects Aster to say it wasn't his, and she'd be inclined to believe him. She prays he makes a good case, she prays this is a trick of the gods, a trick of the real traitor.

"Jean, I—" Aster chokes out. His brown eye snaps around. "I—I didn't mean for it to come to this!"

Aster turns and flees, pushing through the crowd of people, gasps erupting. Ren and Farsing make chase into the woods as others shout out. Scotty falls to her knees, her heart tightening in her chest.

Aster.

Why?

55
DARK NIGHT

Ren and Farsing return soon, Aster having kept out of their grasp on the chase. Ren's chest is tight as he returns to the camp from the thick, orange woods, his head swirling, his flank wounds burning.

Aster. A traitor.

Part of him is relieved because this means Hartwood was framed. Another part of him is confused.

Ren didn't like the deputy when he first joined the team and disliked a lot of his choices, but he always seemed to act out of care for the team.

It was all just a facade.

Ren and Farsing heave as they settle in among their comrades. Aster had weaved through the trees with ease, even in his Panzer Suit. If he wanted to turn and fight, Ren knows he would have easily been able to defeat both Farsing and Ren.

"We should send Scotty and Hartwood after him!" Merryweather hisses. "Track him down and slaughter him like the animal he is! He left his helmet here, his head would pop like a grape!"

"If only I had more grenades," Farsing grumbles, already puffing on a cigarette after the chase. "Bastard would be a smear in the ground!"

"What are we waiting for?" Reagan calls. "He needs brought to justice!"

"He can't run forever," Merryweather says.

"We will *not* give chase!" Jean bellows out.

Anger bubbles in Ren's chest. "Why not?" he asks. "Do you realize what he's done? Do you realize what this means? He's why the others are dead!" Ren's heart aches as he thinks of his old friend, Eliska. "He's why the airships left early!"

Jean paces across the camp, gesturing wildly with his arms, his eyes wide. "What's the point? What's the point in any of this anymore? Why *would* we give chase? We just need to move forward! We just need to move forward..."

Something about Jean's sudden change unsettles Ren. It's like the commander has Cassius's claws in his head. Ren glances around at his comrades, everyone else looking unsettled besides Scotty. There seems to be an understanding in her grey eyes and she's the only one who dares to approach him.

"Jean," Scotty says carefully. "Please, calm down." She places her bandaged hand on the commander's shoulder. "You need—"

Jean swats her hand away and Scotty winces.

"I don't need to hear anything else from *anyone!*" he hisses.

Jean's icy gaze sweeps over the team, Ren thinking he sees paranoia in the commander's eyes. It's as if he expects the rest of the team to turn on him like Aster did. He looks like a fearful young boy, staring into a void of darkness.

Ren frowns. Aster was Jean's most trusted friend, the first and most obvious choice as his deputy.

Without another word, Jean turns away and stomps into his tent — the tent Scotty and Aster had been using to rest.

Ren glances around at his comrades, everyone looking on with concern. Some of the rebels even linger, Bramblewood watching the Raider commander closely.

"We just need to keep it together," Bramblewood tells them. "I know it's... shocking what just happened. But Jean's at least right in that we need to move forward."

"Where's the justice in that?" Reagan asks.

"Justice will come eventually," Scotty butts in. "We'll make certain of it. Don't worry. We can't risk anyone going after Aster. We can't risk more than what we have already lost."

That seems to tame the rage in Reagan's gaze.

Ren frowns and sighs. "Scotty is right," he says. He looks around the team. "We need to get ready for a march again. Focusing on our next goal — getting to the Flight Stronghold — is how we can work towards taking these bastard Valkoeans like Aster down. We must stay strong now! We must stay strong to bring him to justice for his betrayal! For the deaths of the others!" His heart swells. "Eliska! Oliver! Everyone we loved! Everyone we lost!"

"Yeah!" Farsing cheers.

At Farsing's cheer, the other Raiders call out vengefully. Pride swells inside Ren as he looks over the others, his eyes falling on Jericho, the young man cheering loudly. The Raiders' voices die down and Ren notices everyone's eyes still lingering on him.

They are expecting more.

"With this news, I think we can all agree on what needs to happen now," Ren says. His eyes fall on Hartwood, the former tracker of the team and Ren's old friend.

He paces through the Raiders to the edge of the camp, a Ghentian guard watching over Hartwood. The two old friends remain silent as Ren kneels down, producing a knife from his belt and slicing the binds from Hartwood's hands.

Hartwood's hands flex and his green eyes look to Ren hesitantly.

Ren sighs. "I think we all knew deep down that you were innocent," he says. "I'm... I'm sorry. We fell for it. Aster framed you."

Hartwood considers Ren's words and remains silent for a moment too long. Ren holds his breath as he awaits his response.

It's no secret that Hartwood was in love with Eliska. She was the bond that brought the two men together. She was Ren's rival, someone he never got to the level of, even to this day, and she had stolen the tracker's heart. The three of them had been through so much together and Ren regrets not fighting for Hartwood's innocence.

Ren frowns as Hartwood stays silent. "Well, are you going to say something?"

Hartwood's lip twitches under his thick beard.

"I never thought the day would come that you'd say sorry to anyone," Hartwood finally says.

Ren sighs, irritation swelling inside him.

He's back.

Hartwood laughs before growing more serious.

"Aster really did it, huh?" Hartwood says. "I... I had my suspicions, but having them confirmed is strange. He framed me, yet it still feels off. It's Aster for Ludon's sake."

"I know what you mean," Ren says. "If we can't trust Aster, who can we trust?"

"It just doesn't feel right," Hartwood says.

Ren nods. "At least, it feels right to have you back."

Hartwood smiles at him again.

"Oh, Ren," he says. "What's made you so soft over the past few months?"

Ren shakes his head.

Have I grown soft?

He looks over at the others, the lingering rebels having dispersed away to let the Raiders deal with their situation. His eyes fall on Jean's tent near the water.

He looks at the rest of the team. First to Cosette, the quartermaster. Would she be taking over Aster's position as deputy? Or Merryweather, someone who's been nearly a lifelong friend to Jean? Ren's eyes fall on Scotty. Ren isn't sure why Jean has trusted her so much since she first joined, but the clansman has proven herself to Ren with her prowess and undying loyalty. Jean needs someone comforting right now. He needs someone he can trust.

"Scotty," Ren says. "Can you go check on Jean? I... don't think he should be alone."

"Of course." Scotty nods and no one argues with the decision to send her over to the tent.

Ren sighs as she walks off, looking at the others.

We need to be kept together right now. Jean's not in the right mind to do it, so I'll do the best I can.

———

Scotty steps towards Jean's tent, worry swelling inside her gut for the commander. Katze pads at her side, a soft fall breeze rolling off the lake. Scotty is shaken by Aster's betrayal, but it feels like the commander has lost a part of himself by losing his friend.

Bang!

Everyone in the camp freezes as a single gunshot rings out.

Scotty snaps around, feeling naked without Tex or her daggers out in the open, her heart racing. She halts when she notices everyone looking her way and she turns towards the tent again. Gunpowder smoke snakes up from the flap of the tent, the Acros Raiders logo swaying gently to let the smoke out.

Scotty's heart thumps hard in her chest.

Jean!

She races forward, barreling into the tent. She hears footfalls behind her, but everything goes numb as she inhales the fresh smoke and the scent of blood.

Jean lays motionless on Aster's bedroll. One arm is limp next to his smoking gun, the other clutched around his chest. Blood gushes from a hole in his temple, Scotty's stomach churning. She can't believe what she's looking at.

The gun. Jean. He killed himself?

The red aura of Cassius glows over him before burning off entirely, fading into the air like a ghost rising to the skies.

Cassius's words echo in Scotty's head as she trembles.

Someone will give in to me eventually.

Jean's icy blue eyes are open and lifeless and Scotty falls to her knees, her bandaged hand cradling his head. Blood smears on the beige bandages and her fingers ache, but she turns his head to try to spot any life in his eyes.

"Jean!" she shouts.

She knows it's pointless.

"Jean... What did you do?"

He can't be gone just like that, can he? He survived so many battles, Withorn fought to save him with Arlo shot him. Is he really just gone?

Scotty wants to cry out and ask why, but she knows about the god of chaos's grasp on the commander. Aster's betrayal must have sent him over.

The tent flap opens behind her and gasps erupt.

"Jean!" Merryweather cries.

Scotty backs out of the tent, facing her comrades, the open flap revealing the commander to them.

Scotty swallows hard. "Jean... he... he killed himself," she murmurs.

"Jean wouldn't," Cosette says. Tears whelm in her eyes and she brings her hand up to her mouth. Jericho stands next to her, terrified, and grabs onto her arm.

Ren looks on in shock and Farsing paces behind them all.

"No, no no, it's happening again," Farsing grumbles. "Aster must have done this! Aster came back and killed Jean! Where is he? Where's the bastard!"

Withorn pushes through them and pushes past Scotty into the tent.

"I can help!" Withorn insists, throwing his cabinet down. Scotty turns around, her heart aching as she watches the medic pull his supplies out, kneeling next to the commander's body.

"Withorn, he's dead," Scotty murmurs.

"Nikos, help!" Withorn begs. "There has to be something... There has to be something we can do."

Withorn just stares at his supplies, looking back to Jean. He holds the commander's head, hopelessness in Withorn's yellow eyes.

"You stupid bastard," Withorn murmurs. "No one's died under my watch yet."

Connie pushes past Scotty and pulls Withorn back.

"We don't disrespect the dead," Connie says. "Get ahold of yourself."

Withorn doesn't argue and lets Connie pull him away.

"He's abandoned us," Ren remarks.

"It's not like that at all!" Scotty exclaims, turning to face Ren.

She's shocked when she meets his gaze, tears in the usually stoic man's eyes.

"Then what do *you* call it?" Ren asks. "He gave up!"

Scotty's words get caught in her throat. She wants to yell out about Cassius, about the god of chaos's grasp on him, but she doesn't want to tarnish Jean's reputation.

Scotty takes in a deep breath and looks back to Jean's body, the shock ebbing as tears start to roll from her eyes.

He's really dead.

She turns back to the others.

"What do we do now?" she asks helplessly.

56
NEW DAWN

Scotty sits on the shore of Mayhew Lake, staring down Aster's helmet between her hand and her stub. The freshly painted Acros Raiders symbol is bold on the forehead.

Her bandaged thumb brushes over it, her brow furrowing.

Nothing makes sense anymore.

Her stomach jolts when her thumb scrapes blood over the symbol — Jean's blood from her stained bandages. Scotty throws the helmet in the dirt and thrusts her hand into the water, wincing as she tries to wash it away between her bandaged hand and stub.

Lake water soaks the bandages, but the blood remains as a mocking reminder. Scotty stands up and tries to step away from her own hands, from the blood, Jean's dead gaze burnt into her mind. She shuts her eyes, trying to get the image away, but nothing helps.

She sees Aster's bloodied helmet on the ground and grimaces.

This is all his fault!

She yells and kicks the helmet, sending it into the lake. It sits on the surface for a moment before floating down into the depths. Anger swells through her.

The clawing hatred inside her for the Valkoeans bubbles up, but when she thinks about Aster, it feels wrong projecting it on him. She wants to hate him, but everything he's done for her hangs over her head.

She wants to get revenge, but she doesn't want him dead. This is more than how she feels, Aster's evil extends to more than petty revenge. Aster needs to pay for what he's done.

Aster needs justice.

She recalls how Jean said he never wanted the rebellion to end, he never wanted to leave Aster. She hadn't realized how much the deputy meant to him. Was it truly because of Cassius's influence, or did Aster's betrayal just sting him that deeply?

"Who would have guessed that Aster was such a bastard?" Withorn asks, making Scotty turn around. His hands are stuffed in his overall's pockets, a blank look in his eyes.

How long as he been watching?

Scotty looks to her bandages.

"I think my bandages need replaced," she tells him.

Withorn looks at the blood on her hands, the look on his face telling her he knows its not her own. He just nods and leads her to his supplies, taking the old bandages off and cleaning her skin before starting to apply new ones.

Cosette is across the camp, already tinkering on a design for a new hand for Scotty. She said she needed busy work. Scotty won't be able to wear it for some time, but she figures Cosette is using it to distract herself from Jean's death.

"It still doesn't feel real," Scotty murmurs.

"I know," Withorn says. "The others are almost done digging the grave. It's a shame we can't cremate him. It's a shame this spot will always be a reminder of what happened."

"At least he'll get a proper sendoff to Forez," Scotty says.

Withorn finishes the wrap and the two head off to the grave site. Connie has finished preparing the body. If not for the hole in his skull, Scotty could almost be convinced Jean is sleeping.

———

Ren stands over the grave he helped dig, sweat staining his clothes even in the cool fall sun. It looks cold and unforgiving. So many emotions swell inside him. Confusion, why did Jean do it? Anger, why did he leave them? Fear, what happens now?

He chucks his shovel to the side and shakes the emotions away. No. He needs to be strong for the others.

Candles are lit in the dirt around the hole and the Raiders plus some rebels congregate around the new gravesite to pay their respects. Connie gives a speech about the gods and Withorn reads from the Good Book, but Ren goes numb and the words sound jumbled to him. He just looks at Jean's body.

As the medics finish their speech about Forez, Ren prays to his god.

Forez, be quick to receive Jean's soul. May he find peace in your purgatory that he did not find in life.

The prayer is only a thought in Ren's head, but he gets choked up with tears.

He's really gone.

Once the ceremony is over, Ren steps forward and grabs Jean's shoulders. He's not fully stiff yet, his shoulders soft to Ren's touch. Ren almost thinks if he yells and shakes the commander hard enough, he'd wake up and tell them it was just a sick joke.

Merryweather and Farsing support Jean's side and legs as they maneuver him into the hole. Ren and Farsing try to keep their composure, getting harder and harder to do so as Merryweather starts to sob.

Ren wants to lash out and yell at her, but deep down he knows it's because the sorrow disturbs him.

Let her mourn.

The cry echoes through the Greater Asperetti Mountains, the rest of the camp doused in silence.

By the time the dirt is over Jean's body, evening is in full swing. Candles adorn the gravesite, the Raiders standing around it, unsure of what to say. Jean's bayonet is stabbed into the soil as a grave stone, his gun sitting on the rocks marking the shallow site. The rebels have started to clean up the camp, everyone having agreed to move on from this site before the day's end.

The sky is grey as if the gods are mourning with the Raiders. Ren knows it's just another typical fall day, though.

"In a day, we've lost our commander and deputy," Withorn speaks up. "We've paid our respects, we'll be mourning for a while, but as Jean said, we need to move forward. The rebellion will persists and so will the Acros Raiders."

"Who's going to lead us now?" Cosette speaks up as if to finish Withorn's thought.

Everyone goes silent.

"What about Ren?" Jericho speaks up confidently.

Ren freezes, turning to face the young man, shocked to hear his name spoken first. Ren's mouth is agape, the words sticking in his throat.

Jericho's suggestion is immediately met with silence.

"I think he's a great choice," Scotty speaks up. "He has always been brash, but he's always acted in the best interest of the Raiders."

"Ren would lead us well," Cosette says.

Ren's heart swells at the support.

To his shock, no one speaks out against him. At every word of support, he feels the warmth of pride in his chest. His grief for Jean mixes with excitement from his comrades' support, making for a weird mix of emotions.

"I support Ren!" Hartwood calls out.

Farsing shouts out in support and when their voices die down, Ren speaks up.

"I'd be honored to lead you all," he says. "I'll do my best." He swallows hard. There's not much more to say. "I'll try to live up to Jean's legacy and to Oliver's before him."

When their eyes linger on him, he realizes he needs to choose a deputy.

His gaze sweeps over everyone.

Farsing is too unpredictable, and Hartwood is too laid back.

Connie and Withorn need to be medics.

Ren doesn't know Reagan too well. She's an apostle of Yuna, but he needs someone he knows he can work well with.

Jericho, while he has grown a lot, isn't assertive enough.

Merryweather has amazing prowess, but can act without thinking.

He looks to Cosette.

Cosette is a fine quartermaster. She shouldn't have to bear the burden of two important jobs.

His eyes fall on Scotty.

Scotty's skills as a Raider have impressed him since she joined. When Ren failed Jericho after his outburst, Scotty was the first one Jericho turned to. She can act without thinking, but she has great intuition.

"I need someone who will challenge me as deputy," Ren says. "I need someone who is compassionate, who will balance out my brashness." He smiles. "Forez knows I need it sometimes."

He looks at Scotty. "Scotty. Jean saw something in you. You're a selfless woman who has always had the best interest of the team at heart. We worked together well in Salina Village and I know that you won't be afraid to speak out against me. Would you be my deputy?"

As Ren speaks, Scotty's grey eyes widen in shock. She blinks at him. "I-I don't know what to say," Scotty says.

"You'd help lead us well," Farsing says. "We should have listened to you about the traitor. None of us ever though that'd be possible."

"She'll sure keep Ren in his place," Cosette remarks with a laugh.

"Her intuition is as good as Jean's," Merryweather says.

As others speak up in support, Scotty looks like she warms up to the idea more, mustering up the words to say. Ren imagines her mind is swirling as much as his was a moment ago.

"Ren, I will be your deputy," she says.

Ren smiles at her, fear swirling through him. Their gazes meet and he knows Scotty feels the same way.

"We'll lead them well," he murmurs. "We have to."

———

The team packs up their supplies along with the rebels, Scotty grabbing her supplies from Jean's tent. She tries to not look at Aster's blood stained bedroll as she gathers her stuff.

Deputy.

She was so afraid of the idea when Jean mentioned it, but she couldn't escape the fate. Normally, she'd be afraid, but Jean prepared her for this. With his death and Aster's betrayal, Scotty is ready to help lead the team towards bringing Aster to justice.

Withorn helps Scotty get her pack on her back, her bandaged hand and stub aching from all the movement.

She takes up the back of the team as the former deputy did, Ren and Cosette leading everyone behind Bramblewood's platoon.

As they step away from the former camp, Scotty cranes her head back around to give the camp one last glance. The evening sun casts warm light over the land, the peaks of the distant mountains glowing orange.

Her gaze falls on Jean's resting place and a flash of orange catches her eye.

Her heart jolts when she sees a sharfawks pace out of the tall grass, placing his haunches down on the rocks of Jean's grave. Its antlers point to the sky as it watches her with sinister, amber eyes.

Scotty shivers.

Is that Cassius?

She turns and faces her team. She will not let the dark god get to her. She has a new responsibility to take care of. She needs to help Ren lead the team.

We just need to keep moving forward.

ACKNOWLEDGMENTS

I just want to say a massive thanks to Max, my partner of ten years (and husband of one month) at the time of publishing. When I got laid off from my other job, he supported me through finishing this book. I was able to take what's usually two years of work and get it done in under four months.

I've been lucky to have everyone around me be supportive of my career as an author. I hear a lot of creative people be told they'll never make it, and while I'm far from making it, everyone tells me I can do anything I put my mind to. I'm incredibly grateful for that. The constant support helps move me forward!

A massive thank you to all of my beta readers for making this possible! Thank you to Sofia Reynoso, Faye Oliander, Holly Mathewson, and Heather Clodfelter for the amazing notes that helped shape this story into what it is. It truly wouldn't be the same without you all!

I have to give a special shout out to one beta reader, Kate Payne de Chavez. She was my high school Spanish teacher and her class inspired the underdog rebellion aspect on the story, so it was an absolute honor having her help with this.

I'm excited to bring you all the third and final book of this trilogy. If you enjoyed *Down in Flames*, please let me know by leaving a review on GoodReads or Amazon.

ABOUT THE AUTHOR

Sara Tunder is an award-winning author, captain, and gardening enthusiast. Besides writing, she volunteers at a bird sanctuary and a botanical garden. She grew up in the Appalachian foothills, the history and environment having a huge impact on her writing. She has always loved fantasy worlds, creating her first one when she was just seven years old. The passion only grew from there. Now, she lives in Florida with her husband (Max), parakeet (Tobi), and cat (Kobeni) where she works on writing more stories with vivid worlds for readers to explore.

Check out her website and join her newsletter at saratunder author.com or her Instagram @crows.quill to keep up to date on the latest news.

GLOSSARY

Acros - A large, cunning black bird. Their feathers shine a deep blue in the sunlight and they are associated with intelligence.

Alignment - Measurement of time, 350 years. Marks the time it takes for Harkive, its moons (Aurthuras and Nikos) and the solar system to align with each other.

Dewick - A horned humanoid race. They're more muscular and hairier than the other wick, and have below average intelligence. Their bones, especially their skulls, are thick and their faces are more elongated than other races.

Castism - Popular religion worshipping the god Castus.

Ethner - Chemical that creates steam when mixed with water.

Fallion - A sleek-bodied, long-furred hound. Colors range from cream to grey to liver to any combination of the three.

Harkive - The world.

Hywick - Humanoid race. They're the original wick, the dewick and lowick originating from these people. The sub-races include the Ouellettians, the Mountainfolk, and the Snoskal.

Lantern Bellied Frog - Fat horned frog that is dark green with yellow splotches on it. Its belly lights up to attract mates when it sings.

Lowick - Smaller humanoid race derived from the hywick. Sub-races include the Clansmen and Cillvans. They're mostly concentrated on the western coast of South Harkive.

Novaks - Large horned bears of the snowy regions of Harkive.

Sharfawks - A vulpine creature with antlers atop their heads.

Soharism - Popular polytheistic religion practiced by the people of Harkive (See Gods of Soharism at start of book for more info).

Swifts - A large hawkish bird with a forked tail. Menacing and fast, they're used as messenger birds to deliver letters in staggering times and are difficult to take down.

Trollydwarves - A small, furry-shelled mammal. It has a sleep face with pointed diamond ears. The roly-poly shell on its back is covered in muted cotton candy fur and it has a thin whip-like tail with a spiked ball on the end.

Valen - Cervine creature with a speckled tan-green coat. They're big and bulky, being used as mounts or to draw carriages. The males have antlers, which are sometimes trimmed on mounts, and the females have more speckles in their fur.

Weavers - Small, wiry, water dwelling canine. Fur color can range from blue-grey to white and black, and any combination of those colors. If the tongue is split, weavers can mimic speech and have, in some instances, shown signs of understanding the meaning of words.

www.ingramcontent.com/pod-product-compliance
Lightning Source LLC
Chambersburg PA
CBHW050020030726
47506CB00001B/45

* 9 7 9 8 9 8 6 5 4 1 5 5 6 *